glossary of natur... ... shaman

& names / phrases &

Euphemisms | meaning

eg DAY TRAVELER — sun

mythology

proper behavior

med belief

ecology

... peet

courting

personal

relationship

...

of children

way man

ways of women

DAWN LAND

Get
Map library

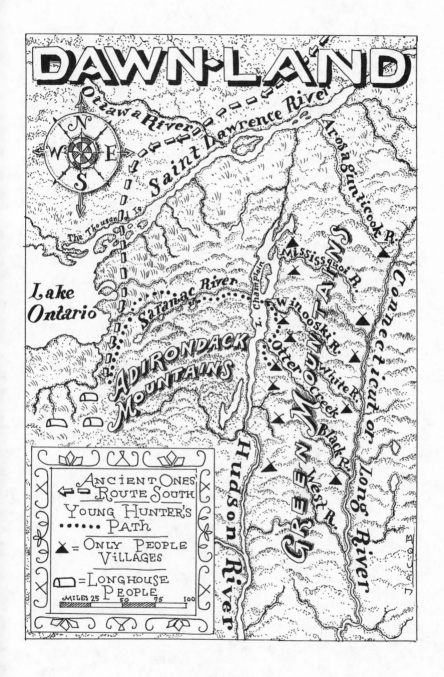

Other titles by Joseph Bruchac

Dawn Land Audio Book
Native American Animal Stories
Native American Animal Stories Audio Book
Native American Stories
Native American Stories Audio Book

Co-authored with Michael J. Caduto

Keepers of the Animals: Native American Stories and Wildlife Activities for Children
Keepers of the Animals Teacher's Guide

Keepers of the Earth: Native American Stories and Environmental Activities for Children
Keepers of the Earth Teacher's Guide

A NOVEL BY

JOSEPH · BRUCHAC

Fulcrum Publishing
Golden, Colorado

Library of Congress Cataloging-in-Publication Data

Bruchac, Joseph.
    Dawn land : a novel / by Joseph Bruchac.
            p.   cm.
    ISBN 1-55591-134-X
    1. Man, Prehistoric—Fiction. 2. Abnaki Indians—Fiction.
I. Title.
PS3552.R794D38 1993
813' .54—dc20   92-54767
                                                       CIP

Jacket design by Ann E. Green, Green Design

Printed in the United States of America

0 9 8 7 6 5 4 3 2

Fulcrum Publishing
350 Indiana Street, Suite 350
Golden, CO 80401-5093

CONTENTS

PART THREE
MOON OF FROST

PART FOUR
MOON OF LONG NIGHTS

Creat

ABOUT THIS BOOK

Dawn Land is, in a way, an historical novel. It draws strongly on the oral traditions of the Western Abenaki, the Haudenosaunee, and other native nations of the northeastern woodlands. Some of those traditions have never been put into print.

The novel takes place in the period not long after the most recent glaciation, thousands of years before the first recorded arrival of the Europeans on these shores. It was a time of many changes and the main character, Young Hunter, may be seen as the prototype of some of the heroes found in the oral traditions of the Western Abenaki—such as Long Hair, Fast Traveler, and White Owl.

About ten thousand years ago, the last traces of the great glaciers left the area we now know as New England. The native people returned to the land from the south and the west where the mountains of ice had not reached. Although archeologists used to say that it was only around that time that the first human beings came into North America by crossing the Bering Strait, hard evidence over the last few decades has pushed human habitation of this continent back more than fifty thousand years. Human beings were always moving, migrating to follow game herds, to find better soil for their crops, or to see what was on the other side of the next range of mountains. Long before Columbus (or Leif Ericson) or the Conquistadores, America was "discovered" by its aboriginal inhabitants and there were pre-Columbian trade routes all across this land.

Dawn Land takes place sometime between the final retreat of those glaciers and the period before the first European settlers (whether Norse or English) came to the area now known as the maritime provinces of Canada and New England. The exact location of the events in the story might be seen as the area between the Connecticut River (*Kwani Tewk*—"Long River" in the Abenaki language) in Vermont, the long valley of the St. Lawrence River, and the shores of Lake Ontario. The native peoples involved are those known today as the Abenaki, a name meaning "People of the Dawn Land," and the Iroquois, who called themselves Haudenosaunee, or "People of the Long Lodges." The grey-skinned giants of the story correspond to a race of people never officially encountered by Europeans, but known to the Abenaki as the *Kiwaskwek*, the Cannibal Giants, and to the Iroquois as the *Genonskwagah*, the Stone Coat Giants. Throughout North America there are stories about a race of giant people who hunted and ate human beings. The area now known as Kentucky is said by the Shawnee still to be inhabited by the ghosts of cannibal giants wiped out by a coalition of tribes who decided to end this threat to their people and waged a war of extermination against the monster people. Regarding very early contact between aboriginal peoples and European sailors, it is documented that Basque and other European fishermen were fishing the Grand Banks off the coast of North America for hundreds of years before the fifteenth century, and more and more evidence keeps popping up pointing to numerous contacts between northern Europe and North America long before Columbus.

Though this story is fiction, it is based on a melding of historical facts and native tradition, as well as ideas about the world and the role of human beings in it. The animals in the story illustrate this. Prior to the coming of the Europeans, for example, there were buffalo in what is now New York State. A buffalo herd in the wild is usually led by an old cow, and though I know of no particular place identified as a "buffalo jump" in the Northeast, driving a herd of buffalo over a cliff was a common method of buffalo hunting in the Midwest and on the Great Plains. Great predatory animals like the cave bear, the sabre-toothed lion, the dire wolf, and even the elephant-like woolly mammoth existed in North America until shortly after that last glaciation. Numerous Abenaki stories make what can easily be interpreted as direct references to those animals that were so dangerous to human beings and would, indeed, fill the nights with fear. The dog is an animal of great importance to the native people of the Northeast. To this day, dogs are regarded as members of a person's family, and it is said in some native traditions that after a man dies, he must go over a path to the sky world that leads to a deep gorge. He must cross over that gorge on a log, which is held in the teeth of that man's dogs. If he treated them well, they will hold the log steady. But if he beat them or starved them ... I know of more than a dozen traditional stories in which dogs sacrifice themselves to save the lives of their masters, and stories in which dogs take the shape of human beings are equally common. Young Hunter's dogs are good, certainly, but they may be seen as nothing more than examples of the best that could be expected from a well-treated Abenaki dog.

It may seem that native life is portrayed in this novel as too idyllic, but this also is based on both historical evidence and traditions. Native child-rearing practices in northeastern North America were extremely caring and gentle. Beating a child was regarded as deviant behavior, not needed discipline. Early English and French visitors remarked in their journals on the openness with which parents lavished praise and embraces upon their children, who were allowed considerable freedom.

To this day, among the native peoples of North America, children are referred to in many native languages as the "sacred little ones." Surrounded by such norms, a native child who lost that kind of loving relationship at an early age, like Weasel Tail, very likely might grow up twisted.

It also should be pointed out that what we now call *ecology* was simple practicality for the indigenous peoples of the American continents. It is common practice even now among the Abenaki people to observe such conservationist practices as not taking the biggest animal or fish, never killing a mother animal with young, and always leaving enough plants or animals in an area to ensure the survival of the species. I have often heard it said by native people that we must think of seven generations to come. This social and ecological balance, as we see in the lives of the Dawn Land People, is the result of past experience, not "divine inspiration." And the grey giants of the Dawn Land are a terrible example of what happens when that connection to coming generations, that delicate and necessary balance, is lost.

To underscore that the comfortable lives of the People of the Dawn Land are not merely a romantic vision, let me cite a recent book by Mark N. Cohen entitled *Health and the Rise of Civilization* (Yale University Press, 1989). He points out that hunter-gatherers worldwide tend to have better nutrition and better health than city dwellers. Many prehistoric hunting and gathering populations were as tall as or taller than the populations that took their places. As Cohen says, "The people of Europe of the 17th and 18th centuries to whom we usually compare ourselves with pride are, in fact, among the shortest people who ever lived." He goes on to say in an article appearing in the Winter 1992 issue of *Anthro Notes* that "many diseases that plague modern populations are also rare or absent" in modern hunter-gatherers. While it is true that perhaps 40 percent of the people in a native hunting and gathering community, like that of Young Hunter's Only People, might die before adulthood, those who survived to be adults were usually in excellent health with a life expectancy into their eighties. Moreover, in Europe in the mid-1800s, perhaps 45 percent of the people died before adulthood and the average life expectancy after becoming an adult was probably much less than that of an Abenaki two thousand years ago. As Cohen so eloquently puts it, "We do not simply progress. Many aspects of so-called 'civilizations'—the adoption of sedentary farming, cities, trade, social class distinctions—are mixed blessings for the participants."

Another example of the native past being different from the stereotyped portrayals of Hollywood, in which women are seen as "squaws," is the roles of women and men. Among the Abenaki and the Iroquois, the roles of women and men tended to be balanced in their sharing of power and prestige. European chroniclers in the 1500s in New England even mention numerous women chiefs. Among the Iroquois, women chose the chiefs and owned the land and the houses. It was usually the woman who proposed marriage by taking a basket of marriage bread to her prospective mother-in-law. When a man married he went to live in the long lodge of his wife's mother, and their children would belong to the clan of the mother, not the father.

There is also a strong tradition of redemption among native people. Rather than a fixed and permanent condition, "evil" in a human being is often seen as a twisting of the mind. Every person contains both the "good mind" and the confusion of the mind that is called "bad" or "evil" in the English language. Even monsters can be redeemed when their hearts are melted by the warmth of a fire. Thus, reforming your enemies rather than killing them is a more desirable solution in many traditional tales.

I am especially grateful for the help given me by my elders, both those who taught me the old stories and those who read early drafts of this novel and gave useful advice. In particular, I must acknowledge Attian Lolo/Stephen Laurent and his wife Margie. *Ktsi oleohneh.* Great thanks.

Because all American Indian languages of the Northeast have been written down by Europeans, some spellings have been Anglicized in ways which seem to me less suitable to the sounds of the words. For that reason, I have opted for divergent spellings in some cases, such as mokasin and wigwom.

Those who are familiar with the oral traditions of the People of the Dawn Land and the People of the Long Lodges may enjoy themselves finding the many places in this novel where I have woven in the strong threads of those ancient teachings. But this story is also intended to stand on its own, to serve, like the old stories, as an entertainment and a lesson. *Olibamkanni.* Travel well.

DAWN
LAND

PART ONE

MOON OF
CHANGING
LEAVES

Vocabulary

Day traveller > the Sun
Sky Walker

Great ones- cave bears (Fear Bear -

only people - -

Oldest Talker -
One who Shaped himself from something

Above Land- "Sky"(?)

Brave One- rattler (?)

bring arrowheads to class

CHAPTER ONE
BEFORE DAWN

The People – tribal names sweat – before history hunting outfits vision

Ketah, Nodah. Listen, hear me. So it begins.

He built the fire before the sun rose. He sat naked in front of it, watching the glow of the stones within its heart. There were thirteen stones, one for each of the villages of the People of the Dawn Land. Behind him was the door of the lodge, open to the east. Beside him was the knife he had napped from the hillside flint the day before, using the one implement he carried with him for his task. That one tool, a piece of deer antler the length of the span from stretched-out thumb to the end of his middle finger, rested in the hollow of a tree near the flinthill place a look away. He had brought nothing with him to this place that was not his own or of his own making. That which was most his own, that which he would soon offer strongly as the Only People taught, was his body.

Behind him, the door of the lodge was open. The lodge was small, the height of a man's waist. It was shaped like the sky dome. The twelve peeled willow saplings that formed its frame were those he had cut and peeled the afternoon before, sharpened and pressed into the soft earth, tied together with the thin tough roots of the woodbine and the grapevine, which grew here in profusion. In the forest around this clearing at the stream's edge, the grapevines were draped with fruit. It was

3

only people [handwritten annotation]

good as he sat, waiting for the stones to grow hot enough, to think of the animal people eating those grapes, to think of the partridge and the jay, the raccoon and the fox and the deer, coming to this place to eat those grapes. But he did not think of eating grapes himself. He thought of not eating. He thought of the stones growing red and then white with heat. He thought of the task before him, the beginning within the sweat lodge. It would be dark within the lodge. The lodge was covered well with the bark of the dead elm, which had fallen by the stream near the base of the hill, taken down by a long-past storm. Within the lodge there were two smells. One was from the dead bark of the elm, its pungent sweetness. The other smell was of earth, the earth he sifted between his fingers as he smoothed the ground, as he dug the hole in the center where the stones would be placed.

Facing the direction where the Sky Walker or the Day Traveler, the great sun, would first show his bright face, and watching the fire turn the wood into sand, he thought of his task, of the honor to be one of the young men allowed to hunt for the people in the strongest way.

All around was the darkness, but it held no fear. The seasons were long past when that darkness had held the Great Ones, the ones who hunted the Only People. Those Great Ones lived only in wintertime stories. It was in the time of his mother's mother's mother when the last of the Great Ones to be seen in the land of the Only People had been killed. The skin of that one, of the one known as Fear Bear, was still to be seen in the lodge of their Oldest Talker. Their Oldest Talker spread it out when it was time for him to speak of the hidden things, when it was time for him to enter his special lodge and call for the Below People to bring him down to their deep land. They would shake his small lodge and speak in their high and distant voices of things faraway.

The hide of Fear Bear was so large it made the skin of the biggest of the bears that still lived look like that of a cub. There had

4

been other Ancient Ones, others as terrible as Fear Bear. All of them were gone now from the lands of the Only People. They were gone or they were shrunk down to the size where they could no longer hunt the human beings. The wintertime stories told how the One Who Shaped Himself From Something took the great animals and stroked them with his hands. He made them smaller so they would not wipe out the human beings.

The darkness around Young Hunter held nothing to fear. So he told himself, calming his mind as he had been taught. That hint of fear at the edge of his thoughts melted away like the ice at the edge of a pond touched by the Sky Walker during the season when the talkers from the sky, the grey geese, returned.

The stones were ready. The Sky Walker had not yet turned the east, the direction of the Only People, to the color of blood. With a green stick, Young Hunter rolled the still-burning logs to the edge of the fire pit. Taking the two forked sticks of peeled ash, he lifted the first stone and carried it into the lodge, placing it in the hole dug in the center. He brought another stone, another, and then a fourth. As he placed each stone, he sprinkled dry cedar needles onto it. The lodge filled with the pungent scent. He sat for a moment, looking at the stones, breathing the strong smoke. Then he brought in the other rocks until there were thirteen. Thirteen, one for each of the cousin villages, the villages of the People of the Dawn Land. Thirteen, one for each of the plates on the back of Great Turtle, the world supporter. Thirteen, one for each of the moons in the long cycle, that greatest circle which shaped the lives of human beings.

Young Hunter placed the stones carefully, one by one. Doing this he could keep his mind focused on the work ahead. He would not think of Willow Girl, of the way she looked at him as he walked out of the village. He would not think of the way her body moved beneath her doeskin dress. He would think of other things than the color of her eyes or the sound of her

role of women

voice. The sound of her voice was like wind whispering among new leaves. He began to laugh. He was thinking so hard of not thinking about Willow Girl that she was all he could think about! True, it was good to prepare to do this work for the Only People, but it was also good to hear the voice of a woman other than his grandmother or his sister-cousins. The voices of women were good to hear and they were full of knowledge. The knowledge women held was the strongest knowledge the Only People had. Their magic was strong. That was why men were always weak before them. The power of women was so great that they could bring new life to the people just as the earth would bring forth new plants in the springtime.

Young Hunter shook his head, still laughing. His grandfather, Rabbit Stick, had warned him.

"Beware of the power of women. They will confuse your thoughts. We men are weak," the old man said, looking out of the corner of his eye at Sweetgrass Woman, Young Hunter's grandmother. Though she was as old as his grandfather and had borne five children who grew to have children of their own, her back was still straight, her hair braided as carefully as when she was first married. Though she pretended to be busy at other tasks, she heard every word said in her lodge. "Grandson," his grandfather continued, "we are weak indeed." He cupped his hand over his groin. "This is our weakest spot, and those women know how to take advantage of us."

Sweetgrass Woman was on their side of the lodge now, and Young Hunter saw that she was holding a pot of water in her hands as she worked closer. There was a smile at the corner of her mouth. Young Hunter leaned back slightly. His grandfather did not notice. "If we could just cut this off," his grandfather said, "as Uncle Turtle did in that story, then we would be stronger than women. But they are too clever. They make us love our weakness." His grandfather leaned forward. "Women are dangerous, boy. Better to stay away from them. Better to—"

6

flute for courtview

Rabbit Stick did not finish his words. The splash of the water over his head from Sweetgrass Woman's pot stopped them. He did not jump up or flinch. He simply sighed. "You see," he said.

Young Hunter understood. He stood up and went outside, leaving his grandparents alone in their lodge. He could hear both of them as he closed the door flap behind him. They were laughing together and there was the sound of scuffling. Then it was silent in the lodge, and when Young Hunter returned from his long walk, his grandmother's face was shining with color and his grandfather wore a suspiciously happy smile.

Young Hunter smiled as he remembered. It reminded him of how much he loved his grandparents. It was because of that love that he had offered himself to be a pure hunter. But to do it properly, his thoughts had to be focused on the task ahead. He spoke to the image of Willow Girl, which was there so clearly in his mind. "Please," he said, "I will come to play my flute behind your lodge soon. I will be there at the end of this moon when the leaves are falling. Then I will no longer be one of the pure hunters. But now I must be alone with my medicine." He saw/remembered her smile. Her image began to walk away from him until it disappeared. A crack of light was coming in through the door of the sweat lodge. He adjusted the pieces of bark, blocking the opening. Now the only light came from the small glowing eyes of the heated stones. Their warmth filled the lodge.

He cupped his hand to carry water from the container he had fashioned from green bark. As the water dripped from between his fingers the stones hissed with power. Clouds of earth breath rose. The breath rolled over him as he cupped his hands again and again and again, pouring the water onto the hissing, singing rocks. "*Ktsi Nwaskw,*" he prayed, "help me be strong enough to do this. To do this all."

7

leaving sweat lodge, like rebirth

When he emerged from the lodge, crawling as a baby new to the world, he saw the first light from the Sky Walker beginning to pulse at the edge of the earth. He lay on his stomach, limbs loose as those of a skinned bear. His own skin glowed. It felt fresh and smooth as peeled ash. It was a weakness that gave him strength. Soon he would follow the track of that deer, the one he was supposed to follow. He would stay close to it for a day and a night without stopping. He would run to keep it running, cutting its circle so that it would not rest. At last, its heart about to burst, he would catch it as it stood waiting for him. Its eyes would be calm, its fear gone. He would speak the old words. He would thank it for its gift. Then his hands would grasp its mouth, holding it shut, cutting the flow of life. Its breath would loosen and its spirit would leave its body, leave its body to give its body to the Only People. It would happen. It had been given to him in the lodge. But there was something else. The vision of it had come to him like coiling smoke, but he could not see it as clearly as he saw the deer waiting for him. Whatever it was, it would come to pass within the next day and night. It had been given to him.

The Sky Walker had crossed the Above Land four times before Young Hunter limped back into the village, the fat deer slung over his shoulder. It was the deer he had been told to take. It was the doe his grandfather had watched for three cycles of seasons, seeing she bore no fawn, gave nothing back to the deer people but simply grew fatter. Young Hunter knew her from the marking on her chest—like two fingers touching together at their tips.

ecology

As he walked into his village, Young Hunter was happy. People nodded to him. He heard their greetings. He loved the voices of his people. His heart was full with his offering, and also with that other thing that had been given to him. The swelling in his ankle was almost gone. The two small red marks from the Brave One's fangs could hardly be seen now. He passed Willow Girl's lodge. Somehow, she happened to be standing outside, purely by accident—though she was breathing hard as if she had just run from some distance to be there. As he passed her, she looked away with such obvious disinterest that Young Hunter knew she wanted him to notice. Tonight the flute.

Now he had completed the circuit of the village and was almost to the lodge of his grandparents. He limped less as he approached the door of the lodge where his grandparents sat. He placed the deer on the mat of reeds his grandmother had laid to the right of the door.

"This one has given herself to the Only People," he said.

His grandmother nodded, but her eyes were on Young Hunter's ankle. She saw the marks there and understood them. She saw too that there was more to understand. Her eyes shaped the question, but his grandfather asked it.

"You were bitten by a Brave One?"

"Uh-hunh," Young Hunter said. "I have a story. I think I must speak it first to our Oldest Talker. That is the right way, isn't it?"

His grandmother looked disappointed. In their small village she was known not just as Sweetgrass Woman, but also as Has to Know Everything. People told her their secrets first because they knew she would eventually find them out anyhow. But as Young Hunter's grandfather nodded, her eyes added their agreement. She would find out soon enough. Bear Talker might be their Oldest Talker, the one who spoke with the ones under the earth, but his tongue always wagged at both ends. It had been that way even when he was a little boy and she had been able to outrun him. She would find out soon enough.

"We will walk together," his grandfather said, pointing with his lips in the direction of Bear Talker's lodge, hidden beyond the western edge of the village circle.

"Uh-hunh," Young Hunter said, moving the index finger of his right hand up and down twice as if tapping a drum.

9

His grandfather stood without using his hands to push himself up. Rabbit Stick was still half a hand taller than his grandson, his shoulders broader, his hips narrower. His stomach was big, but the old man was as light on his feet as a squirrel running on a branch. He put his hand on Young Hunter's shoulder and squeezed it. Young Hunter turned and wrapped his left arm around his grandfather, hugging him, feeling his strength like that of a healthy, old tree. Sweetgrass Woman was standing too now. He put out his right arm to embrace her as well. She was almost as tall as he was, her hair the sparkling silver of a stream touched by the light of the Night Traveler, Grandmother Moon. Tears filled his eyes as he embraced them and their arms formed a circle. He felt strong with the weakness of his days of fasting and running. His head was light, yet full from the work he had completed. So he wept. It was no disgrace among the Only People for a man to weep, to speak his heart in this way.

But there was something more in his tears that filled his eyes like water brimming from a salty spring. A voice in his heart was speaking to him without words, telling him that in the days to come there would be something to mourn. Something was coming to him. Gently, the three of them released the circle. Then, his grandfather at his side, Young Hunter turned his feet toward Bear Talker's visions.

Breathwalking - being alive, alwieves
Breathwalk = Life

CHAPTER TWO
BEAR TALKER

When Bear Talker was young—no longer a boy, not yet a man—he fell for the first time. He fell a long way. He did not stop falling when his forehead struck the earth. The earth opened and he fell through. He fell through a darkness that was not dark to his eyes. As he fell, he stretched out his arms. They slowed his fall as if they were wings. Then his feet touched as lightly to the bottom as a black-capped singer landing on a raspberry bush. There were voices there. He listened to those voices. He did not stay long. He knew he would return. He lifted his arms and began to swim up, up through the darkness toward the two suns overhead. Those suns were his own eyes, open to a sky that he would never again see in the same way.

Bear Talker's father was a man afraid of medicine. His name was Two Sticks—a name given him when, as a child, he was asked to bring in wood. He returned carrying only two slender branches, saying it was all he could carry. Other people's names changed as they grew older and did better things, but the father of Bear Talker had never done anything that the Only People remembered as well as that first evidence of laziness, rooted as deep in his character as an oak tree in the forest earth. After the death of his mother, Bear Talker's life had not been easy. He was never beaten by his father. That would have taken too much effort. But he seldom had enough

11

to eat, and his father's lodge was so poorly made that wind passed through it like water through a fish trap, and no fire could ever truly warm it.

"Take this boy from my lodge," Two Sticks said. "If medicine wants him, I have no use for him."

Those were words the half-starved boy was glad to hear. *Wherever they take me,* he thought, *my belly can never be as empty as in the lodge of a man too lazy even to snare a rabbit.*

So they took him to their Oldest Talker, a woman of the Long River People. It was a journey of as many sleeps as it took the Night Traveler to shrink from being full-bellied to the point where she was cut in half by hunger. The Oldest Talker looked at the boy, and touched the scar on his forehead where his brow had struck a sharp flint stone as he had fallen. "I see," she said, looking into his eyes. "He is a diver like me. He will stay here. When we find the right name for him, I will send him back to you." She ran her hand through his thick hair, from his forehead to the back of his neck. Her hand was strong. The way her fingers found every inch of his skull, probing, knowing, sent a thrill through the boy who was now a no-name. No longer Slow Bird. As the men left without looking back, Oldest Talker peered into the boy's eyes more deeply and smiled. Her strong right hand ran down his neck to his shoulder, her left hand on her own neck. The boy smiled back. His heart beat faster. Despite her name, Oldest Talker was not an old woman. Far from it.

She began by taking him apart. They went down to the Long River that ran below her lodge. There, where no other man or woman lived closer than a whole look away, she made him lie on his back at the edge of the stream. The cool clay squished under his back. It felt as if it were trying to swallow him. She coated his whole body with the grey clay, three fingers thick. It was dawn when she began and as the long-day sun lifted higher, he could feel the clay pulling at every part of his body as it dried. Only his head was free of the clay and he watched her. She held a wooden knife in her hands. Its point had been fire-hardened so that the maple was almost as sharp and strong as stone. She cut lines in the baking clay: a line around each of his ankles, a circle around his knees. On up she worked, cutting him into pieces, taking him apart. She drew a circle around the place between his legs where his penis showed as a lump below the clay.

"Maybe we should just break off this little bump here and throw it away, uh-hunh?" She giggled. She looked even younger then.

The boy tried to remember when he had first heard her name spoken. How many winters ago was it? How many winters old would she be? This medicine work was getting interesting. He felt, for the first time, the incredible mixture of feelings that would be familiar to him as a grown man. The feelings came over him in waves: happiness, uncertainty, fear, sorrow, pity, sexual desire, excitement. All of them mixed together, and all of them balanced by something else that was itself also a mixture of many things: courage, the sort of love felt by the parent for the little one, calmness, and a great certainty. It was like a drink made of many things that normally would not be combined—the juice of many berries swirled together with the soup of a meat stew.

Oldest Talker drew on his chest and his belly. She drew the shapes of his insides, the snake ropes of his intestines and stomach, the wingbeat bird/heart in his chest, and other shapes he did not yet recognize. She talked and sang as she did all this. Then the boy realized something. During the time all this had been happening, the sun had seemed to run across the sky. It was already growing dark. Day Traveler had crossed from horizon to horizon as if he were a soaring hawk.

Oldest Talker straddled him in the dark, still singing and talking. She held a stone in her hand and began to crack the clay, breaking it where each of the lines was drawn, breaking him into pieces and putting him back together again. She pulled him toward her, sliding him between her legs, drawing

13

him out from between her naked thighs, giving birth to him. His body was small and pale and weak. He floated in the water of the river, and she gathered him to her, holding his head to her breast to suckle like a little baby. Somehow the Night Traveler had crossed the sky as swiftly as her brother, the sun. The light of a new day was beginning to show from the east. The boy realized this at the same time he realized that all the while these sacred and powerful things were being done, Oldest Talker had not just been singing and chanting medicine songs, she had also been joking. She was joking even now and the laughter that filled his chest from her jokes also filled him with a kind of awe. This was sacred talk, this teasing. He did not try to answer back. He had been chosen to listen. A pot does not carry itself to the river. And Oldest Talker, her long hair moist and clinging to her broad shoulders as the water washed around them, was both the one who carried the pot and the river itself.

All of that was long ago. Long enough ago that Oldest Talker was no longer breathwalking the earth. Her voice and her presence were within him as he needed her, but a handful of winters ago a dream had called him back to the Long River. He had found her beside her lodge, fallen leaves from the alders caught in her grey hair. She had called him, but done it only when she felt her life breath about to leave her. Perhaps she knew it would be too painful for him. She knew he would try to heal her when no healing was necessary, for her breathwalk was truly finished. But she called him and not the other one.

Oldest Talker had chosen, as every deepfar seer always chose, to teach what she knew, to pass her knowledge on down to another generation. She had chosen to teach only two. One was the boy who was now known as Bear Talker. Bear Talker was the one she chose to call, the one she chose to care for her body. By the banks of Long River, there where the sweet white roots broke out of the bank, he dug the grave for her. He placed her bracelets of pounded copper on her wrists, her

14

no eye contact

necklace of shells about her neck. He wrapped her in bark, placed her stone pipe in the bundle, covered the bundle with earth. He did it laughing and crying. He did it silently, and singing. He built a fire on top of the grave and sat beside it. He could see far ahead as he sat there. He saw a stranger day coming when the river's course would cut into her grave, and Oldest Talker would walk out of the earth, her bone spirit touching the air once more before strangers would return her to the soil for a second time. It was to be that way. Bear Talker shook his head and chuckled. He was so *angry* at her for not letting him come to her sooner. Even when she knew she was dying, she still had to keep on teaching, didn't she?

And now the Long River People came to Bear Talker's valley, as his people had once traveled to the Long River place when they needed medicine help or far seeing. Of the thirteen bands, seven used him as their deep-seeing person. The other six used the woman who was Oldest Talker's other student. That woman.

Young Hunter stood in front of Bear Talker. The deep-seeing man was not looking up at him. He sat there on the huge black robe made from the skin of the last Great One. He played with a handful of penis bones from various animals: otter, bear, wolverine, fisher. He shook them from hand to hand, looked at them, and dropped them on the skin. He cocked his head and nodded as if he were listening to someone speak. Then, suddenly as an otter shooting up from beneath the surface of a lake, Bear Talker stood. He did it in one motion, as if his legs were not needed for him to stand. He thrust his face close to Young Hunter's, as if trying to push him back with his eyes, but Young Hunter did not move. Instead, he stood his ground, remembering it was not polite to stare back into another's face.

Bear Talker's belly was almost touching him. Bear Talker was a very round man. It was as if he were made of circles. His face, his arms, his chest and stomach, his hips and legs,

[handwritten in left margin: Did men have facial hair]

everything about him was round. He had as many winters as Young Hunter's grandparents, but Bear Talker's hair was still as dark as the wing of a raven. A few small hairs grew on Bear Talker's upper lip.

Other men plucked off their facial hairs, but Bear Talker let his grow. He liked to look different from other men, as if his deepfar seeing were not enough to set him apart. *Perhaps,* Young Hunter thought, *he has never gotten over the fact that my grandmother beat him in that foot race when they were both children.* Though it happened before Bear Talker fell through the earth into a new name and a new identity as a deepfar seer, people still talked about that race. So maybe Bear Talker wanted to look as different as possible to make people forget his slow feet.

Whump! Young Hunter heard the thump of Bear Talker's palm against his chest before he felt it. *Whump!* Bear Talker struck him again with the flat of his palm. It was as sudden as the strike of the Brave One, and Young Hunter took half a step backward. "Boy!" Bear Talker growled, "put your mind on what you have come here for. Otherwise," he growled again, "I will tear you to pieces." Then he giggled like a woman. Young Hunter's mouth dropped open. Bear Talker slapped his palm onto the young man's shoulder. "That is an old trick," he said. "Don't mind it, boy. I wanted you to wake up. Now sit beside me for a while before we talk."

As Young Hunter sat, the stiffness in his left leg made him wince. He straightened the leg in front of him, and Bear Talker grasped it before he could bend it back. Young Hunter felt the soothing heat of the healer's fingers pressing the muscle and bone, wiping it clean of pain.

"The healing of your leg is going well," he said. "I am only making it go a little faster." He reached into the bark basket by his side and took out a handful of herbs, rubbing them on the place where the fangs of the snake had pierced the flesh. "How big was this one who struck you?"

16

Young Hunter extended his arms to their full length. "As big around as the thickness of my wrist," he said.

"Hunh. The Brave One must have struck and eaten before it met you. The poison is less then. But most would still die." Bear Talker dipped a gourd cup into the pot beside him and passed it to Young Hunter. The young man hesitated, wanting to smell the liquid before drinking it, but not wanting to offend Bear Talker.

The healer giggled again. It was the giggle he had learned long ago from Oldest Talker. "Water," he said. "Just water. Drink."

Young Hunter poured some of the water on the earth next to the skin, moving the gourd sunwise as he did so. Then he drained the cup in one gulp, turned it in his hands, and passed it back handle first. Bear Talker filled it again, poured water on the earth, and drank.

"Good water," he said. "Water is a strong medicine."

"I have tasted some water that is even stronger," Young Hunter said. Then he bit his lip. He did not mean to speak like one of those who always tries to say something better than the one who has just spoken.

Bear Talker was not offended. He nodded. There was a kind look in his eyes. "The whole story," he said. "Tell it now."

Young Hunter began to speak. He spoke of his desire to be one of the pure hunters, one of those who went with no weapon to take the deer, to bring back food for the people in a way that was specially blessed, to hunt in a way that honored the animal people. Bear Talker listened. The boy was good at telling a story. He didn't hesitate or repeat himself. He described things well, as if he were seeing them as he spoke. Bear Talker had watched this boy for a good many seasons, seen him growing taller and stronger. But he had never before heard him speak, speak like this from the heart. *This young one will do things for the people,* Bear Talker thought.

17

If he survives. For the dark cloud was close, the storm coming. *If he survives.*

Young Hunter continued talking. He described going to the place where the deer would pass, lying, and waiting until the dawn. But then, as he took his first step to follow that chosen deer, he knew something strange was going to happen. When the chosen deer ran, the three-winters doe that had no fawn, she ran straight. She did not circle as another deer might. He could not cut her trail. She was going someplace, faster than he had expected. Late in the day, as he crossed a rocky place, with the doe not far ahead, he met the Brave One. It was not coiled. It gave no warning. It was lying straight as a stick on the stones, its head behind a stone. His foot came down on it as he followed the deer, the deer that had stopped and was looking back at him. He felt the Brave One shift beneath his foot as he stepped, but it was too late to pull his foot back. Its head came around lazily, its fangs extended to punch into the flesh of his calf. It did not shake its head, worrying his flesh as a blacksnake would. It struck and let go, and its eyes held his as it slipped back into a coil, its rattle now singing the warning song too late.

"Why?" Young Hunter said to the snake. "Why?" He stepped back, feeling his death in his leg. Then his foot slipped on the steep slope, and he rolled and slid down the hill, crashing through the bushes.

Water splashed around him, washed over his eyes, and he struggled to sit up. He was in a swamp at the base of the hill, and he was sitting waist-deep in mud. He lay back, breathing hard. He was not sure what to do. His leg throbbed, but not with the pain he expected. He knew of one man in the village of the Flint Stone who had been struck by a Brave One on his arm. His arm swelled and blackened until it burst, and the man died in great pain. He knew that his leg was swelling. The pulse of the wingbeat bird of his heart seemed to have settled in his calf. But the mud was cool. It cooled his leg, cooled his body. He leaned back and looked up. A redtail hawk was circling the little valley in which he lay. It circled and circled, cocking its head to look down at him. He could hear a sound. Bubbling water. There to his right, water was coming from a small spring. The stones around it were red. He pulled himself to the spring, keeping his leg in the mud. The water smelled strong and tasted stronger. He drank deeply and then lay back. He lay there as the sun set.

He must have slept, for when he opened his eyes it was dawn. The deer stood at the edge of the swamp, looking at him. Then she turned and ran. He rose and began to follow. He was not limping much. His leg felt strong enough. He followed her all through that day and tracked her through the night. At dawn the next morning, he caught up with her. She could not stand. He walked slowly as he approached her. Her eyes told him that she was giving herself to the people. He spoke the words of thanks, and then he grasped her. The weight of his body was on her back, his left arm twisting her neck to cut the windchannel in her throat. His right hand covered her nostrils, clamping her mouth. Her eyes were huge. Though he could not look into both of them, for the deer is like the rabbit seeing toward the sides, not to the front like such hunters as men and wolves, it seemed as if all the deer could see was him. Her heart beat harder and harder against his chest. The heartbeat went into him, louder and louder. Then it stopped. He wondered if his own heart had stopped with hers. It was more of a gift than he felt he could bear.

He carried her back to the spring and held her mouth open. He took the water of the spring into his own mouth and let it drip from his lips into her throat. He knew that he would never hunt this way again.

Bear Talker said nothing when Young Hunter finished his story. He reached behind him into his lodge, and pulled out a bundle made of a whole wolf skin. From it he drew out

pipe ceremony video *Bundles*

a clay pipe. He took smoking herb from the bundle and offered it to the four directions, to sky and earth, and the place between. Then he loaded the pipe. He placed the <u>wolf bundle</u> between his legs and did something that Young Hunter could not see. Bear Talker's hands were moving together, but the bundle shielded them from Young Hunter's sight. Then smoke began to rise. Bear Talker held up a handful of tinder and blew through it from the bottom. It blossomed into flame. He held the tinder over the bowl of the pipe, inhaled, and all of the flame went into the pipe and into the smoking herb. He exhaled and smoke rose again, this time from the pipe's bowl. Bear Talker held the pipe up and offered it the seven ways. Then he passed it to Young Hunter.

The pipe was alive in his hands. It was shaped so that the bowl was the head of a marten, the stem the body of a snake. The tip that was to be placed in the mouth was the Brave One's rattles. It was said by many in the village that Bear Talker could make the pipe crawl like a snake and growl like a marten. He allowed no one else to touch it. But now Young Hunter held it in his hands. Bear Talker made an impatient motion, lifting his palms up toward the young man.

Young Hunter held up the pipe and offered it as Bear Talker had done. He lifted it to his lips and drew the smoke into his throat. It was strong smoke, so strong that he saw things. He felt himself falling forward and backward at the same time. His face was as large as the Great One's skin beneath them, his eyes were open/closed. Bear Talker was speaking to him, but his mouth was barely open, and his lips were not moving. The voice that came from Bear Talker's mouth was as high and thin as that of an old woman. Young Hunter listened, understanding things that he could not understand. Things that made him afraid.

CHAPTER THREE
SWEETGRASS WOMAN

She kept the deer's head facing toward the east as she worked her flint knife, taking off the skin. The knife was little more than an edged stone, rounded on one side to fit the curve of her hand, but as it moved with quick, short strokes, her strong hands keeping it going in a rhythm as regular as that of the song she hummed, it separated the layer of tissue between meat and hide so smoothly that it was almost as easy as removing the clothes from a sleeping person.

"*Nolka,*" she sang, "we thank you for giving yourself. This is the way you will help our people as the Forever Great One instructed." She was careful to keep the deer's eyes covered by her skirt as she worked. The deer's mouth was full of tender green grass which she had picked for it. If the deer was not treated with respect, its spirit would speak to the chief of the deer nation. Then the chief of the deer would lead his people faraway and the Only People would go hungry.

Young Hunter's grandfather helped her, but not too much. She was one of those women strong enough not to mind having a man help her, even though she still reserved the hardest parts of the work for herself. Rabbit Stick held the legs as she cut the connecting threads between the joints at the bending places above the hooves. He pulled on the skin each time she nodded her head. They had lived together so long

21

that they could speak more clearly to each other without a sound than any other married couple of the Only People could with many words. On the mornings when the late-winter damp drove its knife into Rabbit Stick's back, and wedged splinters of ice between his fingers, Sweetgrass Woman would be there as soon as he woke, rubbing his back with good-smelling bear grease, manipulating his fingers between her palms until they thawed and woke to strength again. Even before his first sigh, she would know and her strong hands would reach out to him. There were other times when her hands would reach out to him also. In their long life together, he had learned it was always best when he waited for her touch to signal their movements together under the robes, the melding of their bodies, the thrust of pelvis against pelvis as they surged like the salmon thrusting upriver.

Sweetgrass Woman reached out and slapped him on the thigh. "Put your mind on something else," she said. "You are like the rabbit who always wants to jump on his wives. Keep your mind on this gift our grandson brought to the people. Forget that dirty-mind name of yours for once and help me work. Do something useful. Why did I ever agree to come to the lodge of a man named Rabbit Stick?"

Rabbit Stick smiled but said nothing. He pulled again at the skin, and it stripped free from the deer's back as they rolled it. They had only been working for the time it would take the Sky Walker to move the width of two fingers across the sky, and already they had finished skinning this animal which had given itself to their grandson. Now Rabbit Stick would scrape the skin, soak it in the creek, and eventually tie it onto the circular rack by their lodge. They would rub in the mixture of ashes and the soft tissue from the deer's brain to tan it. Then the smoke from the fire and Sweetgrass Woman's hands would soften the hide until it was like the touch of a child's hand. They would waste no part of this animal. The sinew would make sewing thread. The bones would make tools. Every part would be used except for the bones of its skull. Those would be tied to the tree in the place outside the village where such offerings of respect were always left. The deer would be pleased and take back its bone spirit. It would return in the bodies of other animals ready to give themselves to help the Only People.

Sweetgrass Woman began cutting away the flesh from the deer's carcass with her other flint knife, the one with the blade shaped for butchering. As she separated each piece, she placed it in order on the mat woven from marsh reeds. She shaped the animal again, remaking it on the mat. Last of all, she placed its skull facing west, toward where the sun would set, the direction animals and people walked when their breath lives were done. It was the way one went before going up the Sky Trail, on into the Above Land, where all those gone before waited.

She shook her head. The thought had come to her again. Young Hunter had almost walked that trail, almost tasted the strawberries always ripe in the Above Land. He had almost joined his mother, her daughter. Almost joined his father, that happy young man whose face would never be older in Sweetgrass Woman's memory eyes than the day when he held up their first and only child, rejoicing at the circle of life which they had shaped together. He and her daughter, Young Bear Woman.

Young Bear Woman had been her only daughter, but not her only child. Her four sons still lived. Two were in this village, the others with their wives' families in cousin villages close enough for them to come and visit often. But a daughter is a special part of her mother's flesh, an only daughter even more so. Despite her love for her sons, she would never press her forehead against theirs and laugh as she had done with Young Bear Woman. She would never forget how it had been with her and Young Bear Woman as they gathered berries together, as they pulled sweetgrass, as they worked a fish trap in the stream, as they passed back and forth between their fingers the cat's cradle string, changing the shapes each time. Spider web, Sky Bear's cave, baby's swing. When her daughter died, Sweetgrass Woman had not been sure she could continue living. Perhaps she would have died too, had it not been for her daughter's son. Young Hunter had come to fill some of that space left empty in the lodge of her heart. She said things to him and played games with him she had never shared with his uncles. He was less than a handful of winters old when he came to them.

It was Bear Talker who told them. "I've dreamt," he said. "I have seen something. Something very bad happened in the storm which came last night. You and Rabbit Stick need to go and follow the northern trapline trail."

Though there was a fist in her belly and her legs seemed to have been cut away from under her—for she could not feel the earth as she walked—Sweetgrass Woman was not surprised. During the great wind of the night just past, something had come and knocked against the doorpost of their lodge. Looking out, she saw no one there, only the wind and the quick surges of rain, tangling her hair across her face and blinding her. Then, when the calm came, she had heard the call of a Nighteyes. That bird's call meant a death.

Like many trappers, Young Hunter's father had made a small new lodge farther out from the village so that his family could be close to the trapline. It took a day's journey to get from the end of the northern trapline trail to the village, and it was lonely for a man to be without his wife and child. Sweetgrass Woman and Rabbit Stick knew this. They knew this as well as they knew the northern trapline trail, for it led to their family's trapping grounds near the four lakes. There they had camped when their own family was small and Rabbit Stick had followed the line. Each family had its own areas and would not knowingly trespass in another family's trapping grounds. They would trap there one season and then let the tribes of animal people rest undisturbed for the three following winters before returning to trap again.

Young Hunter's father had built their small lodge well. The place where he built it was a good spot for water and no homicide

for the view. It was placed where the rain would not collect and where there was shelter from wind. But he was a young man and he had made a mistake. He had not paid attention to the great dead pine tree set back in the woods to the west of the new lodge. An older and wiser man would have seen it, seen it before the great wind brought it down in a sweep of branches with tips as sharp as spears, striking through the roof of the new lodge. Young Hunter sat beside the broken wigwom. When Sweetgrass Woman and Rabbit Stick came close, he looked up but he did not move. The tree that had killed his parents had not touched him. He sat there in silence.

Almost a whole season passed in the lodge of Sweetgrass Woman and Rabbit Stick before he spoke again.

Sweetgrass Woman shook her head a second time as she remembered it all. She did not mean to complain in her heart about it. It happened that way sometimes. Life and death were close to each other, and Young Bear Woman's voice would always be with her. It was better to be grateful for the good lives the Only People enjoyed now. The time when the human beings were hunted by the Great Ones lived only in stories. Now it was common for a woman to live long enough to know the children of her grandchildren. The villages of the Dawn Land People did not fight wars with each other. It was seldom that anyone heard of a human being injuring another human being badly unless by accident. Many seasons had passed now since that one with the twisted mind had lived among the Only People, and Weasel Tail had been driven away as a result of his own bad deeds. Sweetgrass Woman shook her head sadly. Weasel Tail too had lost his parents in the forest. But how different his heart was from the heart of Young Hunter. She turned her mind away from the painful thoughts of Weasel Tail and his twisted mind to the blessings which the Only People enjoyed. There was plenty of food to eat. The forest gave them roots and plants; there were fish in the streams and

maple syrup *bark baskets*

lakes, and birds and animals of many kinds to hunt. In the
spring there was the sweet sap of the maples and the other
sugar trees to gather. They slashed the bark in the shape of a
spearhead, and placed the new bark baskets at the very point
to gather the sap before placing it in dugout canoes to boil it
down into syrup by dropping in red-hot stones. There were
many celebrations and thanksgiving times. In the warm season's
heart, the cousin villages would gather together. During those
gatherings young people who had not yet met the right person
in their own villages might see a young man or woman who had
grown and changed since the last summer. Then marriages
would take place and young men would leave their homes to
live in the villages of their spouses. It had happened that way
with two of Sweetgrass Woman's own sons.

matri local

There was much to be thankful for. The time of the Great
Cold, too, was only a memory in the stories told in winter. No
one who was breathwalking among the Only People had ever
seen those great mountains of ice which were supposed to
survive still in the Forever Winter Land. There the streams
were so cold that anyone who tried to wade across them was
frozen to the bone after only a few steps.

Nda, Sweetgrass Woman said to herself. *It is not right to
complain in my heart. Our grandson was a great gift to us, and the
sorrow of losing his parents made him value his other relatives even
more. It has made him the kind of young man who is not afraid of any
challenge if he thinks taking it would help the people.* Sweetgrass
Woman sighed. Young Hunter had been gone a long time.
What was that fat man saying to him? Though Bear Talker was
respected and even feared as the deep-seeing man for many
villages, a part of her would always see him as that boy who
could not beat her in running. She would always see him as that
underfed boy who tried to tangle her legs with a stick as they
ran the course that led out of the village and then back
through the break between hills at the head of their valley. The
course covered the distance it would take a grown man to walk

→ looking & finding good in all that happens

26

in the time it took for the sun to climb the width of two hands in the sky. Boys always prided themselves on their running, but sometimes there would be a girl who had that running gift and could beat many of them. Sweetgrass Woman was such a girl. The boy who was then called Bird wanted so badly to beat her that he thrust a stick in front of her to make her fall as they raced. But she jumped his stick and he tripped and fell himself. When he reached the finish long after her, he was given a new nickname which stuck to him for many seasons: Slow Bird.

Sweetgrass Woman now knew enough of men to realize the reason that boy had wanted so badly to run faster than she could long ago. It was not because he disliked her. It was quite the contrary. But back then, all she had had in her heart for him was contempt. Even now, she found herself shaking her head. How did *that one* ever become a deep-seeing person? And what was he saying to Young Hunter? She wished she could fly like a black-capped singer and perch on a limb near them to listen. Whatever was being said, too much had happened too quickly. Whatever was being said, she knew that things would no longer be as they had been before. Things would be different for Young Hunter. Perhaps they even would be different for all of the Only People. Something big was beginning to happen.

how long does it take for sun to climb 2 widths of hand?

CHAPTER FOUR
THE LONG THROWER

Young Hunter watched the smoke rising from the marten's mouth. He saw patterns in that smoke, shapes like the curving lines of trails along a river seen from a high point of ground. And there were other things in those patterns of smoke, things which confused and troubled him as he watched it billow out, first from the end of the pipe and then from Bear Talker's mouth. The smoke shaped a world above him. It was as if things were reversed and the earth was above him, the sky below. He squeezed his hands together in his lap as Bear Talker smoked. He clenched his fists so hard that his knuckles popped. When Young Hunter wrestled with the other young men of his age, his grip was so strong that no one could break free when he grasped them. Though some of his cousins, the sons of his uncle Fire Keeper, were faster runners, no one could beat him at wrestling or make a spear fly farther through the air. But what good would a strong grip do when the things he saw could not be grasped with his hands? When they rose and changed and melted back into the air before he could touch them?

Bear Talker wiped his hand through the smoke. He did it the way the leader of the hunters might smooth the snow before drawing in it the lines that would instruct a group of younger men which ways to go during the late-winter moose hunt. He looked at Young Hunter and it was as if the deep-seeing man's eyes looked into him. They did not stop at the surface, but bored beneath his skin like the red-shouldered beetles that ate what was left after a kill. Young Hunter remembered seeing a rabbit he'd found by the trail along the Wild Onion River at the northern edge of the family hunting grounds. It had not reached the brambles that would have given it cover. The hawk—some of its small feathers were caught in the brambles—struck the rabbit before it was safe, caught it and tore its belly open. But more had happened. That was easy to see, for the rabbit's head was gone. A hawk would not eat the head. A grey fox had done that after chasing away the hawk. The fox's track was there, clearly showing where a mole had stirred up soft earth. Not far from that print, passed over by both fox and hawk, was the last of the rabbit's unborn young. Grey and hairless, its body was smooth to his touch as the softest tanned skin. Its eyes had never opened to a world which promised nothing to the unwary. It was no larger than Young Hunter's thumb. He left it for the red-shouldered beetles. They did their job well, keeping the land clean.

"Now!" Bear Talker said. It was the first he had spoken since taking back the pipe. He no longer used that high, strange voice. His voice seemed to be coming out of a dream, but it was the familiar everyday voice Bear Talker used when people sat together around the fire at night. Sometimes they would sit in groups of their own ages, sharing stories and tales about each other. Other times it would be everyone all together, young and old, especially when it was the time for winter stories. Bear Talker's voice would be heard often at those times.

"Now!" Bear Talker said again. "Now we decide what you will do. I see that something is calling you. That Brave One was waiting for you to test you. It is late in the season now for all of the Close to the Ground People to be out, even on a day when the Sky Walker warms the stones. The leaves are changing colors. Soon they will fall. Soon there will be spider webs on the

29

again finding good — bad happenings

ground shining with ice. Soon the wintertime stories will wake with the first frost and the Snake People will go down to their lodges under the stones and tell their own tales to their children. So that Brave One was a messenger. You did right to ask it why it chose you. You did right to back away from it. That way you found the medicine spring. I know that spring. I have tasted it. It is a place with a lot of spirit. There are stories about that spring. It called you.

"Now I see that you are going to have to walk a long way. You are ready for this journey. Something is coming toward the people." Bear Talker pointed with his chin toward the northwest. "From that direction. I have known this for a long time. I have been waiting for this time. Now I am too old to go and face what is coming. I'm too slow. If you do not believe that, ask your grandmother." He giggled again. "She will tell you how slow Bear Talker is."

Bear Talker reached out his hand, slowly shaped it into a fist, and then thumped it against Young Hunter's chest just where the bones of his ribs ended. "Look through this! Look out of the center of your body. You'll see. All kinds of things are happening and I'm almost the only one who can see them. Except for that … other one, that woman. Hmmph. She has seen it too, even if her eyes aren't strong enough to really understand. Oldest Talker chose her, so I suppose she does have some talent. But it is coming now. Just as Oldest Talker said it would come when I was too old to walk out and face it myself. Ahhh!"

Young Hunter tilted his head to the side. He was confused by Bear Talker's words. But what frightened him was that in the midst of his confusion, he also already knew what the deep-seeing man was telling him. There was a level to his own mind which he had never felt before. It was as if his everyday life were a village built on top of a cave. Now, somehow, he had found his way down into its unexpected depths. *I am dreaming awake,* he thought.

atlatl overhead or slide *Ancient Ones?*

"It is just that you are young," Bear Talker said. Once again, he was speaking as if in answer to Young Hunter's thoughts. "The world is tricky. It doesn't look as if it is changing, but it is.

"There are many more people now than there were when I was young. Maybe someday there will be so many they will make this earth collapse under all their weight. Every one of our thirteen villages has twice as many people as when I was a small child. Each year we go a little farther in our hunting territories. We go farther north too, because it is no longer so cold there as it was in the time of our grandparents' grandparents. Once, not far to our north, it was part of the Forever Winter Land. There were hills made of ice, blue ice. Those hills still exist, but much farther than any of our people have walked. I have seen those blue hills in my dreams and it is true. I know this."

Glacier!

Young Hunter moved his index finger up and down in agreement. If Bear Talker saw it so in his dreams, it was true.

Bear Talker slapped his hand on the ancient bear skin beneath them. "Once," he said, slapping the skin again, "there were many of these Ancient Ones. Many of these who hunted the human beings. That is why we learned how to fight. That is why we learned how to use the spear and the spear thrower. They were hunting us and our Owner Creator saw that it was not right. Ktsi Nwaskw gave us the gift of weapons to protect ourselves against the Ancient Ones. Now that the Ancient Ones are gone, sometimes we use those weapons to fight against other human beings. But that is not the way our Owner Creator meant it to be. We were meant to fight and protect our children from the Old Ones, from Fear Bear and the others. That is why we were given the Long Thrower."

Young Hunter looked at Bear Talker, trying to understand. *What is a Long Thrower?* he thought. Another name for the atlatl? He was proud of his own atlatl. He had made it of springy ironwood, and he had carved the counterweight stone into a

Maliseet moose example

beautiful shape so that the hunted animal would accept its death offering.

Bear Talker giggled. "*Nda,*" he said, "I do not mean your spear thrower, boy. Be patient. I will come around that bend in my story soon enough. Listen now. Things change in this world. You know how Gluskabe helped us and changed the animals. That moose we hunt now in late winter is not the one which walked the earth in the early dawn time. That moose was bigger. Its horns were sharper. It was not afraid to attack us, to trample the people and hook them up on its sharp horns. So Gluskabe shaped it down. He pushed against its horns till they were smaller and flatter. He pushed against its nose till the whole animal was smaller. The old moose looked like the wapiti, but much, much bigger. Now the moose is not so dangerous. Now it is the one that we hunt. The one you like to ride, eh?"

Young Hunter looked down at his feet. It was true that Bear Talker's vision looked everywhere. He saw and heard things people thought were hidden. How else would he know about Young Hunter's game with the moose? In the hot season, when the moose go into the deep water of the lakes to graze the underwater plants, Young Hunter liked to float his dugout quietly toward a feeding moose. When he was close enough and its head was underwater, he would slip out. He would grab the moose's horns and ride it as it swam. His cousins remained on shore, afraid to try this dangerous sport. But Young Hunter was sure none of them had told their elders. If they had, surely someone would have spoken to Young Hunter about it by now, telling him a story to encourage him to show more respect for a game animal as important as the moose. He waited for Bear Talker to admonish him, but the deep-seeing man continued to speak of how things were changing.

"As we move out, as we increase, this land remains big enough to hold us. As long as we keep in balance, do things the way our Owner Creator gave us to do them, our ways will be good. But there are others. We are not the only ones, even if we are the Only People. There are the Shorter People who live far to the south of us. You have been to that place with your grandfather, the place where we leave things to trade with them."

Young Hunter nodded. It was the way they got certain things which they could not find in the Dawn Land. They would go to the trading place at that time soon after the ice was gone from the Long South River. It was a journey of six days and when they got there, to the bank of blue clay, they would spread out a buckskin and place on it the things they had made in the winter to trade. Though they did not see them, they knew the Shorter People were watching them from the other bank. They would put down baskets made of bark, axes and spear points flaked from the chert of their quarry in the north. Then they would leave and come back the next morning. By each of the things on the buckskin something else would have been placed by the Shorter People. Seven blue beads next to an ax, a bark cup filled with ocher near a bark basket, a white quartz spearhead next to the one made of chert. If the trade seemed fair, the Only People took the thing left by the Shorter People, leaving the other in trade. If it did not seem fair, they placed the item left by the Shorter People off to the side and came back the next day to see if something more acceptable had been left in its place.

"The others who are coming toward us now," Bear Talker said, "are not like us and also not like the Shorter People." Bear Talker laughed a laugh with no humor in it. "No, they are not short people! They are not faraway. They are coming close." Bear Talker patted the skin beneath them. "In the time of our grandparents' grandparents, when this Ancient One was killed, when we were given the Long Thrower, a dream was sent to the one who was the deepfar seer. He passed on his dream and the Long Thrower to the one who took his place. So too the next one was given the dream and the Long Thrower to keep. At last, Oldest Talker passed the dream and the Long Thrower on to me. I have seen that dream clearly. I know it is true. That dream says that changes are coming soon. These changes are full of danger for the people."

Young Hunter listened hard. His head hurt. He could never be a deep-seeing man. He could not understand half of the things Bear Talker was saying. Yet some part of himself, another self hidden within his thoughts, was taking in all of Bear Talker's words and changing the way Young Hunter saw the world. It was like the light of the Sky Walker after the Moon of Long Nights. You might not understand what that light was saying, but your skin heard its message and grew darker, no longer as pale as a wood maggot, after heeding the message of the sun.

"The change will also be brought by beings with great power. They will have cold hearts and they will be hungry. My dream tells me that the Long Thrower may help the one who must go out and meet the change which is coming now. You were chosen by the Brave One. The healing spring chose you. You are the best of the young wolves in our village and our village is the best of the thirteen villages. You are the one who must go."

"Go?" Young Hunter said. "Go?" It was the first time he had spoken in a long time. His voice sounded strange and far-away to himself. The smoke from Bear Talker's pipe seemed to be stuck in his head.

"Go," Bear Talker repeated. "You must go and meet whatever is coming toward us."

CHAPTER FIVE
THE VILLAGE

As Young Hunter passed back through the village toward his grandparents' lodge, people nodded to him. He acknowledged their greetings, but his smile went no further than his lips. It was as if two people were now walking in his mokasins. One of them was Young Hunter. The other was a stranger, a stranger who saw everything in the village—from familiar faces to the very earth beneath his feet—as though for the first time.

His best friend, Sparrow, looked up from the log where he sat. He was making a new spear point from chert, pressure-flaking it with a deer antler. His hands moved lazily, but with such practiced ease that he could make a spear point or a stone knife in less time than it took for the sun to move a hand's width. Just five dawns ago, Young Hunter had agreed to walk with Sparrow through the eastern notch in the hills to the watershed where a certain girl of the Salmon People village lived not far from the big waterfalls. Sparrow had seen that girl during the summer gathering. She had told him exactly where her family wigwom was in the village circle, how close she slept to the door, how lightly she slept on nights in early autumn. It was an invitation, of course, but Sparrow did not want to go alone. He needed a friend to walk with him and sit back among the cedars waiting while Sparrow played his flute to invite that

35

arrow-root plant?

Salmon People girl outside where she could get to know him better. That was what he and Sparrow had planned. Now it would not be that way.

Sparrow started to stand, placing his napping antler and the new spear point on the log by his side. But he stopped halfway up and pretended only to be reaching for a new piece of flint near his feet. He had seen the look on his friend's face and knew Young Hunter wished to walk alone. He began shaping a new point instead.

At the eastern edge of the village circle, two men and a woman were working on a new dugout. It was almost complete. They had kept the fire in it going for four days, working with their stone adzes to shape it as they burned out the center. It was going to be a good boat. Young Hunter paused to watch his uncle, Fire Keeper, move the coals with a green stick and then cut away the charred edges with strong, short motions. Young Hunter wondered how that boat would look floating in their lake. He thought of how it would be to use it as they gathered arrowroot, to float silently in it until they were close enough to cast a net over unsuspecting ducks, or hurl the string stones whizzing through the air until they struck and wound around the geese, bringing them down as they began to flap up into flight. It would be a good boat for fishing, too. His aunt was a great maker of fishing gear. She twisted the best lines of sinew and shaped the finest bone hooks in the village. As she worked beside her husband and her brother, the three of them moved as if their six hands belonged to one body. Young Hunter turned and walked away before they took notice of him. He wanted to keep this image of them in his mind forever—or as long as forever might be for him.

A small group of young women were going out to gather food. Willow Girl and her three sisters were among them. The hunting that the men did was important, but it was the women who brought in the bulk of the food for the people. They gathered the chestnuts and beech nuts and acorns, which were roasted and ground into flour. They collected the cattail pollen for the flour to make yellow bread. They pulled the wild leeks and dug the many roots which were good for food or medicine. It was the women who went to the berry patches. They were not afraid, those parties of women, to chase away the bears who thought the berry patches were their own. Often, the bears and the women would gather berries within sight of each other, but certain of the women always carried spears to the berry patches and kept them close at hand.

Three summers before, Young Hunter had heard shouting from the western edge of the village. A party of women was coming back from the berry patches, shouting and singing. It was the Moon of Raspberries. The women had gone out to fill their baskets from a nearby field where they had burned off the dead canes the year before to make the new growth stronger and lusher this summer. But such shouting and singing was not common when women were bringing back nothing more than baskets of berries. Along with everyone else in the village, Young Hunter rushed to see. It was a sight to carry in his mind. Instead of berry baskets, the women were dragging in the carcass of a bear. It was one of those they called a ranger, a lanky, full-grown male. Instead of moving away when the women entered the berry patch, it had charged them, knocked down one woman and grabbed her arm in its mouth, shaking her. That woman had blood on her ripped deerskin skirt and there was a bandage of mullein leaves tied around her arm, but she was laughing and shouting and singing the victory song with the other women. Willow Girl's mother had grabbed her spear as soon as the bear attacked. She had rushed forward and driven her spear into the ranger bear's side. When it let go of the other woman and lunged at her, she braced herself and pushed the spear deeper. The bear felt the spear point's bite and tried to turn and run. But the sharp flint had cut its breath cord. Blood poured from its mouth. Its spirit left it and it fell.

Young Hunter saw all of that again in his mind as the party of young women passed. They joked as they brushed by him. His grandmother had already divided up the meat from his deer among the households of the village. In all of the lodges, Young Hunter's name was being spoken in the way people speak of someone whose work is worthy of praise. As was the custom, that praise behind his back was balanced with teasing to his face. It was important to avoid letting anyone believe his deeds made him taller than all the other people. Some of the clouds around his head lifted as the women began to make their jokes.

"Your lover is thinking of you," one of the older girls said. She pointed with her chin at Young Hunter's feet. He looked down. It was as she said. One of his mokasin strings was untied. A sure sign, the elders agreed, that someone of the opposite sex was interested. As he looked down at his untied mokasin, he stepped on the rawhide string and almost fell. Another of the young women, Snowbird, laughed. She was Willow Girl's best friend. She pulled a root out of her pack and held it up. It was shaped like a penis. "Did you trip over this?" she asked. She had one of those round, laughing faces that changed with each word she spoke. Sparrow had played his flute behind her lodge the last time the Night Traveler was at her fullest brightness in the sky. Many said that Snowbird and Sparrow would soon make their own lodge next to the small wigwom of Snowbird's parents at the south edge of the village. Snowbird did not know about the trip Sparrow was planning to the Salmon People village.

Young Hunter smiled to himself. It was dangerous to court more than one young woman at once. He wondered if Sparrow remembered what had happened to No Teeth, a man now in his middle years. As No Teeth played his flute behind the lodge of the second of two young women he was courting simultaneously, that young woman came out to him in the moonlight. She walked gracefully up to him and then hit him

birch back " tipi "
throwing
sticks

with a big piece of moose meat. It knocked his flute back into his mouth, removed his front teeth, and gave him a new name. That young woman had known she was not the only one having the flute played for her. Young Hunter watched the party of young women as they made their way through the village and disappeared into the forest.

Willow Girl had not looked at him. She was the only one of the girls who had not looked at him. He sighed and continued walking. Soon Young Hunter stood before his grandparents' lodge. He stopped a few paces away from it. He looked at it, trying to carve it into his mind the way a man might cut a design into the hand of his throwing stick. The lodge of Sweetgrass Woman and Rabbit Stick was one of the finest in the village. Some made lazy lodges, but it was not his grandparents' way. Their wigwom was so well made it had lasted three winters and might easily last another three. When the Only People left this village to go to their fish camps by the big lake or to join the midsummer gathering, their lodge would not be one of those pushed down by the rainy winds. It stood strong through the weight of the winter snows. It was made of four maple poles, peeled and leaned and tied together at the top. Another eight smaller poles were spaced between them so that the lodge had the shape of a spruce tree. A hand's width above the height of a tall man, his grandparents had bent a supple sapling in a circle and lashed this ring to each of the poles. It held them firmly together and made a ledge to lay three sticks across so they could store things overhead or hang the hook that held the cooking pot above the fire. The lodge was coated with three layers of birch bark, each layer overlapping the one beneath and then sewn with sinew, with the only break in the bark coming at the doorway to the east. There another pole had been tied as a top frame, and a thick moose skin hung from it to make the door. Usually, as it was now, that skin door was folded back, held open by a string at one corner tied to a peg high up on the lodge. All around the lodge, Rabbit Stick had cut decorations into the bark to make their home more beautiful. They were not the sky decorations of sun and moon and stars which marked the lodge of Bear Talker. The shapes on the lodge of Young Hunter's grandparents were those of weaving stems and the open petals of flowers. The lines and swirling shapes made the whole lodge look like a song. Above the door, the shape of a bear paw incised in the bark told everyone that theirs was a family close to that animal relative.

"*Kuai!*" Young Hunter called.

"Come in," his grandmother answered.

Young Hunter bowed his head and stepped inside. He saw the familiar scene. There were three long logs laid out on the floor to border the fire pit and mark off the sections of the lodge. To the left was the sleeping place for his grandparents. The space at the back of the lodge was where Young Hunter's own bed was made. The skins spread over the fresh spruce boughs looked good to him. He suddenly realized how tired he was. To the right was the space kept open for guests and visitors to their lodge. His grandmother was close to the fire, bent over the two pots cooking there. One held a stew made from the meat of Young Hunter's deer. He would not eat that stew. The other, which was for him and him alone, was a special meal of beaver tail. It was the meal he loved best of all. He realized now how hungry he was. He looked at his grandmother, her eyes looking deep into his heart. Young Hunter felt the moisture at the edge of his eyes. He saw how precious everything and everyone around him was. Even though he did not love everyone in their village—for there were some who bothered him with their ways, people who were lazy or selfish or untrustworthy or too proud—he could not think of a single person of the Only People whose face would not have touched his heart at this moment.

"Come," Sweetgrass Woman said, "eat. Your grandfather will return soon and then we can talk. You can tell us what that crazy fat man said to you."

Young Hunter unhooked the wooden spoon that hung by a toggle from his belt. He dipped into the second pot, then took a small piece of meat from his spoon with his right hand. He threw the piece of meat outside.

"Thank you," he said. "I share this food with you, the Little People."

When he finished eating, he leaned back against the wall and sighed deeply. Before he had finished his sigh, his eyes closed and Sleep Maker sewed his lids together.

He was running among tall trees. The ground beneath him was hard and white. It was harder than snow, but not as bright and shiny as ice. Something was chasing him. He could not see it. His left hand grasped the Long Thrower hard. Bear Talker had given it to him, but had not explained how to use it. It was not heavy enough to be a club. What good was the sinew tied from one end to the other? He should throw it away. It was holding him back, slowing him. But he held on to it. A Brave One was wrapped about his left leg. Its tail rattled a warrior song. Was it trying to encourage him or was it attacking him? He could not tell. He had to find the spring. But the land sloped up. Whichever way he went he was climbing uphill. The spirit of the three-winters doe was speaking to him. *You did not thank me properly,* it said. *This is what happens to humans who forget to thank the game animals they kill.* He tried to speak, to answer the deer's spirit. He wanted to say that he had said his thank-you, he had done all that he should do. But he had no voice.

He looked back. He could not see what was chasing him, but he could see his village. It was far below and faraway. He was high on a mountain, but he remembered no mountain near their village. Then he realized that he was in the Sky Country. Just like the hunters who chased the Great Bear who walked now in the stars, he had run up into the sky. Just like those three hunters—except he was the one who was being pursued. He could not turn back now and go down to his village. Whatever

41

was chasing him would follow. He would not lead it back to his people. He would have to turn and face it. He held up the Long Thrower and as he did so, a great hand reached down to grasp his shoulder, shaking him.

"You have slept long," Rabbit Stick said. He let go of Young Hunter's shoulder. "Your leg is much better. The marks left by the Brave One's strike can barely be seen. You were dreaming?"

"Yes," Young Hunter said. "I was dreaming."

"Bear Talker said I would find you asleep and that I should wake you, even if it seemed that you dreamt. You were moving your hands. Perhaps you were fighting something."

"Uh-hunh," Young Hunter said.

Rabbit Stick smiled. "You must save that dream and tell it to Bear Talker. There will be plenty of time for that. You have some days to rest at home before you must go out again. Ah-hah. I can see from the look on your face that you thought you had to leave immediately to do whatever it is that you have been called to do. You thought Bear Talker would send you out of the village before you had a chance to catch your breath. But the older women got together and went to speak to him. He agreed with them that time was needed before you set forth. Four dawns," Rabbit Stick smiled more broadly. "And four evenings. Four evenings should be enough time for you to practice your flute playing."

CHAPTER SIX
MUSKRAT

He waded into the stream up to his waist. The waters were not as cold as they soon would be when Frost Maker returned from his home in the Forever Winter Land, but they were cold enough to waken every part of his body. He cupped water in his hands and held it up toward the light of Sky Walker, just streaming over the tops of the trees to the east.

"Long Being," he said to the river, "I have come to ask your help. I have given you some of the smoking herb; I hold your water up now to the Great Sky Walker. I give thanks for the lives of my people; I give thanks for the animal people who live within your water, to the fish people and the plants. Now I come to ask for help. I need to be strong in the work I am going to do. That is why I drink your water now and thank you. *Oleohneh.*"

Young Hunter sipped the water from his palms. He felt its coolness become part of his body. Its blessing touched his lips and mouth, entered his throat, and passed down through his chest and into his belly. He pictured each part of his body as the water touched it. Like all hunters, he knew the shapes and names for the organs of the body. He had learned them well since the first time, as a child, that he had watched the older men skin out and open up the belly and chest of a bear. A bear is the same as a man inside. Without its skin, a bear looks even

43

women seduced by Bear stories

more like a man. After that first time he saw a bear without its skin, he could understand the stories about bears who deceived young women by taking off their hairy skins and then singing to lure girls into the woods to be their wives.

When he was very small, Sweetgrass Woman told him the story of a girl who had disappeared that way when she was a child. Her friends heard sweet singing from the edge of the patch of blackberries where she had been picking. When they looked for her, they found her spilled berry basket. They saw her going over the top of a hill, almost a look away, walking beside a bear man. They could not catch her and her new husband. She was never seen again.

Almost every year, Young Hunter thought, *there is at least one who goes out and does not come back, from our village or from one of the other thirteen. One who goes off into the woods alone and never returns.*

That was the way it was. People often felt the need to go far and go alone. It was not just the men or the young people, either. Sometimes women and those who were very old would feel that urge to camp alone or go wandering. It was good to be away from the other people of the village for a time, even those you loved very much. It was good to hear nothing of human sounds, to walk where only the animal people walked, to learn new songs from the birds. That was how it was with Woman Who Walks Alone. Young Hunter still believed that she was not just a story told to children. She was one who never died. She was a woman, just like a human person, but she always lived alone. She was the one who taught the birds their songs. Sometimes a young man might find her as he wandered. If he brought along a flute and played it for her, she might allow him to approach her. She would remove her clothing and let him comb her tangled hair with his fingers. Her own fingers would touch every part of his body, caress his arms and chest and his penis. She would draw him to her and her teeth would bite his shoulder. For a night and, if his lovemaking were good enough, another day, she would stay with him. Then as he slept, exhausted, she would rise up, dress herself, and go over the mountains. She would return to the caves where she slept with her sisters, the wolves. That man would never see her again, but for years the woman he would finally marry in his home village would wonder at the faraway look which would sometimes come to his eyes.

Young Hunter did not want to find Woman Who Walks Alone. His best friend, Sparrow, talked often about her. Several times, Sparrow had gone out to seek that shining mountain where the Woman Who Walks Alone lived. Young Hunter had reminded him of what happened to the man who married a deer woman in one of the old stories, how hard things had become for him as a result, especially when he married a human girl in his home village. Things had not ended well for that man. Sparrow only smiled, then waved his hands like a bird fluttering its wings and said there were some troubles a man would be glad to have.

It was accepted among the Only People that of those who went out wandering, some would not come back. Sometimes a man or woman would leave and then, years later, be found living in another village with a new name. It was a way to start again, perhaps to be a better person this time. It was thought that some even went far to the south and joined the Shorter People, learning their language and taking on their strange ways of living in those warmer lands by the great salty waters. The Shorter People did not like to be seen when they were trading and they never came north to visit any of the thirteen villages, but sometimes a person hunting near the south lands might see a party of them at a distance, recognize them from their short stature and the strange ways they painted their bodies and shaved the hair off their heads, leaving only a ridge in the middle. Young Hunter's uncle, Fire Keeper, once saw such a group of Shorter People as he watched from a mountain slope, well hidden in the trees. He meant them no harm, but

45

Touching the fire ?

knew if he showed himself they would melt away into the forest. There was a much taller man with them. He had his hair cut and his body painted like the others. Like them he wore no clothing at all, but he walked just the way one of Fire Keeper's childhood friends walked before he never returned from a solitary hunting trip. Fire Keeper watched them making their way along the stream that ran through the valley below him until they were out of sight. He wondered for a moment what it would be like to do that, to give up all the civilized ways of the Only People and live with such wild freedom. But it was only a momentary thought. Fire Keeper was happy with his life in the village. If that man down there once had been the man known as He Passes By, now he was someone else. If it was what he wished, it was his business and no one else's. One did not interfere with the making of another's mokasins or try to walk his trail for him.

Young Hunter wiped his face with his wet palms. Then he sat down in the river. The water came up to his chin and he spread out his arms as if he were flying. *There are those,* he thought, *who do not come back because something bad happens to them.* Those who fall through the ice in winter. Those who are killed, like his parents, in a windfall. There were many ways accidents could happen. A fall from a tree or a cliff, getting caught in one's own deadfall trap. There were even those who met something out there, perhaps something stronger than a human being, something with no love for human beings. Perhaps all of the Ancient Ones were gone, perhaps not. Then there were spirit beings, some so powerful that even the mention of their names carried the risk of calling them to trouble the people.

Sometimes, people knew such a spirit was trying to catch them, trying to lure them away to their death. A spirit like the Old Woman in the Swamps, the one with the sweet voice who delighted in calling children into the marshy places and then drowning them. They might hear strange voices in their

Boogey man

46

dreams and know they were being called. That was when they would go to the lodge of Bear Talker to get help. He would go inside his small tent and shut the flap tight. His voice would change, going deeper and farther away. Then many other voices would join his in a powerful chant. The beating of wings would sound from inside, and the lodge would shake until pieces of bark flaked off and the poles creaked and almost broke. Somehow, though, Bear Talker would find the strength to compel those under the earth spirits to help him. He would defeat the spirits which called people in their dreams and those people would be safe to walk in the woods alone again.

Not all of the powerful beings in the forest were dangerous to people. Most of them just ignored human beings. Some of them might even be helpful. There were the Little People, for example. They cared for the berries and the nut trees so that there was always enough for both the animal people and the human beings. One of the stories Young Hunter loved best was one his grandmother told him about the Little People. In that story, a skinny little boy whose parents had died helped one of the Little People. "Come with us," they said, "come in our canoe made of stone." The canoe was smaller than his hand, but as soon as he took a step toward it, the canoe became big enough for him to fit inside. The Little People were big now too, and so was everything around him. When he saw his spear, lying there on the riverbank, looking as long as a big log, he realized that he had shrunk down to the size of the little ones. Then the canoe sank into the water and he was taken to their lodge under the water where they showed him wonderful things. He was gone for only the space of a few days, but when he returned to his village, everything was changed. The people he knew had grown much older and he was now a tall and strong man.

The Little People liked to play by the banks of this same stream. They made shapes out of clay and stone. Just over there, Young Hunter had found such a shape smoothed out of stone. It was like an animal he had never seen before. It was like a bear, but its nose was long. Maybe it was one of the animals which the Little People kept penned up in caves under the earth. After he picked that stone shape up, he left some of his fingernail clippings at that spot. The Little People liked to use human fingernails given them as gifts to tip their spears. That was what Sweetgrass Woman had told him. The little animal shape was in the pouch at his belt. He thought of it as his Helper. Young Hunter lay back in the water and put his feet upstream, letting the current fan out his long hair behind him.

Young Hunter. A voice was calling to him from underwater. Was it one of the Little People? He lifted his head up so that his ears were out of the river.

"Young Hunter!"

The voice came from behind him. He lifted his feet and moved his hands underwater so that he turned slowly, only his eyes and the top of his head above the surface. A lanky man with grey hair was waving to him from the bank. It was Muskrat. Young Hunter put his feet down, feeling the pebbles of the riverbed beneath his soles. He stood and waded toward shore. Muskrat was pulling an old dugout from the bushes. He looked again at Young Hunter and then inclined his chin toward the boat. Young Hunter nodded and climbed into the boat.

The old man stood, his feet certain of their balance. The boat rocked as it was pushed away from the bank, but Muskrat stood firm as a cedar tree rooted on the shore. He held a long pole in his hand and pushed the dugout upstream against the slow autumn current. A few leaves brushed past them on the surface of the water. The sun made patterns of brightness and a single dragonfly hovered, wings clattering. The eastern shore of the river rose more steeply now and Muskrat's eyes were intent on the bank.

Although Bear Talker was called their Oldest Talker, everyone knew that he was not the oldest person in the village. The oldest person was Muskrat. No one knew how old he was.

circle of life

He knew things none of the other elders knew. Many said that when he finally walked the Sky Trail, he would take with him knowledge from the past that no one else carried. "It is sad," some people said. They shook their heads about all the knowledge from the old days that was being lost. "Nowadays young men no longer want to learn things." For some reason, when Young Hunter's grandparents heard such talk, it made them smile.

Young Hunter sat so he could watch Muskrat. The old man seemed to be made of sinew and ironwood. There was no extra flesh on his body, yet his skin was barely wrinkled, except around his eyes and his throat. There his age could be seen, just as the bark of an old cherry tree becomes ridged and folded. Muskrat's black eyes, though, were as happy and filled with life as a baby's. *It is as my grandfather said*, Young Hunter thought. *The very old ones are closest to the very young ones. They have gone so far around on the circle, they are almost back to the beginning.* Some old people Young Hunter knew even went so far that they did become babies again. They had no teeth and had to crawl on their hands and knees. They drooled and their own children had to care for them, clean them, wipe their bottoms, chew food for them to make it soft enough for their old baby mouths to eat. When old people became babies again, they were especially precious. The Only People felt good when there were such blessed ones among them. The Owner Creator showed his love for the Only People by allowing them to live so long they could become carefree as babies once more.

Somehow, Young Hunter knew that Muskrat would not be one of those who became a baby again. He had decided to stay as he was, just as certain other old ones decided to rest and be cared for by their children as they had once cared for their children. Muskrat was walking the great circle in another way. He kept his strength, but he was gradually leaving the weight of his flesh behind. Each year he seemed to be a little thinner, even though he remained strong and supple as those cedars by

49

good fortune to secure smile to live so long —

the river. One day soon, perhaps, he would pull his dugout up on the shore, step out, and turn into a tree. Looking at Muskrat made Young Hunter think of what it might be like when he grew old. Both ways of aging were blessed, both ways made the Only People's hearts stronger. But he knew now which way he would want to choose. Young Hunter frowned. *Perhaps I will not live long enough to see old age.* He looked down at the bottom of the dugout. Perhaps he would go out on this journey and never even return to see the Only People again.

"Hunh!"

Young Hunter jerked his head up at the sound which came from the old man. Muskrat's head was back and he was making a strange noise. His mouth was open and Young Hunter could see the elder's teeth, worn down almost flat, but still strong. "Hunh!" the old man said. "Hunh, hunh!" Was he choking? Then Young Hunter realized he was laughing. Muskrat looked into Young Hunter's eyes and then shook his head.

"Never skin your game until you catch it," Muskrat said. He drove his pole down into the shallow water, pushed, and the boat shot forward like a duck trying to take off. "You are walking so far inside your head, your feet are going to have a hard time catching up with you. Take your mind away from whatever it is that is troubling you, my young friend. Just watch our river."

Young Hunter turned and watched the flow of the river. There were more colors and shapes in the water than there were words for them. The river was alive and it carried life. He let his hand trail in the water and watched as the current brought things to touch his palm—a small stick, one of the waterwalkers, its six legs fanned out on the surface, a white breath feather from the breast of a wood duck. A green tangle of plants floated toward him. He hooked them with his finger and held them up.

"Uh-hunh," Muskrat said. "They are feeding just upstream."

He drove his pole into the mud and looped a rope of twisted basswood fibers over the pole, lashing it to the dugout. Now they were anchored and could begin. They would hunt muskrats. It was how the old man had got his name, for no one could match him in catching muskrats to feed the people. No one ever saw him make a trap or take a spear with him, yet he never returned empty-handed. One of the jokes in the village was that the old man had married a muskrat woman long ago. In return for the respect he showed to them, the muskrat people had agreed to sacrifice their bodies to feed the Only People. Old Muskrat always went hunting for muskrats alone. Young Hunter knew that he was the first ever to be allowed to see what the old man did. He waited and watched, his mind on nothing else now.

Muskrat shifted the braided strap of his basswood basket so that the basket was in front of him and no longer hung across his back. The basket was a beautiful one. Muskrat had dyed the strips of basswood different colors before weaving them together. The basket was very old, but the colors were still bright. Young Hunter had made such a basket himself, following his grandfather's instructions. He had pulled inner bark from a basswood tree after thanking it for its gift with a handful of smoking herb, boiled the bark in water grey with wood ashes from the cooking fire, then stripped the strands across the blade of his stone knife to clean and soften them. He sang the song his grandmother told him the basswood liked to hear and soaked the strips in three pots. Rotten wood in one pot made strips blue as the clear sky. Alder bark in another made a dye redder than blood. Cedar leaves made the third pot of dye as green as a tree frog. Blue, red, and green were the colors Young Hunter's family always used. Muskrat had other colors in his basket: light blue, yellow, reddish brown, and black. The strands had been woven so that they formed patterns as sharp-edged as ice crystals.

51

↳ basket med.

Muskrat's basket was always kept tied shut. He did not use it to carry game. It was too small. It held his hunting magic; that was what people said. Even his four daughters, all of them as old as Sweetgrass Woman, did not know what was inside that basswood pack. Sweetgrass Woman had asked them more than once if they knew what was in their father's pack. If there was any secret to be found out in their village, Young Hunter knew his grandmother would be the one to do it. She was more curious than a mink.

Muskrat began to untie the basswood strings. The strings were thin, but very strong. When Young Hunter was a small child, it had been his game when gathering basswood strips with Rabbit Stick to throw a loop over a low limb, tie it together at the bottom and then sit in it and swing. Even a strip so thin that he could see light through it, and no wider than two fingers held together, could support his weight without breaking. The last knot was undone now and Muskrat was about to reach in. He looked at Young Hunter with those bright young eyes, nodded his head, and then held his hand up to his mouth. Young Hunter understood. It was a secret to be kept, even from his grandparents. Young Hunter nodded back. The old man's thin hand dove into the basket and drew out something small. It was made of two pieces of willow wood and it was no larger than Muskrat's palm. A strip of birch bark was fastened between the two pieces, curling out to either side. Muskrat looked around, then raised it to his mouth. He blew and a chirping sound came out—exactly like the voice of a muskrat. He made the call again, then pointed with his chin.

Young Hunter looked at the water near the bank. It rippled and the head of a muskrat emerged. The old man continued calling. The muskrat swam toward the boat as they sat quietly. The only motion from either of them was Muskrat's cheeks as he breathed and blew. Now another muskrat's head broke the surface, and another. Muskrats were coming from all directions toward the dugout. When they reached the boat,

Muskrat hunting power prophecy

they began to climb up onto it. One fat muskrat pulled itself
over the edge and climbed onto Young Hunter's knee, its feet
cold against his skin. Young Hunter cut his eyes to the old man.
Muskrat lowered the call and shook his head. As soon as he
stopped calling, the muskrats stopped swimming toward the
boat. The one on Young Hunter's knee looked around as if just
waking up. It shook its head and then slipped over the side as
smoothly as water pouring from a pot.

"When they come," Muskrat said, "you need only strike
them with your pole. They think this boat is a log. I have
watched you a long time. I've decided you are the one to carry
this little trick of mine into another generation for the people.
Now you are about to travel." The old man slapped the leather
pouch at his side. "My spirit helper tells me this. It says you will
return, but I may not be here. When a tree is old, even a small
storm may uproot it. So I am showing you this now."

Muskrat handed him the call. Young Hunter turned it
this way and that. He saw how the pieces of wood were cut,
measured them against his fingers, saw how they were pegged
together, how the birch bark strip passed between them.

"Blow here," Muskrat said, "your lips like this. I do not
give you this caller. This one I will continue to use, hunting for
the people. I give you the shape and spirit of the caller. With
them, you can always make one of your own."

Young Hunter nodded. The knowledge of it was within
him now like a design cut into the wood of a tree. But the old
man had given him more than this. If Muskrat's spirit helper
was right, then Young Hunter would return from this journey
to face whatever threatened the people. He took heart, even
though he could not see the shape of the challenge that lay
before him, like the hidden body of a snake stretched out,
waiting to strike.

CHAPTER SEVEN
AGWEDJIMAN = TRY HIM

As he followed the trail from the river that led back to their village on the bluff, Young Hunter felt a presence. He was being watched. He bent his knees a bit more as he walked, turning his body and head with each slow step, his arms held up, relaxed but ready. Suddenly, a brown body leaped from the brush and stood before him. Legs wide, teeth bared in a snarl, it blocked the trail.

"Arrrrhhh," Young Hunter growled, getting down on one knee. "Arrnnhhh!"

A dozen other animals, some the color of new-tanned buckskin, some black as a bear, some mottled with yellow and white, leaped out onto the trail to stand behind their leader. Tongues out, silent, they looked at Young Hunter. He straightened, raised his right hand, and pointed at the ground in front of the leader of the pack. "Lie down," he said.

With a little whine, the big dog did so, rolling over onto its back and showing its throat, its front paws held up to its chest like a puppy.

Young Hunter laughed. "You joker!" he said. He knelt and scratched the dog's wide chest. It rolled its eyes back and kicked with one hind leg. Young Hunter straightened. "Up now!"

The big dog leaped to its feet and began to run around in circles, the others dogs joining in. They were yelping now, fawning at Young Hunter's feet, jumping up for him to scratch them, too. Taking a step backward, he tripped over one of the dogs behind him and fell, laughing, among them. Tongues licked his face as he lay there, buried under an avalanche of dogs.

"*Gaa-shaa!*" he shouted. "Get away!" The dogs leaped back. Only their leader stayed close. Brown, big as a wolf, his eyes circled by white markings, he sat on his haunches, waiting. "Agwedjiman," Young Hunter said, "when I named you *Try Him,* I thought you would be the sort of dog to do whatever your human relations asked you to do. But I never thought you would end up being chief of your whole clan. Look at all your followers!"

Agwedjiman turned his head toward the left and then the right, looking at the others in his pack and then back at Young Hunter with what seemed to be a gaze of perfect, shared understanding. It was that way with dogs. They understood what people told them. They only pretended not to understand when they didn't want to be bothered.

Long ago, dogs and people even married each other. It was known that certain families had dogs for ancestors. The dogs, though, preferred to live in their own way. They didn't like having to work the way the Only People worked. It was better to roam about the village in their own band, doing as they wished. When it was time for hunting, their human friends would call them. Then they would go out with their masters, and when there was food being cooked and the dogs were hungry, they had only to sit near the fires and wait to be given their share. The dogs liked to stay close to the small children of the Only People and watch over them. A dog would even put itself between a toddling baby and the fire when a little one's steps brought it too close to the flames. Sometimes, though, when the people all left the village to go to the fishing falls or to camp for days among distant berry patches, the dogs would not go with them. They would stay in the village, doing as they wished, waiting for the Only People to return. Some said that when the people had gone far enough away, the dogs would even begin to live like human beings.

One story told how a man from the Salmon People went to visit friends in the Spearstone People's village. When he came to the village, he was given a warm welcome. He was treated as a relative and a friend, yet he recognized none of the people in the village. The village chief embraced him and he noticed the cap which the man was wearing. It had ears on it and looked a little like the cap some hunters wore to look like an owl and thus fool the deer when stalking. This cap, though, was different. But he soon forgot about it because the people were so sincerely friendly. His spirit helper did not warn him of danger and so he did not ask impolite questions. He thought that perhaps he had taken a wrong turn somewhere and found a village of the Dawn Land People that he had not visited before. The people sang welcoming songs for him. These songs were new to him, also. The voices of the people rose together in a high, strong series of notes which he tried to learn. As the days passed, he continued to feel welcome. They gave him plenty of fresh game to eat and a good lodge to use. He found himself growing interested in one of the young unmarried women. He had noticed her as soon as he arrived. Her large eyes were a color of brown he'd never seen before. Looking into her eyes, he felt himself becoming entranced but did not fight it. Finally, one night she came into his lodge. He embraced her until morning when she slipped out just before the first light of dawn.

So it went on for some days and the man was feeling very happy. But one morning, he woke and found himself alone. The village seemed to be deserted. The fires were cold. As he stood there, feeling confused, he heard the sound of strange voices. People were coming down the trail. He hid in some bushes to watch and, to his surprise, he saw all of the people he had expected to see when he first came to the village. He stepped out and showed himself.

"Cousin," they said, "welcome! We are just returning from the big lake to the north. We have been gone almost a moon. We've brought back a lot of smoked fish. Did you just arrive, cousin? Why were you hiding?"

"No," the man said, "I've been here for many days. The other people took care of me, the ones who stayed behind."

"How can that be?" said the real Spearstone People. "When we left our village, no one stayed behind but our dogs."

Then the people began to call their dogs.

"Wolf," they called.

"Raccoon! Joker!"

"Hold Fast! Little Bear!"

They called the names of all their dogs. At first the dogs did not come, but when they did, they slunk into the village with their heads down. None of them would look at the Salmon People man. As they crawled past him, the man noticed the familiar shape of the ears on the biggest dog. He noticed that one of the young female dogs attracted him in a strange way. That female dog went straight to her owner, a young unmarried woman who smiled at the Salmon People man as he walked over to speak with her. As the two of them talked, the young female dog came up and put her head into his lap. The young woman of the Spearstone People felt even happier then about meeting this good-looking young man. Even her dog approved of him!

Her good opinion turned out to be justified. He married her and joined the Spearstone People's village. He fit in well and lived there all of his life. The only strange thing about him was that when everyone else left the village to go fishing or berry picking, he always stayed behind with the dogs.

The dogs that had greeted Young Hunter were beginning to drift away up the trail. Only Agwedjiman and two others remained.

"My friend," Young Hunter said, "I am going to make a journey. Do you and your two brothers want to come with me? It will not be easy. It will be dangerous."

Agwedjiman whined and the other two dogs crawled on their bellies until they were at Young Hunter's feet. Neither was as large as their brother, but they were still bigger than any of the other village dogs. Their mother had been a wolf. She had been raised by Young Hunter's uncle, Fire Keeper, after being pulled from the river. She had fallen in, somewhere upstream, and almost drowned. She must have recognized the debt of life she owed, for she remained in the village, faithful all of her days. Only two winters ago she had repaid that debt defending two small girls from a panther, which crept close enough to attack them, as they picked wild strawberries. Malsumsqwa had hurled herself at the panther as it crouched. Fire Keeper killed the panther as it fought with Malsumsqwa. He hurled his spear and it whipped through the air farther than some men could have thrown an atlatl. He rolled the dead panther off the wolf, but her belly and throat were torn badly. She died without whimpering, her head cradled in the arms of Fire Keeper's smallest daughter.

Young Hunter put his right hand on the heads of each of the wolf's children, speaking their names. "Agwedjiman," he said, "Pabetciman, Danowa. Try Him, Ask Him, Where Is It. Do you all wish to go with me?"

The three dogs did not look away. Their eyes continued to hold his.

"We will travel a long way. We will have to go hungry. You will have to be silent and strong. You may not live to return to your families."

The dogs leaned closer to Young Hunter as he knelt among them. Heads side by side, their breath was against his face. Their breath warmed his face and strengthened him. He breathed out, sharing his own life breath with his friends.

The three dogs followed him to the edge of the village before melting off again into the undergrowth. They would be waiting for him on the path the next morning when it was time to leave. Now they would say good-bye to their own families. He would see them again at dawn, the fourth dawn since he had spoken with Bear Talker. It was hard to believe the days had flown by so quickly. It was like one of the old stories in which Sky Walker does not walk across the sky but runs.

Young Hunter stopped. He could feel his heart beating fast within his chest. He felt heavy, as if he were carrying the whole village on his shoulders. He began to take slow breaths, slowing his heartbeat. He had much to carry with him. He smiled, thinking of the many things people had given him over the past three days. Muskrat's hunting secret, mokasins, food, small things to bring him luck. Each day when he woke, he found things left near the door of their lodge in that special way of giving which the Only People followed, a way which did not call attention to the giver. If he were to carry with him everything he had been given, his pack would have to be as large as a wigwom! But he would take little more than could be carried in the packbasket his father had woven when Young Hunter was only a winter old. It was beautifully shaped for the use of a trapper or a traveler. The moose hide strips hung easily over his shoulders, the pack itself balanced perfectly just above the small of his back. It amazed him that his father, who did not live to see his son grown, had made a basket that fit him so perfectly when he was a man. Perhaps his father had seen him in a dream. Perhaps that same dream had even shown him Young Hunter setting out on this journey. Young Hunter shook his head. He was not alone. His burden was a heavy one, but no more than a man of the Only People should expect to carry.

One weight did trouble him, though. It was that of the Long Thrower. Soon he would reach Bear Talker's lodge and the deep-seeing man would give it to him—whatever it was. It was a thing of great power. Of this he was certain. Young Hunter wondered if his shoulders would be broad enough to

59

flute music

carry such a thing. True, he was old enough to be married, to have children. But he was of that age which his people even then called a Child With Children. It was the men of his uncle's age group, those old enough to speak in council, who should be the ones given such a responsibility. They were the ones who would know better what to do and how to do … whatever it was that he was supposed to do. He did not know what it was. He did not even know enough to try to guess. It was like going hunting in a dream. Trails could turn into smoke, rivers become fire, stones grow legs and walk and begin to hunt human beings.

Young Hunter stopped walking again. He shook his head. His thought trail had started to become real. He was seeing something, entering into a dream with his eyes wide open. A long trail and something terrible pursuing him … a man who was no longer a man … huge figures like walking stones … It was as if he were truly seeing ahead as a deep-seeing man would do. But that was not what he wanted. That was not his way. He slapped his own face hard, trying to clear away the spider webs of his waking dream. He sat down by the trail. He needed to put his mind on a new path. He searched his thoughts and then smiled. He had found the memory of the night before.

The light from the Night Traveler was bright. Young Hunter stood only a few paces away from the back of the lodge belonging to Willow Girl's family. Raising the cedar flute to his lips, he began to play.

> *I am lonely, I am lonely*
> *No one listens to my song.*
> *I am lonely, I am lonely*
> *My song is a falling leaf.*

The high, sweet notes of Young Hunter's flute echoed through the village. Strangely, though, no one seemed to be able to

multiple wives

hear that song except for Willow Girl. Her parents paid no attention when she sat up from her bed at the first note. Her mother sighed and her father rolled over and covered his head with his robe. They emphatically paid no notice as she slipped out the door.

The Night Traveler's face was full and her soft light made it seem almost as bright as day, though the edges of things seemed less sharp, more like the texture of a dream. Willow Girl walked straight toward Young Hunter where he stood among the trees. She was tall, straight as a tree herself, graceful as a deer, and the fringes of her dress swayed like grasses in the wind as she walked. Another girl might look down and scuff her feet as she approached the young man come to court her, but Willow Girl was not another girl. As she came to Young Hunter, her eyes were on his face.

For a moment, Young Hunter hesitated and he missed a note in his song. Her face was so serious. Perhaps she was going to tell him to go away. His music was keeping her from sleep. She had no interest in a man who was going away. A bird fluttered in his stomach, but he continued to play, trying to make his music as sweet as ripe berries. He remembered the tales of how Bear Talker had won each of his four wives through his flute playing. Though he knew his own flute did not have the magic powers that the flute of a deep-seeing man had, still, he hoped he was charming Willow Girl. He stopped. He took a deep breath.

"Your flute playing," Willow Girl said, "is awful. I am glad that I know you are a good hunter. Otherwise I would be worried that a man who plays the flute so badly would not be capable enough to provide for our family. It is my plan," she said, "that we have at least four children."

61

CHAPTER EIGHT
FIRE KEEPER

Young Hunter's feet moved him along the trail, but his thoughts kept pulling him back toward the village. There was too much to think about, too much to understand. He tried to concentrate on the simple task of placing one foot in front of the other. The big dog's right shoulder was almost touching Young Hunter's left thigh as it turned its head up to look into Young Hunter's face. Young Hunter slapped his hand affectionately on Agwedjiman's back. He could no longer hear the sounds of the dog's two brothers on the trail ahead. They were scouting the way, silent as wolves. Now and then, one would look back from around a bend or would slip quietly out of the brush by the side of the trail to walk with them a short space before trotting on ahead once more. Truly, when a man was with his dogs he was not alone.

"Agwesis," Young Hunter said, speaking the dog's pet name, "you guard me well. But you cannot guard me from my thoughts. I am all right. Don't worry. But it is fortunate for me that you and your brothers are watching the way for me. This morning I'm like a puppy whose eyes have just begun to open. Like someone who has stared too long into the sky and is now half-blinded by the light." Young Hunter stroked the big dog's head and it whined with happiness.

Young Hunter shifted his pack. He began to walk more purposefully. He would reach the village of the Salmon People before night. There he would be given the second half of the secret of the Long Thrower. He hefted the bundle that he carried in his hand. It was wrapped tightly in a skin decorated with Bear Talker's symbols.

Now, Young Hunter thought, *I will shape my thoughts toward the work ahead of me. I will not let them wander in circles like the water beetles that spin on the surface.* But even as he thought that, he wondered if the heroes of the old stories ever felt as uncertain as he did on this morning. Did Long Hair or the One Who Shaped Himself ever feel confused about whether to go on or return home? They were challenged by monsters and they defeated them. They were attacked by evil magic and overcame it. But in none of those stories was it ever mentioned that those heroes found it hard just to keep walking, one slow step at a time, toward a destination they couldn't name.

It was a cold, clear morning. A good morning for hunting. In less than a moon, the first snow would fall. Not the snow that stayed, but the snow that was a scout for Frost Maker, melting back into the earth, preparing the way. Young Hunter always loved that first snow. He liked the patterns and shapes it formed, the way familiar things became completely new when coated by snow, became secret and hidden. But always before, when it was close to the snow time, Young Hunter had been with friends and relatives. He had known that when the wind was coldest, when the snow piled deep, he would be in a wigwom or a bark lodge, hearing old tales and hunting stories. Always before, he would be in their village or in the hunting camp. He would not be walking toward a strange destiny with only his dogs to keep him company.

The fallen leaves were noisy on the trail. A grey squirrel, its bad memory already preventing it from finding the hickory nuts it had recently buried, rustled in a bad-tempered way through the leaves on the trail ahead of them. It was so

63

involved in the task that it did not notice the man and dog drawing near. Agwesis looked up at Young Hunter, who flicked a finger in the direction of the squirrel. The big dog leaped like a partridge taking off. In two bounds he was almost on top of the squirrel. When he yelped, close to its tail, the squirrel leaped straight up into the air, then ran first one way and then the other before reaching a tree and darting around to the far side of the trunk as it climbed. It reappeared on a high branch, chattering insults down at them. Agwedjiman, who had stopped as soon as the squirrel began to run, sat on his haunches with his tongue hanging out. He yawned, an insulting yawn, then looked at Young Hunter for approval.

"Agwesis," Young Hunter said, laughing, "you are a joker!"

The big dog made a snorting noise which sounded almost like a laugh, and trotted back to Young Hunter's side as they continued their journey toward the west.

There were too many things to think of, that was the trouble. Young Hunter decided to list them in his head and think of just one thing at a time as he walked. Then it would be easy. First, there were the words spoken to him by Fire Keeper just before leaving. Those words were not spoken to him as Young Hunter's uncle. They were spoken as the *sagamon*, the village chief. It was hard for Young Hunter to think of Fire Keeper as a sagamon, one who makes decisions for many. Perhaps it was because Fire Keeper was such a good sagamon. A good sagamon never forced the people to do anything. Each of the village families, with parents and grandparents, children and cousins and uncles and aunts, would follow the words of a sagamon only when those words reflected the will of all the families gathered together. A good sagamon followed the counsel and advice given him by the women. He listened to the old ones, and paid attention to the visions of Bear Talker. A sagamon of the Only People might hold that office all of his life, but he only held it as long as his decisions were not selfish. It was his job to be there when needed, to be silent when there was no need to speak. A sagamon who always drew attention to himself would be as bothersome as a foolish hunter who talked loudly when drawing near to the game animals. It was because Fire Keeper was such a good leader, a leader who followed, that Young Hunter found it easy to forget his uncle was their sagamon. It was now six winters since the women had raised him up into that office when the old sagamon, Slow Walker, had fallen through the ice.

Young Hunter remembered his uncle sitting in front of his lodge. It was clear in his mind, as if he were seeing Fire Keeper for the first time. For the first time he truly noticed the calm way his uncle had of holding his hands around the calumet pipe. For the first time he saw that there were strands of grey in his uncle's black hair, which was coiled on top of his head and knotted with a thong. It was the way a married man wore his hair on formal occasions, not loose about his shoulders, secured only around his forehead with a headband as was Young Hunter's. One of Fire Keeper's small children, the nephew Young Hunter called Raccoon for his curiosity and his quick hands, sat in his father's lap. Usually the boy was quick to run over to Young Hunter, grab him by the legs and throw him down, or climb into his arms and squeeze him tightly with both arms around his neck. But that morning, Raccoon sat quietly in his father's lap as the sagamon spoke. One of Raccoon's hands was held up to his cheek and his eyes were wide as he stared at Young Hunter.

"What you carry with you," Fire Keeper said, "you carry for the people. We have watched you grow, and the oldest women always speak of you as a young man who listens. When you chose to hunt in a sacred manner for the people, all of us who are your relatives felt our hearts grow big with pride. Now, as you travel, we will be with you. Our spirits will travel with you and wherever you go you carry us with you."

Fire Keeper stood and placed his son on the ground. He looked for a moment at his nephew and then motioned with his chin toward the back of the lodge. Raccoon watched the two men as they went behind the lodge, but did not follow them. There was an open space there where Fire Keeper had been working on the dugout canoe. It was finished now and it lay near the head of the lake trail at the other end of the village. It waited there for the first group of people headed in the direction of the lake to notice it and carry it down. No one would be asked to carry that canoe. It would be done because someone saw that it needed to be done. That was why it was there near the trail. It might be done that day or it might not be done until a moon passed. But it would be done.

"You are getting to be a good wrestler," Fire Keeper said. "I have watched you defeat your cousins and the other young men in your age group. You know that I used to play at wrestling."

Young Hunter nodded. Fire Keeper was known as the best wrestler in all of the thirteen villages. After he became a full-grown man, no one ever beat him. It was many winters since he had entered into a contest with another man, but the width of his shoulders and the strength of his hands and arms still were those of a wrestler.

"Come here," his uncle said. His voice was no longer that of the sagamon. It was the voice of the man who used to carry Young Hunter, laughing, on his back when his nephew was only a little older than Raccoon. He would run with him all the way down the path to their lake and then dive into the water with him. It was good to hear that voice. "Here," he said again, "I want to show you some throws you have not yet learned. You can think of these as you travel."

Young Hunter held out his arms and stepped forward cautiously—but not cautiously enough, for he found himself flying through the air to land on his back with Fire Keeper's shoulder against his stomach.

Those were good throws that his uncle had taught him. Young Hunter moved his hands and shifted his hips, doing a little hop and turn as he walked, remembering the feel of them, even the last one which his uncle had not completed.

"This one," Fire Keeper said, "is only to be used when your life is threatened. It is a spirit throw and you can use it against a man who is much bigger than you. If done with strength, it may even kill your opponent. I show it to you because you are going to travel far, Nephew. It will give you strength to have this knowledge in your arms."

Young Hunter went through each of the throws in his mind. Soon he had gone three looks down the trail and the sun was three hands up in the sky. His mind felt clear. *This is a good way to do it,* he thought, *taking one thing at a time.* What would he think of now? Would he think of the farewell his grandparents had given him? Perhaps he should keep that for the times ahead when the nights were cold and he was alone with the wind. He lifted his right hand to touch the knife which hung on his chest, suspended in its embroidered leather sheath by the thong around his neck. The stone knife was a good new one. His grandfather had given it to him and it had only been sharpened once. It would last a long time. Each time a stone knife was sharpened, more of it was flaked away and it grew smaller. The chert of the knife was milky in color, and its shape perfectly fit his hand. It was almost as sharp as one of the slate knives used by the Big Water People far to the south near where the Shorter People lived. Those slate knives were easier to sharpen, for they could be ground to an edge, not napped. But their use was best for the big water animals. The Only People did not hunt such game. Knives of stone were good for them. It was meant to be so. That was why the Owner Creator placed the chert quarry in their land, just as he placed the slate near the place of the Big Water People. He thought of his grandfather making that knife for him. He pictured his grandmother's hands embroidering the sheath with porcupine quills.

He lowered his hand from the knife. *Nda,* he thought. He would save his thoughts of Rabbit Stick and Sweetgrass Woman. Those thoughts were both sweet and sad. Instead, he would find something else to think of, something which was sweet but not sad. He would think of Willow Girl. It would be good, indeed, to think about her. His feet began to move more quickly, almost to a trot. The big dog at his side looked up at him, but Young Hunter did not notice.

In the light of the moon, Willow Girl's face shone up at him. She was so close that he could feel the warmth in the white clouds of breath from her mouth as she spoke. She placed her hands on his forearms.

"Why did you wait so long to play your flute behind my lodge?"

Young Hunter tried to think of what to say. Words usually came easily to him, but now they were like fish that refuse to strike at the bait. He rolled his shoulders and looked down at his feet. As he did so, he saw Willow Girl's legs. Her feet were perfectly shaped for strong walking, her ankles graceful, yet solid, the muscles of her calves rounded and rippled. The fringe of her skirt brushed down over her dimpled knees. He wanted to put his hands on her feet and run them slowly up her legs, feeling her legs with his palms and fingers all the way up to her hips.

"What is wrong?" she said. "Are you thinking of another girl?"

"*Nda!*" The word exploded from Young Hunter's mouth so loudly that he knew everyone in the village, even those so carefully pretending that the two young people were invisible, could hear him. He thought he heard a smothered laugh from inside Willow Girl's wigwom. He took a few steps backward into the shadow of the trees, away from the lodge, drawing Willow Girl with him. Her hands stayed on his arms and she moved as smoothly with him as if she were part of his own shadow.

"You are ... the only one I think about," he said. "I think of you so much, that is why I took so long to come and play my flute here."

"Because you were afraid I would not listen and come outside?"

"Because I was afraid you *would* listen and come outside. Then, just like now, I wouldn't know what to say or do." He shook his head. "My words stick to my teeth like spruce gum."

"Your words are reaching my ears," Willow Girl said. She squeezed his arms with her long fingers and drew him closer to her. "Do you remember how we used to wrestle when we were little children?"

Young Hunter drew a very deep breath. "Uh-hunh," he said.

"I used to beat you then," Willow Girl said. "I was bigger than you. Do you remember what you said? You said that one day you were going to throw me down and get on top of me and not let me up. Do you remember?"

Young Hunter remembered.

"Why did we stop wrestling?"

"It was—" he cleared his throat, for his voice came out high and strained. "It was because we were not brother and sister. We were not cousins. You ... were becoming a young woman."

"Are you happy now that we are not cousins? Are you happy that your family belongs to the Bear and that my family is Turtle?"

"I am very happy," Young Hunter said. His own hands had somehow found their way to her waist. "Cousins cannot marry."

"Are you ready to bring presents to my family?" Willow Girl asked.

"On the day I return." As he spoke those words, a cold wind struck his back. He shivered and Willow Girl pulled him even closer, their bodies pressed together. She moved her hips and now her hands were no longer on his arms, but moving down his side. Young Hunter felt the heat of his own blood. The cold wind was forgotten.

"So this is what you have here," Willow Girl said. "How can it hide under such a small breechclout?"

Young Hunter's hard breathing and the breathing of the dog loping by his side made him aware of how fast he was running. He slowed down and began to walk, looking around. He had come a long way with those thoughts of Willow Girl. He would come back to those thoughts again. And he would return to her as he promised. They would finish what they had begun. They would marry and complete the circle of a family. They would build a new bark lodge with two rooms, connected to the lodge of his grandparents. There would be room for all of them and for the children they would have. As he thought of their lives together, he felt certain that he would return. No matter what he faced, he would return.

Agwedjiman pranced at his side. It had been a good run. He put his nose against Young Hunter's thigh and whined softly.

"Nda," Young Hunter said. "No more running now. I do not want to arrive at the Salmon People village too soon. There are more things I must think about before I speak to their far-seeing woman." He lifted up the bundle that held the Long Thrower. "I must think about this."

CHAPTER NINE
COMES FLYING

"Now," Bear Talker said, "you hold it in your hand. Now you hold the Long Thrower. But it is not yet ready. Let me show you."

Bear Talker reached out his hand and took the long piece of bent wood from Young Hunter's hands. Young Hunter had been turning it, trying to understand its use. It was too long to be an atlatl and there was no place to rest the butt of a spear. And of what use was the piece of sinew tied to one end like a short fishing line?

Bear Talker stood and placed one end of the Long Thrower on the ground, braced against the side of his left foot. He leaned on it and it bent further. Then, with his left hand, he pulled the string of sinew up and hooked it over the other end where a set of grooves held it in place. As he did this, he hummed a song. He held the Long Thrower up, the sinew string holding it in a shape like the hungry moon. With his right hand he plucked the string. It hummed. It was a sound that touched the center of Young Hunter's being.

"It must be held this way," Bear Talker said. It was before dawn, and the light from the small fire in the center of Bear Talker's lodge threw long shadows as he reached across it to hand the Long Thrower to Young Hunter. Young Hunter saw their shadows thrown against the wall by the light of the fire.

71

Those shadows were huge, and the Long Thrower linked them like a rainbow of shadows between two hills. Young Hunter took the Long Thrower in his left hand, holding it at the center. It balanced well that way.

"Hold it at an angle. Uh-hunh, like that. Grasp the sinew with your thumb and leader finger. Pull it back toward your cheek. Keep the left arm held out. Now, let it go!"

Young Hunter opened his thumb and finger and the sinew string hissed back, faster than thought, striking his left forearm and burning it.

"Ahhhh!" Young Hunter said, almost dropping the Long Thrower.

"Bend your left arm a little so that it will not strike you. Uh-hunh. Now, pull back and let it go again."

Again Young Hunter plucked and pulled back the sinew. This time when he released it, the sound it made was a hum and thump. He felt the sound, felt as if something had been released by the sinew string, sent flying from it like a grouse springing up from a branch into flight.

"I begin to see," Young Hunter said. "But what does it throw?"

"First," Bear Talker said, "hear the story." He picked up a coal from the fire between his fingers and held it up. It glowed red, but did not burn his fingers. Young Hunter was not shocked. Bear Talker had a special relationship with fire. He had seen the deep-seeing man juggle whole handfuls of glowing coals, even pick up the red-hot stones for the sweat lodge with his bare hands without being blistered. Bear Talker placed the coal into the bowl of his loaded pipe, sucked in so that it ignited the smoking herb, then flicked the coal out and back into the fire with one long fingernail. He inhaled the smoke and let it rise from his mouth with his words. The story became stronger with that smoke, each breath carrying a phrase which would rise up to be judged for its truth by the Owner Creator.

72

origin story of bow

"It was not long ago," Bear Talker said. The smoke circled his face. "It was in the time of the mothers of our grandmothers. The people noticed that the game was becoming scarce. Then one hunter did not return. And another. Finally, one day, two hunters came upon the tracks. The tracks were in soft earth crossing a trail not far from the village. Those tracks made the footprints of the biggest bear look like those of a cub.

"When they brought word back to the village, the elders understood. Fear Bear had returned, one of the Ancient Ones from the old times. One of the Great Ones that hunted human beings. Three of the best hunters took their dogs and set out on the trail. They were strong men. Each of them could bring down a moose with a single spear cast from their atlatls. Those men and their dogs did not return, and that night the people heard the sound of the great animal walking in the darkness, circling their village. It coughed and its cough was as deep as thunder. Only the fires they kept burning kept the monster away. They kept those fires going night and day, hoping that Fear Bear would leave. But each night it circled the village and each night it came closer.

"One young man, though, had a dream. He saw himself hunting Fear Bear and killing the monster. At dawn he went out from the village, carrying his strongest, sharpest spear. He found the tracks and followed them. He followed them until the Day Traveler was overhead in the sky. Then, as he knelt to study the tracks and figure out how close the monster was, he heard a sound which filled his heart with fear. It was the sound of heavy breathing from the brush behind him. Fear Bear had circled back!

"The man began to run. He could hear the bear coming after him. He went off the trail, through a tangle of grapevines. As he ran, his spear became caught in some of the vines which were wrapped around a young tree. He pulled to free it, for the bear was close behind. The young tree bent, but the vines still were tangled around the butt of the spear, and as he turned,

73

he saw that the bear was almost upon him, rearing up on its hind legs to grab him. He let go of the spear and the vines. The young tree whipped back straight and the vines hurled the spear forward, its point burying itself in Fear Bear's shoulder. As the bear fell back, biting on the spear and growling as loudly as an avalanche of boulders, the young man slipped through the vines and ran. He ran until he was almost back to the village. Then he realized: he was not being followed. Slowly, cautiously, he made his way back to the tangle of grapevines. There he found his spear broken into pieces and a blood trail leading toward the hills. He did not follow, but as he walked back to the village, he was deep in thought.

"That night a dream came to him. A bird flew in front of him; it turned and spoke to him. *Take my feathers,* it said. *I will fly with your spear.* Then he saw the young tree tangled in vines. *Take me,* the tree said. *I give myself to you to help you save your people.*

"The next morning, he went back to the place of tangled vines. He cut down the tree and bent it. He tried holding it in that bent throwing shape with vines, but they broke too easily. Finally he made a string of twisted sinew and strung it across the arc of the bent tree. When he plucked his finger on the sinew string, he heard its voice. Days passed and Fear Bear did not return. The people of the village were glad, but they still feared that the monster was hiding close to the village and they kept their fires burning. Only the young man went out of the village. He went to that place of the tangled vines and there he fashioned small spears. He notched them at one end so that they held the taut string and he fastened to them the feathers of birds, split and tied on with sinew so that the small spears would fly through the air straight. He knew now that this thing he had been given was a powerful thing. It was a Long Thrower.

"He practiced and tried different ways of using it. It could hurl one of the small spears at great speed, hurl them much farther than the longest spear cast. He sharpened them and hardened their tips with fire. Soon he was able to shoot them with great accuracy and they could pierce through a small tree the thickness of a man's wrist. Each day when he returned to the village, he brought back game that he shot using the Long Thrower. But whenever he returned to the village, he had the Long Thrower unstrung and wrapped in hide so that it seemed to be no more than a walking stick.

"Then, one night, another dream came to him. He saw that Fear Bear was, indeed, still alive. It had been licking its wounds and bathing itself in mud to heal. Soon it would come again to hunt the Only People. The next day, before dawn, that young man went to the deep-seeing woman.

"'Grandmother,' he said, 'I have been given a great gift by my spirit helpers. I think I have been shown this so I can help the Only People to live.'

"Then, within the secrecy of the deep-seeing woman's lodge, he unwrapped the Long Thrower and showed it to her.

"'I have dreamt, Grandmother,' he said. 'I see that the Ancient One who hunts our people will return. It seems to me that I must go out and meet him. I must use this Long Thrower to kill him.'

"She held the Long Thrower in her hand and looked at it closely. She looked at it in a way which surprised the young man, for there was no sign of wonder as she looked at it and she nodded her head knowingly. Then she looked at the young man, whose name was Comes Flying.

"'Grandson,' she said, 'you have dreamt well. You must go out tomorrow and meet the Ancient One. I will help you with this medicine. Remember to show this Long Thrower to no one. Start at the place of tangled vines and then go north. As you hunt, remember to listen.'

"'I will do as you say, Grandmother,' Comes Flying said.

"Comes Flying set out at dawn. Only the deep-seeing woman saw him leave. He went to the tangled vines place. There he found fresh tracks of Fear Bear. The Ancient One

75

had returned and Comes Flying knew that its wound no longer was troubling it. He began to follow the trail. Now the sun was four hands high in the sky. He carried the Long Thrower in his left hand and, between the fingers of his right hand, he carried three of the small feathered spears. When he reached a place where there was a big pine tree with a double top and many dead branches near the ground, he knew he had gone far enough. The wind had changed and was at his back. The tracks were very fresh. He knew that his scent had reached Fear Bear. He began to climb the tree, thinking to see Fear Bear from the top. But when he was less than halfway up, the height of four men above the ground, a great roar came from below him and the whole big tree shook. He almost fell from the tree, but grasped a branch and pulled himself back up at the last moment, just as the claws of Fear Bear raked the trunk of the tree only a hand's width below his feet. Reaching up from the ground, Fear Bear could reach almost to the height of four men.

"He looked down into the Ancient One's eyes. They were full of death. The strength of those eyes was so great that Comes Flying had to turn away from them. He quickly climbed higher, as the great bear continued to strike at the tree, clawing to reach him. It seemed the whole tree would soon fall, but Comes Flying kept himself calm. He slung one leg over a branch, braced his back against the trunk, and fitted a small spear to the Long Thrower's string. From where he was, a man could not have thrown a spear down with strength, but as he pulled back the string, he felt the power building within the Long Thrower. He pulled back as far as his ear and then let go! As the small spear struck into the bear's neck, he was already fitting the second small spear to the string. It too dove down to follow its brother. The great beast was so large that the small feathered spears looked like tiny slivers as they disappeared into the Ancient One's fur, but when the second one drove home, Fear Bear's whole body quivered. Fear Bear struck the tree with both paws, its growl the roar of a whirlwind. The tree creaked from its roots as Comes Flying fitted the third of the small feathered spears to the string. Again, his aim was true and the small spear dove into Fear Bear's chest. The Ancient One staggered back and then struck the tree again, biting at it with its huge teeth, sending splinters of wood flying. From the quiver at his side, Comes Flying pulled a fourth arrow. He aimed and let go. It pierced to Fear Bear's heart. The Ancient One fell back and collapsed.

"Comes Flying stayed in the tree for a long time. He watched carefully, but there was no motion, no sign of breath from Fear Bear. He threw sticks down, but they bounced off the great dark hill of the animal's body and it did not move. At last, he climbed down. Even lying flat, it was as tall as his shoulders, its mouth large enough to swallow him whole.

"When Comes Flying went back to the village, he first went to the lodge of the deep-seeing woman. 'Grandmother,' he said, 'I have come back.' He handed her the canine tooth that he had taken from Fear Bear's mouth. It was the size of the bone in a man's forearm.

"'Now, Grandson,' the old woman said, 'you must decide what to do. You have found the secret of the Long Thrower. You are not the first to know of it. It was found a long time ago by those of us who see in the dark. It was decided then that the Long Thrower would not be good for the people. Its power was too great. With it, we might wipe out the animal people. With it, it would be easy to kill other human beings at a distance where we could not look into their eyes and become ashamed at taking another human life. Long ago, others used the Long Thrower to clean this land of the Ancient Ones, those who hunted the people. Now, Grandson, it seems the last of them is gone. What will you decide?'

"Comes Flying did not speak. It seemed that he had heard her words before in his dream. He handed the Long Thrower, unstrung and hidden in its wrapping of skins, to the deep-

77

DAWN LAND

seeing woman. It would be kept until the people needed it again."

Bear Talker slapped his palm down onto the skin beneath them. "This is the skin of Fear Bear. But it is only half of the skin. You see it is as large as the skins of two of the bears we have today. But still it is only half of the skin. The other half was given to be held by the one who keeps the small spears for the Long Thrower. That is where you must go now. You must go to the Salmon People's village and near there you will find ... that other woman. That one Oldest Talker tried to teach. You will show her the Long Thrower. Then she will give you the small feathered spears that she has kept even as the generations before us have kept them."

PART TWO

MOON OF FALLING LEAVES

CHAPTER TEN
THE CROOKED KNIFE

There were thirteen villages, thirteen different bands of the people. They had spread throughout the Dawn Land long ago, moving back to the north and the east after the great mountains of ice returned to the Forever Winter Land. As the land changed, the great inland sea shrinking, the people learned the land's ways and became part of the land. Each place where they lived, they became part of the land, giving back to it in equal measure as they received. They were called by the other nations to their south Dawn Land People, but they simply called themselves *Alnonbak:* Human Beings. They greeted each dawn with thanks for all they were given.

Some of the village bands had names which reflected their relation to the giving land. The Spearstone People lived close to the quarries of chert stone which made good lance points. The Salmon People lived near the falls of the Long River. There the best places could be found for spearing the salmon as they made their seasonal run. Two men with spears could catch enough to feed the village for a week in the time it took for their torches to burn out.

Young Hunter had visited the Salmon People before, during a spring salmon run. He had not fished the way the Salmon People fished and his grandmother wanted him to learn.

81

Winter Stories

"Your uncle Fish Hawk will welcome you," Sweetgrass Woman said. "He married a woman of the Salmon People and settled in their village. His sons are close to your age and they will welcome you too. When you see your uncle, tell him that his mother wonders what his face looks like."

That visit had been three winters ago. Young Hunter had stayed through the whole salmon run. He had learned how to make a night-fishing torch by tying together a bundle of birch bark strips, frayed at the edges, and wedging them into the end of a pole of green wood. He had learned from his uncle how to make a fish spear. As the older man fashioned a spear for his nephew, binding the two curved pieces around the point so they would encircle and hold the body of a speared salmon, his hands moved quickly in a way that seemed familiar to Young Hunter. Fish Hawk moved his hands in the same swift, sure way his older brother, Fire Keeper, did when working in a dugout. Fish Hawk, though, was not a sagamon like Fire Keeper.

Big Story, the sagamon of the Salmon People, was a very thin, very straight man of middle years who seemed to be a special favorite of the small children in the village. Everywhere he went, Big Story was in the midst of a crowd of little ones. Young Hunter had soon learned that the sagamon's name was an apt one. He was the best storyteller in the village. During the warm moons, he would sit by the side of the river in the bright light from the Night Traveler and tell of the many things that had happened to the people, things as recent as the past winter and as far in the past as the time of their grandparents' great-great-grandparents. Young Hunter enjoyed listening to those stories as much as the little children did, but he knew that the best stories, the very best ones, were the ones which Big Story saved for the winter moons. Then, when the snakes were asleep and the land was resting, Big Story could tell the legends of the Before Times. Young Hunter vowed to himself that he would come back sometime to the Salmon People when the snow blanket was spread, to hear those old and powerful tales.

punishment

As Young Hunter came closer to the place where the hunting lands of the Only People gave way to those of the Salmon People, he thought about his relatives and wondered how they were. He thought of his uncle Fish Hawk and his cousins. It was only two moons since the summer gathering-together time, but as was always the case because people came only when they felt like coming, not everyone had been there. There were no rules to be followed when it came to the time of gathering all the people together. People came or did not come as they wished. It had been two summers now since his uncle or his cousins had come to the gathering-together. *Perhaps*, he thought, *they are now taller than I am. Perhaps ...*

Suddenly, Agwedjiman stopped. The hairs on his back stiffened and he spread his front legs wide and growled. A sound came from the left of the trail and Pabetciman and Danowa came out, backing toward Young Hunter. Their legs were stiff too. Young Hunter tensed, listening. He could hear nothing, smell nothing. Though his sense of smell was not as good as that of his dogs, he could still scent a deer or a moose from a distance. He knew the smell of those animals when they were startled. The scent of the bear, the rabbit, the fox, certain birds, all of those were familiar to him. So too were the odors of the plants of the forest. He was always aware of those scents, even without thinking of them. He could smell nothing, yet there was something in the air, something which was fearful. It was as if he had another sense than smell or hearing or sight. He remembered how Bear Talker spoke of the kind of smelling that a deep-seeing person could do, a smelling that scented out lying and fear. Once, when two men of different families had come to Bear Talker with a dispute, he had been quick to scent out the one who was lying. That man, who had hunted in the territory of the other's family without their permission, was told to leave the village and not come back for four winters.

Young Hunter could feel the hairs on the back of his own neck standing up. He moved slowly, shifting his position so

83

that his legs were wider apart, placing the bundle that held the Long Thrower on the ground. His spear thrower was between the heel of his right hand and his two small fingers. He fitted the shaft of his spear into the atlatl and cocked his arm back. He listened, smelled, watched the dogs. But nothing happened. Nothing came. The dogs were now facing in three directions— north, west, and south. Something was out there, but it was going away. With that other sense, Young Hunter felt it going. It was as if eyes had been watching them and now those eyes turned elsewhere. He thought of how a deep-seeing person could send his or her spirit to watch things faraway. Yet, somehow, he felt that what had been close was like no human being he had ever known, even one who could send a spirit shape to spy.

It is going, Young Hunter thought. And another voice inside him spoke, saying, *It will return.* Then, like the air suddenly clearing after being heavy with the threat of thunder, it was gone. The dogs relaxed and Young Hunter stood straight again.

Young Hunter resumed walking. The three dogs stayed close. It was near the end of the day. The Day Traveler could only be seen through breaks in the trees. It was still another half-day's walk to the Salmon People's village. Young Hunter began to look for a good place to camp. As always, he looked up to the treeline first, scanning it for broken snags and dead branches. Although the dreams about that night his parents died no longer visited him, he could still call back that memory and see again the sharp fingers of the great tree piercing the top of their lodge. That memory always stood by his side whenever he set up a new camp.

There was a slight rise ahead, and a spear's cast away from the trail, an indentation in the south-facing hill. The drainage was good there, the ground dry. He began to cut poles, using the stone knife which he took from his neck sheath. Soon he had fashioned a lean-to frame. He cut boughs from the hemlocks and wove them into a covering. Other boughs spread on the floor made a good sleeping mat. It was dark by the time he was done. He sat on the boughs and the three dogs curled up behind him. It would be good to feel their comforting warmth this night. Above, the little stars were already visible, but it was a night without the Night Traveler. Grandmother Moon would not be back in her place in the heavens for another two days. And then she would be thin and hungry. Young Hunter wondered where he would be by the time she looked down on him full-bellied and strong. He wondered how many times she would vanish and then return to her place in the sky during his travels. He would be going a long way, this he knew from what Bear Talker told him. The heroes of the old stories—Long Hair, Fast Runner—they made journeys halfway around the world in a day. They went carried by great winds or flying on the backs of giant birds. He felt glad that he would not be traveling that fast. Somehow, he knew that he would reach the destination where danger was waiting for him all too soon.

As Young Hunter thought all of this, his hands were busy. From the pouch at his belt he had pulled forth his fire bundle, unwrapping the large clamshell and opening it. Still hinged, the shell was lined inside with blue clay. A small hole had been bored through it so that even when the shell was tied tightly shut, there was space to let the smoke breathe out as the piece of rotted wood, which had been burning slowly all day within that shell, kept his fire. It was wood from the yellow birch, the tree that is the best friend to fire. In such a specially prepared shell, one could keep fire for more than a day. He placed the gently smoking spunk at the base of the pile of tinder he had prepared, the twigs and dry bark shaped like a tiny lodge. Leaning down, he blew on the spunk and the smoke curled up thickly with each breath. Then the bright red flame flared up and caught the tinder sticks. He placed other sticks around those until the fire was large enough to warm his hands and face. From the top of his pack he pulled out chestnuts he had gathered. He would roll them into the coals when the fire had burned down. He had eaten as he walked, chewing some of the dried meat Sweetgrass Woman had packed for him, so he was not very hungry. But the making of a fire and the preparing of food were good to do. These things calmed him. His heart had been beating fast as he started to make the fire, but as soon as it began to burn, he felt his body relax. He had been tenser than he had known. He shrugged his shoulders and stretched his arms. The sinew cords in his back popped as he did this. He reached up to massage the back of his neck, leaned back against one of the supports of his lean-to, breathed in deeply, and sighed.

A broken maple sapling was close to his leg. He twisted it to break it free and then reached into his pack to take out his crooked knife. The knife was a good one, its handle made of ironwood, its blade the incisor tooth of a large male beaver. He began to use it to strip the stick, his thumb against the handle, drawing the blade in toward himself.

With a crooked knife, one could do many things—planing, hollowing out, shaping down—just as the beaver could carve the hardest wood with its yellow teeth. The beaver was the one who gave the Dawn Land People the crooked knife. Once, long ago, a trapper found a mother beaver caught in his snare near the water's edge. She was dead, but a live young one clung to her fur. The trapper took pity and brought the young one home. He made acorn mush for it and fed it each day and it grew strong. It followed him around during the days, playing with him as a dog plays, and it slept by his side at night. When he left it alone in the lodge, it would take his clothing, and anything else it could drag, and put the things into piles as if it were building dams and lodges. Finally, after the passage of several seasons, the beaver was little no longer. It was fully grown. It had learned to travel with the man by riding in his pack, its head and forepaws outside so that it could watch everything. It was the spring of the year, and the trapper saw

86

how all the animals were with their mates. He began to realize that the beaver should be with its own people. So, one day, he placed it in the pack and carried it to a distant pond.

"Here," he said, "is a place for you to live, Brother. I will not trap here. This is the hunting territory of my family and no one else will come here to trap. Here you will be safe. Here you can have a family and live with your people."

The beaver looked up at the man as he spoke, as if it understood every word. Then it turned and went into the water and swam slowly away without looking back. The man was sad to see his friend go, even though he knew this was the way it should be. Still, he was surprised to see it go so willingly from him without even looking back. He had cared for it and fed it for so long. That night, the man had a dream. In his dream, his brother the young beaver came to him and spoke. He did not look like a beaver, but appeared to be a man. Still, the trapper recognized him.

"Older Brother," the beaver man said, "you see me as I appear when I am among my own people. When you trapped my people before and killed my mother, you did not know my people well. You saw me, a helpless baby. You took pity on me and saved my life. So I forgave you for the harm you caused to my people. You did nothing evil. It was only the natural way and you were trapping to keep your own people alive. But when I became your brother, you treated me with love. At last, when I was grown, you returned me to my own people. So I have come to you in this dream. I have seen how you struggle to make certain things with your stone knife. When you wake, return to the shores of my pond. There you will find a special gift."

When the man woke, he knew the dream was a true one. He went back to the shores of the beaver's pond. There, at its edge, he found a knife. It was the long tooth of a beaver set into a curved wooden handle carved in the shape of a beaver's tail. The tooth was set tightly in place by sinew bound and glued. The man picked up the knife, and as he did so, he thought he

sweet grass basket *brick bark basket*

heard the slap of a beaver's tail on the water. He looked and saw only the calm surface of the pond, but he spoke his thanks aloud. So it was that the Dawn Land People were given the crooked knife long ago.

Young Hunter turned the stick in his hand. It was smooth enough now and the slanted notches carved in at either end would hold. He put the crooked knife back into his pack, then stuck two forked sticks into the earth on either side of the fire and laid a third stick across them for a crossbar. By his side was the bowl he had fashioned earlier of birch bark, folded, and then sewn together with cedar roots from the coil he carried in his pack. The bowl was filled with water from the spring near the base of this hill and in it were pieces of his dried meat, a handful of greens gathered near the spring, and a small cake of maple sugar. The maple sugar had been given to him by Willow Girl in a small basket of sweetgrass. "Take this and you will think of me as you travel," she had said. He took the piece of wood he had shaped and fitted one of the slanted notches over the crossbar, then hung the basket on the bottom notch. It hung above the fire at just the right height. The green bark would grow hot, but it would not burn, and soon his stew would be cooked.

All of the fear which had edged close to him was gone now. One of the dogs in the lean-to behind him stretched its legs, pressing them against Young Hunter's back. He would not think of tomorrow now. He would hold the sweetgrass basket close to his face and smell it; he would enjoy the warmth of his fire, and soon, the taste of his food. It would be enough. For now, it would be enough. Tomorrow he would reach the village of the Salmon People.

CHAPTER ELEVEN
RED HAWK, BLUE HAWK

Ktsi Nwaskw, oleohneh. You who are great, thank you. Thank you for this new day. I am able to move about. I am able to see my breath in the morning air. I lift my arms and drink this water. It is a great gift to have this water. It is a great gift to move into this new day. Oleohneh.

Twice during the night he had wakened. He woke as one wakes when sleeping in the forest. Not by sitting up in a quick motion, but by opening one eye slowly. Fully awake, feeling every part of his body, but not moving. Looking, only looking. What he saw each time was the alert shape of one of his dogs. Pabetciman the first time. Danowa the second. Sitting with head erect, ears up, back to the fire, and looking into the forest, looking for anything that might threaten the four of them. Each time, as he watched, the dog turned its head back toward him, feeling his gaze. And in the gaze of the dog he saw no fear, only reassurance. *We are watching. Nothing comes. Sleep.* He leaned back and closed his eyes, thinking of the story Rabbit Stick had told when he was only a small boy about the hunter who was good to his dogs.

There was a man who always treated his dogs well. He fed them as much as they wanted to eat, petted them, and spoke to them with warmth and respect. He even allowed them to

89

sleep in his lodge with him. When that man hunted, his dogs often found game and drove it to him. In that same village, there was another man who had only one dog, but he did not treat that dog well at all. He beat the dog and hardly fed it, and it never found any game.

One night, the man who was kind to his dogs was wakened by talking outside his lodge. His dogs were gone and he crept to the door to look out. There, by the embers of the fire, he saw his dogs sitting. With them sat the dog which was always beaten by its master. The dogs were talking to each other and the man could understand their words.

"Our man treats us well," his dogs said. "That is why we take such good care of him."

"Ah-hah," said the other man's dog. "My man is very cruel. He beats me and gives me only small scraps to eat. But whenever he takes me hunting, even though I am the greatest hunter of all the dogs and I smell many animals, I never let him know those animals are there. I always lead him in the wrong direction. If I had a man like yours, I would help him become the best hunter of all the people."

The man had heard enough. He slipped back into bed and pretended to sleep. When his dogs crept back into the lodge, he paid them no notice. But when the next day came, he went to the lodge of the man who treated his dog badly.

"I would like to trade you something for that dog of yours," he said.

"You are a fool," said the man who was cruel to his dog, "but one should never argue with a fool. Give me your best bear robe and you can have this worthless animal. My advice to you is to kill him and eat him. That is the only way he will ever be any good to you."

The man who was kind to his dogs gave the other man his best bear robe. He called his new dog to him and it came gladly. He petted it and gave it a piece of meat. He took it home with

Marker trees

him and soon it was the leader of his dogs. It always brought him to the game animals and with the help of that dog, the man became the finest hunter of all of the people.

Young Hunter opened his eyes. The first light of the Day Traveler was brightening the eastern sky. His three dogs sat on their haunches, waiting for him to rise. He removed the support poles from the front of his lean-to and laid the roof down flat on the ground. He smoothed with his hands the ground where his fire had been. He hung his pot-hook in a bush and placed the birch bark pot upside down beneath it. Now there was little sign that a camp had ever been made there, though when he returned he could set up camp again with little effort. He shouldered his pack, picked up his spear thrower and the bundle with the Long Thrower in it in his right hand, and his spear in his left. Then he set off down the hill toward the trail to the village of the Salmon People.

As he reached the trail, a deer lifted its head and bounded away. The dogs looked up at Young Hunter, awaiting a hand signal to send them in pursuit. Young Hunter shook his head. "*Nda,* brothers," he said. "This is not the hunting territory for my family. We are only passing through. We will not hunt without the permission of the Salmon People."

The dogs turned without a sound and headed down the trail before him.

The sun had walked far into the western side of the sky by the time Young Hunter reached the first marker tree. Cut into its bark was the shape of a leaping salmon with a fish spear poised above it. Marker trees were found at the edges of each village. There, in simple but eloquent shapes, the name of the village and its people would be inscribed for anyone walking the trail to see. Such trees too were to be found at the heads of the trails to trapping grounds and berry-picking places. Other trees were used for messages, especially dead trees without bark, on the sides of which a person could leave a message with

91

the fire-blackened end of a sharp stick. The circle of the sun with three lines, the snake-shape of a stream with an arrow pointing up it, the rough sketch of a canoe and a beaver might indicate that a man had gone upstream to trap beaver, for three days. There were many signs. Much could be told on a marker tree, and more than once Young Hunter had written his own messages for friends or relatives following him.

As Young Hunter proceeded, he knew he was being watched. But he did not feel, as he had before, that the eyes which observed him were strange or hostile.

"Ho!"

The voice came from the left of the trail just ahead. Young Hunter stopped and signaled his dogs. All three of them trotted back and lay down behind him, mouths open, ears pricked up.

"Hey!"

The second voice came from the right of the trail and was louder than the first.

"*Kuai!*" Young Hunter called, cupping his hands around his mouth. "*Kuai, nidobak!* Hello, friends!"

Suddenly, a young man leaped from the brush to stand in the middle of the trail only a few paces from Young Hunter. His long, thick hair was bound back by a strip of softened basswood tied about his forehead. He was long-nosed and lantern-jawed and he stood there without moving. He was almost close enough to reach out and touch Young Hunter with the spear that he held tightly in his right hand.

From the look on his face, Young Hunter thought, *he is proud of having crept so close to me without being noticed. He doesn't know that my dogs and I sensed him and his companion long before this.*

As suddenly as the first, a second young man leaped from the brush on the other side of the trail. He too was long-nosed and lantern-jawed and wore a similar basswood headband, ornamented like his companion's by a shape that looked like a diving hawk. Like his companion, he had a belt of ash withes wrapped around his waist to hold up his deerskin loincloth and his pouch. He too stood without moving, staring at Young Hunter. He held his spear tightly in his left hand.

Both young men looked to be about Young Hunter's age, perhaps seventeen winters. They were a hand taller, but their shoulders were not as broad as his. Their arms were longer than Young Hunter's, but not quite as muscular. They held themselves with the grace of men accustomed to running long distances. Their knees were slightly bent, their arms held out from their sides as if ready to leap or thrust with their spears. Their faces, though narrow and hawklike, bore some resemblance to Young Hunter's own face. Each wore around his neck a cord of milkweed fibers from which hung a stone. The two stones were flat and the holes in them seemed to have been made by nature, not bored out with an awl. The two stones were blue with flecks of gold, exact twins of each other, as exact as the two men were twins of each other.

The one to the right spoke first. "Why do you dare to come to our village carrying weapons?" he said in a harsh voice. He pointed with his chin at Young Hunter's spear.

"I think he is afraid," said the one to the left. "He is afraid to face us without his coward's weapons. Perhaps if we put our spears down, then he will be brave enough to attack us."

Young Hunter did not move. He stood watching them.

"Hunh!" the one to the right said. "He is still afraid, even though we have put aside our spears. Perhaps if we turn our backs, then he may be brave enough to attack."

Young Hunter yawned. He stood there, leaning on his spear, his legs crossed.

The two young men turned back to face him.

"Coward!" the one to the right said.

"Puss-face," said the one to the left.

"Fish belly!" said the first one.

"Skunk lover!" said the second.

"Unnnhhh..." said the first. It was clear that his brother's insult had just surpassed the one he had in mind.

"Are you finished?" Young Hunter said.

"*Nda!*" said the first young man. "Now you must fight us. You must beat us if you wish to pass into the sacred ground of our village."

"But I warn you, my brother and I have never been defeated. No man has ever gained victory over us!"

"Have any *boys* ever gained victory over you?" Young Hunter said.

"That," said the first young man, "is beside the point!" He leaped forward and dove for Young Hunter's midsection, trying to grab him about the waist and wrestle him down. Young Hunter dropped his spear. Placing his hands in the middle of the first young man's back, he kicked his own legs back so that his full weight bore down on the other, now hopelessly out of balance. Whoompf! The first young man landed on the earth belly first and all of the wind was knocked out of him. Young Hunter leaped up lightly to his feet.

"Wicked one!" the second young man shouted. "I see now that you are not a human being. You are an evil spirit. But I will not let the death of my brother go unavenged." He leaped at Young Hunter as if trying the same move. At the last second, though, he shifted his weight to the side, grabbing Young Hunter's arm and pulling so that he ended up behind Young Hunter. "Hah!" the young man shouted, wrapping his arms around Young Hunter's chest from the back. Young Hunter shifted his hips to the left, then quickly went to one knee, pulling his attacker's arm forward as he did so. The second young man flew through the air. Whoompf! He landed on his back next to his still-gasping brother.

Young Hunter dusted off his hands. The three dogs, which had sat quietly through the wrestling match, got to their feet. Agwedjiman went to the second young man and nuzzled his face.

"Agghhh!" the second young man said in a strangled voice. "Now he sends his wolf to tear out the throat of the man he has defeated by treachery." He reached up a hand and began to scratch behind the dog's ears.

Pabetciman and Danowa ambled over to the first young man, who still lay on his belly, arms and legs outstretched. They began to lick his face from either side. He rolled over and put his arms around both dogs.

"Pabo, Dano! *Kuai*, friends! It's been a long time since we have seen you." He stood and reached a long arm out to pull his brother to his feet. Both of them, grey with the dust of the trail, smiled down at Young Hunter.

"Welcome, Brother-Cousin," the first young man said.

"Welcome," said the second. He held out his arms and the three young men embraced.

"It is still not fair," said the first young man. "Now that we are finally taller than you, it is not fair that you can still beat us in wrestling. No one else in all the villages can beat us."

"Together or separately?" Young Hunter said. Then he laughed. "Red Hawk, Blue Hawk, I have missed you both, Brother-Cousins. How is my uncle? How is your mother?"

As the three young men walked toward the village, they spoke of their families. The news was easy to carry. No one in their families had died or been seriously ill since they had last seen each other three winters ago. The past summer had been a good one. Each village looked forward to a winter-coming time with many blessings. Plenty of fish were expected in the pools below the falls, much game would be found in the hunting territories. In the last two years, both villages had grown. There were new mouths in almost every family lodge—though there were no other sets of twins. Red Hawk and Blue Hawk remained special in that way. Twins were not common in any of the thirteen villages. When they did come, they were regarded as a special blessing from the Owner Creator. Sometimes the womb sharers were a brother and sister.

Twins = womb sharers

woman —
Oldest Talker

Clan mother or red.?
woman

Identical twins

Sometimes they were of the same sex. More rarely, they were like Red Hawk and Blue Hawk, two who shared one face. All of the Dawn Land People were good at reading the moods of others, understanding the unspoken languages of posture and gesture, but those like Red Hawk and Blue Hawk were known to be able to speak without speaking. Their senses were almost like those of a deep-seeing person, for each seemed always to know what was happening in the other's mind, even when they were out of sight of each other. But they were seldom out of sight of each other. One of the jokes in the village was that they would never be able to marry unless they found twin sisters. Young Hunter remembered the words spoken to him by Bear Talker. The numbers of the people were growing indeed.

"Have many gone to seek new hunting grounds?" Young Hunter asked.

"Our father speaks ... " Red Hawk began.

"Of going beyond the Forked Hill to trap," Blue Hawk continued.

"But our Oldest Talker ... " Red Hawk said.

"She says we must wait," Blue Hawk said.

Young Hunter had been as far as the Forked Hill. It marked the westernmost boundary of the hunting and trapping grounds of the Salmon People. Young Hunter had been there three winters ago. He had stood on the Mountain Near the River and looked across at that place beyond which the Salmon People did not travel. His grandparents had let him spend two seasons with his uncle Fish Hawk's family. It was during that time that the three boys had begun their wrestling contests. If it were up to Red Hawk and Blue Hawk, Young Hunter knew, their contests with Young Hunter would go on for many winters to come.

He thought of the two old men whom everyone jokingly referred to as "the Wrestlers." Both of them were greyhairs. One was from the Spearstone People's village and the other, Hard Thrower, was of the Only People. Hard Thrower was a

great maker of atlatls. Young Hunter's own spear thrower had
been made under the old man's guidance. Hard Thrower and
the Spearstone village man, whose name was Combs His Hair,
were brother-cousins. Each year, in the Moon of Raspberries,
either Hard Thrower or Combs His Hair would make the long
walk to his brother-cousin's village. Young Hunter noticed
that Hard Thrower always seemed to know each year when
Combs His Hair was on his way. Hard Thrower would braid his
own hair tightly and then paint designs on his body with clay
and paint. Those designs looked like twining snakes. He would
wrap his belt more tightly about his waist and then sit in front
of his lodge. He would work on an atlatl, perhaps, with his
crooked knife, but he would not pay attention to his work in his
usual way. Always—and Young Hunter remembered seeing it
happen four times—his brother-cousin would arrive before
the middle of the day. He too would be painted and his long
hair would be braided and tied on top of his head.

Without a word, Hard Thrower would stand and the two
old men would walk to the open place between the lodges and
start to wrestle. They would be stiff at first, but as they warmed
up, their moves would sometimes not seem to be those of old
men. They would seem, at times, to have the grace and
quickness of the young. But those moments were few. Frankly,
neither of the old men was a good wrestler. In fact, as Sweetgrass
Woman whispered (a bit too loudly) to Young Hunter one
year, the reason they loved to wrestle each other was that
neither of them had ever been skilled enough to beat anyone
else. Finally, for it never happened quickly, one of the old men
would throw the other and hold him down long enough to
claim victory. Then, their arms about each other's shoulders,
they would walk down to the stream. They would wash off the
clay and paint and the dirt from their wrestling. They would
wash their cuts and scrapes and laugh. Back at Hard Thrower's
lodge, his wife would be shaking her head and smiling as she
prepared a meal for the two aged warriors.

Young Hunter smiled at the thought of himself and Red Hawk and Blue Hawk still wrestling when their faces were wrinkled, their arms thinned by age.

"I am glad," Young Hunter said, "that you two are the first ones I have met. It was good luck that you happened to be on the trail."

"*Nda,*" Red Hawk said.

"There was not luck about it," Blue Hawk said.

"Our Oldest Talker ... " Red Hawk continued.

"Medicine Plant ... " Blue Hawk added.

"She saw you were coming," they concluded in one voice. "She sent us to meet you."

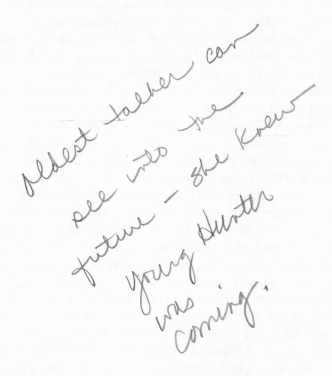

Oldest talker can see into the future — she knew young hunter was coming.

[handwritten marginalia: Special dreaming abilities = deep seeing person — Oldest Talker]

CHAPTER TWELVE
MEDICINE PLANT

[handwritten: Soul travel]

It was because of her dreams. All children dreamt, but not as she did. She saw things in her dreams. At first she did not tell her parents what she saw. What she saw was not frightening, it was simply that it was so real that she felt there was nothing strange, nothing to tell them about her dreams. It was as if when she closed her eyes into sleep, she simply walked out of their lodge and went about the village. But her body did not go with her as she walked. *[handwritten: Astral Planing]*

One day, she spoke to her mother about something that had happened the night before while she slept. "How," her mother said, "did you know that?"

"I was there," she said. "I saw it."

They took her to the Long River village, to Oldest Talker. In those days Oldest Talker was in her late middle age. It was a handful of winters after Bear Talker, no longer a boy, had been sent back to be the deep-seeing person for his own village. He had wanted to stay, after growing to manhood under her guidance, but it was time for him to go. When there were two deep-seeing people in one village, things might grow confused. Even when those two slept together as Bear Talker and Oldest Talker had done for seven winters. One deep-seeing person was enough for any village. People would worry if there were two. *[handwritten: Why?]*

99

Oldest Talker took the girl's face in her hands. "I have seen you walking about at night," she said. "You know that?"

The girl nodded.

"I have seen you come into my lodge at night. I have seen you standing by the doorway watching me, even though you thought I could not see you. Do you know what it is that you have been doing?"

The girl shook her head.

"There is a light," Oldest Talker said. She pressed both hands against her chest, just above her navel. "It comes out of you when you sleep. It is part of you. Letting it out is a little like giving birth. It is that light which has been walking through your village and beyond, even here to the Long River People, while you sleep. So you have been going about and watching. You have been seeing things you should not see. If people hear of this it may frighten them. They may send you out of the village. So, you must learn to control this. When you do this it must be to help the people, not just for your own curiosity. Do you understand?"

The girl looked up at Oldest Talker. The older woman's hands were very large, but they felt warm and comforting. The girl shook her head. She did not understand.

Oldest Talker smiled. "That is good," she said. "You are honest. And no one ever really understands before they begin to learn. Today you will start to learn."

She was a good learner. She knew this. She knew that she was a quicker learner than Bear Talker had been. She felt proud of that. She was proud to be chosen to learn. It was an honor to be learning in the lodge of a deep-seeing person. She knew too that Bear Talker—even though he had not returned to the Long River village—knew she was now learning what he had learned and learning it faster. She knew he was jealous. That made her feel good too.

cultural change from stone bowls to birch bark baskets

Oldest Talker looked at her as if reading her thoughts. Oldest Talker shook her head. "You know so much," the older woman said. "That can make it hard for you to learn, girl!"

Oldest Talker picked up her bowl. It was a beautiful bowl, the only one like it in the village of the Long River People. It was made of stone, and the one who had made it long ago had taken more than one winter to do so. No one remembered anything about the man who made that bowl, except that his name was Hurt Fox and he lived in the time of Oldest Talker's mother's mother's mother. The people still knew how to make such bowls, but they seldom made them. A bowl made of bark could be completed in almost no time, and such a bowl would carry as much water as one made of stone or clay, but weigh less. A bowl made of new bark could even be used for cooking. Hung at the right height above the fire, it would last for the making of many meals. Still, the Long River People were glad to have such a stone bowl in their village. It was good to see such beautiful things. Knowing they could make others like it was enough for them. And it was good to see such a bowl in the hands of their far-seeing woman.

Oldest Talker held the bowl out to the girl. "Fill this with water from the river," she said.

The girl did as she was told. She came back with the full bowl. It was heavy and she was tired from carrying it.

"Now," Oldest Talker said, "go fill it again."

The girl hesitated. "What shall I do with the water already in the bowl?"

"Do you mean you cannot fill it when it is already full?"

"*Nda,* there is no room."

"Uh-hunh!" Oldest Talker said. "You understand that. That is good. Now, why is it that you do not understand you have to empty your mind of such things as knowing a great deal and being proud of all you know before I can start to teach you the things you really need to know?"

101

Plants talk

She understood. She poured out the water. She let go of the pride she had gained from two winters of learning from Oldest Talker. She poured out her feeling of superiority about being a better student than Bear Talker. Then, only then, did she really begin to learn.

One day, as she walked in the forest, she heard voices. They were small and came from close to the ground. The voices came from the plants which could be used for medicine. She listened closely and realized that each plant had its own voice. Those plants were calling to her. When she returned to the village, she told Oldest Talker.

"Uh-hunh," the older woman said. "You have found your name."

All of that had happened to Medicine Plant many winters ago, before Oldest Talker followed the last trail which only spirits can walk. Medicine Plant had been with her, had returned from the village of the Salmon People to be there by the river near her teacher's lodge. She had held the older woman's hand and felt the calmness. Like a bird ready to fly to the Always Summer Land, Oldest Talker's spirit was spreading her wings.

"Granddaughter," Oldest Talker said. Medicine Plant leaned closer. She was not sure if she was hearing with her ears or with her heart. "You will not bury me," the old woman said. "That must be left for my grandson to do. I have called him. He will soon be here. When my breath is gone, leave me here where he can find me."

Medicine Plant understood. There was no jealousy in her heart anymore. There was no feeling of triumph when it came to Bear Talker. Bear Talker was weak in the ways men are weak. He needed to be the one to do the final things for this old one who had been his teacher and lover and spirit grandmother. Oldest Talker breathed in one more time and then the bird in her chest fluttered its wings and was gone.

Medicine Plant walked away from the lodge. She stood near a cedar tree on a nearby hill. Soon, a short round man

What happens at death?

came running along the path which led from the village of the Only People. Medicine Plant wanted to talk to him. There was so much he did not understand. But she knew his heart would be too full of sorrow and love for her words to reach him. He did not see her on the hilltop. The eyes in his head and in his heart were blinded by what he felt. Medicine Plant turned and walked away.

As Young Hunter walked with his brother-cousins he wondered what he would see, what he would be told. Medicine Plant was not a deep-seeing person in the same way Bear Talker was. Bear Talker lived in the village. He had wives and children. He would sit and joke around the fire like everyone else. It was only when the spirits came to him, when his special strengths were needed, that his voice would change. He would divide himself into another person then, enter his small lodge, and wrestle there with the ancient deep ones under the earth. There were certain times too when he would cast his soul out of his body to travel far, to see things happening in distant places. But aside from those times, Bear Talker was like an uncle.

Medicine Plant was different. Like her teacher, Oldest Talker, she lived in a lodge far from the village. Her wigwom was near a waterfall in a wild place where the people did not like to go. It was said that the animals came to her there. Even panthers would act like her dogs when they came there. People spoke of seeing her in the woods with a fox trotting by her side. It was not that the people were afraid of her. Everyone knew that she always used her powers to help them. But they respected her just as they respected fire. Fire had its own place. Only a foolish child would place a hand in the heart of the flames.

As Young Hunter walked with Red Hawk and Blue Hawk, he thought of the words spoken to him by his uncle Fish Hawk. He thought of the advice given him by Big Story, the sagamon of the Salmon People. Both of them had told him to wait a few

Dreams guide behavior

sleeps before visiting Medicine Plant. He had taken their advice. It was now the third dawn since his coming to the Salmon People's village. He had rested from his journey. He had eaten well and played games with his small nephews and nieces. He had thrown the stick at the hoop as he gambled with his brother-cousins and the other young men of their age group. He had laughed when people teased him about how certain of the young women in the village looked at him—or looked away from him a little too slowly.

"You have come here … " Red Hawk said.

"To steal our girls," Blue Hawk said.

Young Hunter had spent time with his relatives. Being with them had taken away some of the weight he felt from his coming journey. He had done as a good guest should do, but he knew the trail was waiting for him. It led to the north and to the west. The dream had come again to him and this time he saw himself farther along that trail. There was sorrow to be found there in a place where cliffs rose like the walls of a deadfall trap. So he spoke to his uncle Fish Hawk.

"This dawn," Young Hunter said, "I must go to see your deep-seeing person."

Power of Dreams

His uncle nodded. He knew that his nephew had dreamed.

Young Hunter embraced his relatives and gathered his few belongings. He accepted the offer of his cousins to walk with him along the way. They would act as his guides, though he knew the way well. He had been there once before. It was not the first time he had visited Medicine Plant.

The trail wound along the river. The water made a powerful sound as it rushed over the stones. The colors of the stones changed as the waters washed shallow and then deep above them. He watched the river as he walked. Rivers had always fascinated Young Hunter: their always motion, their way of hiding and then disclosing, their way of taking away and then giving. His foot scuffed a piece of birch bark into the stream. It floated and spun into an eddy, twirled, and then

Beginning of birch bark Canoe ?

broke free to roll over a little falls made by two rocks close together. It still stayed upright, high on the water. It rode higher than any dugout could ride. A dugout in swift water might swamp or even break when it struck rocks at great speed. The birch bark bounced lightly down the stream as if it were a boat. Young Hunter felt his mind moving toward an idea. A new sort of boat. But it was an idea for which he had no time now. Still, it was an idea to keep in his mind.

"Wake up," Red Hawk said.

"You are sleeping as you walk," Blue Hawk said.

Young Hunter shook his head. That piece of birch bark in the river had almost taken him away with it downstream. He had turned around and was walking backward without even noticing it. He shook his head again as if his skull were a basket and he had to empty out pieces of rotten bark from within it before using it to load. His mind had to be clear if he was going to see such a one as Medicine Plant, even though he had seen her before.

Dugouts used before

105

CHAPTER THIRTEEN
WEASEL TAIL

intimate knowledge of landscape

The first time he had met Medicine Plant had been three winters ago, when Young Hunter spent the summer with Fish Hawk's family—that summer when he roamed the lands of the Salmon People with his two brother-cousins. By the end of that summer he knew the faces of all the people in the village as well as he knew each hill and brook, beaver pond and cattail marsh within four days' walk. He knew all the new stories of the twenty different family lodges. He knew that Sweetgrass Woman would spend many happy nights hearing him tell about those people, asking him questions about relatives and friends. She would want to know who was angry with someone, which unmarried girls were being visited by young men, which married men were not acting as married men should act. The stories would make her laugh or nod her head or say hmmph! But there was still one person whose stories Young Hunter had not heard, one person of the Salmon People village Young Hunter had not met. Medicine Plant.

"It is not that people are afraid of our far-seeing person," Fish Hawk explained. "It is just that they *respect* her so much." Fish Hawk laughed as he said this and looked over his shoulder, even though he was sitting inside his lodge. It was a nervous laugh. "Our far-seeing person," he continued, "likes to live alone. So we do not wish to bother her." He laughed again,

view of lesbians

Description of Med Plant

oldest Talker

more nervously than before. He did not talk further about Medicine Plant, and Young Hunter could see that it would do no good to ask any more questions.

Stories were told about Medicine Plant, but in very soft voices. She was a sister in spirit to the one called Woman Who Walks Alone. She was not the same, of course, for that ancient spirit being never grew old, while Medicine Plant did age. Though she was younger than Bear Talker, her face had deep lines of wisdom. Her thick hair was no longer the color of the deepest shadows. It was silver like spider webs and moonlight. She was still straight and strong, as strong as most men. But she had no interest in men, it seemed. People joked—softly— about the games she played with Oldest Talker, the old woman who was her teacher and who had gone to the spirit world. They did not criticize the two women. There was nothing wrong in what they did together. Plenty of other women chose to be with men, to bring children into the world from their own bodies. Medicine Plant's way of bringing children into the world was by helping those mothers when the birth time came. She would appear at a birthing mother's lodge. She would bring the right medicines and help. In all the years of Medicine Plant's midwifing, no mother among the Salmon People had lost a newborn or died giving birth.

midwife

Each village had a midwife, and the knowledge shared among midwives was great. Yet none could match Medicine Plant. She knew what to do when a birth was difficult—when there was more bleeding than normal, or when a baby came out backward, too eager to place its feet on the earth. She could tell if the birth cord was twisted around the child's neck and knew how to prevent it from strangling that child at birth. It had been so four winters ago with the firstborn of Fish Hawk's oldest daughter, Swan. Medicine Plant's sure hands had set things right. That child, a boy named Strong Singer, could be seen running about the village, naked and happy, with the other children.

107

Deviant behavior = twisted mind thing

There were more children in the village of the Salmon People than in Young Hunter's village. That was as it should be. Food was more plentiful here by the river. There were unused hunting grounds farther west. As he walked toward Medicine Plant's lodge, he remembered the words spoken to him by Bear Talker. The people were increasing. They were spreading across the land, farther to the north and the west. But they did not know—as he now knew, as Bear Talker saw— that something waited for them. Something with no love for human beings.

He turned his thoughts away from that direction. He would think instead of Medicine Plant, of why she preferred to live alone. It had been said by some that she lived this way, away from men, because of a bad experience with a man when she was young. A man from another village had tried to force himself upon her. But that man soon found out that the slender young girl was not defenseless. In fact, he was no longer sure that she was a girl at all and not a mountain lion! It took him a long time to recover. Though he had been a loud and boasting person before, he became very quiet and respectful to all women after that.

Young Hunter wondered why any man would try to force himself on a woman. It was a twisted-mind thing. Young Hunter remembered a certain day when he and his grandfather were hunting. His grandfather was teaching him how to use the strung-together stones. Young Hunter had practiced with them to the point where he no longer struck himself in the head or wrapped them around his own arm when he tried to throw. Rabbit Stick smiled at Young Hunter's shout of delight when he first succeeded in sending them spinning until they struck and circled around a young tree, the rawhide cord hissing in the air, the small stones winding fast about the tree and knocking against its bark as they wrapped tight. But Young Hunter had yet to try them hunting. Today he would try to take a duck with the strung stones. They were coming close to the marsh where his grandfather knew a flock of mallards had been feeding. Suddenly, Rabbit Stick held up his hand, palm forward. Young Hunter stopped. Although his head reached no higher than his grandfather's waist, he already had a hunter's heart. He stopped without a word, still as a tree. He listened.

A sound came. It was like the cry of a rabbit grabbed by a fox, a strangled cry. But it was not a rabbit's voice. His grandfather began to run. Young Hunter followed. They ran toward the cry. It came from the place where fire had burned the marsh the summer before. There the grass was new and soft. The trees held themselves around the clearing like hands cupped around a fire. It was a private place, a place where young men and women sometimes came when they wished to be alone, when they were trying to make the decision about whether or not to marry. It was the proper way to do it, to know each other well. Sometimes a girl might even become pregnant and have a child before she and her young man decided. Sometimes that girl would decide he was not the right young man for her. Perhaps too she would decide after having a child that being a mother was not right for her yet, either. No one would suffer from her decision. Her aunts or her sisters or her mother would take that child. Few children ever felt the lack of mothers or fathers among the Only People. So that clearing was a place where young people went and often the sounds which came from that place were sounds of joy.

But the inarticulate sound which Young Hunter and Rabbit Stick heard yet again as they ran was a cry of fear and pain. Rabbit Stick was running so fast now that Young Hunter could not keep up with him. Yet he knew that as his grandfather ran, his eyes and ears were open. He would not rush headlong into danger like the field mouse frightened at night by the owl's call. Rabbit Stick ran in a crouch, holding in his right hand that throwing stick which had given him his name. At the edge of the clearing Rabbit Stick stopped and Young Hunter caught up. His grandfather was on his belly, parting the tall grass to peer through. Young Hunter saw what his grandfather saw. He saw it in the time it would take a drop of water to fall from the tip of one of those grass blades and strike the ground. Yet there was so much in that quick seeing that it was as if a whole day passed before his eyes. He saw at that moment the possibility of things which he had never thought of before. He understood, for the first time, how the same thing could happen quickly for one person and seem to take forever for another.

A young man and a young woman were there in that clearing of new grass. The grass was soft and pale green. The sky above them was clear except for a single cloud. That cloud was shaped like some kind of new animal, part bear, part snake. Young Hunter wondered what that cloud animal saw during its brief life. No breeze blew. The whine of a summer tree-singer cut through the air from the trunk of one of the maples farther back in the forest. From far off, a crow was talking. Dragonflies criss-crossed the air and Young Hunter could hear the tiny clatter of their wings. The sun was very warm on his bare back and the back of his head. He realized that he was holding his strung-together stones so tightly that they hurt his hand. He could feel the coolness of the air coming into his lungs and he heard the throbbing of his own heart in his ears. Rabbit Stick moved one leg slightly and Young Hunter saw the strong muscle in his grandfather's calf tighten.

Yet what he saw and heard most clearly of all in that long moment were the young man and the young woman there in the clearing. The young man was from the village of the Onion Land People. His name was Weasel Tail. He had been visiting his brother-cousins for two moons. He had shown some interest in the girl there in the clearing with him, Swaying Reed. But Swaying Reed had shown little interest in Weasel Tail. It surprised Young Hunter to see them there together. But other things he saw surprised him more. Shocked in his seeing, he saw that Swaying Reed's hands were bound together by a piece of rawhide. Her wrists were red and swollen. Her deerskin skirt had been torn off and thrown aside. She was curled on one side, trying to protect her woman's place between her legs. Her eyes were on Weasel Tail who stood there, reaching for her. Her eyes were not fearful. They were dark with anger. Had she been able to speak, Young Hunter knew she would have been insulting Weasel Tail. But she could not speak. A basswood headband tied across her mouth stopped her from making anything other than that strange cry which had drawn Rabbit Stick and Young Hunter here.

Weasel Tail loomed over Swaying Reed. He was a tall young man, much taller than Young Hunter's grandfather, much taller than the other young men of his age group. It was a strange thing, that height of his, but it was not the only strange thing about him. There was a great scar on his right shoulder in the shape of a crescent moon. It had been left when some fierce animal, no one knew what kind, had killed his parents as they slept in their solitary hunting lodge in the northernmost part of their watershed. The boy had been wounded, but whatever had killed his parents and dragged off their bodies did not take him. Though but a small child of five winters, he had walked back to the Onion Land village. His relatives went back to the lodge and found it torn apart. There was blood everywhere, but when they followed the trail it ended among the rocks and they could follow it no longer. They asked the boy about what had happened, but he shook his head. He never spoke about it. Perhaps, the people thought, it was not a natural beast but something from the spirit land. No one hunted again in that territory. And though Weasel Tail grew, and grew tall, cared for by his relatives, it was as if something had been taken from the boy that night when his parents were killed.

Young Hunter knew Weasel Tail's story. It was told at night around campfires by the older boys to frighten the younger ones. He felt sorry for Weasel Tail, for he too had lost

111

his parents. But Weasel Tail and he were not alike. Weasel Tail enjoyed killing things.

Weasel Tail had a talent for cruelty to living things. It did not matter if they were large or small, game animals or the insects crawling on the bark of a tree. One day, Young Hunter and a group of small boys came upon Weasel Tail as he crouched by the banks of the Onion Land River. He was spearing small frogs with a slender ash-pole spear with a fire-hardened point. He saw the boys out of the corner of his eye and motioned them to come closer. Then he caught another frog with his hand. He held it up, smiled, and took a hollow reed from the bank. As the boys watched, fascinated and horrified, he thrust the reed up the frog's backside and then blew, filling its belly with air. He dropped it back into the water and laughed as it tried to dive and swim. At last, tiring of the game, he pierced it with his spear. Young Hunter felt sick. The other boys stayed, but he went back to the lodge where his uncle Fire Keeper was talking with the other men.

There were more things that Weasel Tail did that day as the boys followed him, watching. He twisted the bellies from ants and watched them circling, trying to carry their own abdomens back to their lodges. He thrust a sharp twig through a striped snake, pinning it to the earth, and laughed as it twisted, striking at its own pain. He was encouraging the few remaining boys—for most had run home by then—to fight with each other, to strike each other with clenched fists, when Fire Keeper found him. Fire Keeper led him to Bear Talker. Together, the sagamon and the deep-seeing man spoke to the young man. They saw that his mind was twisted. They saw that something had been lost from the center of his being. They wanted to help him regain that which was gone from his spirit. It was ten winters now since the loss of his parents, but clearly some part of him was still lost and wandering in the forest. Bear Talker could seek it out for him if he wished. He could try to call it back and make him whole once more. It seemed to Fire

(soul loss   112

Keeper that the tall young man was listening. He could see that in his face. But Bear Talker could see deeper. There was a struggle going on deep within the young man. It was no simple thing.

Just as Fire Keeper thought his words were touching the young man's heart, a change came over Weasel Tail's face. A shadow crossed it, and for a moment, Bear Talker was not certain that he was still looking at the face of a human being. Weasel Tail looked down at that crescent scar on his shoulder and then laughed, a high, strange laugh like the sound of a storm wind. He stood up, still laughing, and walked away from them. Just before he disappeared into the forest, it seemed to Fire Keeper as if the laughing turned to weeping.

"*Nda*," Bear Talker said. "We cannot follow him. If he is to be helped, he must want to help himself."

Then Bear Talker and Fire Keeper gathered the boys who had followed Weasel Tail and spoke to them for a long time. Even though it was not the season for storytelling, they related the tales that explain why humans must respect the animal people. Just like human beings, every living thing from the greatest to the smallest was made of both body and spirit. That spirit could leave the body in dreams. If the human or animal person was a deep seer—and there were such among all the animal nations—that spirit could do things, even bring harm to those who did not show respect. Sickness would come to a hunter who killed the deer and failed to give thanks, failed to show respect by hanging the skull from the offering tree. They told such stories as the one about the man who once killed many frogs for no reason, and a flash flood rolled down the valley and swept away his people. When the two men finished talking, the Sky Walker had gone beyond the western edge of the world. Many parents as well as children sat in the circle around the elders. Everyone in the village was there— except Weasel Tail.

When he returned, after spending the night somewhere in the forest, Weasel Tail was more silent than before. No one saw him doing those things anymore. Perhaps, Fire Keeper hoped, he was touched by the power of the stories even if he had not listened to them. But Fire Keeper also hoped that Weasel Tail would grow tired of visiting his brother-cousins and return to the Onion Land People. Otherwise, he said, something bad was going to happen.

Young Hunter heard his uncle's words again as he and Rabbit Stick saw what was happening in that clearing. Weasel Tail loomed over the girl. He had undone his belt and his loincloth lay on the ground. He was turned slightly and Young Hunter could see that the young man's penis was erect. It was thin and twisted, more like the bony penis of an animal than a man's. Weasel Tail held his spear in his right hand and touched his penis with his left. No words came from his mouth, but what his eyes spoke made Young Hunter feel sick.

All of this was seen in the time it took a drop of water to fall. Rabbit Stick stood up. He came out of the tall sweetgrass like a bear rising out of the berry tangles. He came out like a hawk bursting from a cloud. He stood with the smooth grace of a salmon leaping up the long falls. Young Hunter had always seen his grandfather as an older man, one who moved with careful deliberation. But there was nothing old in his motions now. There was simply an ageless, elemental strength.

"*Nda!*" Rabbit Stick shouted.

Weasel Tail twisted toward them. His feet seemed to be stuck to the ground. His face was strange as he saw them.

He does not see us as human beings, Young Hunter thought.

Rabbit Stick's left hand, the hand closest to his heart, was raised. He held his palm out toward Weasel Tail. It meant peace. It meant that what was happening must stop. Rabbit Stick's right hand was low, held against his thigh.

Weasel Tail shifted his feet and lifted his arm, the arm which held the spear. He spoke a word. That word and the way he spoke it made Young Hunter feel hot and cold at the same

114

time. It was the word for a game animal. Weasel Tail meant to kill them both. He would hurl his spear through Rabbit Stick's belly, then pull it out and pierce Young Hunter with as little emotion as he had shown when torturing the frogs.

Before Weasel Tail could bring his arm forward, Rabbit Stick took two quick steps with that flowing swiftness Young Hunter had never seen before. He whipped his right hand, all of the momentum of body and shoulder going into a powerful underhand throw. His stick whistled through the air, whirring like a maple seed spinning from a branch. As quick as thought, it cut the distance between them and struck the young man full in his groin with a sound like that of a flat rock striking water. Weasel Tail screamed and fell forward. Blood gushed from between his hands as he clutched at his groin. The tip of his spear dug into the ground and snapped.

Rabbit Stick untied the hands of Swaying Reed. He lifted her to her feet, took the headband from around her face, and pulled the grass from her mouth. Young Hunter handed her the torn deerskin skirt. It fell from her hands as she wrapped her arms around Rabbit Stick's waist. She pressed her cheek against his chest and wept like a small child. Young Hunter pressed his own cheek against her shoulder and patted her back. He felt his grandfather's hand on his head, the old man embracing them both.

"Granddaughter," Rabbit Stick said. "Clean yourself in the small stream. Then we will take you home."

Swaying Reed straightened. Young Hunter picked up her skirt from the trampled grass. She took it from his hand, touched his cheek, and then walked to the small stream.

Rabbit Stick went to the edge of the bog. He pulled up two handfuls of moss and went back to where Weasel Tail lay writhing on the ground. The blood no longer spurted from between his fingers. A moaning sound, low as the wash of wind over cold stones, came from between his clenched teeth. Rabbit Stick pulled Weasel Tail's hands away from his groin.

Young Hunter could see torn flesh. Rabbit Stick pressed the moss against the wounds.

"We will come back with Bear Talker," Rabbit Stick said. "He will help you to heal."

Swaying Reed was coming from the stream. Her head was high and her back was straight. Rabbit Stick reached down and picked up his throwing stick. He looked at it and there was sorrow in his eyes. He hurled it high overhead. It rose and rose and it seemed to Young Hunter as if the stick were going to join the sky. But instead it fell, deep in the center of the marsh where no one walked, sinking out of sight.

When Bear Talker and Rabbit Stick returned, there was blood on the grass and traces of blood led into the forest. They finally lost the trail four looks from the village. It was hard to believe a person wounded that way could go so far. The trail led straight north. Bear Talker was troubled.

"The twisting inside him is strong," Bear Talker said. "I see something coming from this which will make our people weep."

CHAPTER FOURTEEN
THE CLIFF TRAIL

Young Hunter shook his head. It had been many winters since Weasel Tail had disappeared. He was losing himself again in his thoughts. It had been this way ever since the Brave One bit him and he drank from the medicine spring. It seemed as if he were sleeping and walking at the same time. Still, there was a thread that sewed all of these strange things together. His thoughts about Medicine Plant had linked him to that old memory of Weasel Tail, a memory which had been buried so long that it surprised him with its clarity.

A hand grasped his shoulder and shook him.

"Are you awake now?" Red Hawk asked.

"Or are you still dreaming?" Blue Hawk added.

Young Hunter laughed. He hoped his laughter did not sound as strained to his brother-cousins as it did to his own ears.

"I am wide enough awake to wrestle you both again, even here on these hard stones."

The two brothers shook their heads. It was like seeing the doubled image one might see when a person stood over clear water.

"*Nda,*" they said, speaking together. "This time we will take pity on you."

The trail was climbing now up the cliffs from the river. It led toward the notch between the hills. There one could look and see ten times farther than from any other place in the lands of the Salmon People. There was where Medicine Plant had her lodge. There was the place where Young Hunter had come three summers ago on his last visit to the Salmon People.

He had been following the trail of a fox. Its footprints in the sand at the stream's edge started his tracking. Young Hunter was proud of the way he was able to follow the small traces of its passing, even up here where earth gave way to stone. Though he had never climbed this trail before, he did not think of that. Following the tracks filled his mind. He had picked his way through a tangle of blackberry bushes, come out on a game trail, and where the trail wound in among big pines, seen the red flash of a fox's tail. He had felt the hunter's thrill in the center of his being and moved more quickly. He was not hunting this fox to catch it, only to see how close he could come, but his heartbeat quickened. The game trail opened onto a wider one, one which looked to be walked by human feet. It leveled out for the length of a spear cast, crossing an exposed rock face.

Young Hunter had stepped onto that stone, and as soon as he did so, he saw the woman who stood there ahead of him. It was as if she had risen up out of the stone itself. Her long hair hung loose about her shoulders and was the same silver as the moon. Like many of the other women of the village, she was bare-breasted, but though her hair was the color of an elder's, her breasts were like those of a young woman. They did not hang down like the breasts of a woman who has fed children. She wore a deerskin skirt that hung past her calves, decorated with unusual designs, shapes that made Young Hunter think of stars and the night sky. Around her neck was a thick rawhide cord from which hung a flat stone with a hole in it. She held her arms out to either side of her body, almost the way one

Shape changing [handwritten]

might hold out one's arms before looking up toward the Sky Land to give thanks to the Owner Creator. But her hands were not empty. In her high hand she held a stick with deerskin wrapped around one end. In the other she held a hoop drum. Her eyes, which had been lifted as if looking for something in the clouds, suddenly shifted down and her gaze pierced him. He felt as if a cord had been stretched between her eyes and his. His whole body quivered from the intensity of her stare. Then, bringing her hands together in front of her body, holding her drum chest high, she had begun to play. The drumbeats were deep and slow. The stones trembled under his feet. She began to sing.

> *Nopassamek, the storm hears my drum*
> *Walking far away, the storm hears my drum*
> *Nopassamek, my drum calls the storm*
> *My drum calls, my drum calls the storm.*

Young Hunter stood still, even though he knew he was supposed to turn and run. He knew who this woman was. She was Medicine Plant, the far-seeing one of the Salmon People. The fox was her fox, perhaps even her spirit walking in the shape of that animal. Her drum was warning him. Her song was warning him. Turn and run. Any other child in the village would have done so. Yet he did not run.

Perhaps it was because he had heard the drum of the storm at its fiercest. He had felt the power of the storm as it brought down that great tree on their lodge, killing his parents and leaving him alive. For a long time he had sat silent after that, thinking of the power of that storm, a power which held no anger. When the next great storm came, he had been living in the lodge of his grandparents. He walked outside and stood there, the wind whipping his hair about his face, the rain beating down on him. The great shouts of the Thunder Beings filled the sky. Their spears of light flashed down close by. And

119

he was not afraid. He stood there in that storm without moving until he felt a hand placed on his shoulder. It was the hand of Rabbit Stick, his grandfather. But the old man did not try to pull him away from the storm and bring him inside. Instead, the two of them stood there through the storm, feeling it circle them, cleanse them. When that storm was over, Young Hunter felt a weight taken from him. His tongue was loose again in his mouth and he could speak.

So it was that, four winters older than when that storm had given its wordless message to him, washing away his fear, deepening his respect for the many powers all around him, Young Hunter had not been afraid of Medicine Plant's storm song or the thunder of her drum. So it was that he did not run.

Medicine Plant began to walk toward him. She walked with such slow power that her feet sank into the stone and her long dress brushed against the rocks. Deeper and deeper she walked and then she screamed. Her scream was like the scream of a fox, that sound which can terrify even the bravest hunter when it shatters the peace of the woods late at night. The scream pierced to the very roots of Young Hunter's hair at the nape of his neck, yet he was still not afraid. His eyes still held those of the deep-seeing woman, and as he watched her, he knew that she was watching him watch her.

Medicine Plant stopped walking. She looked down at the serious-faced boy who was now only a double arm's length away. Then she smiled and stood up straight. As she stood, she did so in a way which made it clear to Young Hunter what she had done, showing him her secret. Her feet had not sunk into the stones at all. She bent over slightly so that her face was close to his. Her breath smelled like the spruce trees. Her face was broad, her features large, as if they had been carved out of wood. It was a face which could easily hold a smile. Her eyebrows were very dark, and so thick that they almost met above her nose. One of her eyebrows was raised now, arched like the back of a wary bobcat. Young Hunter did not move. He felt like two people. One was looking up at this woman. The other was standing apart from them both, watching and remembering this meeting on the trail, seeing this small boy, short for his age, and this very tall, broad-shouldered woman leaning down to him. A smile flickered across Young Hunter's face as he realized how they looked together.

"Hunh!" Medicine Plant blew her breath into his face. *"You are laughing at me?"* Young Hunter lifted his right hand and moved it back and forth, saying no. It was all that he moved. Even his eyes stayed fixed on the big woman's face.

"Henh!" Medicine Plant said. She began to laugh. "What kind of boy is this who faces me without being afraid? It seems that even the Ancient Ones, even the Cannibal Giant, the Forest Wanderer would not be terrible enough to frighten this one."

She reached out one hand and placed it on Young Hunter's bare chest. Then she placed her other hand on his forehead. Young Hunter felt the heat of her hands.

Then her hands felt cold, cold as spring water. It was a shock how cold her hands suddenly felt, but even as he noticed it, they felt warm again. Now they were so warm that it seemed they would burn his skin. He could feel the heat and then the cold running through his body, circling from one hand to the other. But he did not move.

Medicine Plant lifted her hands from the boy. She shook her head.

"So," she said, "you are not afraid of me. How do you feel about this old woman, then?"

"I like you," Young Hunter said.

Medicine Plant threw her head back, placed her hands over the center of her stomach, and laughed. Her whole body shook with laughter. When she stopped laughing, there was moisture in her eyes.

"I see," she said. "I see, indeed."

Young Hunter understood. The way she spoke of seeing meant more than just understanding his words, more than just

121

seeing the boy who stood before her. It was a kind of seeing which was like a path leading into the distance, a path which circled many ways.

"There are things I have to tell you," Medicine Plant said. "But I cannot tell them to you yet. You have to go back to the Only People village. There you have to listen to that One Who Loves Food More Than Women."

Young Hunter nodded. He knew she was referring to Bear Talker by his joking name. It was the way people of equal rank sometimes spoke about each other. Such names were not always spoken to someone's face, but people knew their own nicknames. It was yet another way the thirteen villages had of keeping people from getting too proud. It reminded even the most important people that they were no better than anyone else. Those nicknames were given you by people in your own age group and they tended to stick throughout life, though new names might be added later. His own grandmother, Sweetgrass Woman, was known as Has to Know Everything, and Tongue Wags at Both Ends. His uncle Fire Keeper was also called Log Killer by his friends. The nickname referred to the time when he was camping with some friends on a hillside. Perhaps something in his dreams had been talking to him, for when he rolled over in his sleep he rolled a bit too far and went rolling down the hill.

Along the way, he rolled into a log and became tangled up in its branches. In his confusion, he thought the log had attacked him. He began wrestling with it so loudly that he woke the other men who came down the hill to watch him. He wrestled that log a long time, even after he was fully awake. At last, without saying a word, he dragged the log up the hill to their fire and stuck the end of it into the heart of the flames. He stayed up the rest of that night, pushing the log into the fire until it was all burned. That was how he came by his nickname.

"It is good for you to listen to that fat old man," Medicine Plant said. "He has things to teach you. The time will come,

122

though, when you will need the words of this old woman. I will be happy to see you then. You will be welcome." She began to turn as if to go, then stopped. "Remember," she said, "the fox is my sister."

Young Hunter had understood. He would never again hunt or trap a fox. He watched the deep-seeing woman walk away until she was lost between the folds of her high hill.

That had been three summers ago. Since then his shoulders had broadened, his chest thickened. He had added four hands in height, though he was still shorter than many young men of his age. But that did not bother him. He had been listening well to Bear Talker and the other elders. One did not need to be tall to see the stars.

The place where Young Hunter had first met Medicine Plant was behind them now. They were climbing up into the notch between the hills. The land spread out behind them like the palm of a hand opened to show what it held. The three young men looked back. It was like this early in Creation, Young Hunter thought, when the Owner Creator took the One Who Shaped Himself up on the mountain and they looked wide-eyed at the beautiful land.

"Our village ... " Blue Hawk said, gesturing by lifting his chin.

"Is there by the river," Red Hawk said.

"Uh-hunh!" Young Hunter understood their words. They were not just locating their place, they were praising it. They were acknowledging their connection to that land. And there was more in their words and that gesture. Though they might not know it, his brother-cousins were turning their eyes away from the road that Young Hunter soon would follow. For a time, he had hoped that they might be able to come with him. It would be easier than traveling alone. But he saw now that it was not to be that way. The journey to come was his. They would go back down this mountain. He would continue on and down the other side toward the west and the north. Young Hunter shifted the weight of the pack on his back. He could feel the Long Thrower, still hidden in the wrappings of skin.

"*Gagwi Io!*"

The shout came from so close behind them that Red Hawk and Blue Hawk both lost their balance and slid a few yards down the stone slope. Young Hunter's own heart leaped into his throat, but his feet stayed firmly on the stone and he did not flinch. Instead, he turned to look into the familiar eyes of Medicine Plant a few yards above him.

She had come up behind them as noiselessly as the mist drifting over the hills. It was as if she had risen up from the rocks like smoke from a fire. Her eyes held Young Hunter's and then traveled along his body, from the top of his head to his mokasins and back up again. Then she smiled and took a step down toward him. He could see that he was now a hand taller than she. He could see too that she was not as old as he had thought when he first met her.

Medicine Plant nodded and then looked down the slope toward the two brothers. They had straightened and were trying to show some semblance of dignity. Yet they were leaning close to each other. *Just as they did when they were small children hearing a ghost story around the fire at night*, Young Hunter thought.

Medicine Plant gestured with her hand. It was like the gesture one would make to a dog.

"Go back home," she said. "This young wolf and I need to speak alone."

It took courage for them to do so, but Red Hawk and Blue Hawk hesitated, defying the deep-seeing woman for a moment. They looked to Young Hunter.

Young Hunter nodded. "We will meet again, Brothers," he said. He gestured toward the trail with his chin.

"We will meet, Brother," Red Hawk said.

"We will meet, Brother," Blue Hawk repeated. They turned and began to descend the trail. They looked grateful to do so.

CHAPTER FIFTEEN
THE SMALL SPEARS

She looked across the fire at the young man and nodded her head again. The twelve seasons that had passed since she had last seen him had been good to him. His shoulders were broader than those of most men in their prime. The strength in his arms could be traced in the ropes of sinew and muscle, and his legs were just as powerful. But the strength that was easiest to see was in his face, just as on the first day he had met her. His eyes did not look away. He only looked at the earth, as was proper, when he spoke. That was the way the Dawn Land People always spoke, grounding their words in the earth.

Now, though, there was new strength about the boy. He had grown. There were things in his face not to be found in some men twice his age. The Owner Creator had been speaking to this one. It meant that he was ready to carry the weight of the secret of the Long Thrower. She and Bear Talker were in agreement. This strong boy was the one to go out and meet the danger coming toward the people. But she knew, also, that what he would meet was great and terrible. She could not tell if he would return. She could only point him on the path to follow.

She lowered the shoulder bone of the moose over the red-hot coals, holding it by the piece of wood she had wedged into the joint end to make a handle. The heat darkened the bone. The cracks in it widened, easy to read. Medicine Plant nodded to herself. A good one, the lines clear, joined solidly together. She held it out to Young Hunter.

"Here is the way you must follow." The index finger of her right hand traced a line from the burned spot which represented her camp. "You will cross the river moving toward the sunset and the Forever Winter Land. You will cross the Waters Between the Mountains. Whatever you must meet lies beyond there. Though this line here shows you will meet something before you cross."

"Uh-hunh," Young Hunter said. Then he waited. There was more to be said to him.

"This is as far as I can see," Medicine Plant continued. "That which comes toward you is great and powerful." She paused. "It is also not good. But you have done as I have told you these past days and in the years since we first met. You have listened to your dreams. You have shown respect to the animals. You have not hunted the fox."

Medicine Plant lifted the pouch which lay near the fire. It was made of the whole skin of an animal, not a fox, but a fisher. She reached in through the opening of the pouch which was the animal's mouth. As her hands searched for something, Young Hunter allowed his eyes to take in more of their surroundings inside Medicine Plant's lodge. He did not move his eyes or his head. That would not have been polite. But he widened his vision to see more of what was around them. It was the first time he had been in Medicine Plant's lodge and there was much to see. Medicine plants hung everywhere. Some he knew. Some he had never seen before. Some were both familiar and strange. Just there, close to the smoke hole, hung a plant which he recognized as the red flower that grew by the stream, the one the same color as the redbird. For a moment, the image of that bird stayed in his mind, then seemed to shift, to become a woman's face. Then that almost-seen face was gone and he was looking at the dried redbird flower. But this flower was not red, it was white. Clearly the Creator had marked this one flower for a special purpose.

Young Hunter's eyes took in the way the medicine woman had rigged sinew and sticks so that by pulling on a cord which hung by her side, she could adjust a flap of birch bark to open or close the smoke hole overhead. This was good. On the days when there was no fire and rains fell hard, it would be easy to close the smoke hole and keep the rain out. *Someday*, Young Hunter thought, *I will make such a flap for the smoke hole when I build a lodge. I will do it when Willow Girl and I make our first small lodge next to the lodge of my grandparents.*

Medicine Plant coughed and Young Hunter pulled his thoughts back. He was walking ahead in his mind again. Medicine Plant was holding out something taken from her fisherskin bag: a fox cut from a piece of birch bark. She placed it on the palm of his left hand, the hand closest to his heart. The warmth of his palm made the bark move and twist as if the fox were trying to walk.

"This fox," Medicine Plant said, "she is my helper. Now she will be your helper, also. There may be times when you cannot find the way. Perhaps, at those times, a fox may come along.

"I see," Medicine Plant continued, "you are one of those who notices things. That is good. By seeing much, you may see things which you can bring back, things which may help the people. But do not try to see it all at one time. Now, bring your mind together, aim it in one direction. Watch what I do."

She pointed with her lips at the Long Thrower which lay, unwrapped now, at Young Hunter's side. He picked it up and passed it to her around the fire. Medicine Plant held the long stick in front of her, her hands far apart at either end. Then, slowly, she began to bend it. The Long Thrower did not bend easily, though Young Hunter knew it was meant to be bent. The long muscles in Medicine Plant's arms grew taut, as did the muscles across her chest, lifting her breasts that were still as firm as those of a young woman. Young Hunter could see now that her strength was greater than that of most men. He wondered if she knew how to wrestle. He liked the thought of wrestling with her.

He remembered how Medicine Plant had touched him before he entered her lodge. She had made him lie flat on the ground on his belly. Then she had massaged his body from the top of his head to his feet. Her hands felt hot and then cold, as if made of ice and fire. Her fingers were powerful and seemed to dig in beneath his flesh, stripping the muscles from his bones, tearing him apart, putting him back together again. Her hands even reached down into his groin, but he had not responded as he did when Willow Girl touched him behind her lodge after he played his flute. Instead, he had relaxed as Medicine Plant's powerful fingers grasped him and then reached deeper, as if to pull out the long loops of intestine in his belly, as if to empty him of his guts. When she was done, he felt like a bird just broken out of its shell. A fire burned in every muscle of his body, and he thought his skin must be glowing like that of a snake when it has shed its old scales.

Medicine Plant braced the end of the Long Thrower against her foot. Her right hand pulled the sinew string from one end to the other, wrapped and looped it so that the curve in the Long Thrower was held taut. She plucked the string of it as Bear Talker had done. Again it sang out that thrilling note which touched the center of Young Hunter's being. She reached over the fire to Young Hunter's right and pulled a bundle out from under a basket. The bundle was made of the same sort of skin as the wrapping used to cover the Long Thrower. They were pieces, Young Hunter could see, of the same hide. Holding the Long Thrower in her left hand, she unfolded that skin bundle, disclosing a number of straight sticks. She lifted one and held it up toward the roof of her lodge. Young Hunter could see that it was like a small spear. Its point was sharp and dark brown from being hardened in fire.

At the other end, split feathers had been glued and bound onto the small spear in a spiral shape. He remembered the story of Comes Flying.

"The feathers," Medicine Plant said, "help it to fly straight when it goes far."

Young Hunter wondered how one could throw such a small spear. It was not much bigger than the spears which his grandmother's stories had told him that the Little People carried.

Medicine Plant lifted the small spear and placed it so that its feathered end was against the sinew cord of the Long Thrower. That end of the little spear was notched so that the string fit into the groove. She pinched the thumb and forefinger of her right hand around the string and the notched end of the small spear, looping her middle finger around the string just below it. She motioned toward the left with her head. Young Hunter moved aside. From her place at the back of the lodge Medicine Plant could now see through the open door.

"Watch," she said. Holding the Long Thrower firmly, she thrust her left arm out and pulled back on the string with her right until only a hand's width of the small spear still rested against the wood just above her clenched fist. "It will go," she said, "with your breath." She breathed out, letting go with her right hand. The string twanged and the small spear was gone. A blur of motion faster than a hummingbird's wings and it was gone.

Medicine Plant lifted another of the small spears. "Watch," she said. Young Hunter watched. She drew back the string, and as she let go her breath, released it. The string whipped forward, thrusting the small spear into flight, throwing it out through the door of the lodge in a line straighter than the cast of any spear.

"And again," she said.

Young Hunter watched even more closely. He saw how she held the Long Thrower, angled so that the small spear stayed in place as she drew it back. He saw how her left eye

[handwritten margin notes: "why did 2 diff people had the bows & arrows so they'll not easily"; "mis used."]

closed and her right eye looked along the small spear. She released her breath and this time his eyes followed the quick flight of the small spear out through the open door of the lodge. He saw it strike among the trees.

"And one more," Medicine Plant said. A fourth small spear sped after the first three.

"*Tobi!*" Young Hunter said. "It is a weapon!"

Medicine Plant looked into his eyes. There was much to read in her look. With such a weapon as this, one might kill off all the animals in the forest. With such a weapon as this, a man would have great power. Such a weapon was a great weight to carry.

Medicine Plant put the Long Thrower down on the skin wrappings. Young Hunter followed her out of the lodge. They walked through the trees. It was even farther than Young Hunter had realized. They found the small spears lodged in the trunk of a dead pine, buried deep in the punky wood. Young Hunter pulled them free. He had to place his left hand around each of them and then pull back with his right to work them free. He handed the small spears to Medicine Plant, but she did not take them from his hand. Her palm-down gesture told him to keep them.

"*Tobi,*" she said. "A weapon."

As they walked back toward the lodge, Young Hunter saw everything around them with even more clarity than before. He felt the stiffness of the pine needles underfoot, how they still held some of the morning frost in the shade beneath green boughs. He heard a hatchetbeak give its long repeated call from the forest to the north of the lodge. That call made him see in his mind the bird's broad black-and-white wings and its red headdress. It was good to hear the hatchetbeaks that lived near the lodge of his grandparents. He could see them swooping through the trees, hammering their powerful beaks against the pitted trunk of a tree such as that pine where the small spears had struck. Medicine Plant's hand tapped him hard on his chest. They were at the door of the lodge.

130

Walk in balance

"When we walk," she said, "we always walk with one foot in the spirit world. But we also walk with one foot on the earth of this world. Then we walk in balance. You must keep that balance to reach your destination. You dream often as you walk. That is a good thing, but be careful not to lose yourself in your dreams. That is part of the message the Brave One gave to you."

She pointed with her lips toward Young Hunter's leg. He looked down at the scar. It had been many days since he had looked at it or even remembered what had started him on this strange path. The leg was no longer swollen, but he remembered now how it had looked. Twice normal size, it had felt as if it would burst. Only the mud and the cool bubbling waters had kept it from bursting into flame. Then he had taken the sharp stone he found at the edge of the mud, reached down and cut his own flesh with its sharp edge, cut it so that the mud and the spring water would draw the poison out. The scar was there. It was healed now. The last of the scab had fallen off. Young Hunter saw its shape. It was a pale twisted line, thick as his little finger. Its shape was the shape of a snake.

Medicine Plant reached into the lodge and drew out the Long Thrower. She handed it to Young Hunter. "Now," she said, "you must learn."

Young Hunter fitted the small spear again to the string. His left forearm burned where sinew had whirred against it again and again. The thumb and forefinger of his right hand were red and swollen, blistered at the tips. He paused and put his hand again into the bark bowl where the deep-seeing woman had dissolved a mixture of dried herbs in warm water.

Leaning against the side of the lodge where she usually sat, Medicine Plant continued to play with the cat's cradle between her hands. With each pull and twist she made a new shape. Sky Bear's Cave, the Fisherman's Spear, Turtle's Lodge ... Young Hunter watched and remembered each shape as she formed

131

it. He knew there was purpose in everything the deep-seeing woman did when he could watch, even if she did not overtly call attention. She was not just playing.

It was like the winter stories he had always loved. Those stories might delight or frighten the children, but they also taught lessons. Like the story of the old woman with the sweet voice who hides in the swamps and drowns those children foolish enough to venture in alone. It was a good story to keep most of the children out of those dangerous places. Although such stories did not always work. Young Hunter smiled. He remembered the morning when his grandmother had found her seven-winters-old grandson setting out toward the swamp. Over his shoulder he carried a pole which he had fashioned into a spear, sharpening its tip with his small knife and then hardening it in the fire.

"You are walking far, Grandson?" Sweetgrass Woman said.

"I go to the swamp, Grandmother."

"Uh-hunh. And what about the old woman who waits there to drown the children?"

"It is all right, Grandmother. That is why I am going to the swamp. I am going to find her and kill her with my spear. Then she will trouble the people no longer."

Neither Sweetgrass Woman nor Rabbit Stick—whose attention during this conversation was focused on a very interesting piece of bark on the wall of their lodge—told Young Hunter not to go into the swamp. But as the boy vanished along the trail, a significant glance passed between the old people.

When Young Hunter came back, worn out and covered with almost frozen mud at the end of the day, neither of his grandparents said anything to him. Rabbit Stick was leaning against the side of the lodge, his head back and his eyes closed, breathing hard as if he had just come running from somewhere. Young Hunter looked at him intently, but the old man said nothing. Then Young Hunter put down his spear and went down to the stream to wash. When he returned, he sat by the fire in the lodge with his grandparents and helped himself to the food from the cooking pot. Finally, he cleared his throat.

"I think," he said, "that Woman Who Lives in the Swamp saw me coming. I heard her thrashing around in the marsh like a wounded deer. Each time I followed her sound, my spear ready, she fled before I could see her. At last, I chased her out of the swamp. I heard her running away! I know it was not a deer, for I found footprints, almost as large as those of a man."

Rabbit Stick reached one hand behind himself to pull the pile of deerskin robes more securely over the muddy mokasins he had hidden there.

"I think," Young Hunter continued, "I have chased her away. I think she will no longer bother the little children in our village."

"Perhaps we should no longer tell the children that story about her," Sweetgrass Woman said.

Young Hunter thought for a moment and then shook his head. "*Nda,* Grandmother," he said. "I think the story should still be told. Even if Woman Who Lives in the Swamp has gone forever. I discovered today that there are some dangerous places in that swamp. There are places where a small child might fall in and drown. I think it is good to still keep telling that story so we frighten the little children away from the swamp."

"I think you are right, Grandson," Sweetgrass Woman said.

Rabbit Stick said nothing. Leaning back against the wall of the lodge with his eyes closed, he was fast asleep.

Young Hunter pulled the sinew string back to his cheekbone. The muscles of his left arm bulged as he held the Long Thrower firm, sighted, released. The small spear flew whistling across the clearing and buried itself next to its four elder brothers in the rotted pine. Young Hunter smiled and flexed his right hand. The days of practice had sped by and his blisters were now calluses, his fingers no longer stiff. Two handfuls of days had gone as quickly as the flight of the small spears toward their target. He thought of his three dogs in the village of the Salmon People down by the river. By now, he thought, they have taken control of the whole tribe of Salmon People dogs. He laughed out loud. If any of the bitches were in heat, then there would surely be more than one pup born with white markings about its eyes. It was the first time he had thought of his dogs since coming to Medicine Plant's lodge. He had left them behind for he knew that the deep-seeing woman's fox was used to walking undisturbed. But his thinking of them now told him that it was almost time for him to leave.

The Night Traveler was no longer thin and starved in the sky. She was full-bellied and happy, her grandmother face bright in the night. Flights of hawks had been passing overhead, many nations of hawks gathered together for their annual migration to the Always Summer Land. Two days ago there had been four eagles with the hawks. They passed low over the top of Medicine Plant's mountain, and Young Hunter, resting on his back high on the mountain after much practice with the Long Thrower, had felt the wind of their wings as they passed, close enough to touch. As the last of the four eagles soared by, it turned its head and looked into his eyes. Then, angling its wings like the others, it passed around the mountainside out of sight. But from the sky something floated to land in front of him. A white-tipped tailfeather.

Young Hunter lowered the Long Thrower and placed his hand on the pack by his side. The eagle feather was in that pack, along with his other things.

"You have been an easy guest," Medicine Plant said.

She placed something in front of Young Hunter.

"This can be hung over your shoulder," she said. "It will hold the small spears. You can reach in easily to draw one out."

She began to place the small spears Young Hunter had made into the quiver. The marks of his teeth were on the shafts, for he had copied Medicine Plant's way of making them. He had watched her one night as she made two of them, heating the shafts over the fire, sighting down them with her eye, and then using her teeth to straighten them. He had watched as she split feathers and attached them with the glue she made of powdered bone, fastening them firm with thin sinew. It took him four nights of trying before he could make one of his own properly. Now he had made many.

Young Hunter walked to the rotted pine and drew out the five arrows. He took them back to the lodge, squatted down, and gave them to Medicine Plant. The first arrows he had tried to shoot from the Long Thrower and the last arrow he had made. The silver-haired woman wrapped them in the skin. She looked up at the sky. The days were shorter, the wind beginning to come from the northwest. She stood up and walked to the other side of the clearing. Young Hunter sat back on his heels, watching.

Medicine Plant lowered her head to look at the earth. Then, suddenly, she looked up, moving only her eyes. She looked at Young Hunter with a gaze of such power that he fell backward. She took a single step. She stepped with such force that her foot sank into the earth up to her knee. She lifted her head and smiled. Then, almost as if she had done it accidentally, she pulled her foot up from the ground and shook the dirt from it. Walking as lightly as a deer walks when it comes into a meadow, she came over to Young Hunter and embraced him, her bare breasts pressing against his cheeks.

"Remember," she said, "keep your eyes open in both worlds."

She pulled Young Hunter to his feet and shook him hard. She slipped his pack over one shoulder, his quiver over the other. She placed the Long Thrower in his left hand. Then she turned him around and pushed him.

Young Hunter felt as if his feet were not touching the ground. He was light as a white-winged seed lifted by the wind. He floated down the path which led between the hills to the river. He did not look back. It was only when he reached the river that he felt his feet beneath him again. He looked back up the trail. Something small and red slipped back into the trees.

PART THREE

MOON OF FROST

CHAPTER SIXTEEN
THE WOLF

Hunger/anger in his heart, he looked down into the valley. There were seven lodges of the new people there, seven of those long lodges that he had first seen less than a handful of winters before. The lodges were close to the river. Some of the men were in the river, fishing in the cold water. In another two moons the edges of the river would all be ice, only the center flowing free. But the people of those seven lodges would never see that.

Beyond the lodges were the fields. It was still a strange sight for him to see, the way those people cleared those wide places, leaving only the blackened stumps of the larger trees after cutting and burning. The blackened stumps could not be seen now, though. The food plants of the new people were tall, their dry yellow stalks covering all of that wide rolling land which edged the river beyond the seven lodges. The hunger/anger grew stronger in him. He wanted to go down with a firebrand in his hand, touch it to the stalks of those plants, and watch the fields fill with flame, the smoke lifting, the fire wiping them off the face of the land. But that was not his job. The Great Ones would do that. His job was to be their wolf. His job was to see but not be seen.

He had been taught the hard lesson of what his job was to be, taught it in a way he would not forget. Though it twisted his heart, he did as he was supposed to do. If he wished to continue to live, it would be only by doing as he was supposed to do, by being their wolf, their dog, their slave, their pet. If he did well, sometimes they would let him have the woman he stole. Not keep her. *Nda.* That was not their way. He closed his eyes, shutting out the thought of their way. As he closed his eyes tight, his right hand moved, without his being aware of it moving, first to his shoulder where the scar was shaped like a crescent moon, and then down to his groin where he felt the ridges of scar from his belly to his left thigh. He pushed down against his manhood, keeping it, though twisted, still hidden in his loincloth of filthy deerskin.

He opened his eyes, studying the lay of the land once again. He saw the places a man could go without being seen as he crawled on his belly in the night. He saw which of the elm bark–covered lodges would be the easiest to sneak into, and then smiled as he saw a woman enter that very lodge. The shape of her body and her long, dark hair showed that she was the right age. Although he had never seen them laugh, he knew that what he was going to tell them would make those who owned him glad. He crawled backward. The Great Ones were waiting for him. He would come back with the night.

Night. Four mouths breathed sleep within the elm bark lodge. Didn't they have ears to hear him? Didn't they have noses to catch his scent? He could smell them. Their scent was not the same as that he remembered the Dawn Land People having. It made him feel easier about what he was going to do. These were not real human beings. Even their language was not that of real people.

He held the slate-bladed knife in his left hand. Its edge was ground sharp enough to cut a moose hair lengthwise. He moved on his belly like a weasel, circling toward the door of the lodge. The door flap was propped open to let in the cooler air. The man whose throat he had cut in the bushes as he stood there relieving himself had just come out of that door. *These almost people are as foolish as rabbits,* he thought. *They deserve what is coming to them.* Low to the ground, he slid into the lodge.

The glow of the banked fire in the center of the small lodge was almost bright enough to blind his night-sensitive eyes. He looked away from it, waiting for his eyes to adjust. Then he looked around. This lodge was not round, not like the lodges real human beings lived in. This one had corners and edges— almost like the stone lodges of those who owned him. He pushed the thoughts of the Great Ones away from his mind. Those thoughts confused him at times such as this. He let his hunger/anger grow until a redness seemed to wash over his vision. He could see clearly now. On either side of the fire were sleeping places. A man and a woman, both of middle age, slept on one sleeping rack. On the other side of the lodge were two more sleeping racks. On one of them was a very old woman. On the other, a rack wide enough to hold two people, was the young woman he had watched earlier. The young woman was the one to take. He imagined how her soft flesh would feel, how her breath would be hot and moist against his palm as he clasped it over her mouth to keep her from crying out. The redness of his vision grew stronger and a drumbeat filled his head.

He breathed hard as he wiped the blood off his knife onto the old woman's clothing. As always, the slate blade had cut easily through their throats, parting the cord of their breath as easily as a hollow reed. He looked at his blade, making himself think not of the lives he had taken but of the sharpness of his blade. It was a good weapon. He pulled the bag from his waist. The old woman, he decided. Her neck was the thinnest. It would be easy. He had done it before and he did it with surprising speed. Then he closed the skin bag and tied it, heavier now, to his belt.

The firelight glinted off the wide eyes of the young woman. It lit her deerskin dress and he could see the shape of

141

a redbird painted clearly on it. The gag across her mouth was tight, her hands firmly bound behind her back as she stared up at him. *Perhaps,* he thought, *she thinks I am a spirit of the night, something not human.* He smiled at that thought, showing his teeth. *When she sees the Great Ones, then she will truly know how a spirit of the night looks.* He lifted her up and slung her over his bony shoulder as easily as if she were only a small child. He slipped out of the lodge, taking care to leave a clear trail. He wiped the blood from his hands on the bushes, scuffed his feet on the soft earth.

When he reached the ridge, he stopped, dropping the young woman on the ground. He untied the bag at his waist and opened it, letting its contents roll out onto the earth. Then he picked up the stick he had prepared and left behind him, the stick sharpened at both ends. He drove the stick into the earth. He took that which had been in the bag and impaled it on the stick, turning it so it would face down into the village. When they saw it, they would stop thinking. Anger would blind them. They would follow, blind with anger. They would follow his trail until they reached the spot between the cliffs. They would follow into that narrow place. Then, when they heard the sound which was like that of the storm wind, the howling of great wolves, then their anger would become fear. But it would be too late.

CHAPTER SEVENTEEN
THE RIVER TRAIL

Young Hunter sat by the river watching the Day Traveler move toward its highest point in the sky. He had no need to hurry. He was on the trail now and would not turn back again. The trail would take him soon enough to meet that which was dangerous to the Only People. And on a dangerous trail it was never a mistake to walk with care. He looked back toward the hill where Medicine Plant had her lodge. Its crest was barely visible beyond the three bends in the river which he had walked. He had come down from that hill and looking back at it, he could see it was firmly connected to the earth. But on his way down it had been as if he were coming down from the sky. His feet had felt as if they were walking between the stars.

Young Hunter nodded. He understood now how it must have felt to the Man Who Lived With the Deer. That one had gone and lived with them, seen the magical things they did, taking the shapes of human beings and then four-leggeds. But when that man returned to the Only People, even as he told them his story it must have seemed like something that happened to someone else a long time ago. And that was how Young Hunter felt now.

All this thinking. Young Hunter shook his head, wishing he could chase all of these many thoughts away as if they were a wasp buzzing near his ear. Not try to kill it, just shoo it away so that it would not distract him any longer. But the thoughts stayed with him and like the wasp, those thoughts could sting. The thought of not being strong enough or wise enough to carry the burdens that were now his. The thought that it was all a mistake. The thought that it was not. The thought that he would rather be back home in his grandparents' lodge.

He stood and picked up the bundle which held the Long Thrower and the small spears. It was awkward to carry them this way, wrapped and hidden in the skin bundle, the Long Thrower unstrung, even the quiver made by Medicine Plant kept out of sight. But it was right to keep this secret hidden. He thought of all that he had seen in the watershed of the Salmon People. Their lives were full and good. The game animals were plenty. Bear, moose, deer. Plenty. And the smaller animals—rabbit, squirrels, muskrat, raccoon, and beaver. Plenty to provide for the people. Salmon and sturgeon in the river could be speared easily and caught in fish traps. Then there were the many plants to gather in the different seasons, the roots to dig. The berry season had ended and the harvest of nuts from the trees was almost all brought in. The hickory and chestnut, the acorn and beech were being ground into flour. Each season had its special gifts for the people. There was no time when the people needed to go hungry. Everything they needed was here for them. They needed no new things like the Long Thrower and the small spears. With a weapon such as this they might be able to wipe out the animals which now blessed them. Such a weapon was only for one who was going out to face something out of the time when the Great Ones walked and the people were afraid at night. Such a weapon was like those magical weapons in the stories of Long Hair and the One Who Shaped Himself.

Young Hunter pounded his fist against his thigh. He did not like the thought of becoming a part of such a story. Was this the way one walked into a story? His stomach growled and he felt the pressure at the bottom of his belly. He laughed aloud.

But where in any of the old stories do we hear of a hero who has to take time to empty his bowels? Young Hunter left the trail looking for a good spot to scuff away the leaves and squat down and shift his breechclout to ease himself. He no longer felt like someone in an old story. He felt very human and it was a good feeling.

As he washed his hands in the river, his eye was caught by a stone. Its shape was that of a spear point, but smaller. He picked it up. It was not the chert stone, which could be easily flaked into a point. It was the soft brown stone that broke when you tried to shape it. Its shape had been given it by the river, not by human hands. Young Hunter studied it and thought of the small spears in his pouch. Their fire-hardened tips could pierce wood. What if he were to make a spear point of this size and fasten it to one of them? What would it be able to pierce then?

Young Hunter placed the small stone carefully on the riverbank. "I thank you," he said, speaking to the stone and the river. He put down a small piece of the acorn cake he had brought with him in his pouch from Medicine Plant's lodge. "I give you this in thanks." He climbed back up the bank, shouldered his bundle, and began to walk toward the village.

"We are not curious … " Red Hawk said.

"About what happened to you," Blue Hawk said.

"We do not want you to tell us," Red Hawk said.

"We will not even listen if you try to tell us," Blue Hawk said.

Young Hunter smiled.

"So tell us!" both brothers said.

Young Hunter smiled more broadly. It was good to be back with his brother-cousins. He no longer felt as if he were walking with one foot on the earth and one in the sky. He wished he could take Blue Hawk and Red Hawk with him when he set out again toward the north and the west.

Red Hawk grasped Young Hunter's right arm.

"We will not force you … " he said.

"To tell us your story," Blue Hawk added.

"But we will beat you to death ... " Red Hawk said, twisting Young Hunter's arm behind his back.

"If you remain silent," Blue Hawk said.

Young Hunter bent his knees and took a deep breath. Then he stepped back with his left leg and swung it forward so that it caught Blue Hawk behind his heels, knocking him to the ground. Young Hunter ducked and swung toward Red Hawk, pulling his arm so that the second young man found himself lifted into the air on Young Hunter's broad shoulder.

"If you put me down I will not hurt you!" Red Hawk said.

Blue Hawk, whose breath had been knocked out by his fall, said nothing. Young Hunter put Red Hawk down and reached out his hand to pull Blue Hawk to his feet.

"You are fortunate," Blue Hawk said. "We have decided to take pity on you."

The three of them laughed. It was good laughter, laughter that carried Young Hunter's heart the way a stream carries a piece of birch bark, bobbing and dancing in the light.

"Did she speak to the spirits?" asked Red Hawk.

"Did she change into a fox?" asked Blue Hawk.

"Did she cut you into pieces ... " Red Hawk said.

"And put you back together again?" Blue Hawk said.

"Yes and no," Young Hunter said. He held out both arms. "Here," he said, "beat the story out of me."

The two brothers looked at each other and each took a step back from Young Hunter.

"I am not interested in his story. Are you, Brother?" Red Hawk said.

"Not at all," said Blue Hawk.

Agwedjiman whined softly. He had sat quietly, waiting by the side of the trail as the three talked, but he could contain himself no longer. He was too dignified to fawn on Young Hunter and roll at his feet when he was in another village, even another village where he and his brothers had bullied every other male dog and established themselves as chiefs. But the whine, almost like the whimper of a small puppy begging to be picked up, could no longer be held within.

"Agwesis!" Young Hunter said, his voice soft. He went down on one knee and stroked the dog's large head. "*Wli gesu,*" he said in a long, caressing tone. "You are a good creature." He held out his other arm and Pabetciman and Danowa came quickly from where they had been waiting a few paces behind their leader, Agwedjiman. Young Hunter petted and praised all three of them. *Soon we will walk a dangerous trail together. Soon.*

Red Hawk cleared his throat. "It is fortunate you have returned," he said.

"Our dogs have been badly bullying your dogs," Blue Hawk said.

"Uh-hunh," Red Hawk said. "We were afraid they would run away."

Young Hunter stood up and threw his arms around the necks of the two brothers. "I wish," he said with a laugh, "you two could travel with me. You make my heart as light as the wings of a butterfly."

The two brothers smiled.

"We have much to do here in our village," Red Hawk said.

"We have to get up in the morning," Blue Hawk said.

"We have to eat and sleep," Red Hawk said.

They paused and looked at each other.

"We will go with you," they said in one voice.

Young Hunter shook his head. "*Nda,*" he said. The laughter left his voice. "Medicine Plant has helped me hear my dreams more clearly. I must walk to the north and the west. I must walk there alone."

147

Creation Story

CHAPTER EIGHTEEN
THE TRACK

Big Story nodded his head. "I speak," he said, "for all of the families gathered together.

"Long ago, the Owner Creator walked with the One Who Shaped Himself From Something, the One Who Gathered Himself Together Out of the Dust. The two of them walked together to the top of the highest mountain. They looked out together over the land. They saw that it was beautiful and they gazed wide-eyed. 'All of this Creation came to be,' the Owner Creator said, 'because I spoke.' Then the One Who Gathered Himself cleared his throat. 'I too wish to make something happen,' he said. 'I wish to make the wind.' Then the One Who Gathered Himself spoke. He tried and he spoke and a wind did come up. It bent the grasses. It shook some leaves from the trees. He was pleased with himself. 'That is good,' the Owner Creator said. 'Indeed,' said the One Who Gathered Himself. 'Can you also make the wind?' 'I shall try,' said the Owner Creator. Then he whispered one word. '*Kzelomsen,*' he whispered. Then the wind began to blow. It was a great wind. The clouds flew across the sky like swallows. The great trees bent as flat as the grasses. It blew so hard that it almost lifted the One Who Gathered Himself from the mountaintop. It blew so hard that it blew all of the hair right off the head of the One Who Gathered Himself and he stood there bald."

148

Big Story looked down at the earth and rubbed his hands together as if dusting them off. The story was done. Young Hunter understood. The One Who Gathered Himself was more powerful than any human being. But even his words were weak compared to a single whisper from the Owner Creator. Young Hunter was carrying something strong, something which had to do with the lives of all of the people. He was doing something great, but it was not big when compared to that which was truly great. And even as it made Young Hunter feel humble, it made him feel stronger. The weight he had to carry was not that great after all. The story would stay with him. It would help him along his way.

Young Hunter stood. The others who had gathered around did the same, turning to go to their daily tasks. They would not escort Young Hunter in a crowd to the edge of the village. That was not the way of the Only People, the Salmon People, the Spearstone People, the Onion Land People, the Fallen Bank People, the Broken Away People—none of the thirteen villages. It would be an interference to escort someone that way. Most people wished only to be with family or a few good friends when leaving on a journey. Coming back, that was another story. Then there would be dancing and celebration. Joking and questions would greet you then. But not at the beginning of something, not at the time of going away.

Fish Hawk and his wife each embraced their nephew. Then Young Hunter walked with only his brother-cousins to the lodge. He gathered his pack, tied his belt around his waist. Red Hawk and Blue Hawk put their arms around him and around each other. They leaned their heads together until their foreheads touched. None of the three young men spoke. This good-bye was not just for his journey, it was a farewell to those carefree times when they were children with no responsibilities more than to listen and learn. Perhaps by the time Young Hunter returned, the two of them would have children of their own and their eyes would hold that wider gaze

149

territorialety

which was in the eyes of Fish Hawk as he stood watching from a distance, seeing and remembering his own parting from the days of youth.

Young Hunter stepped back, breaking their circle. He placed his right hand over his head and swung it, palm outward, toward his brother-cousins. Red Hawk and Blue Hawk did the same. Then Young Hunter turned and walked to the edge of the village where his dogs joined him. Red Hawk and Blue Hawk watched until he was lost from sight.

Young Hunter went the fast travel way. He walked for as long as it took the Day Traveler to go a hand's width across the sky. Then he ran for that same amount of time. Going this way he quickly came to the divide which marked the edge of the watershed of the Salmon People. The Day Traveler was just at its highest point in the sky, though not as high as it had climbed only a moon before. The days were shorter now, the nights cooler. It was the time of frost. As he traveled, Young Hunter saw in his mind the trail he was following. He knew the way well.

This was land well traveled by the people. Each village had its own watershed, but there were also lands in between that were the hunting territories of no one village or another but shared in common. There was plenty of room between the village territories so the people could grow. If a village ever seemed too crowded, it might divide itself in half. Some of the people would remain while the others trekked to a new territory that no one yet claimed. That was how the Broken Away People were formed five generations ago. But even the land they had gone to was part of the wide territories that were well known. There were no unknown places in their territories. Each place had its own story, even those places where only the deep-seeing ones went or places that were avoided for special reasons—like the places where the Little People lived. The Little People did not like uninvited visitors. There were stories of people who tried to camp in such places, such as the white cliffs near the Spearstone People's village. As soon as they camped there, stones began to rain down on them. They looked up to the top of the cliffs, and there they saw the thin, small faces of the Little People looking over the edge as they hurled down rocks. The intruders left and no one ever tried to camp there again unless called there in a dream. And even then their visits were brief and gifts of smoking herb were always left behind to thank the little ones.

So Young Hunter knew his way well. He knew that just before darkness covered the land, he would reach the lean-to he had built when traveling to the Salmon People village. Though he could travel farther into the night, that was the place that would be best for him to make his camp. From that point he would strike out the following dawn. Not back toward his village, but onward toward the north and west. On to cross the top of the long lake they called the Waters Between the Mountains. Then, when he came to the other side, he would be in a new land, in a place where he and the Only People had not traveled. From then on he would have to follow the way that had been shown to him by Medicine Plant's divining—or by his own dreams.

There were a few villages of people on the other side of the Waters Between the Mountains. They were good-looking people, almost as good-looking as the people of the thirteen villages. They had a strange way of speaking the language of human beings, but they were not hostile. Over many winters, it had been worked out that the people on the sunrise side of the lake, Young Hunter's people, would not fish beyond the middle or cross over to the other side except to trade. In return, the people on the sunset side kept to their own half of the lake. Neither of the two groups spent much time in the very middle of the lake. There was an Ancient One who lived within its waters and people did not like to be too far from shore, just in case it was in a bad mood. Even in the winter, when the surface of the lake was frozen over, the people from either side

151

kept within their own boundaries. It was said that those who fished on the ice and fell in and were lost had been taken by the Ancient One. Perhaps it was only a story to frighten young children away from dangerous places such as the lake ice in winter. Still, story or not, the big lake saw few people crossing it at any time of year.

Young Hunter had seen the big lake once before. Remembering it, he could see it in his mind and feel with awe its size and depth. There was great power and great beauty there. He understood why the One Who Shaped Himself had returned to the big lake long after having made it. He returned and fashioned an island and then sat on that island and turned himself into stone. Young Hunter had seen the island when he and his uncle Fire Keeper had crossed over to it. Fire Keeper had used a dugout canoe kept hidden where no one else could find it. If Young Hunter wished to cross the lake, to visit the island, *Wujahosen, the* Guardian's Rock, he could use that canoe.

The sun was now only a hand's width from the western edge of the sky. Soon the Day Traveler would enter his lodge to sleep through the night. Young Hunter reached the top of the hill and found the marker which showed the way to leave the trail and find his lean-to. The tips of two bushes were broken and braided together as he had left them. He was about to step off the trail when he heard Agwesis's warning growl. The dog shouldered its way in front of him and stood stiff-legged, facing the direction of the lean-to. The hair on his ruff stood up and he bared his teeth. His growl was low and steady. *Something there. Something dangerous.*

The other two dogs pressed against Young Hunter from each side to guard him. He pushed them gently away, touched Agwesis on his shoulder, and gestured toward the left. The dog looked up at him, then slipped into the undergrowth to the left. Young Hunter gestured to the right and the other two dogs went that way. He fitted a spear into the atlatl and held it ready. There was no time to take out the Long Thrower and string it. He placed his pack by the side of the trail. Then, with the toe-heel step of the stalking heron, he moved forward.

It was dusk now, but Young Hunter saw clearly. He glimpsed Danowa and Pabetciman off to his right, brown shadows flickering through the autumn bushes. It was easy to move quietly through this section of the forest, for the trees were tall here, shading out the smaller growth. It was not like the cleared places where people made openings and burned the brush to encourage the growth of the berry bushes and the new shoots for the deer to feed upon. Now, as he moved from tree to tree, he was within view of the lean-to site. He could not see Agwesis, but he knew the big dog was waiting on the other side of the small opening where the lean-to had been made. Young Hunter could smell something now. It was a strange, musky scent, a scent new to him. He lowered himself slowly to his stomach, watching. Nothing. He listened. There were no sounds, not even the noise of a squirrel rustling leaves or a chickadee calling. That too was not as it should be. But his senses told him that whatever it was that had been here was now gone.

Young Hunter whistled. Agwesis came out of the bushes and walked stiff-legged to the collapsed lean-to and began to sniff at it. Young Hunter stood and went over. The strange smell was stronger now. He saw that the poles of the lean-to had been dragged and chewed. They were still usable, but splinters of wood stood out from them. It was not a beaver or a porcupine that had chewed the poles, chewed them in the places where the sweat of his hands had been left. The marks were those made by some animal with teeth like those of a wolf or a bear.

Young Hunter turned slowly, looking all around. He remembered that feeling of being watched as he had approached the village of the Salmon People. But he could find nothing within reach of his own senses that was threatening. He whistled twice and Pabetciman and Danowa came out of the trees. The three dogs sniffed the torn places on the lean-to. Then, with a loud *whuff*, Agwesis walked away from the lean-to. He circled the clearing, lifting his leg to mark each of the trees around it. When he was done, it seemed as if something had gone away. The strange smell was fading, the feeling of danger almost gone.

Young Hunter slept, but his sleep was light. The three dogs did not sleep. They sat outside the circle of fire, looking toward the north, the south, and the west. A dream came to Young Hunter. He was floating upward, beginning to fly. He flew over the trail which he had thought to follow, the trail which led to the northern part of the long lake. There, where the cliffs were close to the water, he saw a dark shape far below, waiting in hiding near the trail. It was shaped like a black cloud, red-eyed and filled with anger. It clawed at the sky to reach him, but he was too high in the air. Then Young Hunter felt himself being drawn back down toward his sleeping body as if by a thin strong thread.

He opened his eyes. It was morning. He looked up at the canopy of trees overhead, wondering if he had looked like a spirit light when he flew in his dream, like that light that some people sometimes saw coming out of Bear Talker's lodge when the deep-seeing man was seeking guidance. He sat up. The three dogs still sat in the same positions they had taken the night before as he started his fire by cradling the ember carried in his clamshell fire-holder, blowing it into flame in the pile of cattail fluff and grapevine bark tinder placed beneath the sticks piled like a wigwom.

Young Hunter stood and stretched. He yawned and then bent his knees and swayed from one side to the other like a tree in the wind, reached up toward the sky like a bear clawing the trunk of a pine, spread his arms like a hawk on the circling wind. He looked toward the east, drew in a long deep breath. The cool air of the morning filled him, giving him strength. There was nothing left in that air of the scent of fear which had been there the night before. He let out the breath.

Opening his pack, he brought out some of the food given him by his aunt. He broke off a small piece and tossed it into the bushes. For the Little People, the forest people, the earth. It was important to share food that way, to give away the first piece. He broke off three more pieces and fed one to each of the dogs. They came to him slowly, with dignity, and took the food from his open palm. Each looked into his eyes as he fed them. Most dogs would not look long into the eyes of a human being. Agwedjiman, Pabetciman, and Danowa were different from most dogs. Perhaps it was the wolf in them. Perhaps it was just their special pride in Young Hunter, their friend. As they looked into his eyes they said things without needing words to make their meaning clear. *We will guard you. You can trust us. We will hold fast.* It was always this way each morning when Young Hunter was on the trail with his dogs, but this time their gaze held his a bit longer. He felt, more strongly than ever before, that his life depended upon their help. Last night, perhaps, he would not have survived without them. Something which could not be seen had seen them. Something which could not be described now waited for him. His dream told him this was true. Somewhere, something was waiting. It burned with anger and hatred. The red eyes of that dark cloud. It was waiting for him. Sooner or later, it would try for his life.

Young Hunter circled his arms around the three dogs. "Brother-friends," he said, "you have done well. We see another dawn together. Now, I have dreamed. My dream has told me to take another trail. We will not follow the path which takes us under the humpbacked mountain. We will go straight to the big lake, to the place where the One Who Shaped Himself sits. There we will cross."

The three dogs looked at him, intelligence in their eyes. He did not doubt they understood his words. He felt that he did not even have to say his words aloud for them to understand. But speaking aloud helped him feel more sure of himself and his decision. "We will go straight west," he said.

155

"That way if something is following us we shall lead it that much sooner out of the lands of our people."

He stood and made a hand motion. Danowa looked up at him, as if in agreement, then shouldered his way through the undergrowth toward the western trail. He vanished into the forest and only the bobbing heads of a few late-summer flowers showed he had passed that way. They were the small, orange flowers shaped like little fists, the ones that were good medicine against the swelling when one touched the three-leafed burning plants. As Young Hunter looked about the small clear space near his lean-to, he noticed how many of the plants around them were strong medicine plants. The bushes next to the lean-to were those with the strong sweet scent that cleansed one's hands when rubbed between one's palms. Under the taller trees were many of the Strong Medicine Plant, the five-leafed one whose roots cured many things, giving strength to anyone who needed it. Its red berries were bright in the early morning sun. Perhaps whatever had bitten at the lean-to poles had been unable to stay in this place because of those medicine plants.

Perhaps their strong, healing spirits had driven it away. That thought made Young Hunter feel more sure of himself. Whatever it was that hunted him was not brave. It might be strong, but it waited in ambush. It would not attack from the front. He knelt near the medicine plants and saw what he had not seen in the dim light of the evening. The Strong Medicine Plants were clustered together around their leader, the tallest and strongest of them. It was the Mother Root of the others, the sort of plant which the Only People never picked because it seeded many young. One of the smaller plants below the Mother Root was broken and partially uprooted where a foot had stepped. Young Hunter looked closely at the disturbed earth. The print was that of an animal he did not recognize. It was as large as that of a ranger bear, but not a bear's. Its shape was almost that of the paw of a weasel. It was many times too

156

large, though like the weasel's track its claw marks were visible in the soft earth. It was not the print of a long-tail or its cousin, Pezo, the lynx. Those animals pulled in their claws as they walked. The track was sunk deep and Young Hunter saw that this new animal was a heavy one.

It was strange. Young Hunter knew all the tracks of the animals found in the lands of his people. Tracking had been a favorite game for him when he was a child. Tracking was of such importance to the people that one of the few strong rules given to children was that they should never make false tracks. They should not take the foot of a dead animal and press it into the earth or snow to make a false trail. That would offend the spirits of those animals. They would go away from the places where human beings could hunt them. Young Hunter was one of the best trackers. He could tell not just the type of animal, but the age of the track when he found it. He could follow tracks across hard earth or even, when fresh, across a rock ledge. If the track were very fresh he could lean close and smell the animal's scent still held in its print.

Looking closely, he could see other tracks less visible than this one, and saw from the space between them that this animal was a large one indeed. Its stride was wider than that of a big bear. The tracks were not that fresh. They had been made the day before, early in the morning. They led away toward the north. He nodded to himself. His decision to go to the west was good.

The exposed root of the smaller Strong Medicine Plant was broken and the leaves had wilted. Young Hunter reached down with his left hand, the hand closest to his heart. He carefully separated the broken root from the piece still left uncovered. Now he held the plant in his hand.

"I take you, Brother," he said. "You are giving yourself to me."

With the fingers of his right hand, he brushed earth back over the root left in the ground.

"You will live, Brother. Your people will continue to help the human beings. This is how the Owner Creator meant it to be."

157

tobacco offerings

Young Hunter opened his pouch and took out a pinch of the smoking herb, placing it on the moist earth.

"I leave this *kinnikinnik* here. I thank you for giving yourself to me."

A small breeze came up and the leaves of the Mother Plant bowed low, as if dancing toward him. The leaves touched his cheeks and his forehead. Then the breeze passed and the Strong Medicine Plant stood erect again. Young Hunter folded the leaves of the small plant so that they circled the stem. He coiled the plant like a piece of twine, put it into his bag and stood. It was time to follow the trail west.

CHAPTER NINETEEN
THE LAKE TRAIL

The Day Traveler was in the middle of the sky. Young Hunter looked down into the valley of the beavers. The valley opened like the palm of a hand and the range of mountains to the north lifted up like fingers. It was a good place to stop, to see all that was beautiful below them. He had been running without pause since the first light and he needed to rest. He sat down with a sigh, leaned back, and closed his eyes. Perhaps he slept, for when he opened his eyes again it seemed as if the Day Traveler were farther toward the west and Danowa was sitting there next to him, silently waiting, holding in his jaws a fat rabbit he had killed.

Young Hunter made a small fire and when it had burned down to glowing coals, he placed the whole rabbit in them after removing its insides. It cooked within its own skin and when he raked it out again, the blackened flesh was sweet to taste. He and the three dogs ate it slowly, savoring the quiet peace of the valley. Then they walked down to the pond where Young Hunter swam in the water while the three dogs played and rolled on their backs on the bank.

Young Hunter took a deep breath and let his feet lift so he was floating. He looked up and saw two hawks circling above. Their tails were spread wide and held the red of the sun. They circled, crossing each other's paths, dancing with the sky.

Young Hunter's own arms were spread wide like their wings and he whistled up to them, whistled the long greeting whistle of the sun-tailed hawk. The two big birds circled lower until they were close indeed. They cocked their heads, each of them in turn, to look at Young Hunter. Then they flapped their wings and lifted again, rising higher until they disappeared in the westward-verging light of the Day Traveler.

Young Hunter drifted close to the edge of the pond where a beaver had been working on a small birch. He reached up and broke free a piece of the tree's red inner bark and placed it in his mouth. The taste was good and he chewed it, thinking of how good a tea this bark would make. He could see bushes covered with ripe blackberries in the meadow above the beaver dam and he climbed out of the water. Soon his hands were stained red by the sweet fruit and he had eaten his fill. He heard a sound behind him and turned to look. There, less than a spear cast away, was a very fat black bear, stripping mouthfuls of berries from the bushes and grunting with pleasure. It had plainly come out of the woods from the eastern side of the pond, downwind from the dogs sprawled and dozing near the water—and too intent upon a feast of berries even to have smelled the dogs. The bear turned to look at Young Hunter just as he turned to look at it. A surprised, foolish look came over the bear's face. It too had thought itself alone. Then it made a sound, a low sound which Young Hunter knew to be a greeting. Young Hunter repeated that sound and the bear bowed, swung its head back and forth, and then went back to eating. It had accepted Young Hunter as another bear.

Slowly, still on his hands and knees, Young Hunter made his way out of the berry bushes back down the slope. When he reached the pond he looked back. The bear was gone. Young Hunter looked at the surface of the pond. It held the quiet reflection of the Owl Mountain. From its top he would be able to see the expanse of the big lake. The reflection wavered and then broke as a beaver swam slowly across the pond. Halfway across it slapped its tail and dove, rising to the surface and then slapping its tail again. Not in warning, but in play. The three dogs paid the sound no mind. Agwesis rolled on his back and kicked his feet in the air as if trying to run across the sky. Danowa sighed and yawned. Pabetciman crawled on his belly like a small puppy and thrust his big head into Young Hunter's lap.

Young Hunter let his feet dangle in the water. This was a good place, indeed. The cold nights had lessened the numbers of the little biting ones, the ones too small to be seen, the yellow-eyed ones with the piercing beaks. There was no need to smear more bear grease on his skin or to make a smudging fire. He watched as the Day Traveler drifted toward the west. Now the sun was close to the tops of the trees and soon would sink down to his rest. A piece of the brown forest at the edge of the pond moved and stepped into the water. A female moose. She looked back and grunted and a calf of that year's spring came bouncing out to the edge of the water, hesitated, and then jumped in with all four feet at once. Young Hunter laughed softly and the dogs glanced at him. He motioned, palm down. The dogs lay back and watched the two moose.

The mother moose now stood in water up to her stomach. She dipped her head under the water and when she lifted it, her mouth filled with water plants, the water streamed off her head and shoulders, and the light of the Day Traveler painted her many colors. She looked like the bright sky arch which formed a trail across the sky when it rained with sun in the sky. She shook her head and that rainbow glowed about her in a circle. Some of the plants broke free and floated toward the calf who stood in the shallows. It reached out delicately with the tips of its lips to feed on the water plants.

So they continued until the darkness was so complete that they could no longer be seen. Yet Young Hunter could still hear them as they splashed in the shallows. He could hear too the beavers working in the stand of aspens at the pond's north end. It was their time to be fully awake. It was his time to sleep.

The dogs' bodies were warm around him. He lay back with his head on Agwedjiman's stomach.

"Brothers," he whispered, "this is a very good place. When we have done whatever it is we must do, we will come back here. We will camp and fish. We will bring Willow Girl with us and then we ... " but his voice trailed away into a dream.

They were up before the dawn and traveling. They traveled until the sun was halfway up in the morning sky and then they paused by the Crooked Stream that cut down toward the big lake. Young Hunter's stomach was growling and neither the spruce gum he chewed nor the handfuls of berries he stripped as he ran had stopped his hunger. He signaled the dogs to sit and then crept close to the stream. He lay down and slowly let his right arm sink into the water, his fingers drifting under the bank. Now his fingertips could feel the throbbing of fins in the water. More than one fish lay quiet under that bank. One moved and brushed against his wrist. His open hand slid slowly past it and his palm ran along the side of one fish and then another. Not the largest one, that one should always be left. His hand slid now along the belly of a fish which was the length of his forearm. He slipped his index finger and thumb into its gills and guided it, without a struggle, out to where he could see it. In the rippling water the colors of its sides were brilliant, the same bright red and green as the sparkling stones in the current.

"Fast Swimmer," Young Hunter said, "I thank you for letting me take you. I need you to stay alive. I need your strength so I can help my people live."

He lifted the trout from the water. It relaxed in his hand, even when it was clear of the water. He placed it on the moss and it moved back and forth. With one quick, clean blow of the stone in his left hand Young Hunter broke its neck. The trout quivered the whole length of its body and became still. Young Hunter slid the strong nail of his thumb into the trout's vent at the end of its body near the tail and slit upward, cutting open the fish's belly. He reached in and pulled out the intestines, the stomach, the still-quivering heart. He broke free the gills and then placed them back into the water. It would not be respectful to leave them where they would dry up on land and be eaten by flies.

Taking his stone knife from its sheath about his neck, he began to strip free the bones from the fish, placing them into the water also. The swirl of the stream took them down and out of sight. Now he had two fillets. The head and skin of the fish went into the water. He placed the meat over his thigh and broke a piece from it, placing it in the blueberry bushes near the stream.

"I share this food," he said. He looked toward his dogs. They were not interested. They preferred the taste of fish after it was cooked. He offered them a piece and they sniffed it and turned away.

"You are spoiled little children," Young Hunter said. "I have no time now to make fire. Look, this is good." He ate some of the raw fish. He felt the living strength of the trout entering him. He pulled his cup from his waist. The cup was carved from the burl of a maple and was hard and smooth as stone. It gleamed from years of use. It was shaped like the bowl of a spoon with a short handle. The handle was pierced, and through it a strong piece of rawhide was tied to a crosspiece, which acted as a toggle to be thrust under a belt. Everyone carried cups that way, using them to dip food from the pot or drink water. He brushed the surface of the stream with his hand and then thrust in his cup. The water was so cold it made his eyeteeth ache. It tasted of the old ice still held in the highest places. He dipped his cup and drank again.

This too would be a good place to camp, he thought. But even as he considered it, a feeling of uncertainty came over him. He lifted his head and listened. Nothing came to his ears but the sound of the wind and the water. The sky above was clear blue and cloudless. It was peaceful here, and yet he knew that he did not wish to sleep in this place. That second voice within him, which was his own and not his own, was telling him to fear the dreams—or worse than dreams—that would come to him here in the night.

He looked toward the west. The trail divided here. The shortest way, the way he had planned to go, led down the mountain, over the hills below him, and then, half a day's journey farther, through narrow cliffs. The longer trail swung south around the mountain shaped like a snake before it turned back to the big lake. The voice within him spoke again and he listened to it. They would not take the cliff trail. Something was waiting there for them.

"Let us go, friends," he said to the dogs. "The way before us is clear for fast traveling. Tonight our Grandmother Moon will shine and we can continue through the night."

It was just before dawn of the fourth day since leaving the Salmon People's village when Young Hunter and the three dogs stood on the hill that overlooked the bay where the One Who Shaped Himself sat on his island. Young Hunter took a deep breath, his eyes quickly choosing the way they would take to reach the place where the dugout was hidden. They would have to go as quickly as they could. They were being followed. He had slept for a brief time waiting for the Night Traveler to rise and make the way bright enough for them to continue. As he had slept, sitting upright with his back leaning against a cedar tree, his dreams had told him that the thing which had been waiting in ambush near the cliffs to the north no longer waited there. It had backtracked and cut their trail. In his dream Young Hunter had seen it, a dark cloud with red eyes. It circled the valley of the beavers, it came to the stream where Young Hunter caught the trout, and it tore at the blueberry bushes there with teeth and claws. It was hungry with anger. It was coming closer.

164

He motioned and Agwedjiman went down the slope and was lost in the tangle of hackberry and beech saplings. The Night Traveler no longer shone her pale light off the surface of the big lake. She was gone behind the mountains. Then the first light before dawn was glowing at Young Hunter's back and the shadows were about to run across the land toward the west. Young Hunter breathed deeply and looked back over his shoulder. He could see nothing yet, but he could sense it. Danowa whimpered and nuzzled Young Hunter's thigh. Pabetciman whined and looked toward the east. Their noses were better than his, but Young Hunter understood. It was close enough now for them to smell it.

"Uh-hunh, my friends," he said. "You wish to try to hold back that being which comes closer?"

He put his hands on the heads of the two dogs. "Go, my friends, slow it down if you can, but do not give away your lives. This is not the old story of the hunter and his dogs and the fierce beast."

The dogs looked up at him and then turned to run back in the direction from which they had come. Young Hunter faced the west and began to make his way quickly down the hill, angling toward the headland where his uncle had taken him four autumns before. As he ran, a part of his divided mind retold him that story of the hunter and his dogs. The rhythm of his grandmother's voice speaking the tale blended with the soft beat of his running feet.

CHAPTER TWENTY
THE FAITHFUL DOGS

There was a hunter who always treated his dogs well. He gave them food before he ate. They slept with him in his lodge. He petted them and spoke kindly to them often. They were always gentle with him, but when they hunted they were fierce. There were four dogs. One of them was white as the new snow. One was black as a night without moon or stars. One was brown as the earth at planting time. The last dog, which was the leader dog, was grey. It had two spots like another pair of eyes on its forehead. Together, the four dogs could kill even a full-grown bear.

One day, the hunter went farther north than he had gone before. He went toward the great white mountains of ice and snow. He went into a part of the Dawn Land where no human person had gone before. It was said that terrible creatures lived there, but with his dogs by his side this hunter feared nothing.

After many days of traveling north, the hunter and his dogs came to a part of the woods where a great windstorm had passed. There were fallen trees everywhere. The trees were tangled together and it was hard to fight through the windfalls. Finally he found a game trail and was able to make his way through the hardest places. Soon this trail became very wide. It became wider than any game trail he had ever seen before.

Along the sides of the trail the trees were all broken and bent. His dogs stayed close to him as he went along and the man thought of turning back.

Then he shook his head. He would not turn around.

"*Nda!*" he said. "My dogs and I are afraid of nothing."

At last he came to a great clearing. There the grass and bushes had been matted down as if trampled on by great feet. Beyond the clearing was a great tree, the largest tree the man had ever seen. Even though it was dead with a broken top, it was twice as tall as any other tree. The man came closer and saw that the tree was hollow. He came closer still, and he could see that something was inside that hollow tree. It was coming out from the top of that tree. What he saw frightened him. The man's dogs whined and the leader of his dogs took the hunter's sleeve in his teeth and pulled the hunter back.

"Uh-hunh," the hunter said. "We must leave this place quickly."

Then the hunter and his dogs turned and went back up the trail. They went as fast as they could, but the trail quickly grew narrow. The undergrowth was thick and held them back. They could only go slowly. Now the hunter could hear the brush and the trees breaking behind him. The earth was shaking from the footsteps of that which followed. He was more frightened than before.

"My brother," he said to the leader of his dogs, "what can we do?"

Then his dog spoke to him.

"My friend," the dog said, "I will tell you what we must do."

The man was greatly surprised. He did not know his dog could talk.

"*Kitchi nidoba,* my great friend," the dog continued, "the fierce beast is close behind us. It is the fiercest of all the beasts in this northern forest. My brothers and I were worried when we came to this part of the forest. We were afraid that it would catch our scent. Once it catches the scent of anything which is alive, it does not stop until it has caught it and torn it apart. Now it is after us. All you can do now is try to escape."

Then the leader of his dogs made a growling sound. Immediately, the white dog turned and ran back down the trail. "Strong Teeth has gone to try to slow the fierce beast," the leader dog said. "Perhaps we will be able to reach the wider trail. Then we can run faster."

Before the hunter could say anything, the sounds of a terrible battle began back down the trail. He could hear the growling of his dog and the awful noises made by the fierce beast. His dogs pushed against him and the hunter turned and began to run. He stumbled through the tangles and the windfalls. At last he came to the main trail which led south. Just as his feet struck that trail he heard a piercing yelp from far behind followed by a terrible howl. The hunter looked down at the leader dog.

"*Kitchi nidoba,*" said the leader dog, "my brother Strong Teeth is dead. The terrible beast has killed him. Now it will begin to follow us again. You must run as fast as you can."

Then the leader dog made a growling sound. Immediately the black dog turned and ran back down the trail.

"Hurry," the leader dog said. "My brother Bear Killer will hold him back for a time and perhaps we can reach the Long River."

The man hesitated, watching his black dog go down the trail to give away its life. But the other two dogs pushed against him and he turned and began to run. He ran faster than he had ever run before. His dogs were by his side, urging him to run faster. As he ran, the Day Traveler moved across the sky. It had been low on the dawn side of the land, but soon it was directly overhead. In front of him the man saw the sparkling waters of the Long River. Just as he reached that river another piercing yelp split the air from far behind him to the north. Again, the awful howl sounded. The sound was so awful that the hunter fell to the ground.

The leader dog came and nuzzled him with its nose.

"*Kitchi nidoba,*" said the leader dog, "my brother Bear Killer has given his life. He has slowed down that terrible beast. I think he has weakened it. But it is still strong enough to pursue us. Now you must go faster than before."

The hunter shook his head. "*Nda,*" he said. "I am too weak and tired to run any farther. I cannot even stand."

Then the two dogs began to lick the man's feet. As they did so he felt the strength returning to his legs. He felt as if he could run a great distance without stopping.

"*Kitchi nidoba,*" said the leader dog, "now we have shown you one of our secrets. Now you know why we lick our feet when we grow tired. You have enough strength now to run a great distance. If you run quickly, you may be able to reach the narrow valley. Now my brother and I will go back and fight. If I am lucky, you may see me again."

With that, the two dogs turned and ran swiftly back up the trail.

Tears came into the hunter's eyes as he thought of the sacrifice his two dogs were making. He turned south and began to run. He ran with greater strength than before. His feet were almost flying. The Day Traveler continued across the sky and now it was in the west. There, ahead of the hunter, was the narrow valley. He was back at the northern edge of the hunting grounds of his people. Perhaps he was going to be safe. Suddenly, from behind him to the north, another piercing yelp split the air. He knew another of his dogs had died. The awful howl sounded one more time. It was not far away!

The hunter stood there. His legs would not move. He felt he could run no longer. Now the fierce beast was closer than before. It seemed that his dogs were all dead. He heard a noise approaching through the underbrush and he grasped his spear and waited. Then a head thrust out of the brush. It was the head of the leader dog.

The leader dog came slowly out of the brush. There were wounds all over its body, but it carried a bloody piece of skin in its mouth. It dropped the piece of skin, sat down, and licked its wounds. Then it looked up at the hunter.

"*Kitchi nidoba*," said the leader dog, "all of my brothers are dead. Strong Teeth is dead. Bear Killer is dead. Hold Fast is dead. The fierce beast is still alive and it is following us. We have hurt it badly, but we have not stopped it. Our sacrifice will mean nothing if you too are killed. Now you must do as I say. I am going to hide here and wait until the creature passes by. Then I will leap out and attack it from behind. It may be that I will be able to stop it. Perhaps you will be able to reach the flint cliffs. If you reach there, you will be safe."

"My friend," the man said, "I will not leave you here to die."

"*Nda*," said the leader dog. "You must run. If you stay here, the fierce beast will certainly kill you. It may kill me, but I will fight well. I think it will not get past me. There is only one thing which I would like you to do for me, *kitchi nidoba*."

"Tell me and I will do it," the hunter said. His eyes were full of tears and he could hardly speak.

"There is one dog in our village. You will know her when you see her. She is the brown-and-white dog and her owner does not treat her well. She is my wife and will give birth to our children within two moons' time. I ask you to take care of her and our children. Now run and do not look back. Quick!"

The man turned to run toward the south. The magical power the dogs had given by licking his feet was almost gone. He could barely move his legs. He had hardly taken a step before he heard the sound of heavy feet thudding on the trail behind him. He knew the terrible beast was close behind, but he did not look back. He continued to stumble forward. It was almost on top of him and he could feel its hot breath on his neck.

Suddenly, there was a loud growl as his leader dog leaped out of the brush onto the terrible beast's back. The man began to run faster and he could hear the sounds of an awful battle behind him. He ran and ran and still he could hear them fighting. The Day Traveler was sinking behind the trees to the west and it was growing dark. When he could run no longer he heard a sound from far behind him. It was the dying yelp of his leader dog. He listened, but the awful howl did not follow it. It was so dark that the man could see nothing. He did not know how far he had traveled. He was so weary that he could barely move, but he kept walking, his vision clouded by tears as he wept for his faithful friends.

Then, through the darkness, he saw light. He blinked and stepped forward and saw the light was coming from a fire in the little valley below him. He had reached the flint cliffs and the light was coming from his own village.

Two days later, after resting and telling his story to his people, the hunter took the trail to the north. Other hunters went with him. They traveled for four days before they came to the place where his leader dog, Do Not Quit, had fought the fierce beast. Trees were uprooted there and the earth was torn up by their battle. Do Not Quit lay there, dead. There were wounds all over his body, but he held in his teeth another piece of flesh torn from the body of the fierce beast. The blood trail of the fierce beast led away toward the northwest. Half of the other hunters followed it for a long time. There was more blood than it seemed any animal could have in its body. It was clear that the fierce animal was dying of its wounds. At last, the trail came to a swamp and the hunters followed it no further. Perhaps it died of its wounds or was drowned in that swamp, for such a fierce beast was never seen again.

Meanwhile, the hunter whose dogs had sacrificed themselves bound up the body of Do Not Quit in birch bark. He made a scaffold in the trees and placed his dog's body there where no animals could disturb it. Then he and the other half of the group of hunters continued toward the north. They traveled for four days before they found what was left of Hold Fast on the other side of the narrow valley. Only his bones remained. The hunter placed the bones of his dog in a basswood pack and they went on. After four more days they found the bones of Bear Killer on the other side of the Long River. Again, the hunter placed the bones of his dog in the basswood pack and they went on. Four more days passed before they found the bones of Strong Teeth at the end of the wide trail.

Carrying the bones of his faithful dogs, the hunter went back to his village. There he buried their bones and there too he buried the body of his leader dog, Do Not Quit. He planted four small trees in a circle around their grave, honoring them as one would honor a chief. After that, he went back to the village and spoke to a certain man. That man thought the hunter had lost his senses to trade so many fine deer skins for a worthless, pregnant, brown-and-white female dog. But when the four puppies were born, no one thought that again. One of the puppies was white as the new snow. One of the puppies was as black as the sky without moon or stars. One was as brown as newly planted earth. The fourth puppy was grey and had two white spots on its forehead which looked like eyes. Those four dogs grew up to be the best hunting dogs anyone had ever seen, and that grey dog with the white spots on its forehead became the leader of all the dogs in the village. The four dogs slept with their master inside his lodge, and sometimes at night, when people passed by that lodge, they thought they heard more than one voice speaking from within—even though that hunter and his dogs lived there alone.

CHAPTER TWENTY-ONE
THE DUGOUT

With the story in his mind, Young Hunter ran. He ran with the story. He ran on feet strengthened by the story. It made his running easy. His breath was smooth. The water was close now. He could smell the lake. He entered the wooded headland where his uncle had taken him. At certain times of year, there was a small village here. This was not the time for fishing, though. The Lake People were inland, getting ready to move into their winter hunting grounds.

A sound came from the small cedars ahead of him. Young Hunter stopped, raised his spear. Agwedjiman stepped out and looked up at Young Hunter. *The way ahead is clear,* his eyes said. Then the big dog swung his head to look back up the trail in the direction from which Young Hunter had come. His ears pricked forward. He could hear some-thing coming. Young Hunter turned and cupped his hands behind his own ears, directing his hearing as a deer does. He could hear it, very faintly. A battle was going on. His two dogs were fighting something beyond the top of the hill he had descended. Agwedjiman looked up at Young Hunter. There was a question in the dog's eyes.

"Go," Young Hunter said, waving his hand. "Help your brothers."

The big dog sprang forward, his feet kicking up small pieces of sod as he gathered speed, seeming to flow rather than run up the long hill trail.

Young Hunter hurried down the trail toward the lake. A turn and another turn and he was in sight of the water again. There, to his right, was the hollow cedar tree. Young Hunter stepped up onto the branch which was waist high, looked into the hollow, reached in. He brought out a bundle wrapped in deerskin and tied with basswood cord. He leaped down and ran toward the steep bank. He slid down it to the edge of the shore, knowing he was very close to the place where the boat was hidden. As he ran along the shore he untied the bundle, revealing a strong, finely carved paddle. His feet scrabbled on the loose stones. His eyes took in everything around him. It seemed as if he remembered every rock. It was all as it had been when he and his uncle had come here. No, there were some small changes. The top of that cedar tree had been broken. The trunk of that beech had been worked upon by one of the big red-headed drummers. The small alders there were thicker. But it was as familiar to his eye, to his nose, to his feet, as if he had never left this place.

He waded out and placed his bundles and the paddle on a large flat rock that stood out above the waist-deep water. He waded farther, following the line of the shore toward the north as the water grew deeper, until his feet found it. He bent over, his head and shoulders underwater, and reached down to shift the stones, hooking his toes under the edge of it to keep himself in place. The stones were large and smooth to the touch.

It was not easy to move them and roll them, one by one, to the side. He lifted his head to breathe and looked back toward the shore, a spear throw's distance away. He could not see the dogs yet, but he knew the way they fought. They would work together as a team. One would run in and attack. Then, as whatever it was they fought turned its attention that way, another would attack from behind. So they would continue, keeping it turning and striking, trying to lead it away.

Young Hunter shook his head to clear the water from his ears and listened. There was no wind and the waters of the lake were as calm as a meadow. The sound of the fighting came to him. It was closer. Soon whatever it was would come into sight where the trail opened to the shore. He took a deep breath and bent again, rolling out two more large stones. The shape beneath him shifted, lifting slightly. It trembled like a big animal starting to wake from sleep. Young Hunter rolled out another stone as large as his own torso and the dugout began to rise. It rose beneath him, lifting him as it rose. Water streamed around it as it bobbed up, carrying Young Hunter and the few remaining stones to the surface. Young Hunter jumped out and rocked the boat to tip out the last stones and much of the water inside. He began to push the dugout back to the big flat rock where he had left his things. Even before he reached it he gave a long two-note whistle, calling the dogs.

He threw the bundles into the middle of the boat and pushed it toward the beach, its stern grinding into the gravel. He placed the oar in the stern and picked up a long stick that came floating toward him. It had been cleaned of bark by beavers. It was strong and would not break. It was a gift to him. He could use it to push the boat out quickly. He breathed a prayer of thanks to the beaver people and the Creator.

Suddenly, so close to each other they seemed to be one animal, the three dogs came spilling over the bank. Their feet sprayed the sand and loose gravel and splashed through the shallow water as they leaped, one after the other, into the boat. They lay down quickly, silent except for their panting.

Young Hunter bent his back into it as he shoved the dugout into deeper water. He leaped in and began to push with the pole. The dugout was heavy and moved slowly at first, but it picked up speed as he poled without stopping, hand over hand. First to one side, then to the other.

Young Hunter heard something come over the gravel bank behind them. Its feet struck the earth heavily and crunched loudly on the gravel. He did not look back. Hand over hand, he poled. But he could see the eyes of his dogs looking back behind him. He could see the raised fur on their necks and hear the soft growls in their throats as they tensed, ready to leap. He heard water splashing loudly behind them as whatever followed reached the lake, but he did not turn back to look. He knew that even that much of a pause might be too much, for it was close to them. The pole bent as he shoved it against the bottom and the dugout glided now, cutting the water smoothly. Now he could no longer reach the bottom. He swung the pole into the boat and in the same motion grasped the oar and made the first quick, shallow stroke.

As he paddled the song came to him. He did not look back. Looking back would make that which pursued them stronger. He could barely hear the splashing of water as it swam toward them and he knew it was falling behind. He did not look back. He sang.

Kweh hah'yu wey
ha' yu way hi'
Kweh hah'yu wey
ha' yu way

Again and again he sang the song, and as he sang, he paddled. There was nothing but the song and the water and the motion of his arms and his own deep breathing. That was all there was and it was all one. Now they were past the headland. Young Hunter lifted his oar and breathed deeply. His back ached, his arms burned, and he could not feel his own fingers.

But it had not caught them. They were alive. He looked back. The light was so bright upon the water that it was hard to see clearly what was there. But he could see the dark head of something that swam. It swam strongly, but it was still falling behind. It was slower than the dugout.

Young Hunter flexed his fingers, shrugged his shoulders forward and back, and then picked up the paddle once more, lengthening the distance further. When he looked back again he could see it was no longer following them, but was angling back toward the headland. Young Hunter watched as it reached the tip of land. Even from this distance he could see that the animal was large. It was larger than a great bear. Its shape was different from a bear's, different from any other animal he knew. It was far away, yet he knew that it still watched them. He could feel its fierce eyes, trying to will itself over the distance between them. The hunger of its anger touched the pit of Young Hunter's stomach as he saw the animal rear up on its hind legs. It clawed upward as if trying to rip the Day Traveler from the sky. Two heartbeats later its howling scream reached them. The howl chilled Young Hunter to the bone. It was the same scream he had always heard in his mind when the story of the fierce beast and the hunter and his faithful dogs was told.

Young Hunter looked away. He no longer wanted to see that creature that had followed them this far and would follow them again. He turned his eyes toward the island of the Guardian.

CHAPTER TWENTY-TWO
THE GUARDIAN'S ROCK

Long ago, after the One Who Shaped Himself From Something had traveled all over the land, he returned to the beautiful lake. Of all the things in creation that he had done, this was the work of which he was proudest. He looked at the Waters Between the Mountains and thought it the most beautiful place in creation. He looked at the deep waters. He looked at the green islands. He looked at the ledges and stones beside the lake. He looked at the mountains to the dawn direction. He looked at the mountains in the direction of the sunset. Truly, there was beauty all around him. This was where he wished to sit down and rest. So he shaped an island. He placed it in the water off the headland. Then he stepped onto that small stone island and sat down. He turned into stone himself. There he sits to this day. He looks back at the land of the Dawn Land People. He guards this place. His place is the Guardian's Rock.

Young Hunter thought of the right words to speak as he came close to the small island. He heard in his mind the words his uncle Fire Keeper had spoken when they came to this island the last time, the only time he had been here before. His words were simple words. They were thanking words. Young Hunter spoke those words.

"Great One," he said, "I come to visit you. Long ago you did many things which made this land a good place for the

178

Only People. I thank you for everything you did. I thank you for watching over this place. I thank you for helping me to cross safely to the other side."

As he spoke, he sprinkled some of the smoking herb from his pouch. It made a shiny place on the water and the many colors of the sky arch were there. The small waves which were washing against the side of the dugout, pushing them back from the Guardian's Rock, began to smooth. The wind, which was pushing them away, stopped blowing. Young Hunter picked up the pole. The water was shallow here, for the Guardian's island sloped into the water, a long ledge going down into the green depths. Young Hunter pushed the dugout toward the island.

As he came closer, he saw again how much life was here. Though the island was all of stone and it seemed that nothing should be able to live there, still there was life of all kinds. The waters were filled with fish all around the island. Birds of many kinds had flown away as the dugout approached. There were insects walking on the surface of the water and other insects of many kinds to be seen on the stone itself. And there were bushes growing out of the cracks in the stone of the Guardian's Rock. They grew out where the layers of stone changed colors and shifted shape—at the base of the stone layers, which seemed like a huge, crouching figure. A figure of one neither human nor animal, three times the height of a tall man. A figure holding great power, but also holding nothing of menace. As Young Hunter poled the dugout closer, he saw that among the bushes at the base was one that was brilliant green. He searched the seeing of his memory and could not find that bush there at the time he and his uncle came to the Guardian's Rock. It was just the sort of bush he needed. Its green leaves were a strong astringent, good for stopping bleeding and cleansing wounds.

"I thank you, Great One," he said. "Truly our Creator did well when he allowed you to shape yourself out of the dust."

179

Young Hunter swung his dugout so that it slid against the sloping stone. He stepped out and pulled enough of the boat up onto the ledge so that it would not drift away. The stones were uneven beneath his feet. It was no place for a human to stand long, no place for one to camp or wish to camp. But the strength of the place was good. It welcomed him. He placed some of the smoking herb among the folds of stone at the base of the Guardian, where he imagined the feet of the One Who Shaped Himself From Something to be. The dogs stayed behind him in the boat. Agwedjiman and Danowa lay on their stomachs, heads up, tongues still out. They watched and listened. Pabetciman lay on his side. The bleeding was less now, but he was very weak.

Young Hunter carefully stripped leaves from the green bush. He brought a double handful of them back to the dugout, rolling them between his palms to crush them and release their healing water. He motioned with his head and Pabetciman lifted his front paws and rolled slowly, without a whimper, onto his back. His brothers shifted to either side to make room.

The three wounds on the left side of the dog's belly were long. Two had sliced only through the outer skin, but the middle cut was so deep that a bulge of intestine had been thrusting through when Young Hunter first saw it. Young Hunter pressed the leaves against the cuts. The green healing water went onto the edges of the wounds. He wondered again at the claws of that terrible creature. They cut as clean and deep as the ground edge of a slate knife. He shook his head in admiration at the courage of his dogs. They had held it. They had kept it from him. They had come back to him alive. Only Pabetciman had been injured. It was his stubbornness, Young Hunter guessed. He was always the first to attack and the last to let go.

He had noticed the cuts when he saw Pabetciman turned away from him on his side, licking his wounds. The dog had looked up at Young Hunter as if apologizing for causing trouble by being hurt. Licking his wounds was medicine too. Young Hunter knew that often a dog could heal its own wounds just by licking them. In the time of his grandparents' grandparents a man had been injured while hunting and was saved by his dogs. The dogs had taken his clothing in their teeth and dragged him into a cave. They licked his wounds each day and caught food and brought it to him. When he recovered, he returned to his family—which had thought him dead—and told his story.

Perhaps even this wound of Pabetciman's eventually would have healed from the dog's licking it. But the wound was deep. They still had far to travel. Young Hunter had to help. The medicine water of the leaves had cleaned the wound. Now it would not swell or grow bad-smelling. The only thing left was to close the wound. Young Hunter took the bone needle and the thin sinew from his bag. He began to pierce the edges of the wound, working the sinew through each hole. He did this many times, pulling the skin together tightly. Pabetciman did not whimper. He lay there as if he were a small puppy again, his legs flopped back, his eyes on Young Hunter.

Young Hunter finished his sewing and tied the sinew together. He gently ran his hand across the soft skin of the dog's stomach. He felt in his memory the many times when he was younger and these three friends were puppies, picking them up to hold the softness of their small hairless bellies against his cheek. He laughed. In his memory he had just seen the time when he picked up Pabetciman to hold his belly against his cheek and the small puppy had emptied its bladder right in Young Hunter's face.

Young Hunter helped the dog roll back onto its side. He looked into its eyes.

"My friend, you will be strong again. You will heal quickly." He shook his finger in the dog's face. "But you will not pull with your teeth at those stitches in your belly! Do you hear?"

181

The dog glanced at him and then turned away with a guilty look. Young Hunter knew that Pabetciman had already been planning to start chewing at that sinew right away. Dogs were like that. Great hunters. Loyal friends. But like little children.

"It is all right, my friend," Young Hunter said. "I know I can trust you not to chew at your wound. Continue to lick it with your tongue; that will help it heal. But wait until the leaves have dried there. They will taste bad if you lick your wound now."

Young Hunter climbed out of the boat and walked again to the base of the Guardian. There was so much he did not understand. This great one of stone here on his island, surely he knew the answers. But Young Hunter knew it would do no good to ask. The Owner Creator had made it so that human beings could not rely on the ancient great ones to solve their problems. Human beings had to help each other and help themselves. The concerns of the Guardian were not those of Young Hunter. His eyes of stone were open to the beauty of this place, the beauty of this creation.

Young Hunter squatted down on his heels and looked toward the headland where they had been. It was twice as far away as a look would be when one climbed a hill in the watersheds of the Only People, but it did not appear that far. It seemed it would not take long to swim from here back to that headland, but Young Hunter knew that was not so. Those huge trees looked so small. If he tried to swim that distance his arms would be very tired and the Day Traveler already long at rest in the west by the time he reached shore.

There was no sign of the black creature that had followed them and almost caught them. Young Hunter knew what it would do now. It would not cross the lake here. It would go farther north until it came to the strings of islands. It would cross there and then come south to cut his trail once more. Young Hunter saw this clearly in his mind. He was not sure how, but he knew he would have to kill it. He stroked the bundle that held the Long Thrower. He could not see all that was coming, but he saw the edges of it. It was as if he were being given some of the strength of vision that was held on this island by the Guardian.

He still had far to travel. Young Hunter turned and looked toward the west. There, on the other side of the Waters Between the Mountains, Young Hunter would be in unknown lands. There, to the west and the north, he would meet what was coming to endanger the Only People. Whatever it was, he knew that the black beast which now hunted him was part of it. It must have come from the north. Young Hunter nodded to himself. He understood. That terrible beast was one of the Ancient Ones. One of those that used to hunt the people. It had been sent to kill him. It had been sent by a *medawlinno*, by a far-seeing person.

He had not spoken this to himself in his mind before, but he knew it to be true. The eyes he had felt upon him were distant eyes. He had felt the gaze of one whose body was far away, but whose vision had traveled to find him. Then, after finding him, it had sent the Black One to stop him. He knew too that the far-seeing one whose gaze had been upon him was not the same as he was. It was not a human being as he was. This was not a strange idea to him. It was well known among all of the human beings that there were deep-seeing ones among the animal people too. And among the Ancient Ones that hunted human beings.

Something that had walked this earth long ago was coming toward the Dawn Land. It had dreamed his coming just as Young Hunter and Bear Talker and Medicine Plant had dreamed of it. It meant to stop him.

Young Hunter lifted the bundle he had been stroking with his hand. *Perhaps*, he thought, *perhaps this is what I have been given this for*. He realized he must string the Long Thrower now, place the holder of the small spears over his shoulder, and have it ready as soon as he reached the other side of the Waters Between the Mountains. He stood and placed his hand against the side of the stone that was the Guardian. The rock was warm to his touch. It was warm from the Day Traveler's rays, but it seemed also as if that warmth came throbbing up from somewhere deep within the layers of stone.

CHAPTER TWENTY-THREE
THE TWO DREAMS

He woke as he often woke. He was in the midst of a dream, yet it was not a dream. He lifted his hands up slowly in front of his face until he could see them. They were still the hands of a human being.

He sat up and looked around. He was in a lodge, but it was not a lodge. He had gathered pieces of elm bark and dragged them into this place. They paid no attention to him as he did this, no more attention than a man would pay to a dog playing with a stick. He had propped the pieces of elm bark against the walls to make the place seem like a real human being's lodge as he slept. But it was not that. It was made of stone. All around him the large stones were piled together, stones larger than a human being could lift. They were fitted so closely together that no light shone between them. The stone, which closed the door and kept him inside, was rolled away.

He had dreamed and wakened, but he was still in the midst of a dream. It was the time of day when the hunger of his anger was least, when it was only a faint presence in his belly. He did not look to his right, but he reached back, feeling the empty place there. The place where the woman had been only the night before. Now she was gone. He did not want to think about that. He did not want to think about where she was now. The stone in front of the door had kept her captive in here with

185

him. And he was as much a captive himself, even if he was their dog. Even if he would never be able to live among real human beings again. He would not think about where she had gone.

She had been braver than other women he had stolen for them. She had not whimpered or sobbed. She had not screamed as he dragged her along the path to lead the pursuers to the place where his masters waited in ambush. She had not screamed when she saw the old woman's head placed on the stake. She had not screamed when she saw his masters. She had not screamed or gone crazy when she saw what they did to her people, leaving none alive. And that was bad. The killing was bad, but what came after that was worse. That was when some of the women he stole for them became crazy. One had become so crazy that she began to stuff her mouth with twigs and grass. Then, after her first night in the stone cave, she began to stuff the twigs and grass into all the other openings in her body. It disgusted him and made him feel pity. The pity and disgust made his own hunger/anger greater, made his own pain worse. Yet he had still felt the same horror and loss when he woke one morning, reached beside him, and found out the grass-stuffing woman was gone.

He struck the ground with his fist. It was wrong! It had only been two nights. It was too soon. The Great Ones always let him keep a woman longer than that. Four nights at least. And this one, this one with the red design painted on her dress, was so good-looking and young and strong. He knew his own strength was greater than that of most men, though his strength was nothing compared to that of his masters. But it had been hard for him to force her legs apart. When he rolled off her she had tried to strike him with a stone. He finally had to tie her hands behind her to keep her from trying to kill him. And she had not stopped talking. She had not screamed, but she had talked.

All of the time she had talked. She talked softly in that strange language that the plant-growing people used. It was not like real human-being talk. He wanted to learn none of it. Still, though she spoke softly, though he knew none of her words, he understood what she was saying. He read it in her eyes. She would kill him if she could. That was what she kept saying.

It made him want her that much more. It made his own body feel warm—and not as cold as stone like the bodies of his masters. She was so alive with her hatred. It matched the hunger of his own anger, his anger which was turned against himself. Last night it had been even better than the first night in the stone lodge. He had thrust himself into her as she continued to speak. She bit his cheek and it bled and that was good also. He held her wrists tightly and pressed the top of his head against her cheek so she could not bite him again, and still she spoke.

But now she would speak no more. They had taken her. But they had feasted less than two days ago. It was not time yet. He knew there was no way he could speak to them, yet he wanted to protest. He was of use to them. That was what kept him alive.

He knew their secret. For all of their power and cunning, they were cowards. They were not good hunters. That was why they killed the way they did. He had seen them burn whole forests just to drive a few small herds of curved horns over the cliffs. They were wasteful, too. He had watched as they ate only parts of the animals they killed, tearing open the bellies with their strong fingers to rip out the livers, or ripping out the tongue and leaving the rest of the animal to rot. Surely the Creator must not be pleased at their ways, and so they kept themselves hidden from the eye of the sky. They were not good hunters, but they were always hungry.

Most of all, they were hungry for human beings. But they were not good at hunting humans. They were powerful, but they moved slowly. Humans fled from their fires and escaped, unless they found other ways, used other ways. So it was that they caught him and kept him and made him do as they wished. Made him to be like them.

He still wondered at that. Wondered at how they had made him this way. Then he would remember the single eye of their Oldest Talker boring into him, touching the center of his being. He would hear again that powerful speaking without words. They had marked him when he was only a small child, marked him and left him to grow. Left their mark to grow on him and within him. And when he was grown, and that which was within him drove him out of the places where human beings walked, he had come to them. He had been drawn to them.

He wondered about other things too. It was not always that he wondered. Most days he thought little, tried to keep himself from thinking. Most days he would just drift, letting a grey cloud mask his mind and his spirit. But when thoughts came into his mind again, unbidden and sharp, those times he asked himself other questions. Why were there so few of them? Why were there no young ones among them? How old were they? Why were there no females? So he would wonder until he felt the touch at the base of his skull, a touch unconnected to flesh. Then he would close his mind once more, knowing that in some way old One-Eye was hearing his thoughts and was waiting. Waiting perhaps for his anger to flame to the point when he could no longer control it, when he would strike out against them or try to run. If the two sparks of hatred for them and hatred for himself grew larger and turned into a flame, a flame fanned by too much thought, then he would run as the heavy-shouldered curved horns ran before their driving fires. He would run, but they would catch him. He would be of no more use to them. Except in one way.

He crawled out of the stone lodge. Two of them stood there. Their skins were grey as the stones. Hard-looking. Like dirty ice at the edge of water. He stood, and though he was taller than other men, his head only came up to their waists. He kept his eyes on the ground. One of them made gestures at him. He did not know which of them it was. He did not try to tell them apart. Except One-Eye. It bent toward him, pointing with a long, clawed finger. It breathed out as it bent and the heavy smell of its breath washed over him. It was a smell that always sickened him, though he did not show it outwardly. He looked where it was pointing. It was pointing at the stone that they had just rolled away to unblock the door of the stone lodge where he and the woman had been placed night before last. He looked and then he understood. There was blood there. The creature touched the blood and then made a sweeping gesture toward the hills. She had squeezed through the small space between the blocking stone and the doorway of the hut. He looked back at the doorway and saw where earth had been scraped away to make more space. She had forced herself through that space, scraping her skin as she did so. It was a good thing that the Hunter was away. Had it been here, sleeping outside his stone hut as it usually did each night—for when he was in the hut alone that stone protected him as much as it kept him prisoner—she would be dead by now. But she was not dead. She had escaped.

The one who was making signs to him waved a hand toward the hills again and then pointed at him. He was being told to go and catch her. He nodded. His left hand stroked the scar on his inner thigh. He would bring her back. He would hear her soft talking again for a while, until ... but he would not think of that. He would bring her back and hear her voice again.

The one making signs waved its hand again, impatiently this time. He nodded and took the trail.

Young Hunter looked across the water and shook his head. The strange awake dreaming had come to him as he touched the stone of the Guardian, as his eyes took in the many colors and ripples on the lake. He wondered at the place he had

189

seen. He had not seen it clearly, but with the blurred seeing of one who has fever or has been struck hard on the head. But he had seen enough for it to trouble him. He had seen the square houses of stone, the tall shapes which were like men but not men, like figures of grey stone which moved. He had felt the awful fear and anger and hunger which were held like burning coals in the mind of the human being through whose eyes he saw all this.

It was all connected. This dream and his journey and the terrible beast and the Long Thrower. He looked at the waters, and though it was a warm day, felt as if a cold wind blew over his body. He felt very small.

Then he shook his head again and looked up. The Day Traveler had gone the width of two hands across the sky as he stood there lost in his dream seeing. There would be just enough time now to cross to the other side and find a sheltering place for the night.

"Old One," he said, placing his hands on the stone a second time, "I thank you for allowing us to come to you. Thank you for guarding this place."

Young Hunter looked around. He found a stick no bigger around than his small finger and the length of his arm. Like his pole it had been stripped clean by a beaver. There were gull feathers floating on the surface of the water. He picked up the stick and four of the feathers. With a small piece of sinew he bound the feathers to the end of the stick. Then, carefully, he wedged the other end in a crack in the stone and stepped back. The wind fluttered the feathers at the end of the stick. It made him think of a prayer.

The dogs were waiting patiently in the boat. Agwedjiman and Danowa sat with their heads up and alert, looking in different directions. Pabetciman straightened himself on his side and looked guilty.

"So," Young Hunter said, "you were thinking of chewing at that sinew which holds your belly together. Is that not so?"

The dog put his paws over his eyes.

"You are a bad one. I should throw you into the lake."

Pabetciman pressed his paws more tightly over his eyes and whimpered.

"Miserable one!" Young Hunter said. He reached out his hand and stroked the dog's head. "You are a good friend. You fought to save my life. Now I ask just that you let yourself heal. Do you hear me, *nidoba*? Lick your wound but do not chew at it."

Pabetciman licked his hand and then lay back.

Young Hunter pushed the boat free and jumped inside. Standing in the stern, he poled it away from the Guardian's Rock until the bottom dropped below the pole's length. Still standing, he picked up the paddle. It was long-handled, designed to be used either sitting or standing. Standing, bending his knees, he could put more strength into each stroke. The dugout moved steadily toward that shore where Young Hunter had yet to walk—except in his dreams.

CHAPTER TWENTY-FOUR
THEIR DOG

He was their dog. They had marked him and then called him to them. In the center of his being, there was darkness. It was not bright and clear, not the pulsing light that a deep-seeing person would recognize as the center of one in balance with his own life and the life around him. The center of his being was tangled like the thick web of a spider spread between trees. He was not one of them, but he was enough like the Great Ones so that he could almost understand. And he heard when he was called.

Their deep-seeing one was the one with the single eye; where the other eye had been was only a mass of scar. The eye had been torn out long ago by the claws of a great ice bear far to the north, torn out as it wrestled with the great white bear until it broke the bear's back. He had seen that, been given that seeing by One-Eye. He had not been told it. They had no spoken words for him or for each other. Only that seeing from mind to mind, seeing as if he were there. It was so vivid that he lifted his hand up to touch his own right eye and was surprised to find it not gone but still whole.

One-Eye had called him. He was feverish from the wound made by the old man's stick when it struck him in the groin, limping as he followed that call out of the swamp. He had followed it many days and nights, hearing it whisper to him

A little farther. One step farther. He came at last to the stone of a tall cliff. He stood there, staring as the voice still called. Then he saw the narrow way within and he entered the cave. He followed that whisper deeper and deeper. It spoke to the dark center of his being. It spoke of great power. *This power can be yours. You will be one with us. The other small ones run from us; they run if they see us. You can bring them to us. We are not many, but we are strong. We are old. Older than the trees. Only the stones are older. You will join us. We will feed you.*

So he listened and walked and crawled through darkness until he found himself following a shadow. A tall walking shadow. He followed as the light increased and he saw the one he followed. But he did not run away. They came out of another cave mouth into the jumbled hills and he walked behind. He followed, walking farther away from the Only People. His wound healed and became another scar like the scar on his shoulder. He had no name now. He was their dog, placed each night in one of their caves with a stone rolled tightly into the mouth to keep him out of their way. He was now one who walks behind, eating the scraps or digging roots, stripping bark from the trees and chewing it. Walking without thought. His mind more cloudy. Clouded from the fever at first that came with his wound, but the fever did not leave when the wound healed. The fever stayed in his mind. His thoughts twisted and stuck. There were spider webs across his eyes and his mouth. He breathed through those webs.

And he heard One-Eye's whisper inside his head. It was not words nor was it pictures. It was like another thought that was also his own thought. He followed. He did their bidding and he ate. They had fire and they cooked. They always had fire. It was their friend. Everything they caught was thrown into their fire and burned black, even if it was as small as an insect. Throw it into the fire. Alive. Watch without emotion as it squirmed, their eyes wide as the squirming grew slower and slower. He saw them take a rabbit, thrust a stick through the skin of its back and then hang it over the fire as it screamed. All aflame, it broke free and ran in circles outside the fire until it stopped and the flame began to die out. They threw it back into the fire again.

Their skins were thick and the fire did not burn them when they reached into it to take out their food. Their skins were grey as moss, grey as certain stones. They would reach into the fire with their long-fingered hands and pull out the blackened food and twist it, tear it with their sharp fingernails. If blood still dripped, they would toss it into the fire again. And when their great bellies had been filled, One-Eye would toss him the scraps. Hungry, he ate. He always ate. He was their dog. He followed them.

There—his thoughts broke as he saw it. He dropped to one knee and stared. The print of a woman's heel in soft earth, earth still settling into the print. She was not far ahead. She would be tired by now, weak from hunger, for she had not eaten their food. But he had eaten and grown strong.

His thoughts had returned him to that first morning when they had rolled away the stone and One-Eye beckoned him to come out. One-Eye spoke to him with his hands and the gestures were similar enough to those used by the Dawn Land People for Weasel Tail to understand. His belly was twisted by hunger, and he ate the meat that was handed to him.

How many of them were there? Even that first morning when they all gathered around, looking at him with no sign of any emotion, he had been unable to count them. They all seemed the same. Only One-Eye was distinguishable. All of them were twice the height of a human being. All of them seemed as old as the grey stones of their wigwoms. Their muscles were great slabs, their hands huge, their fingers like claws, fingernails like slate blades. They wore no clothing. They had grey hair on their heads and on their bodies, though the skin showed in many places. Because they were naked, he saw that all of them were males. There were no females. How many of them were there? Ten, twenty? He never knew for sure. When he tried to count, it seemed that One-Eye always stepped in front of him and looked at him. Spoke with the gestures of his huge hands, looked deep into him, and then whispered without words to his mind, telling him where to go, what to do ...

He felt happy as he followed the woman's trail. She must be very tired now, for there was no longer any attempt made to conceal her tracks. They were as easy to follow as the tracks of the big-headed curved horns that first time they took him to hunt with them.

They had walked toward the setting sun until they came to a place where the land opened into a wide plain. A river cut through it, and along the river in the small valley below them, there were many of those animals. They were animals he had never seen before. Their hindquarters were small, their heads huge and shaggy, their horns black as late-summer berries. One-Eye placed him at the base of an oak tree and motioned him to climb into its branches, to stay. He did as he was told, for he knew that he would not live long if he remained on the ground. The eyes of One-Eye's pet, the fierce animal he now knew as the Hunter or the Black One, were on him. Hungry red eyes. He climbed to the tallest, thinnest branches and watched.

All of them, even the Hunter, seemed to vanish into the hills. One moment they were there, the next they were gone. It was silent for a while, then he saw the bigheads moving, nervous, smelling the wind. The wind was at his back, but he could smell it too. Smoke. Then he saw the fires. They came from either side of the valley, filling it, sweeping toward the bighead herd. The Ancient Ones were behind the fires, directing the fires toward the herd. Trees and grasses exploded into flame, the sky grew dark with smoke. The land was red with fire. The bigheads ran down the valley following the thin stream of water until they came to the cliff. The fires blocked all other ways to go. They kept running, running toward the cliff, running over it, a dark waterfall of flesh. All of them went over the cliff. All of them were killed.

They moved their camp whenever an area was empty of life. Everything burned. Everything dead. They followed their hunger and they were always hungry. Though they killed much, they used only a part of it. They did not dry meat or carry food with them. They burned and killed and ate. Then they moved on. Somewhere, deep inside, under the dark sticky webs which blinded the eye of his heart, he was sick. But the other sickness, the hunger of his anger, was stronger. One-Eye's whisper in his mind strengthened his weakness. He ate as they ate.

Once they had been men. Perhaps. Or like men. Ancient Ones like human beings. But this living had made them this way. Perhaps it would change him also. When there was clear water in a lake or stream he would look into it, study his own face. Was it still human? He thought it was still human, even though many winters had passed since he had first become their dog and followed them, walking toward the setting sun and then toward the Forever Winter Land. Perhaps he would not become like them in the way he looked. Perhaps his skin would not become grey as stone. Perhaps they never had been men. Perhaps they were the last of their kind, from ancient times. But they were still powerful. Powerful enough to wipe out the animals as they traveled and hunted with fire. They changed the living land to a dead place and they made the skies dark with smoke. Rain followed them, hissing in the ashes. And he was their dog.

He led them. He scouted for them, leading them away from the sunrise, leading them toward the sunset or the winter lands. The Dawn Land was still within him, hidden deep in his heart. He would try to lead them away from his people, even though his people were no longer his people. Now, though, they had circled back toward the sunrise and a part of him worried about whether he could keep them heading in the direction of the Always Summer Land, not toward the long lake between the mountains. It would be hard for them to cross the Waters Between the Mountains as he had crossed. Perhaps they would be satisfied here, hunting these new people. These ones who had come from the land toward the summer land, toward the sunset. These new ones with their long houses of bark, with their fields of strange plants, these were the people he would continue to help his masters to hunt. He would lead them into ambush and the fires would burn hot. Then they would eat. And when they had wiped out these people, they would continue toward the direction of the Always Summer Land and the sunset. They would not enter the Land of the Dawn.

There! A small branch of a raspberry plant was broken back. It marked where the woman he followed had pushed off the trail. Her footprint was faint in the earth among the leaves. She had heard him. She was hiding from him in fright, holding her breath, hoping he would pass by. He smiled and it was a smile not good to see on a human face. He would catch her now. He would not be quick to bring her back to his masters. He would spend some time with her. She was a good one. She was strong and young. Sweet. Were it not for his fear of his masters, he would never bring her back. Instead he would keep her and he would ... His thoughts whipped back at him like a branch striking his face on an unfamiliar trail in the night. What was it he was thinking of doing to her? And it came to him that though his face was still that of a human being, his heart was no longer human. For his thought was this: *He would kill her and eat her himself.*

But he would not do that. He shook his head. He was too afraid of them. Afraid of them and of the dark one, their Hunter. One-Eye had sent it somewhere, sent it with a command from his mind. It was fierce, but it did as One-Eye wished. Why had it been sent toward the east? Had One-Eye seen something coming in a dream? Had they sent the Black One to meet it?

The Black One was an Ancient One. Smaller than his masters, but larger than a great bear. It was blacker than smoke, its body like that of a long-tail, though its tail was just a stub. Its eyes had found him that first day when One-Eye carried him into their camp. Its eyes had found him and he could not move. Those eyes caught him like the eyes of a rattlesnake catching a chipmunk. The Black One recognized him. He was its food. And he, in turn, recognized the Black One. It was every evil dream of darkness kept hidden in the hearts of real human beings. But One-Eye had cuffed it like a puppy, picked it up by the scruff of its neck, and looked into its eyes. Spoken to it with its mind. So it stayed away. It did not touch him. But he felt its eyes on him as he sat near One-Eye. It was waiting. A time would come.

He knew how it would happen. He had seen it done now more than once. Seen men brought into the camp who were caught and not killed. Seen them placed on their feet, pushed. Run! And they ran. But not far. The Black One yawned where it lay near the fire. It opened its jaws wide so that its fangs, three times the size of the largest bear's, glistened in the firelight. It rose lightly to its feet, its mouth still open, and it bounded in pursuit. Its motions were lazy, dreamlike, as it ran, yet it was always on the man in less than four leaps, rising on its hind legs, its front paws coming down on the man's shoulders, its teeth piercing the skull as the man screamed. As it rode him down, the heavy muscles of its neck rippled with one last killing shake. Then the sounds of its eating. He did not look away. He no longer looked away from anything.

He shook his head. He would not think of the Black One. He would follow this woman. He would catch her. He would beat her and then play with her for a while before bringing her back to his masters.

He began to follow the trail as it led into the thick bushes, but his thoughts were clouded and he did not see clearly. He did not see, as he followed the woman's trail, the place where she had walked backward in her own prints and then stepped off to the side of the trail so that he passed her. He did not see her.

But he heard the sound of her breath. He heard it behind him and to his right as he bent to look at the trail, following like a weasel on the track of a rabbit. He heard the sudden inrush of breath and turned toward it quickly, raising his arm as he turned. But not quickly enough. The heavy branch in the woman's hands struck his shoulder and drove him to the ground. She struck again at his face. He heard the thick sound of the wood striking the bone of his cheek. It filled his head with searing light and then he heard nothing more.

CHAPTER TWENTY-FIVE
THE NEW LAND

Young Hunter, at first, was not sure how he felt about the new land, these plains which opened to the northwest beyond the mountains. At first, the wide spaces seemed strange after the closeness of the woodlands, and he felt exposed. He knew that the beast which had pursued them might still catch up to them, and in this wide land there seemed fewer places to take shelter or avoid being seen. Though the days were still warm, the trees were bare of leaves and on three mornings there had been frost on the grass. One dawn when he woke, he saw that he had been gripping the Long Thrower so hard in his sleep that his knuckles were as white as that frost.

Then a day came when the sun was bright in the afternoon sky. The frost had been melted back into the earth by the sun's heat and it felt like late summer. Young Hunter was resting on a small rolling hill, lying back in the soft, wind-flattened grass, the three dogs at his feet. Pabetciman was almost completely healed now. The ten sunrises that lay between them and the Waters Between the Mountains had been good to him.

As they lay there, Young Hunter heard a sound from the sky. He looked up. A sun-tail hawk was there. It was playing in the sky, circling and diving. He had heard its whistle, heard the *fwut!* of its wings. It had not yet joined its relatives in the long flight to the Always Summer Land. It was staying late, but it was playing in the sunlight. It locked its wings to hover directly above them, no more than a spear's cast above Young Hunter and the dogs. It cocked its head to focus one eye on Young Hunter.

As he had in the valley of the beavers, Young Hunter spread his own arms wide as he lay there. He felt the pull of the hawk's wings in his own chest. He did not close his eyes, but he felt himself going beyond his own vision. He was lifting with the hawk as it began to rise and circle. He went higher and higher and he turned to look down. He saw with eyes more acute than his own. Even the smallest blade of grass far below was visible. He rose higher, the earth opening below him like two hands held together to cup water. He saw the plains rolling on toward the mountains back in the direction of the Dawn Land. He saw past the mountains to the glitter of light which was the Waters Between the Mountains. Beyond, he saw the watersheds of his people. Looking back this way, with the hawk's eyes, he saw how close everything was on the earth. He saw how plain flowed into mountain, how river became lake. Everything was always becoming, everything was still and in motion. It was all connected. He and the land and the sky were one and would always be one. He knew that what he saw was a great gift. He would never be far from home, wherever he traveled. The earth was one great, breathing being beneath the sky. It held him on its back and he would never leave it, in life or in death.

No people and no sign of people. It was strange. There was plenty of food. Though the touch of frost had come, many of the bushes still bore berries. There were many nut trees. The streams were filled with fish and there were animals everywhere. It was easy to eat well. But there were no signs of people. It was as if something had wiped the people out—or kept them from entering this place. It was the way the Dawn Land had been in the old stories, the stories about the time of the

Ancient Terrible Ones, the ones who hunted human beings the way a weasel hunts a rabbit. Young Hunter was calm as he walked. The second voice that spoke within him and his dreams had told him the same thing. The black, long-toothed beast had not turned the way they had turned. It no longer followed them. For now, said that inner voice and his dreams, they were safe. But only for now. And with that in mind, though he remained calm, he stayed watchful and continued to practice with the Long Thrower.

Young Hunter went on across the wide land, heading south as his dreams had told him. On the twelfth day from the Waters Between the Mountains, he heard a sound like thunder and felt the earth shaking beneath his feet. He climbed to a hill and looked down. A great dark river of animals flowed through the valley. They were not as tall as moose, but had broader shoulders. Their heads were big, their flanks narrow. The hooves of the bigheads pounded the earth and Young Hunter's heart leaped at the surging of their strength. He watched without moving, the three dogs quiet at his side. The sun moved the width of a hand before the last of the bigheads passed. He followed them to the shores of a lake. It was not as big as the Waters Between the Mountains, but it was the biggest lake he had seen in his travels through the new lands. The bigheads licked the earth at the lake's shore, then rolled in the mud, kicking their feet in the air.

Young Hunter watched from upwind. He moved his feet, imitating the way the bigheads pawed the earth. This would be something to tell Willow Girl and his grandparents about. He would try to dance this for them when he got back to the Only People.

The wind shifted and carried his scent to the animals. Heads turned in his direction. Animals stopped rolling and stood to sniff the air. Several of the old females detached themselves from the rest of the herd and began to walk toward him. He did not move and the dogs sat on their haunches behind him. There were four of the female bigheads and now they were less than a stone's throw from him. They swung their tails and pawed the earth. Young Hunter had seen an outcrop of stone three times the height of a man not far behind him. He could be safe there with one quick dash, but he did not turn and run. He opened his mind to them. He did not hunt them. He wished them no harm. He only wanted to learn their dance.

An old, old cow came forward and the four who had first approached stepped aside. Danowa whimpered, but Young Hunter motioned him to silence. The old cow's coat was thin in places. The hair on her great head was tinged with silver. Her horns bore many marks on them. But she walked with great dignity. The mother of a clan. She came so close that Young Hunter could smell her breath. Her eyes were huge and dark. He heard the crunch of the gravel beneath her feet as she walked. She looked at him and looked into him. Another step and she blew out a breath. The mist of her breath touched Young Hunter's face. Then she turned and slowly walked back down the hill. The other bigheads also turned back. It was as if Young Hunter and the dogs were now invisible.

Young Hunter watched them until the Day Traveler was low in the sky. Then he walked up to the rock outcrop and propped some branches against the stone to make a frame for a lean-to. When he finished the shelter, he made a fire and its warmth reflected from the stone. His eyes still saw the calmness and power in the eyes of the ancient bighead cow. The three dogs sighed as they drifted into their own dreams, and then he too slept.

When he woke the next morning, the grass and the gravel were both white with frozen dew. He walked out, barefoot, down the hill to the lake. The bighead herd was gone, leaving only their dung, the marks of their feet, and the places where they had rolled in the mud. Silently as mist they had melted away, their trail leading back to the north. Young Hunter walked to the place where he had seen them licking and chewing the earth. It was white there too but not the white of frost. He reached down and scooped up some of the white crystals, moistened a finger and touched it to them. They clung to his fingertip. He touched the finger to his tongue, savoring the biting tingle from the crystals.

Young Hunter rested by the lake with the dogs. He made a fish spear, tying the two curved pieces to either side of the point so they would grasp about the body of the fish. At the place where a stream ran into the white crystals lake, the fish were running up to spawn. He speared one, drew it out, smiled. He made a fish rack and built a fire under it so the smoke would rise in the proper way. For three days he fished and smoked the strips of fish meat on the rack. Then, his pack filled with good food, he began to make his way north again. He followed the trail of the bigheads.

The Day Traveler crossed the sky twice before they caught up again to the bighead herd. The land was jumbled with hills now. It was as if this were a place where the Owner Creator had thrown handfuls of great stones, letting them shape the land as they fell. In some places the earth fell away and Young Hunter stood at the edge of a cliff, looking out over the new land. He saw nothing dangerous to a person. In the calm of this new land he almost doubted the words of Medicine Plant and Bear Talker. But that doubt was only on the surface. It was like a leaf floating on a river that flowed toward rapids and waterfalls. For almost one whole day he floated like that leaf, not thinking of the danger of those rapids yet to come. His mind was on Willow Girl and the stories he would tell her, the places they would see together. He did not see his dogs as they walked before him until they stopped, blocking his way, and his knee bumped into Agwedjiman's chest. He looked at his dogs and they looked back at him. The look in their eyes was a look of uncertainty. The sun was at his back. Without realizing it, he had allowed his feet to begin to carry him back toward the

Dawn Land. Then he knew that he was no longer listening to his inner voice. In a brief moment of panic, he remembered that he was in a strange place and that death might come to them at any time. This calmness, this lack of caution and awareness, was as great a danger as any other he had to face.

"My friends," he said to the dogs, "thank you for watching over me like a baby about to walk into the campfire. I will not walk sleeping again."

Each day after that, he unslung the Long Thrower and practiced as soon as he woke. Each day his aim grew better. Soon he could knock a leaf from the top of a tall tree. One mid-afternoon as he walked along one of the streams which flowed through the jumbled land, the dogs startled a flock of geese. As they rose in a clatter of wings he had a small spear fitted to the string and was ready to loose it in the space of a single breath. But he relaxed and did not let it go. He felt the connection held in his power between the small spear and the center of the bird's breath. It was as if a cord were tied between them. But he was carrying enough food for now. There was no need to kill.

He began to practice his speed in fitting the small spears to the string and letting them go. At first it had been hard to have even two of them in flight at the same time, and when he shot with speed he could not shoot with good aim. Now his fingers were as quick as the blurred strike of a Brave One. He was able to have six or seven of the small spears in flight and all would bury themselves in earth less than the width of a hand apart.

The fire-hardened points of the small spears were tough and did not break easily. When he made targets by placing small pieces of wood upright, his spears would pierce those pieces of wood, even splitting them in half. But he tried now to see if the idea which had been given him of fashioning a stone point on the small spears would work. His first try failed. The point was too heavy. The next was better. And the next better still. Soon all of his small spears were stone-tipped and he had extra points to carry with him.

The days passed quickly in this way. He walked, following the direction pointed out to him by his dreams and the words of the oldest talkers. As he went he marked the ways behind him as well as the ways forward. He made note of the places where he could make a quick and concealed camp, the places where one could make a trail that would confuse any pursuer. He learned the land as he walked through it. He saw it and felt it, understanding how he could call on it to help him when he was in need. He made friends with the land, measuring the distance with his stride and his eyes. He knew how long it would take to walk from this lookout hill to that cave in the piled stones, from this three-trunked, great pine to the waterfalls that were thin and straight as an atlatl shaft.

The eye of his mind went back often to that dark animal that had pursued him and the dogs all the way into the Waters Between the Mountains. He could see it more clearly now through the eye of his memory. It was bigger than a large bear, yet it moved like a long-tail. But its tail was short. He saw its teeth glistening as brightly as the fire of hate in its eyes. Its teeth were longer than those of any animal he had ever seen before. It gaped its mouth and roared at him from the shore and those teeth shone. He had a name for it now in his mind. The Black Longtooth. The other voice in him told him that he would see it again and not just in memory. He practiced daily with the Long Thrower.

The Day Traveler quickened his pace a bit more each day toward the western edge of the world. He was more eager for his rest than he had been on that first day when Young Hunter began trailing the bigheads. Each day Young Hunter had to look sooner for a camp before the darkness came, and each night it seemed a little colder. He was close behind the herd. Staying with them made him feel more comfortable, as if they were guiding him, showing him the way into their land. There was no harm in them. He watched them from hilltops as they grazed. They were the land in motion, brown as the earth. At times it was as if they were one single being moving together. Then, when they stopped, he could see them as individuals, especially the old cow who always seemed to be at the head, leading the way.

From the top of the hill he watched them for a time. Then he went back down to the place he had chosen to make camp for the night. A slab of rock had slid down next to a ledge. It made a natural lean-to against this hillside which faced south and east. He would not have found the place had not Danowa led him to it as he chased a rabbit, which found shelter, disappearing among the rocks. The dogs were waiting in the shelter. Young Hunter sat and leaned his back against the sun-warmed stone. The world outside seemed close and small through the slanted door shaped by the leaning stone. Some animal had brought leaves and grass into this place and it was easy to make a comfortable bed. A trickle of water flowed next to Young Hunter off the face of the ledge. He took his wooden drinking cup from his belt and held it under the trickle. Drop by drop the cup filled. He tasted it. It tasted of stone, but it was a good taste. It was dark outside. The dogs pressed their backs and their feet against him. He shifted his body, moving the dry grass and leaves to make them more comfortable. He slept.

CHAPTER TWENTY-SIX
BLOOD

When the Owner Creator finished shaping the earth and the many living things upon it, then it was time to make the people, to make the human beings. The Owner Creator looked around for something to shape the people from, something which would make them part of the earth. There were the stones. So the Owner Creator began to shape the stones. Soon they had arms and legs, bodies and heads, hands and feet. The Owner Creator breathed upon the stones and the new people began to move. They began to breathe. They were great beings, big as huge boulders, heavy as great stones. They moved slowly.

At first the Owner Creator was pleased. But the new people were hard-hearted. They did not care where they stepped. They crushed everything beneath their feet. When they killed for food, they spoke no words of thanks. They killed more than they needed. As they moved through the forests, they pushed over the trees. They had no love or respect for the rest of creation. Each place they went, they brought destruction.

The Owner Creator saw this. The people made from stone were not good for the rest of creation. The Owner Creator took them and broke them into pieces, returning them to the earth as stones. Then the Owner Creator tried again, making people out of the ash trees. These new people had hearts which were growing and green. They were as supple as the trees and they danced like trees in the wind. They were in balance with creation.

He woke with his face pressed hard against a stone. Feeling the pain which knifed through him, he rolled to his side. He could not open his eyes. Something covered them. He reached up his hand, feeling his hand tremble as he did so. He wiped his hand across his face. He felt his hand and his arm move, but he felt nothing else, not even their touch against his own face. His hand felt moisture and he wiped it from his face. Now he could see, but only with one eye. He could see his hand covered with blood. His own blood.

He felt the eye he could not open. No pain, but it was broken and torn. He blinked the eye which could see. Something moving in front of it. Close to his face. A many-legs. He reached out his bloody hand and grasped it with his finger and thumb. He felt pleasure as his fingers squeezed and the legs moved frantically till the inside of the many-legs' belly squeezed out like pus from a wound and it stopped moving.

He tried to move his other arm. It was caught under his body. He remembered now how he came to be here. *The woman*. He began to feel his body again. No strength in it. His belly knotted. He pushed against the ground with his good arm and rolled over farther. Now he could free his other arm, bring it beneath him. Waves of fire washed across the side of his body, down the back of his neck. Another many-legs was there in front of him. He reached for it. The pleasure of killing it took his mind off his body's pain for the space of a breath. Then he put his hands beneath him and pushed. He pushed. It was the hardest thing he had ever done. He lifted himself to his knees and his belly began to act like a fist, opening and closing. He began to vomit. His back arched as he did so and the pain in his back almost stopped the vomiting. Almost. He vomited and he did not look at what came out of his mouth, that which made the earth foul. Nothing was left in his belly, but he heaved and heaved again until he felt as if his heart would come out through his lips. Would it be made of ice or stone now? But it did not come out.

He fell back as if there were no bones in his body. He slumped to his side, not touching his back where the pain was greatest. He touched his right eye again. Where his right eye had been. Blood flowed there, but no vision. Only a dull ache. Only darkness. Darkness that swallowed up the sight from his good eye as well.

When he woke again, the taste of vomit was in his mouth. He felt like a gutted animal. He saw the hill from which the many-legs came. There. He dragged himself over to it and began to pick them up, crushing them, placing them in his mouth, swallowing. Their taste puckered his lips, but he continued. Catching, crushing, eating. The taste of vomit went away as he ate.

Rain had fallen. His body was wet with rain. The blood had washed away. He fell back to his side. He shivered, feeling many knives driving into him all at once. His head was close to a muddy pool of water, a pool of stone. The water was red with his own blood. He leaned over and drank in long gasps. Bits of stone and gritty earth came with each drink. He drank until the pool was empty. Then he sat up. He had remembered the woman again.

The woman. The Day Traveler was now on the other side of the sky. He had lain there for a whole night and much of the next day. She was beyond his reach now. His body felt as if it were on fire. It was not the pain of his wounds. It was another fire. It was anger and hunger, deeper than ever before. She had tried to kill him. She had struck him many times as he lay there, struck him on his face, on his back as he rolled over. His eye had burst like the belly of a frog pierced by a spear. He remembered it. He saw it as if he had been a watcher, floating above his own body. She had turned from him as he lay there, seeming to be dead, her face fierce with triumph and fear. He felt at one with her in that moment. Then that look left her face. It became calm, human again. He no longer felt at one with her. She turned toward the southwest and began to run.

Then his spirit sank back down into his body, back down into the darkness.

He levered himself up, pushing with his hands against the stone until he stood. He was bruised in many places, wounded. Half his sight was gone, but he saw clearly. She could not kill him. No pitiful human could kill him. He was One-Eye. His skin was becoming stone. He was wounded but would be stronger now. They would suffer. All the pitiful humans would suffer.

He turned and began to walk back toward his masters. He was their dog, but he was more than that now. He knew their hearts more clearly. He picked up his spear where it had fallen. The woman had not taken it. He would find her again. He and his masters would find her as they continued to wipe out the weak ones. He would find her. His pain linked him to her like a thread.

As he walked, his heavy feet startled a rabbit. It took two quick leaps and then stopped, head up near the edge of the trail. He threw his spear and it struck the rabbit in its hindquarters, pinning it to the ground. He limped forward. The rabbit was squirming. He pulled the stone knife from its sheath around his neck, grasped the rabbit with his left hand. The rabbit screamed. He slit its belly open and dropped the knife. Blood covered his hand. He pulled out the entrails. The rabbit's mouth opened and closed. The one who was no longer a human being began to eat.

CHAPTER TWENTY-SEVEN
FIRES

Young Hunter rolled to his back and looked up at the slanted roof of the rock shelter. He could see the Night Traveler, Grandmother Moon, full in the sky. She was there in the west, her face beautiful as she watched over the night. He traced his hand along the lines of Agwedjiman's head. The dog sat with its head up, smelling the air, its back against his right side. Pabetciman and Danowa were also awake and watchful.

He wondered what it was that had woken them. Some faint sound? Some feeling of something close? The sight of the Night Traveler reassured him. Still ... he sat up and gathered together the branches he had brought into the shelter. He knelt at the opening and thrust the bases of the larger ones into the cracks in the stone. Then he wove the smaller ones between. He continued until the opening was screened shut. The dry leaves on the crossing branches filled in the spaces so that the light of Grandmother Moon barely slipped through. It was easy to do, for the space there had been just wide enough for himself and the dogs to slip through. He felt better now, but there was more that he could do. The wind was blowing now, a cold wind that came through at the base of his screen of branches.

Where the spring dripped down off the ledge there was a small pool of water. The earth there was moist and sticky. He took handfuls of the moist clay earth and molded them along the base of his screen. There were some larger flat stones inside the shelter. He placed them along the bottom of the opening, overlapping each other like the scales of a fish. Even a big wind could not push through now. From the outside no one would be able to see in, even if they stood next to the place.

Young Hunter buried himself in the leaves and grass again. The three dogs settled back down, the heat of their bodies joining his. The warmth of this place was even better now that the wind no longer blew in. He could easily make a small fire and it would be warmer still. There were dry sticks. But he remembered how dry the grasses of the rolling land on the other side of the hill had been. Sparks would blow up and might carry and start the grass burning. It would take only a small fire and the right kind of wind to set that prairie ablaze. It would not be good for the bigheads if such a fire started. And there was another thing too: a fire could be scented by anything outside their shelter. There was no need for a fire. He leaned back, his head on Danowa's neck. The small feeling of uncertainty had not left him completely. It was still there, like the drip of water down the stone face. But it was softer now. He closed his eyes.

The second time he woke, the feeling was stronger. Again the three dogs were already awake, their heads up, their bodies tense. He reached up a hand and made a small opening in the screen of branches to look out. The Night Traveler was farther along the sky. A huge cloud moved toward her from the north. It looked like a great hand. It was open and it grasped the Night Traveler, squeezing her light out of the sky. Young Hunter took a deep breath and lay back. He slept again, but his sleep was troubled.

When he woke the third time, he knew what had woken him. It was the dogs. All three of them were nudging him. But he did not come awake with a start, leaping up and exposing himself to danger. Instead he was suddenly awake, fully awake, reaching out with every sense toward the danger which he had sensed, but not yet seen.

Then he knew how he had sensed it. It was the smell. Faint, but growing stronger, something he had never smelled before. An animal smell and not an animal. The scent of the bigheads had been new, but not like this. Their new scent fit easily into this land. This smell was different. It was wrong. It was a smell that was sickening and cold. A scent that should not be here. And with it came the beginnings of another scent. A familiar one this time. Just edging the air. Smoke.

He sat up slowly. *Something outside.* He listened. He heard the dogs breathing. He listened. It was quiet outside. The smell of smoke was growing stronger. It was as if he could hear the smoke. *Something out there, waiting.*

He could see through the small opening in his screen of branches. Only darkness. The light of the Night Traveler was still hidden by cloud. The dogs breathed. His own heart beat louder, like the beat of a loud drum. Was it loud enough for what was outside to hear? He did not move again. If he moved, it would know he was there. The dogs stayed as they were, listening, their only motion the rise and fall of breath.

Young Hunter began counting the beats of his own heart. As if they were strokes of a canoe paddle taking him across a wide expanse of dark water. His eyes still looked out through the opening in the screen at the darkness. *Then the darkness moved.* It shifted. It was the body of something large, something that leaned away now so that the darkness of a sky less dark outlined its huge hunched shape. A wide back bent low over something, bending away from their shelter.

"Whoooough-whey-yo-yo-yoorruuugh!"

The terrible cry coming from that bent dark shape seemed to split the stones. It seemed to come from the world of spirits. It pulled the breath out of Young Hunter's body. He did not move and the dogs did not move, but he felt a part of himself being torn from him by that awful, awesome cry. It was the cry of wolf and owl joined together. It was as cold and powerful as the storm wind of winter. Yet it was not owl nor wolf nor storm wind alone. There was something almost human in that voice and that made it even more terrible. It was a voice without pity, without words. It was colder than the wind.

Young Hunter felt the cry pull a part of himself, a part which could see and not be seen, out of that shelter. He could see the dark shape more clearly now as it bent, a shape twice as large as any human being. Below, on the prairie, he could sense other shapes like it crouching and waiting, spread out from each other like a net around the herd of bigheads. And that terrible cry was repeated by each of those shapes in turn, filling the night with fear.

"*Whoooough-whey-yo-yo-yoorruuugh!*"

"*Whoooough-whey-yo-yo-yoorruuugh!*"

"*Whoooough-whey-yo-yo-yoorruuugh!*"

"*Whoooough-whey-yo-yo-yoorruuugh!*"

The herd of bigheads woke and their feet began to move.

Suddenly, light filled the crack in the screen of branches. It was so bright that it drew Young Hunter's vision back into his eyes, and then blinded him as that light moved toward their shelter and was lifted up and away. Young Hunter knew that light for what it was now, knew why the smell of smoke had come to them. Fire making. That was what the creature had been doing, making fire there in the lee of the hillside near the entrance to their hiding place. And now it was lifting its torch high, higher than the top of a small tree. The torch moved away from their shelter, moving down the hill, down toward the dry grass of the prairie. The light wind was growing stronger and the cry came again. It was answered in that circle as a net of flames was woven and spread, spread to ensnare the herd of bigheads. Through the crack in the screen the wind blew stronger, carrying the smell of smoke.

The fire was strong. It was covering the plain and sweeping up into the dry brush of the hill toward where Young Hunter and the dogs were concealed. The only sound to be heard now was that deep whisper of flame, hungry flame swallowing the world. Smoke swirled in through the screen. The brush and leaves of the screen were smoking and soon would burst into flame. There was no way to get out. The dogs pushed back against Young Hunter. They whimpered. They wanted to be brave, but this enemy was one they could not battle.

Young Hunter slid back to the small pool of water. He pulled the dogs to him and began splashing them with water, making them roll in that pool which was just large enough for the body of a single dog. He dug with his fingers in the soft clay, trying to make the pool deeper. The dogs were digging now also. The heat grew much stronger. The laced sticks were in flame and smoke began to curl from the grass and leaves where they had slept. Young Hunter kicked the grass and leaves back, clearing the floor of anything that would burn. He dug more of the moist earth free and pushed it toward the entrance. The dogs kept digging and he pushed the earth higher, making a bank between them and the heat of the flames. His basswood pack began to smoke. He pulled it toward him and splashed water on it, slid the strap of it and the case for the Long Thrower across his shoulders.

He kept his face close to the surface of that small pool of water. It was hotter now than it had ever been in the sweat lodge. The water was growing hot. He drove his arm deep into the earth near the base of the cliff, trying to pull more clay free to protect them. But his arm broke through and the water drained into the hole made by his arm. The water that might have saved them drained away. Young Hunter dug with both hands. The dogs dug next to him, *shunk-shunk-shunk-shunk-shunk*, the sound of their paws in the gravel. Their fur was smoking, as was the hair on Young Hunter's own head. He felt the skin of his back blistering. The straps of the basswood pack and the Long Thrower were searing lines across his shoulders. Firebrands.

He jabbed with his spear at the earth. There were stones wedged there. If he could move them and break through ...

The dogs were next to his face. All of them digging, pushing, the fire a circle around them. Young Hunter could no longer breathe. He knew that the next breath would be so hot that it would sear his throat, fire would fill his body, and he would be hollowed out by it. Then the stones gave way! They fell and Young Hunter fell with them, sliding with the dogs down into a darkness which seemed to have no end. A stone struck his chest, spinning him onto his back. His head struck hard against something, making a sound that reverberated inside his skull like the sound of a drum. Darkness closed deeply around him as he dropped into the center of the world, sliding, falling forever.

When he opened his eyes, he knew where he was. He did not think he was dreaming. No dream could make his head hurt so much. He did not think himself back in the lodge of his grandparents. The weight pressing down on him was greater than the weight of his bearskin sleeping robe. He did not think that warm moisture on his cheek was the mouth of Willow Girl about to whisper into his ear. He did not think those things, and yet he did think them. He thought them even as he knew that he was deep inside the hill. He was on his back, his head lower than his feet. Above him, how far he could not tell, above the scatter of stones on a steep, slippery slope, he saw a shaft of light sifting in where they had made their hole and then fallen. He could see the heads of his three dogs and feel their breath on his face.

"I am alive, my friends," Young Hunter said, reaching out an arm to pat their heads. The dogs whimpered in response to his words and his touch. He tried to move his other arm but it was caught. He tried to move his legs, but they wouldn't move.

"Help me, friends," he said.

Agwedjiman began to dig at the earth and rock that had tumbled down the slope with Young Hunter as he fell, burying all of him but his head and one arm. Pabetciman and Danowa joined in and as they dug, Young Hunter realized that it had been their bodies pressing close to him that had kept the earth from covering his face and smothering him. He tried to help, but the throbbing in his head made it hard even to move. No Oldest Talker had seen anything like this coming to him and he wondered if this was the end of his trail. He wished that he had never been chosen for this hard road, that he were back in the lodge with his grandparents. His heart filled with despair and he stopped struggling. *I will die here,* he thought. *They will not free me.* Then, suddenly, the stones at his side began to give way where the dogs were digging. His other arm came free and with it the bundle holding the Long Thrower.

Young Hunter reached down toward his legs. There was no feeling in them. A huge flat rock was covering them and he couldn't move it. He wedged the Long Thrower bundle under the stone and pushed. Slowly the stone lifted and then he found himself sliding backward again, stones cascading around him, his legs freed. But this slide was only a short one and he was not hurt. He came up against his packbasket at the bottom of the slope and it broke his momentum before he struck the stones of the cave floor. His dogs pressed close and he reached up and grasped Agwedjiman.

"Help me right myself, Brother," he said. Then, as the dog braced itself, he pulled himself to a sitting position. He shifted his hips, using his arms to turn himself, to straighten his legs out. Now they were straight in front of him. They did not seem to be broken, but they were as lifeless as bags of deerskin filled with meat. He began to massage his legs. The dogs licked his feet.

"You are good," he said to the dogs. "You are good." He caressed them with his words and with his thoughts, trying not to let the fear overwhelm him again. He felt the warmth of their bodies and the warmth of their concern for him. Then, like the pricks of hundreds of small knife points, feeling began to return to his legs. Young Hunter groaned, a groan that became a laugh.

"Ahhh," he said, "I am like the One Who Shaped Himself. I must make my legs before I can walk." His legs were burning now. The backs of his calves and thighs were tender, burned from the heat of the fire. He massaged his legs for a long time. The light from above changed its slant and he knew the Day Traveler had moved at least the width of three hands across the sky. Finally he was able to kick with one leg and then the other. He rolled himself to his knees and stood looking up. The roof of the cave was high above, dimly seen in the thin light. It was as if the whole hill were a lodge. He looked carefully at the slope where they had fallen and slid to safety. It was not too steep to climb. But he knew that he should wait. Agwedjiman pressed his head against Young Hunter's leg.

"My friend," Young Hunter said, "this is the second time I've fallen and found good luck. You weren't with me the first time, when I found the medicine spring, when the Brave One marked me." Young Hunter reached down to feel the place on his ankle where the scar had formed. He could close his eyes and still see the snake's head turning, the fangs piercing his skin. But now there was a scar there, formed in the two moons that had passed since he had been bitten.

Young Hunter turned back to look at the cave. There were curves of stone on the floor, shapes, as if water had frozen the surface of a wide rippling stream. He began to walk. His legs were weak as he walked, but he was drawn by the beauty around him. He had never seen this place before, yet it seemed as familiar to him as if he had walked it many times. *Perhaps*, he thought, *I was here in a dream I do not recall.*

The water that had dripped down the side of the cliff in their small shelter was flowing here, flowing along the floor of the cave. It was a thin flow, almost like sap from the maple trees in the time just before the buds turned green. He followed the flow of water, felt it leading him onward. It flowed into a narrower passage where there was not enough light for him to see. But he could hear the water dripping farther inside, calling him.

219

Young Hunter turned and walked back to the place where his pack lay at the bottom of the slope. He took out his fire-making kit. With his knife he split the end of a stick the length of his arm. Then he wound dry grass and bark around the end of it until there was enough to make a good torch. He leaned it against his leg and then took the firestick and began to twirl it in the piece of willow wood that was its base. It was in the willow that the animals hid the fire when they stole it long ago from the stone people to give to the pitiful human beings. Thinking of that old story, of the great shape he had seen in the darkness making its own fire, Young Hunter paused for a minute. Then he began to twirl the stick again. Its point curled up smoke as the friction built up brown dust which finally became a tiny coal in the hollow at its base. He took his stone knife, eased the coal into his tinder bundle, then lifted the bundle and blew through it gently until it burst into flame. He lit the torch. The eyes of the dogs glowed from the flame. He motioned them to wait. The water was calling him alone.

He crawled, holding the torch before him. The passage was smaller now, no wider than his shoulders, and it twisted and turned. The flow of water was between his knees as he crawled. Then the passage suddenly widened. Young Hunter stepped out and straightened. He felt like a newborn child taking its first breath. A chamber encircled him. Its walls were flat and it was large enough to hold perhaps a dozen men. But what he saw on the walls of the cave made it seem larger than that. The walls were covered with drawings, shapes pecked into the stone.

There was a shape at the center, high and close to the ceiling of the cave. A tall man with wings. Farther down was a shorter, broader shape of a man. Next to him were three dogs. The shapes were roughly done, but the spirit of them was strong. Young Hunter knew they had called him here. He held the torch up to look farther, to follow the story. This was a message, like the message a friend might leave on the clean side of a marker tree, shapes which would tell someone following him which stream he had gone up, how long he would be gone, what his name was.

This message, though, had been made a long time ago. Young Hunter felt that it was longer ago than the lifetime of any person. Long enough ago for the wind and leaves and the earth to have closed up the cave entrance until he and his dogs had opened it. This message had been waiting.

Young Hunter stopped. What he saw on the wall made the hair rise on the back of his neck. There again was the shape of the man and the three dogs. Close to them were many four-legged ones with large heads. The bighead herd. Rippling lines rose all around them, lines which made Young Hunter see that fire again. And there, in the hands of that man with the three dogs, was the unmistakable shape of a Long Thrower. A small spear had been shot from it and it hung there on the wall of the cave, halfway between the one who shot and a figure that was like that of a human but stooped, claw-handed, gigantic.

Young Hunter placed his hands and his forehead against the wall. It was cool and moist. He felt its coolness entering him, calming him. He did not know what words to speak. He wondered at the way his journey had led him from place to place, how he had come to this spot at this time. If he had not made his shelter next to the stone, he would not have found these Speaking Walls. Despite his own uncertainty, despite his fear, he had followed the path he was meant to follow. He had made the right choices when the times had come for him to choose.

"*Oleohneh*," he said. "Thank you. I am small and weak, but I see that I am part of something which is great. I will do my best to continue on this journey. I will go on and meet whatever threatens the Only People."

He stood there for a long time before he turned and went back into the passage that led away from the Speaking Walls. He did not look back. There was no need to look back. He carried it within him now.

221

CHAPTER TWENTY-EIGHT
FIRE HUNTERS

He saw the smoke of their hunting. It rose in the sky far to the north. That was where the herd of bighead animals had gone. He had passed the edge of that herd as he followed the woman.

It would not take him long to reach their camp now, but he did not move quickly. The pain from his broken eye, from his lacerated back, was great. He moaned as he walked, pain washing over him. And as he went, he thought of not returning to them. He thought of running in another direction—south, perhaps. But there was nowhere he could go as long as he lived. As long as he lived, One-Eye would be able to find him, to scent out his spirit.

Like the dog that returns to a bad master, even though it knows it will be beaten for having lost the game animal it was sent to bring down, he continued on his halting way. He passed the place where the grass was blackened and the bodies of the bighead animals lay piled at the base of the cliff. He came like a dog, walking sideways, knowing that his master already knew of his failure.

At the edge of the ravine that led to their camp, he paused. His hands fingered the leaves of a willow tree. The leaves stripped off easily in his hands. They were yellow, ready to fall. There was no other place to go. He took a breath and made the sound they had taught him, the long ululating yell.

It was not as terrible as when it came from their throats, but it was like no human sound he had ever made before learning it. It made his throat feel hard. He listened, knowing they heard. There was no answer. He began to walk.

He rounded the place where a rock jutted out like a great knee. One-Eye sat there. His eye was turned to the direction of Weasel Tail's arrival and that single eye was knowing. Weasel Tail stopped. He felt again all the human fears that had come over him the first time he had seen them. He had only been a child then. They had come out of the storm and taken his parents, lifting them up with their great hands and gutting them like deer. They did this as he sat there, too stunned and full of fear to cry or speak. He saw their grey skin like stone, their thick features. Then the one-eyed one looked at him and reached for him with giant hands, lifted him. He did not cry or speak. If he had cried or spoken, he would have been killed.

The one-eyed one had held him in one hand and crooked out a long finger on the other hand. The nail on that finger was sharper than the claw of a bear or a stone knife. That fingernail cut into his shoulder, marking him. Still, he did not cry out. It cut his skin, made a shape there as blood welled up. And he did not cry out. A voice that was not a voice, a voice with no words, was speaking to him inside his own thoughts. Though he did not know the words, he knew the meaning. *You belong to me.*

Then the one-eyed one had put him down. They had left him there, carrying the bodies of his parents off into the storm. The confusion swirled then in his mind. Fear, anger, and a terrible excitement. They left him. But he knew that he belonged to them. That they would claim him again. That they would find him and draw him to them. And they did.

One-Eye held something in one hand. His other hand reached for Weasel Tail, pulling him close, half-lifting him from the ground. It was not a gentle grasp, but Weasel Tail did not cry out. The giant's left hand was filled with some plant that Weasel Tail did not recognize. It was crushed so that juice dripped from between One-Eye's thick fingers. Then that hand passed over his face, the juice of the plant filled his broken eye. It burned him and he struggled to free himself. One-Eye shook him as a hunter might shake a dog returning with its muzzle filled with porcupine quills. *Stand still,* that shake meant. Then the juice hand was pressed again, pressed against the throbbing circle of pain which had once been an eye. Weasel Tail did not try to break away. He screamed, but his scream was silent. It was a scream which he held within him. He felt it hardening his heart.

Young Hunter felt the hurt of it. It was not like the burning his own people did to clean the berry places of the old canes and make the next year's growth green and full. Yes, the grass would be greener here next spring, but this burning had been an evil thing. The carcasses of small animals were there in the grass. Usually they would run from such a fire as this, but they had been driven back into it. His feet and the feet of the dogs crunched the charred vegetation as they walked, leaving prints behind. There were other footprints here, larger than those of a human being. Much larger.

Young Hunter looked at the prints. He decided there were not many of the creatures. They wore no mokasins and it was easy to tell one set apart from another by their stride and the shape of the prints. Much like the feet of real human beings, but so much larger. As he looked at the prints, the dogs spread out, scouting to either side and ahead. Nothing would take them by surprise here. But Young Hunter was certain that the beings who had done this were gone now. He and the dogs had waited within the cave for another night to be sure of this.

The trees were broken and burned, the bushes crumbled into ash. Here and there smoke rose from burning roots where the fire had gone deeply into the earth. The burning made a circle and then had been pushed by the wind, pushed toward the east. It continued until it reached a great cliff where the land

fell away. There the burning ended and there too the tracks
ended. Young Hunter looked over the edge. There lay the
herd of bigheads. The bodies twisted and still, piled on top of
each other, legs, backs, necks broken. The whole herd had been
driven here, driven to leap to their deaths. They had fallen
perhaps six times the height of a man. Young Hunter shifted
the weight of his pack and the Long Thrower and began to
climb down.

As he walked among them, Young Hunter knew that no
words of thanksgiving had been spoken to them for the food
their deaths would provide. And these were beings that could
give so much to the human people. He felt the hair on their
shoulders. It was thick and warm, perfect for robes or the
covering of lodges. Their horns were black and beautiful.
Every part of these animals was beautiful. They would help any
human nation that lived close to them and remembered to be
thankful. But it had not been so with those who had made the
fires and driven the bighead herd over the cliff. The huge
footprints of the fire hunters were here. They also had come
down that cliff to look at their kill. But they had taken almost
nothing; most of the bigheads were untouched. Some of the
animals had their tongues ripped out. A few small ones were
disemboweled. That was all. So much waste. It was as if what
they hunted was not life for themselves, but death for anything
else that lived.

Young Hunter heard a sound coming from the piled
bodies closest to the cliff. It was the sound of moaning breath.
One was alive there. He climbed through the bodies. So many
had fallen there that the ones below had cushioned the fall of
those who went last. He saw it as it had been. The bravest ones
went last. They turned to face the flames, face the fire hunters,
until they were forced over.

Where the bodies were three and four deep, he found the
source of the rough breathing. There, caught between the
bodies of two others, was the old cow. He knew it to be her from

the white markings on her head. She was wedged in, her legs in the air. She kicked and rolled her head, but she could not rise, caught by the deaths of the others. As Young Hunter came close, her right eye focused on him. Breath exploded from her and foam flecked her mouth. But she was caught. The dogs were by his side now. Young Hunter motioned them back. He slipped off his pack and put down the Long Thrower. He crawled close to the old cow. She did not struggle, though her breath came hard.

Young Hunter slid in between her back and the chest of a young bull. He put his back against her and his legs against the chest of the dead bull. "Grandmother," he said, "we will try together." He inhaled deeply and then pushed. Once, twice, and then she moved, rolled. Her hooves caught in the pile, she kicked, stumbled, half-ran, and fell from the pile of animals to stand on the earth. Young Hunter lay for a moment where she had been and then sat up to look down at her. The hair of her head was burned. She had faced the flames and the fire hunters, and did not leap in fear like the others who pushed past her. She would have led her people to safety through the flames if they had followed her.

The old cow began to walk around the edge of the pile of animals. There were so many of them. As many as leaves from a big tree. She stopped and made a sound, a deep coughing. It was like the sound of a stake being driven into earth. *Come back,* that sound said, *come back.*

Young Hunter could feel the spirits of the dead animals trying to answer her call. But they could not return to life. She walked, making that coughing noise again and again. Four times. The dogs turned to look toward the place at the base of the cliff where there was a tangle of brush and a small grove of the trembling-leaf trees. Out of those trees a small bighead came walking. It limped as it came. It had seen no more than one winter, but it was alive. It was smaller than the older ones, its weight not as great, so the fall had not killed it.

Behind it, others came. There were not many, but there were others. All of them were small, all of them were young. Now there were as many as the fingers of four hands. They came up to the old cow. They touched their noses to hers and she licked them.

Then the old cow turned and began to walk. She walked the direction of the sun, circling the great mound of dead animals, and the young bigheads followed her. Young Hunter did not move. He knew it to be a dance, one of sorrow and farewell. He sat on top of the pile of dead animals and the dogs sat next to the edge of the killing cliff. The old cow walked and stopped, walked and stopped. Each time she stopped she looked at one of the bodies of the dead bigheads. One of her children, a brother, a sister. Young Hunter saw it all, saw it with his eyes and with that other way of seeing which needed no eyes. He saw something else, also. It seemed that as they walked that herd behind her grew larger. There with the small shapes of the young survivors were the shadow shapes of many others until it seemed, when he looked with those other eyes, that the herd was complete again.

The old cow turned to the south and began to walk. The few survivors walked with her. They would leave this land now, but they would return. New grass would grow deeper and sweeter than before. Where the heavy feet of the fire hunters had sunk into the soil, the earth would rise again and their footprints would disappear from the land. The old cow did not look back as she went.

Young Hunter climbed down from the pile of dead animals. His dogs came to his side. He understood more clearly now the danger that he had been sent to meet before it came to the Only People. Somehow, the Black Longtooth was part of this.

"My friends," he said to the dogs, "I do not know how we can succeed against giants like the Forest Wanderers in the stories my grandmother told."

Agwedjiman put his head under Young Hunter's hand and his two brothers leaned against Young Hunter's legs.

We are with you, they said without words.

Young Hunter sighed and again turned his face away from the rising sun.

The Day Traveler crossed the sky two more times as they continued to the west. Young Hunter wondered at what he had seen in the place behind them near the banks of the wide slow river. There had been a village there before it was burned. It had been a village—before its destruction—like Young Hunter had never seen before. The lodges had been larger and longer than those of any of the Only People or their cousin nations. And there were fields full of the dry stalks of a strange plant, taller than cattails, like giant grass. But there were no people there anymore and the footprints around that village were those of the fire hunters. Had those who lived in this village all been killed or had some escaped? Were they people like real human beings or were they strange like the fire hunters? Whoever they were, Young Hunter longed to see them. It had been too long since he had seen another human face. Soon the white blanket of winter would cover the land. It would not melt away with the Day Traveler's light as it had done this morning when they woke with a finger's width of snow covering them. It would be good to find friendly people, even if they were strangers, good to find a place to rest and plan. His dreams were leading him this way and seemed to tell him that such a place, where he could rest and think, was ahead.

He had dreamed last night. An old woman walked toward him. She wore a heavy robe of thick dark fur. She spoke to him. *My people and I shall survive. We thank you for your help. Now you must continue to walk toward the place where the Day Traveler sleeps. You will find a helper there.*

The old woman turned and began to walk away, walking toward the sunset. She stopped when she reached the hilltop.

She looked back at him and she was in human form no longer. She walked on four legs and her robe was now the heavy coat of a bighead. She turned away and walked over the hill and was gone.

Pabetciman stood straddle-legged in the middle of the trail. They were in a place among hills again, after another four days of travel, following the weave of a little valley. The ground dropped away before them and there was a wide and pleasant valley. More trees here now, more streams flowing. Pabetciman's nose was close to the earth. Young Hunter bent to look at what the dog was smelling. The print of a foot. A smaller print than that of most men. The mokasin shape was unfamiliar, like none of those made by the Only People or their cousin nations. The print of a young man or a woman, it had been made that same morning. The one who made it could not be much farther than a look ahead.

Young Hunter studied the print and the next and the next that followed it. This person ahead of them was following the trail they were on, going in the same direction. The stride was not even. Here were the marks of a hand touching the earth, the indentation of a knee. It was the trail of one who fled and continues to flee, even when the strength to run is almost gone.

Young Hunter straightened and walked back to where Pabetciman and Danowa stood. He tapped Pabetciman's shoulder lightly and motioned, then tapped the other dog and motioned in the other direction, describing a circle. The two dogs went off the trail to either side. Soon they could no longer be seen. Each would circle ahead, cutting the trail of whoever was fleeing before them. *It will probably be there*, Young Hunter thought, *at the place where the valley narrows*.

Young Hunter turned to Agwedjiman and swung his right hand away from his left shoulder, palm out, toward the way they had come. Agwedjiman went back up the trail. Now nothing would come up on them unawares from behind. Perhaps they would cut the trail of someone—or something— who hunted this small-footed person who fled. Perhaps that person or thing had lost the trail or given up the hunt. Perhaps not. Young Hunter would take no chance.

He began to follow the trail, slightly bent as he ran. His eyes turned the tracks into a line connected to his own breath. He read the story of it as he ran. The one whose tracks these were was a strong person, determined. There was weariness in that stride, but strength of spirit. Even with that strong spirit, the person was weakening. And close.

Young Hunter stopped. He sat and leaned back against the trunk of a maple tree. A red leaf floated down past his face and he caught it in his hand. He listened, for it seemed to him that a voice was coming to him. It was fainter than the sound made by that maple leaf as it fell, but he heard it. Perhaps it was only in his memory, but he heard it. It was the voice of Bear Talker. *Be careful,* it told him. *Do not show what you are carrying.*

Young Hunter looked around him. His eyes took in everything, each stone, each tree. He heard the call of a redbird from the treetops, the rustle in the leaves of a hunting shrew. He looked and listened. Then he saw what he needed. He stood and pushed through the brush at the edge of the trail until he came to where a circle of bushes grew around an old, old maple. He knew those bushes. They were sweetscent bushes. They cleansed your hands when you rubbed them between your palms. Rabbit Stick had showed him, when he was very young, how to put them into the water which would be poured on the stones in the sweat lodge.

Young Hunter knelt down and pushed aside one of those bushes. It had covered the hollow at the base of the maple tree. The hollow was just barely visible through the fallen leaves. Young Hunter brushed them aside, and felt inside. The hollow went up into the tree a long way. It was dry and smooth inside. He took the Long Thrower from his back, pulled its deerskin case from his basswood pack, and wrapped it. He placed the Long Thrower and the bundle of small spears inside the hollow tree, arranged a few sticks across the opening, and brushed the fallen leaves back where they had been. Then he slid backward, took a few paces, and looked. There was no sign of that hollow. It was hidden well by the sweetscent bushes. Now he could continue on his way.

CHAPTER TWENTY-NINE
TORN-DRESS WOMAN

Bear Talker came out of his lodge so quickly that he stumbled, striking his shin painfully. He did not stop, but continued through the village, limping a little as he went. Those who saw him go past so early in the morning in such a hurry shook their heads in surprise. Straight to the lodge of Sweetgrass Woman he went, pausing only at the door to call out the word *"Kuai!"*

"Come in," Sweetgrass Woman said, barely finishing her words before Bear Talker's head and shoulders pushed aside the skin door flap. She stood up from where she knelt by the fire. Rabbit Stick pulled his legs in to allow his friend to make his way around the fire to the guest's place. He saw that the deep-seeing man's face was flushed and that he was breathing hard, as if he had been running. It was hard to imagine Bear Talker running. Rabbit Stick smiled at that thought.

Bear Talker made his way around the fire and sat down, favoring one leg as he did so. It would be bruised tomorrow, but he gave no thought to that. There were other things to speak of and he was eager to speak. His heart was pounding, but he struggled to maintain his dignity, especially in front of Sweetgrass Woman. It was not proper to speak first and he would wait.

The three of them sat there without speaking. There was a smile on Rabbit Stick's face. Bear Talker wondered what that

232

smile was about. His friend was looking at his foot. Bear Talker looked down and saw why Rabbit Stick was smiling. He had only one mokasin on. In his excitement he had left the other one in his lodge. He slid that foot beneath him.

"Older Brother," Sweetgrass Woman said, finally. Her voice was very kind with barely a hint of laughter in it. Bear Talker could not recall her speaking to him with that tone of voice before. It settled him. "Older Brother," she said, "you are well?"

"I am well, Sister," Bear Talker said. The gracefulness of her words had restored his balance. "Are things well with this lodge?"

"We are well indeed," Sweetgrass Woman said. Rabbit Stick nodded. The smile was still on his face, but at least he no longer looked toward Bear Talker's now hidden bare foot.

Bear Talker took a deep breath. Now he could speak. He had been a deep-seeing man for many winters. He was old with his knowledge. But there were still times like this when he felt himself to be like a small child who wishes to convince his older playmates that he has, indeed, seen the tracks of a moose, that there really is a giant trout in the pool near the red rocks, that an eagle flew low above him as he sat in the field. Bear Talker let out the breath. "I have traveled," he said.

The smile left Rabbit Stick's face. He leaned forward. "You have seen our grandson," Rabbit Stick said.

"Uh-hunh," Bear Talker said. "I have seen him. He is far beyond the other shore of the Waters Between the Mountains. There are strong enemies around him, but he is safe. His heart is good and he is well and healthy."

Sweetgrass Woman reached across the lodge and took Bear Talker's left hand in both of her hands. Her hands were small, but very strong. Her hands were warm, not cool like those of some older women. Very warm. She squeezed Bear Talker's hand hard. There were tears in her eyes. Rabbit Stick reached out and took Bear Talker's other hand with his left hand. He placed his right hand on the hands of his wife. They sat that way for a long time, the three of them. The circle they made in that small lodge was strong.

The trail left by the one with the small feet was very fresh now. Earth still crumbled into the edge of that track, there in the soft soil. The tracks were clear. Too clear. As if the one being followed knew he was coming. Tracks such as this were sometimes meant to lead one on. Young Hunter saw that as he ran but did not break his stride. He continued to run as if he were blind to everything but that trail. As if he were blind to that small motion there off to the right at the edge of his vision.

Young Hunter threw his body to the side. Something *whished* past his head. He swung his right hand up and back, grasping the hand that had swung the club, pulling forward the one who had tried to ambush him. As he pulled his attacker from the hiding place, he swept his left leg toward the attacker's feet, and the one with the club came down flat, Young Hunter firmly on top. The club flew free as strong muscles twisted beneath him. But there was no match here. His strength was much greater. Young Hunter had both of this small man's hands pulled behind his back now. But it was not easy to control him. He struggled like a wildcat. Young Hunter pressed down more firmly, forcing those hands back down. *Hanh-ah!* He saw what he had not had time to realize until now. It was not a small man beneath him. It was a woman.

Young Hunter let go of her hands and stood, taking his weight from her. *Willow Girl would be jealous,* he thought, *seeing me wrestle this way with another woman.* It was a quick and foolish thought, one that darted through his head like a small bird through the leaves. The woman stood up slowly, as if not understanding why she had been released. She turned to look at him and it seemed as if surprise were in her eyes, as if she had expected to see someone other than Young Hunter. Something—was it anger or fear?—lessened in her eyes. But wariness remained. Her eyes traveled over Young Hunter, taking in every detail. It seemed as if she recognized his way of dressing. Perhaps, he thought, she has seen other men of our thirteen villages. Perhaps too, he thought, she has not liked what she saw in them.

Her dress was torn, but Young Hunter could see it was not the same as the dresses of his people. Her mokasins were different than those of the Only People and their cousin nations. Her face, perhaps the way it was shaped, was different also. Not exactly the same as the faces of his people. Though it was a good-looking face, even if it was very dirty.

He bent over and picked up her club. It was a rough one, made of a small tree which had died, its roots loose in the earth. His own people made clubs such as this one. The roots were strong and heavy, forming the head of such a club, each root cut off to be no longer than the width of a man's hand. Her club was an unfinished one. She had made it without tools, it seemed, twisting it from the earth and breaking off the handle to make it the right length. But it was still a good weapon. Good enough to break any man's head. He held up his right hand and dropped the club on the ground between them.

Torn-Dress Woman looked at his open right hand and at the club on the ground. He pushed it toward her with his foot. She looked at him and again at her club.

"Uh-hunh," Young Hunter said. He gestured toward the club with his open hand.

Torn-Dress Woman reached slowly for the club, her eyes on him. The fingers of her right hand closed firmly about it as she bent. Then, in a motion as smooth as an otter sliding into the water, she swung it up at Young Hunter's face. He moved his head to one side and the club missed him. The momentum of her strike carried her two stumbling steps past him. She turned and looked.

Young Hunter shook his right hand from side to side. "*Nda*," he said.

Torn-Dress Woman looked down as if dejected. Then, sudden as a stooping hawk, she stabbed at his belly with the club. Young Hunter sidestepped and pushed her in the middle of her back as she went by. It was a good strike she had tried. Wherever she came from, whatever her nation, her people were good fighters.

She turned again, not giving up. She feinted at his left shoulder and swung back toward his knees. Young Hunter jumped high and the club went below his feet. He stepped back. Torn-Dress Woman stepped back also. *Some part of her,* Young Hunter said to himself, *is happy to be fighting. She comes from a people who would rather fight than run.*

Torn-Dress Woman looked at him. Her shoulders sagged with weariness. She let the head of the club fall to touch the ground. It was no use. She could not defeat him. Young Hunter waited, trying not to smile. She took half a step away from him, turning her body. Then she pivoted her hips, whipping her hand from her side so that the club came flying at him, spinning in the air like a rabbit stick. Young Hunter hurled himself backward, dropping to his back. The club flew over him and struck a small birch tree, ripping off a chunk of bark the size of a man's hand.

Young Hunter stood, walked over, and picked up the club. He looked at Torn-Dress Woman and smiled. She looked back at him and shrugged. She did not smile, but it seemed that when she did her smile would be a good one to see. Young Hunter smiled at her again. He liked the way she fought. He liked the way she thought clearly enough to set an ambush, thinking he was the one who pursued her. He liked the way she stood there, looking proud even in her torn clothing.

Young Hunter again held up his right hand, making the sign which showed he had no weapon, meant no harm. He pointed to his heart and made the sign for friend. He gestured toward Torn-Dress Woman and held up two fingers. He was not sure she could understand his signs, but he tried to speak with his eyes as well. He opened his heart. *You and I,* he said with signs, *travel together to your village.* He handed her the club.

Torn-Dress Woman did not move. She took a strong grip on the club with her right hand. Young Hunter sighed. Then he smiled again. He closed his eyes, relaxed his arms, and turned his back toward her. Perhaps this would convince her. She was a few steps away from him, and he would hear her if she stepped close to strike. But she moved more silently than he had expected. The handle of the club prodded him lightly in the small of his back.

Young Hunter turned to face her. Torn-Dress Woman stood there. Her left hand held the club by its head. Her right hand was held up to face him, palm open.

CHAPTER THIRTY
REDBIRD

Although Torn-Dress Woman was old, more than twenty winters, she traveled quickly. She was as light on her feet as the young women of his own age. Young Hunter thought this as she walked slightly ahead of him. She knew this trail and Young Hunter had signed for her to show the way. It was interesting the way the muscles of her legs and hips moved as she walked. *Perhaps*, Young Hunter thought, *I have been wrong in thinking that people of that age are really old*. After all, it was common for men and women of the Only People to have more than sixty winters and still be strong and straight. But Torn-Dress Woman was much older than he, old enough to have children.

Torn-Dress Woman stopped. They were at the top of another hill and she scanned the way below them, choosing the best path to follow. Down the slope to their right he could hear the sound of a stream flowing over rocks and falls. Young Hunter waved his right hand, seeking her attention to ask a question. He made the sign for child and then pointed toward her breasts. She looked at him with that look of hesitance he had seen before, the look a person might give to one who was not quite human—an animal in the shape of a person, or some spirit of the forest. Then she sighed, held up two fingers, and scooped those two fingers under the palm of her left hand. Two children. Dead. Then, before Young Hunter could say anything—although his sympathy for the loss of her children showed in his face—she made signs that were clear to Young Hunter. What was his name?

Young Hunter tapped his chest, made the sign for young man and the sign for hunting. Man-Young-Hunting-I. He said the words aloud. Torn-Dress Woman repeated the words. It was the first time she had spoken and Young Hunter was surprised. He had thought she had no voice. But she certainly did not say his name well with what voice she had. It was hard to believe a human being could speak real language so poorly. Young Hunter laughed.

Torn-Dress Woman smiled. She said words that he knew must be in her own language, pointing her chin at Young Hunter as she did so. His name in her tongue. Young Hunter tried to repeat those sounds and she laughed harder. They stood there, both smiling, and then Young Hunter asked with hand signs: What-Your-Name?

Torn-Dress Woman hesitated. Giving your name to someone, even the common name that everyone in your village knew and not the secret name you kept only for your family and closest friends, meant giving that person the power to call you. Only those who were very foolish or very strong would give their name to a stranger. She looked down at her dress, her hands touching what had once been some kind of pattern on the leather, some shape painted there, which had been worn away as her dress had become more tattered.

Just then a redbird fluttered out of bushes heavy with dark berries and landed on a branch just over Torn-Dress Woman's head. She looked up at the bird and her eyes filled with wonder. Young Hunter understood. That bird was her name.

"Redbird," Young Hunter said.

He pointed at the bird and it flew. Torn-Dress Woman looked at him and nodded. She pointed to herself and to the bird in flight and spoke her name in her own language.

Young Hunter tried to say that name. It was hard to keep his lips stiff as he did so. It was hard, indeed, to believe it was human speech. Redbird shook her head and said her name again. Young Hunter repeated it, making a sound like the moaning of a bear. Redbird began to laugh. It was a good laugh to hear and as she laughed, Young Hunter saw that she was much younger than he had thought, no matter how many winters she had lived.

"Redbird," he said in his own language, "that is your name."

She repeated her name again and Young Hunter said it, a bit better this time. That name changed her, made him see her in a different fashion. He could no longer think of her as Torn-Dress Woman. Then he remembered something. He held up a hand, waved it, and then sat down on the trail, digging in his pack. Redbird watched. She was still smiling and there was something in her eyes that had not been there before, a different sort of trust between them. He pulled out a small bundle and handed it to her. Redbird unwrapped it and her smile grew wider. It held a bone needle and a ball of sinew. Now she could sew her torn clothing.

"*Niaweh,*" Redbird said. And though Young Hunter had never heard that word before, he understood her thanks. She sat down by Young Hunter with the sinew and needle in her hands. Young Hunter took his stone knife from its sheath about his neck and handed it to her. She cut the sinew to the right length and began to sew together the rips in her torn dress. As she did so, she hummed a song under her breath. The song blended with the sound of the stream down the slope.

I will learn that song, Young Hunter thought. *When I return home I will give it to my grandmother. Then she will be able to use it to help her as she sews.*

Here and there, patches of snow were spread on the hills, but the light of the Day Traveler was warm on that hillside. Young Hunter leaned back and closed his eyes. It was good to hear the sound of Redbird's song and to feel her presence there beside him. The sunlight on his chest made him feel warmer and more relaxed than he had been in many days.

When Young Hunter opened his eyes again, the Day Traveler had jumped far across the sky. He sat up. Redbird was no longer by his side. He listened. He heard the sound of the stream. He stood and looked around. Then he whistled once. Half a look down the slope, where he had lain waiting for Young Hunter's call, Agwedjiman raised his head out of the long grass. Young Hunter held his hand up high and motioned down with it. The big dog lay back into concealment. His two brothers were farther down the hill, waiting among some little trees which lined a ravine. Redbird had not seen the dogs. They had been close, watching the fight between Redbird and Young Hunter, but they had obeyed his signs and not broken cover. Then, still doing as he told them, the three dogs had followed them at a distance without being seen.

Young Hunter wondered where Redbird had gone. Had she not trusted him after all? There, on a flat stone near the place where she had been sitting, he saw the bone needle and the ball of sinew. He bent to pick them up. The bushes rustled behind him. Redbird stepped out. In her hands she held a piece of birch bark folded to make a basket. In the basket were two trout.

The swelling was gone from his eye and it no longer ached. The clay that One-Eye had packed over it had drawn out the swelling and the pain. But the eye was sunk within the socket, a dead thing without vision. Though that was not entirely so. When Weasel Tail closed his eye that saw the light, it seemed as if he could still see. But what he saw was dark, the world reversed. He could not walk with that vision, but he could follow it with his spirit. It led him to the place where the Great Ones, his masters, walked. It was a place with no women, no young ones. It was an ancient place where they were always alone. There, their hearts grew harder each season. They were hungry, but never hungry for laughter or beautiful things. Their hearts found joy in death and ashes. Any who came close to their footsteps learned that. Only Weasel Tail and the Hunter could come close to them and still survive.

The Hunter had returned. Where it had been, Weasel Tail could not guess. But three dawns after One-Eye had doctored his wounds, Weasel Tail sensed that the Hunter was returning. He quickly found a tree and climbed into its highest branches. He knew that it would kill him if it caught him. One-Eye might cuff the Hunter for killing his dog, but that would be all. The Ancient Ones cared nothing for him.

But the Hunter cared for him. It wanted his blood. Some nights, when he sat close to One-Eye by the fire, he saw its eyes watching him from the other side of the flames. Those eyes followed him as One-Eye carried him to the tree and placed him in its branches to climb up to safety. Running its tongue over those long fangs, it would prowl the tree beneath him. It was too heavy to climb to the top branches where he tied himself in each night. Muscles rippled under its dark skin like big stones under a flowing stream's surface. It sat and yawned and its eye teeth shone like great knives.

Weasel Tail felt his skin crawl as he watched it watching him, but he could not look away. It too was an Ancient One. It was one of those out of the oldest stories. Pitiful human beings were its natural prey. Only the grey-skinned giant One-Eye could keep it under his control. His spirit could speak to it. Perhaps his spirit even went into that great black beast, which was larger than the largest bear and moved like the long-tail cat. Its eyes gleaming, it sat at the base of the tree, and still was sitting there when Weasel Tail finally slept. In the grey morning, waking stiff and cold in the top of the tree, he looked down to see it gone. The smoke of their fires lifted with the dawn breeze.

Four more sunrises and they would reach the big village. The Hunter would range ahead. It would kill any human it found alone, though it would not attack a group. One might escape and tell the humans what was coming toward them. The Hunter would circle the village, killing those who had strayed too far out alone. Like its masters, it was too much of a coward to show itself to many. It would ambush, strike out of darkness. It would stay at the edge of their nightmares. When the way was clear, it would return to One-Eye, who would hold it back as Weasel Tail made his own visit to the village.

As Weasel Tail climbed down out of the tree, he thought again of the woman. He hoped she would reach a village before the Hunter could catch her. He wanted to be the one to take her. He wanted to feel her body beneath him while she still lived. He would follow behind the Hunter now. He knew, because of some command given in some way he could not understand, the Hunter would not bother him while he was acting as their dog, their scout. It was only when he was done with his work for his masters, in some unguarded moment, that the Hunter knew that it could try to take him. It would not interfere with Weasel Tail when he did his work for the Great Ones, when he went into the next village to draw them out as he had done with all the other villages many times before. Weasel Tail breathed hard as he thought about the work he would do. He closed his eye which could see the light and stared into the growingly familiar darkness.

The night was bright with the cold. High above, the small, far-off ones in the Sky Land glittered. The Night Traveler was gone from the sky when it began. Points of light like spears of fire streaked down across the sky. It happened each year at this time. The *Awatawesu* would descend to earth, the Sky People coming down to visit their relatives. Redbird and Young Hunter sat close to the fire and watched. He motioned for her to sleep, but she shook her head. *What she might see in her sleep*, he thought, *has made her afraid to close her eyes.*

243

When the morning came, Young Hunter looked out from the small shelter he had made of bark and bent saplings. Redbird was awake, sitting in front of the door. She stared at the place where the fire had been with a look that Young Hunter knew to be sorrow. *In spite of herself,* he thought, *she has dreamed.* He hoped that in her village her people would have a deep-seeing person. The weight Redbird carried in her heart was a great one and she would need help. And even as he thought that, a part of Young Hunter wondered how he was able to see with such certainty into the heart of someone he had just met. Young Hunter crawled out and sat next to Redbird. He poked the ashes of the fire, coaxing them back to life with small twigs and pieces of bark. The sun was hazy in the morning mist, the ground patched with white where the spider webs were frosted with ice crystals. Young Hunter's breath was a cloud about his face.

They had been traveling for three days. Before they had begun their travels from that hilltop where they shared each other's names, Young Hunter had scouted back while Redbird waited. He had made a small travois, tied it to Agwedjiman, and placed the bundle holding the Long Thrower on it. Each evening, when he scouted back after making camp, he untied it and hid it until the next dawn when he would harness it again to the dog. Redbird had not yet seen his friends and showed no surprise about what he was doing. It was only common sense to check that no one was trailing close behind them.

This morning, though, he had slept too late. The trail here was well used and he knew that soon they would come to a village. Perhaps it was Redbird's own village. The look on her face was that of a person who is close to home. The land here was good land. It had the look of land that was being cared for by human beings. They had passed hills covered with berry bushes, which he knew, as was true with the bushes in the lands of the Only People, had been kept healthy by autumn burning to clear away the insects and dead canes and make the earth sweeter for the new roots. It would be better here to have the dogs stay farther behind and to leave the Long Thrower hidden in the place where he had stashed it the night before.

They were a day's journey past the place where Redbird had been captured. The place had been her brother's village. It was there that her husband and two children, who had come with her on her visit, had died. Young Hunter knew this from the signs she made when they stopped there. Only burned stubs marked the edges of the long lodges. Fire had wiped the village away. Of the people, only bones remained. He felt a churning in his stomach even now as he remembered. Some of those bones had been cracked to get the marrow out of them. The fire hunters were eaters of human beings. He understood now why he had seen no other human beings as he traveled in the new lands.

He had helped Redbird bury the bones. She did not weep here, as she had done each night when sleep finally claimed her, but he felt the sorrow in her. There was no way he could console her by words, by touching her. He sensed that also and knew that the best he could do was to follow her lead as she gathered the bones and placed them in the breast of Mother Earth. As he did so he wished that, like the heroes in the old stories, he could speak magical words and have the bones come back together, the people return to life. But he did not know such words. He helped gather the wood to make small fires on top of the graves. Then, as they stood there, he spoke.

"You people," Young Hunter said, "you who died here, you were not my relatives, but I will not forget you. You have returned to our mother, the earth, but I will remember you. I will do what I can to end this."

Redbird stood by him as he spoke. Though she was silent, Young Hunter sensed her approval and her hand rested for a moment on his shoulder before they turned from the graves.

Young Hunter had seen around that small village, for the second time, those fields of tall grass. He saw how they grew out of mounds in even rows, and understood that the people must have placed them that way. They were doing it to grow food. They were doing more than the Only People did, more than just sprinkling back into loosened soil the seeds of medicine plants or food plants after gathering them.

Young Hunter wondered about this as he and Redbird left the ruins of that village. There were many things to learn. He was thinking again of those fields as he and Redbird set out on the trail. All around the dead village were the tracks of the fire hunters. As Redbird walked she scuffed her feet angrily at those tracks, trying to wipe them out. Young Hunter followed her, giving her space for her anger. They began to climb a hill and soon the village was lost from view. There was a large boulder in the trail ahead of them. As always, Redbird led the way. As she reached the boulder, a smile came to her face. She looked around the boulder, and as she did so, she gestured back with one hand to Young Hunter. *Follow me.*

Young Hunter felt something tighten in the center of his chest. He knew that another man might turn now and run. He grasped his spear a bit more tightly, but he followed Redbird. He stepped around the boulder. Six men stood there blocking the path. Their faces were painted black and red. Their eyes seemed to look at him out of night and the setting sun. Redbird's hands were resting on the shoulders of the shortest of the six men. Her face was happy, but the painted faces were grim as death. They held spears tipped with finely shaped points made of white stone. They lifted their spears and pointed them at Young Hunter's chest.

PART FOUR

MOON OF
LONG
NIGHTS

CHAPTER THIRTY-ONE
THE WALLED VILLAGE

From his perch in the tree he watched them. They moved in the early morning like stones coming back to life. He saw in his crooked mind, like wisps of smoke, parts of the old story. The Creator made beings from stone, but they did not return his love. So he broke them into pieces and made new beings. But perhaps he had not caught all of those first people. Some had escaped his eye. These ones still lived. Weasel Tail did not know how old they were, but he knew they were older than human beings. Sometimes when he dreamt, he knew that he was sharing One-Eye's dreams. One-Eye dreamed of walking through a land where the only brightness was the flare of fire. Everything was white, ice, snow. There were other beings in that dream who were women, so perhaps there once had been both male and female among the grey giants. But now there were men only, with skins of stone, unable to die as humans and animals die.

From his perch in the tree he counted them again. Now more than two times the number of fingers on his hands. So few. Yet each of them counted for the death of at least one village; each had such a hunger that the death of all the living, moving beings in the world would not satisfy it. The death of all the human beings in the world would not satisfy it. As he thought that, Weasel Tail felt the division in his spirit. Some part of himself that was still human feared for his people. But that part was small and growing smaller. The other part, that part which had grown within him since One-Eye had first placed his scar upon him, that part was strong. It was the part that grew stronger with each cruel act, that rejoiced in his part in the death they carried. He was their dog, their scout.

Below him they began to break down their shelters. Made of long sticks propped together with brush piled onto them, they were rougher than the roughest human lean-to. The big central fire they kept always burning gave them as much heat as they needed until the time came for them to return in the deep winter season to their caves. In the caves they stored food. Hung it where the ice stayed all year-round.

They broke the shelters down with their feet, crushing the poles, sweeping the brush into the fire. Fire would burn away all traces of their having been here. Fire. If there was one thing they loved as much as they loved killing, it was fire. Each of them carried fire. Within the roughly tanned skin of an animal they each carried two shells, tied together to hold inside the glowing spunk held in slow-burning moss. Easy to blow into life. He had never seen them make fire from nothing, only carry it with them and wake it into life with their breath.

One-Eye came to the base of the tree. The Hunter was nowhere to be seen, but Weasel Tail was not taking any chances. In the last few days it had hidden itself twice and leaped out, almost catching him as he descended. It was as if it were particularly hungry to kill a human, as if it had missed a chance and was now trying to make up for it. One-Eye struck the tree with his fist and looked up. Weasel Tail began to climb down. When he was close enough, One-Eye reached up, grabbed him roughly and placed him on his shoulders. They were going to travel fast. This way, their dog would not hold them back.

The broken shelters were burning as the wind touched the flames. Sparks began to rise, falling into the grove of pines a spear's cast away. There was much dead wood there and it too would catch fire. The whole forest would burn. One-Eye began to run. His long, loping strides carried him out of the ravine. He would travel as far as a man could go in a day in less time than it took for the Sky Walker to travel two hands across the sky. Behind, the others were coming. Their feet crushed everything they trod upon. On the giant's shoulder, Weasel Tail breathed in the cold morning air, sharing their power.

Young Hunter walked ahead of the six men. He could hear Redbird's voice close behind him. She was speaking so fast that even the few words he had learned from her language—especially those words which meant his own name—were being spoken with such speed that he could not be certain he really heard them. The men were saying little in response, but he knew her words were having some effect. He felt the tension behind him lessening, and when he looked back, he saw that they were no longer holding their spears so tightly that it turned their knuckles white. His back was bleeding in several places where they had prodded him with the points of those spears as he walked. Those white stone points were as sharp as the claws of a lynx. The wounds were not deep, but he felt the warm moistness of his own blood on his shoulder blades.

Redbird was at his side now. Her hands were filled with moss. She began pressing it on his back where blood flowed. She was still talking as she did so. It was hard to believe this was the same woman who had spoken so little in the four days they had traveled together. Young Hunter could see now why she was called Redbird. She made as much noise as that bird which sings and sings and sings. She looked up at him and her face became stern. She was not pleased at the smile he wore. She wanted him to be serious! The short man who was closest to them reached out a hand to pull her away from Young Hunter's side. She wrapped her left arm firmly around Young Hunter's arm and slapped the short man's hand hard, shouting

251

something at him as she did so. He winced and backed away. She began to speak more loudly and even faster, moving her hands as she did so. Young Hunter could see that she was telling the story of how they had met. They were climbing now, toward what looked like a blank rock face high in the hills. But, at the last moment, the trail turned twice, first east and then south. On the southern side of the cliff a cave opened into the hillside.

As he passed it, Young Hunter noticed its size and a strange feeling came over him. It was as if he had seen this place before, or as if he were seeing something which had not yet happened here. He shook his head to clear his vision, but the spear point touching his back forced him to keep moving, to climb and turn another corner in the trail. Then, as the rest of the party stopped to look into the long valley below them, Young Hunter stopped also.

The valley was hidden well among the hills. The dip of streams winding through the valley, many tall trees, narrow trails through the rocks—as they walked, Young Hunter felt this was a place where people had spent more than one generation, but he could see it was not a place that an outsider would find easily. As they went farther into the valley more people joined them, coming out of the brush, appearing where trails joined. The six men who escorted Young Hunter did not stop, and although people hailed Redbird and tried to speak with her, she did not stop either.

Young Hunter liked the looks of these new people. They were straight and strong, proud-looking. They seemed to be taller than the Only People, their faces more angular, but they were not bad to look at. Some were almost as good-looking as the people of his own village. There was something else about these people, though. There was a wariness about them. It was like the wariness of animals that have been hunted hard. It made him think of the story his grandmother told about the man who was lost in the woods and was adopted by people who turned out to be deer. In their own villages, away from the eyes of most humans, deer and other animals would do that—take the shape of human beings.

Now they were at a place where fields opened out along a wider stream. Wide fields stretched over the flat land, which was covered with snow. The stubble of the tall-grass plants poked out of that snow. A trail made by many feet had worn the snow down to dark earth and there was something ahead of them which Young Hunter had never seen before. On the hill above them was a great wall, encircling something. It was a wall made of newly cut trees, their branches stripped, their bases buried in the soil which had only recently frozen to hold them even more securely. From the look on Redbird's face and the way she touched the wall with one hand when they reached the top of the hill, it was something she had not seen before, either.

These people, Young Hunter thought, *know that there is something terrible for them to fear. Their new barricade might help to protect them from the Black Longtooth, but even these walls will not keep out the fire hunters.*

His first sight of the walled village itself was through an opening just wide enough for a man to pass. It showed him, even before he passed through, that this was a village bigger than any he had seen before. There were so many lodges, all of them big ones with long sides and smoke coming out of the holes in their roofs, that it made Young Hunter feel dizzy. And the number of people! There were as many as one would see when the thirteen cousin nations gathered at the big fishing falls when the salmon came upstream. But Young Hunter kept his face calm and his back straight.

They stopped in the very center of the village. All of the many people in the village had surrounded them in a great circle. A group of old women came up to them. They felt Young Hunter's arms and legs—with approval, he thought. They looked into his face. Redbird stood by his side, holding his arm but saying nothing. Two of the old women took her

253

and moved her away from him. She did not protest. Young Hunter stood and said nothing. He saw a movement out of the corner of his eye, there through a chink in the log wall behind one of the lodges. It was Agwedjiman, creeping close enough to help if called but still concealing himself. Then Young Hunter realized what he had missed. There were no dogs in this village. It was strange to see people with no dogs. He raised one hand, as if to scratch his nose, then let his hand fall to his side in a sweeping motion. Agwedjiman crawled back out of sight, understanding the signal to leave and come only when called by Young Hunter's whistle. Young Hunter looked around to see if anyone had noticed. But everyone's attention was on Redbird. People were embracing her and some were weeping. A tall old man and a group of old women encircled her now and she was talking to them earnestly, making signs which Young Hunter understood. She was telling them of the grey giants, those who hunt with fire.

Young Hunter was taken again by the arms and led by the six young men who had escorted them into the village to a small, empty lodge made of logs in the very center of the village. Redbird did not follow. She and the old women and the tall old man walked away from him to a large lodge at the west end of the village.

Young Hunter was kept in the long lodge two sleeps, visited only by one or another of his six guards, who opened the door, made of tough woven saplings, twice each day to bring him food and water. And though he was not certain what would happen, he thought that the elders of the village must be discussing what to do with this strange young man who had been brought to them. That second voice within Young Hunter told him that he should only wait, be patient and wait. He tried to occupy his mind with thoughts of Willow Girl. But when he looked for her in his dreams, he saw the figure of a young woman walking away from him. He followed that young woman and grasped her by the shoulder, but when she turned, her face was not that of Willow Girl.

On the morning of the third day, the door opened and the tall old man who had been speaking with Redbird entered. Seen close, the old man's face was strong and funny at the same time. He wore a strange cap which covered the top of his head and had an eagle feather fastened erect on it in such a way that the feather moved as he moved. He looked down into Young Hunter's eyes.

"*A-ho*, Grandfather," Young Hunter said. He knew the old man would not understand his words, but he saw that his tone was understood. The old man nodded. He reached out his right hand and took Young Hunter by the arm, drawing him out of the lodge. Everyone in the village was gathered, from the smallest children to the very old. The old man took his hand and tapped it twice against Young Hunter's chest, saying something very loudly as he did so. Young Hunter saw Redbird where she stood among the old women. Her eyes caught his and she gave an almost imperceptible nod. Things were going well so far.

The old man stepped back and stretched out his long arms. He motioned with them. Young men and women came forward with that motion and formed two lines facing each other down the center of the village. They stood shoulder to shoulder. They all held ball sticks—much like the ones the Only People used to play shinny and lacrosse—or branches. None of them held anything as heavy as a war club. Young Hunter saw what was intended. Redbird did not join the line, even though someone offered her a stick. She still kept her eyes on Young Hunter and slowly raised her hands in front of her face. She was not blocking off her vision. She was showing him what to do.

The old man stepped back up to Young Hunter. He held a stick now and with it he struck Young Hunter a sharp quick blow on the shoulder. Then he gestured with his head toward the long double line. He spoke and his words held a question, which Young Hunter understood.

"Uh-hunh, Grandfather," Young Hunter said. "I will let your people try me." He walked toward the waiting lines and took a deep breath. He lifted his hands up to protect his eyes and began to run.

They traveled for two days without stopping. Their power was like that of the rocks themselves, and as he rode on One-Eye's shoulders, he felt their power coming into him, driving out those useless human feelings which twisted at his heart and weakened him. He wondered again why his masters had such fear of showing themselves. Why was it that they hid in the dark places and only struck from ambush against those weak ones which they could so easily have wiped out?

Twice, as they traveled, the Hunter came to One-Eye's side. It rubbed against him and looked up with hungry eyes at Weasel Tail. *Throw him down to me,* those eyes said. But One-Eye only pushed the Hunter away and waved it onward. Weasel Tail saw now that it was only a matter of time before the Hunter would take him unless he took action first. He began to make a plan. He would find a way to kill it. He knew with cold certainty that if he were ever caught by that black creature, even within One-Eye's sight, once those huge jaws were gaped open and the fangs, longer than spear points, touched the base of his skull, his master would not save him.

But One-Eye kept him close. He was still useful. A good dog. When they stopped at a spring, One-Eye stood over him, straddling him as he drank. He buried his face in the water. When he looked up he saw, only the length of two arms away, the dark head of the Hunter lifting from the other side of the pool. Its eyes held his and then it opened its mouth and yawned. It reached out its paws and stretched. Weasel Tail felt himself falling forward, his limbs weak. Even if he could stand, it would be only to walk toward those hungry eyes, to give himself to black death.

One-Eye's hand grabbed him roughly by the shoulder and lifted him. He stood, legs shaking. The Hunter looked at him and Weasel Tail thought he saw mockery in its eyes. One-Eye made a sound that Weasel Tail had not heard before, a sort of coughing. He looked up. The giant was laughing, laughing at him. An anger harsh as the coldest blast of winds in the Long Nights Moon swept over Weasel Tail. If he had the power to do so, he would kill them all. Pitiful humans, cowardly Ancient Ones, black monster, all of them. Everything around him turned the color of blood and he screamed. He screamed and screamed until One-Eye shook him, once, twice, silencing him before lifting him once more to his perch on the giant's shoulders.

It was late in the day when they stopped again. For a time, as they traveled, Weasel Tail's mind had spun like a leaf falling from a tall branch, but he had gradually brought himself back to a cold clarity of thought. His eye was alert as they went, looking along the edges of the trails, trying to see a certain plant. He did not know much about medicine, but this one plant he did know. He watched for it and shaped a prayer in his mind. *Show yourself to me, Little Helper. I will give you a present. Show yourself to me, Little Helper.* He knew that One-Eye could, in a way, sense his moods if not his thoughts, so he tried to think on two levels. One was on the surface, foolish, bobbing as a small duck might bob on a pond with no thought of the great pike rising toward it. The other level of thought was deep, like a loon disappearing in the depths far from the sight of any hunter who might cast a spear or throw a stone. It was on that deep level that he formed his plan.

As soon as One-Eye stopped, they heard the scream. It came from the north, farther along the line of walking giants. As they traveled, the giant grey-skinned ones did not walk together. They spread themselves in a long line, driving everything before them, killing it if it came close. He had seen one of the other Ancient Ones kill a bear that way, breaking its neck with a single blow as it tried to run past, then ripping it open with clawed fingers to drag out the steaming entrails and gnaw upon them.

There was a small valley toward the north and One-Eye walked to its edge to look down. Along the rim of the valley the other Ancient Ones stood looking down. The scream came again. There in the valley below, the Hunter had caught a man and was playing with him. The man ran and the Hunter loped behind, batting at his legs to knock him down. The Hunter's claws were sheathed to make its game last longer. They were too far above for Weasel Tail to see the man's face. He felt no pity for the man, but the fear began to gnaw within him like a squirrel in a hollow tree. The Hunter struck the man a glancing blow and he rolled over and over. When he rose to his feet he did so slowly, and he looked up toward the giant shapes of the Ancient Ones lining the edge of the ravine. Then, instead of running, the man turned and faced the black shape that stalked him. No longer did he act like a frightened rabbit or a little striped one. He bent to pick up a stone and held it in his hand, even though it would be of no more use than a pebble would be against a bear. The Hunter feinted a charge. The man did not move. The Hunter crouched and its short black tail switched back and forth. Then, so suddenly that its motion was blurred, it leaped. Its paws pressed the man's head down and it gaped its jaws, driving the fangs into the man's neck. Weasel Tail heard the crunch of bones and the rip of flesh as the muscles bunched on the black animal's shoulders and it tore the head from the body.

The Hunter lifted its eyes up toward the top of the ravine, two long spear casts away, and it looked up at where Weasel Tail sat on One-Eye's shoulders. Weasel Tail looked away at distant hills. He felt no sorrow, no pity for the man who had died in that valley. Yet he kept it in his memory that the man had not screamed at the last. He had stood and faced the Hunter.

I will give you a present, Little Friend, he said to himself again and again. *Show yourself to me.*

CHAPTER THIRTY-TWO
THE LONG LODGES

His shoulders were streaked with red from many small cuts. His back was bruised in many places from the heads of the clubs. He turned, ready to run the length of the line yet again. The tall old man stepped in front of him and placed his hand on Young Hunter's chest, holding him back.

Young Hunter stood there, his chest heaving as he breathed. His upper arms ached. The smallest finger on his left hand throbbed and was standing out at a strange angle. The old man grasped his hand and pulled. The finger slipped back into joint with a pop. It would swell now. That knuckle might grow larger in size as had other knuckles on his hands when he had dislocated them in past seasons while wrestling. But none of his injuries was serious. The blows struck at him by the many young men and women had been testing blows, not blows struck in anger. He had run the length of their gauntlet with no panic in his steps, and when he had reached the end and turned to look, he had seen the tall old man motioning him to come back through it again. He had not hesitated.

The old man slapped Young Hunter on the chest and shouted. All of the people gathered around shouted something back. One of the old women came up to him. Her face was that sort of face which an old woman with many grandchildren is sometimes given. The many lines of caring in it made her face familiar. Her eyes were very clear and their color was strange. They were the color of new grass. Young Hunter had never seen such eyes before. She draped a bear robe over Young Hunter's shoulders. The people around them shouted again. Then she took Young Hunter by the hand and led him out of the village, the people following, until she came to the stream. She broke the ice with a stick and made him take off his clothes and walk into the stream. Then, knee-deep in the icy water herself, she washed him.

When she brought him out she seated him on the bearskin and wrapped it about him, acting like a grandmother taking care of a well-loved but stubborn child. People were drifting back to the village now. Only a small group of the older women were there with them. The old woman put a hand on her own chest and then reached out to grasp a handful of dry reeds at the water's edge. She pulled a single reed free and held it up, pointing again to herself and speaking a word in their strange language. Young Hunter understood. That word was the word for the reed and the old woman's name. She spoke the word slowly and Young Hunter repeated it as best he could.

The old woman nodded and patted his head. She circled her hand to indicate the other women gathered around and then touched the bear skin. She did it again and then included Young Hunter in her circle. Again, Young Hunter felt he understood. This was their clan. These women were the clan mothers of the Bear Clan. They had adopted him. Reed spoke the word for bear and Young Hunter nodded.

He had heard the word before. As he and Redbird walked the trail she had tried to teach him words from her language, beginning with the names of the animals.

Reed lifted him to his feet if she were helping a very small child to stand for the first time. Young Hunter leaned on her like a child. As he stood he saw Redbird. She was standing back from the Bear Clan women, arms folded, a satisfied look on her face. The shortest hunter stood next to her and Young Hunter noticed how much his face resembled hers. The shortest hunter too seemed pleased. As Redbird stood there Young Hunter noticed that she even looked younger now. She had put on new clothing and her hair was carefully combed and braided. Her face shone and her cheeks were very bright. *Women,* he thought, *they always want to make themselves look even better.* He had crept up, as a small child, to spy on the older girls as they used the punky wood of the pine tree to make their cheeks shine and took the sweet grease of the bear to make their hair more glossy. *But then again,* he thought, *we young men take some care to look good also.* He wondered how his own hair looked now after his bath in the icy stream.

After walking with him a few paces, Reed made him sit. She pulled the robe down off his shoulders and she and the other Bear Clan women began to fuss over his bruises and cuts. They cleaned each cut with water, dabbed it with clay. All the while, Redbird stood there watching. She looked very satisfied. And much younger.

Reed lifted Young Hunter's left hand and looked at the swollen knuckle. She wound a piece of skin around it and bound it to the finger next to it. *Not one of the fingers I need to use the Long Thrower,* Young Hunter thought. And as he thought that, other things came into his mind. The way ahead would be hard.

The Sky Walker had crossed the sky many times since they had stood at the top of the valley and watched the Hunter kill the lone man. It had eaten that man as they watched, crushing the bones with its powerful teeth. Only the head was left behind. Weasel Tail now slept each night even higher in the trees, lashing himself in with a basswood strap. The Hunter stayed close. It had almost caught him as he was eating a rabbit he had caught one dawn. He just managed to scramble up into a tree, leaving the rabbit behind. The Hunter played with it, tossing it up as if to taunt him, then swallowed it whole.

Sometimes, from his tree perch he would look down and see one of the Ancient Ones looking up at him, its eyes pale and emotionless in the fire's glow. The Ancient Ones did not sleep as much as human beings, but would sit through the long nights around their fire without moving, their eyes open. Sleeping or not at night, each morning when they started again with the dawn, they would move with that same long, tireless stride, covering great distances as they went. They had passed two more villages as they made what Weasel Tail saw now to be a great circle. Both villages were empty, the people having fled. Even though the settlements were deserted, the grey-skinned giants set fire to the villages. It was as if they were feeding their fire by allowing it to burn free wherever they went. If there were more of these Ancient Ones, Weasel Tail thought, the whole world would be turned into ashes.

As they traveled he continued to chant his prayer. *Show yourself to me, Little Helper.* Then one day, as they crossed a small river, he saw it there on the other bank. He felt it answering him. He slapped his hand twice on One-Eye's left shoulder. It was the one sign that the giant always heeded. It meant that Weasel Tail had to empty his bowels. One-Eye surged out of the water on the far bank, water streaming from his waist and legs as if he were a grey stone in the river suddenly come to life. He dropped Weasel Tail on the bank.

Weasel Tail scuttled down the bank and squatted. As he did so, his hands played idly—or so it seemed—with the plants there. But he was grabbing handfuls of that plant he recognized, that one which was to be his Little Helper. It burned his fingers with its bitter juice and he wrapped his handfuls in the fern leaves that also grew there, making a packet which he shoved under his waist band. He wiped himself with his other hand and washed both hands in the running water. A sharp-edged stone was there just under the water. He picked it up and drew it quickly along the edge of his thumb so that blood flowed. He dripped the blood onto the earth where the roots of that plant he had gathered remained. *Little Helper,* he whispered in his mind, *I give you this present for showing yourself.*

He crawled up the bank and One-Eye scooped him up. As he settled himself on the giant's shoulders, he knew it would be easy now. He had only to catch another rabbit. He would stuff it with his Little Helper and then pretend not to notice as the Hunter crept up. Now he needed to catch another rabbit.

It was food like no food he had tasted before. It was the color of sun and sweeter to the taste than the bread his grandmother made from the pollen of the cattails. He looked up from his bowl and the pleasure in his face was so obvious that the old woman laughed.

"You like?" she said. "Good food? Uh-hunh?"

Young Hunter stared at her. Reed was speaking words that he could understand. They were not being said exactly in the way the Only People said them, but like one of the cousin nations far to the east and north. She was not speaking the words badly; it just was a different way of saying them. He listened more closely and her words seemed to become clearer.

Reed laughed again and poked him in the arm. "Eat, child," she said. "You I tell how I speak your people words. Eat." Then she repeated her words in the language of the People of the Long Lodges.

Young Hunter ate, knowing that Reed would tell him her story only after he had finished his food. As he ate he looked around the long lodge of the Bear Clan. He was sitting to the south side of the central fire that was placed in a walking area in the middle of the big lodge. There were four other fire pits, two to each side down the length of the lodge. Upright poles marked off the compartments of families, each compartment as large as a lodge of the Only People. Sleeping racks lined the walls and the smoke holes in the roof were higher than he could reach, even with a high leap. There were many people in the lodge now that it was night. None of them paid special attention to him. Now and again someone might pass by and show him something, speak a word to him, make a gesture to communicate in some way, but it was not as if he were a stranger or an enemy. It was as if he were now one of them. All around him the people were busy with their own families and their own lives. Here a woman prepared food or worked on a tanned skin. There a young man used the sharp edge of a rock to smooth the shaft of a spear. Children were all around. Some were working like the adults, copying their elders. Others played as children always play. Only Reed paid special attention to Young Hunter. She had brought him to the central fire, made him sit and combed his hair. She had given him the new clothing he now wore, clothing which, he had gathered by signs, had belonged once to a son of hers who had been killed. She brought him a sweet-tasting drink and this new food. And now she had spoken in words he could understand.

Young Hunter ate and watched and waited for the story that was to come.

"My father," Reed said, "loved to walk far. A Dawn Land person, from the sunrise and the Forever Winter Land. His eyes this color, as mine. You see my eyes."

Young Hunter nodded agreement. The more she spoke, the smoother her speech was becoming as his ears grew accustomed to it and as her voice became familiar again with words she had not spoken aloud for many seasons.

"My father came among these good people. They adopted him and he remained. He had seven children. I am the last alive. So I carry his eyes and keep his Dawn Land language. I speak it well. I remember it so that I can remember this story which his father gave to him. His father's eyes were the color of the ocean. His father traveled even farther than my father to reach the Dawn Land."

Reed's voice was taking on a different rhythm. It was the rhythm of the storyteller's voice, one who tells a strong old tale, a tale which tells itself. Young Hunter leaned forward to listen even more closely.

"Long ago," she said, "my father's father lived with his people in a land on the far side of the ocean. They were great fishermen and their boats were as large as this lodge. They traveled far in their boats to find the fish and they caught them with long lines. Their boat had wings, like those of a gull, and it could go fast across the water. They would live for many sunrises on their boat, sleeping and eating as it crossed the great water until they came to the place where the ocean was shallow again and there were many fish. In that place of shallow waters, in the middle of the great water, there were others fishing in big and small boats. There, in that shallow water place, they spoke many languages and traded things sometimes.

"Then, one dawn, a storm came. It tore the wings from their boat, it drove them across the surface of the great water toward the sunset. It drove their boat onto shore and the waves destroyed their boat. My father's father and his friends survived, but their boat was destroyed. As they climbed up that shore, half-killed by the water, they saw around them many big grey stones. Then those stones began to move. They were not stones. They were giant men.

"My father's father and his friends were afraid. But the giant men made signs with their hands. They spoke no words, but they acted as friends. It seemed they did not want to harm my father's father and his people. They took them to lodges made of piled stones. There were fires burning there and my father's father and his friends were happy to feel that warmth. They were tired and half-killed by the water. One of my father's father's friends was coughing and coughing as if a bone was caught in his throat. It was strange, this coughing. He was sick and could not stop coughing. The giant men gave him stew, which they had made from the plants of the seashore. They made beds of dry moss for my father's father and his friends.

"There were not many of these giant people. They seemed old in the way stones seem old. There were both men and women among those giants and even a few children, but those children were taller than the tallest human. Although they did not speak, but only made signs with their hands, my father's father saw that they thought and felt as human beings. The kindest of them was a giant who wore a white bear skin about his waist. One of his eyes was gone. He told, with signs, of how the bear whose skin he wore had clawed out his eye when it attacked him as he slept. But he rose up and killed it with his hands.

"My father's father and his friends used their lines to catch fish from the cliffs. They shared the fish with the grey giants and all went well for a season. They were like bears, those giant people. My father's father said they would dig with their hands to find roots, just like bears. So my father's father decided they would stay for the winter among the giant men. He and his men did not feel well. Now all of them had the coughing sickness. It is a sickness we do not have among our lodges. It made the men of my father's father's nation weak for many days, but if they were cared for and kept warm, they grew well again.

"The giant people cared for them in their sickness, and one by one, my father's father and his friends grew well. They were strong enough to walk again by the cliffs, to watch the rush of the waves against the many colored stones, to delight in the calls of the many birds. Though the land was rocky and there were few trees, it seemed a beautiful place and a good one. They understood why the giant people lived here, why they would sit throughout the days without moving, only looking out at the waves, the giant men and women and their children leaning against each other like big stones.

"Then a terrible thing happened. It happened so slowly at first that my father's father did not see it. One of the giant children began to cough. It coughed harder than my father's

266

father and his friends. It coughed for many days and blood began to come from its throat as it coughed. Soon, all of the young ones were coughing. But the sickness did not pass from them as it did from the fishermen. It caught them and held them, it twisted them until it twisted out their lives. It was a pathetic thing to see. Those tall and strong children, bigger than any human, all died of the coughing sickness. And before the last child died, the women also were caught by the sickness. The coughing shook them like great trees in a wind. They spat blood and they died. All of them died and so too did many of the giant men. But not all of them. As many survived as the fingers on four hands and among them was the One-Eyed One.

"The One-Eyed One was their dreamer. He spoke to the spirits. And when he was well enough again to walk, he climbed to the highest headland and sat there for a long time, looking not at the sea, but inland. Those giant men who survived all looked no longer toward the sea, that same ocean that had brought my father's father and his people and their coughing sickness. One by one, those giants who had survived climbed to the headland and sat there with the One-Eyed One, all of them looking toward the sunset.

"My father's father and his people were sad, but could do nothing to help. They were well again now, and from the wood which washed onto the shores, they had been making a boat. It was not large, but they thought it would carry them far enough to reach the shallow water place where others came to fish. There they might find their own people and return to their homeland. The boat was now made and they decided they would leave the next morning. They went to their sleeping places inside the stone lodge of the giants.

"When they woke next morning, my father's father opened his eyes with the feeling that something was wrong. He had dreamed terrible dreams. He sat up and saw that the door to the lodge was blocked with great stones. He and his people could not move those stones. They could see down to the shore between the cracks. On the shore their boat was on fire. Then the grey giants came and rolled the stones away from the door. My father's father buried himself in the moss of his bed. His dreams had spoken to him about what was going to happen. 'Do not go outside,' he said to his friends. But they went outside. And as they went outside the giants grabbed them and carried them to the great fire which burned now higher than ever before. The giants threw them into the great fire. When they were dead and burned, the giants dragged their bodies out and ate them.

"My father's father stayed hidden in the stone lodge, hoping they would not see him. As he hid he wept. He wept for his men but he wept also for the children and the women of the giant ones. He wept for the hardness of heart that had come to these giant people who had been so gentle before he and his men came with the coughing sickness. The door of the stone lodge darkened. The One-Eyed One stood there. It looked down, seeing my father's father where he sat weeping. My father's father said he felt something touch his thinking, touch the sorrow he felt for the lost children and women of the giant ones. He looked up and saw a single tear flow from the giant one's eye. Then the One-Eyed One turned and walked away. When my father's father came out of that lodge at last, the giant ones had gone. Their trail led toward the Forever Winter Land. My father's father walked toward the south.

"Farther south, he came to the Red Paint People."

She paused and Young Hunter nodded. He knew of those Red Paint People. They lived at the edge of the Forever Winter Land and their language was close to being like that which real human beings speak. Some of the young men in his own father's time had traveled north to trade with those Red Paint People.

"The Red Paint People were kind to my father, even though he was different from them. He was adopted by them.

He learned their language and their ways, married, and had children. He began to hear stories of fierce monsters, forest wanderers, cannibal giants with stone coats who lived to the north, who killed and ate solitary hunters. Stories to frighten children. But my father's father knew they were not just stories. His son learned his story. As I said, he too loved to travel. He carried that story here."

Reed paused again and cleared her throat. "He also carried some of the language of my father's father. This is how it sounds." Then she spoke. It was the strangest thing Young Hunter had ever heard. It was a growling language, like bears talking, harsh to hear. "That," Reed said, "is how they talk on the other side of the great water. My father's father gave that to my father and he gave it to me just as he gave me that story of the giant people."

Reed looked into Young Hunter's eyes. "And now I have given you that story for I see that it is one you will need. For I see the giant people have come to our land now. I have told this story before, but the People of the Long Lodges have always thought it was like the stories from long ago. Its truth was nothing that could touch our lives now. Now they see it is different and they have built the walls around the Village Between the Hills. Something hunts us, kills our people when they are out alone. And when they go too far toward the north, even in groups, we never see them again. Now when young men go out to hunt, they never go in parties of less than six men and they do not go far to the north, never beyond that pass between the hills. Our small villages have all been destroyed. Many of the young men thought all our warriors should go out, try to find these enemies, and wipe them out. Our deep-seeing one died two winters ago and no one was here to take his place, so it is hard to make decisions as we did when his eyes could look far and guide us. But our clan mothers and our sagamon thought long and hard and counseled against seeking our enemy. If our warriors go out and leave the village with little protection, the enemy may come and wipe us all out as happened with other villages. So it was decided that we must watch and wait. Other eyes may come to show us what to do."

Reed looked hard at Young Hunter as she spoke those last words and he felt a shiver go down his spine. He understood. He saw who the fire hunters were and the greatness of their danger to all the people. He saw that they were beings to be pitied and feared. He saw too that his own weak seeing was needed now to help these people of the Village Between the Hills, as well as his own Dawn Land People. He saw something of the purpose for which he had been given the Long Thrower— even if he still was not sure his strength was enough to use it well. Then another shiver went down his spine as he saw what could happen if, someday, such sickness as the people of Reed's father's father brought with them should come again across the great water to the Only People. That danger might be even worse than the fire hunters.

CHAPTER THIRTY-THREE
SNOW SNAKE

Though the People of the Long Lodges were not the same as the Only People, in many ways their lives were similar. Despite the danger that everyone knew was waiting outside the walls of their village, they still rose with the Sky Walker's first light and gave thanks for each new day. Within the walls, their children ran free and were treated with kindness. The old ones were listened to with respect. And here too as in his own village, Young Hunter found that the young men loved to play games to test their strength and skill. He had wished to be on his way as soon as possible, because he sensed that whatever awaited him, the place to meet it was not in this village. Each evening he said to himself, *Tomorrow I will set forth on the trail again.* But each night as he slept, his dreams had spoken to him, saying, *Not yet, not yet. Wait....* So, instead of departing, he would climb the wall and look out into the distance, looking for some sign. And his gaze always ended up resting on that place where the trail ran up between the hills to the narrow pass north of the village.

His swollen finger was no longer stiff and the other young men, eager to test this new brother, now found that Young Hunter was a wrestler like no other they had encountered before. More often than not, it seemed that Redbird would chance to be passing by just when Young Hunter was wrestling and for some reason he seemed to do even better as she watched. One by one, he threw the best of them. No looks of anger came his way. Instead, each of the young men he defeated seemed pleased. They had done well in adopting this one!

Finally, he found himself facing the biggest of the young men in the village. His name was Burden Carrier. He was the nephew of the tall old man who had first greeted Young Hunter on his arrival at the Village Between the Hills. The old man was their sagamon. His name was hard to pronounce. Young Hunter could barely say it, and then only very slowly. *Sah-dah-ga-eh-wah-deh.* It meant Even Tempered.

Ho-da-sha-teh, Burden Carrier, was a head taller than Young Hunter, though his shoulders were not as broad and his upper arms not as thick as Young Hunter's. Burden Carrier's arms were very long, though. When they grappled together, it seemed as if his arms wrapped themselves twice around Young Hunter. The two strong young men stood there, straining against each other, like two deer with locked horns. Their feet slid in the snow, but they did not unlock their grasp on each other. It seemed as if neither could get an advantage. Then, with a sudden twist of his hips and an ankle trip, Young Hunter used one of the throws Fire Keeper had taught him and threw Burden Carrier to the ground.

Burden Carrier came up laughing, his hair covered with snow. Behind him, some of the other young men were exchanging those things they'd wagered on the match. The shortest of the men, the same short hunter who had greeted Redbird with such excitement on the trail, seemed to have won all of the wagers. His name was Walks Soft and he was, Young Hunter now knew, Redbird's younger brother. He winked at Young Hunter.

Of all the young men, Burden Carrier was the best at the winter game the People of the Long Lodges loved the best. It was the game they called snow snake. The day after he wrestled Burden Carrier and threw him, Young Hunter was taken just outside the walls by the tall young man to watch them play.

Below the hill on which the palisade stood, along the edge of the longest and flattest of the fields, a special playing place had been made. A heavy log had been dragged in the snow to make a straight groove and water had been poured in to coat that groove with ice. The length of that groove was truly great. It was twice as long as the distance Young Hunter could shoot one of his small spears from the Long Thrower. He thought also of the Long Thrower itself, hidden in another hollow tree only a look beyond the pass through the jumbled hills that led down to the valley of these Long Lodge People. He thought too of his three dogs. They came quietly to him each night and he gave them food, passing it through the space between the logs to the other side of the stockade wall behind the Bear Clan long lodge.

The men began making ready to play. Each had his own stick carefully wrapped in deerskin. Each took his stick out and spoke to it, rubbed it with medicine. Then each began taking his turn. A long run, an arm thrown back, and then—*whhhhissss*—the stick would go sliding down that long runway. The one that went farthest in the groove would be the winner, and if a stick bounced out of the runway, it would be marked at the place where it left the track. The sticks truly seemed to be living things, like snakes gliding through the snow. They played for a long time. Always, it seemed, Burden Carrier's snake sped the fastest and went the farthest. The Sky Walker was now in the middle of the sky, having moved the width of three hands since the playing began. It was a good game to play, and Young Hunter stood close to the runway to watch the snow snakes as they flew across the ice.

Burden Carrier came over and took him by the arm. He held out his snow snake and placed it in Young Hunter's hand, motioning with his chin toward the runway. The other men looked surprised. Young Hunter looked at the snow snake. He could see how finely it was made and the weight of it felt strong, its balance such that it seemed ready to leap out of his hand on its own. Young Hunter looked at Burden Carrier as if to ask the question—*Are you certain you wish me to use your own special snow snake?* Burden Carrier made the sign for brother and spoke. His words were slow enough for Young Hunter to understand.

"*Tsiateno:sen, kate'nien:tens,*" Burden Carrier said. "Older Brother, try."

"*Niaweh,*" Young Hunter said. He could speak a few handfuls of words correctly now, thanks to Redbird and Reed.

Burden Carrier motioned to another of the young men, the one called *Gah-gah,* which meant Crow. Crow was almost as tall as Burden Carrier, but perhaps two winters younger. Crow came over to Burden Carrier and the two spoke together. Then Burden Carrier held up his right hand. In it he held a necklace of bear claws. Crow held up his right hand. He held a smooth stone with a hole in it and a rawhide cord looped through it. They placed the two items down on the snow. Burden Carrier spoke, making signs with his hands as he did so, and then held up four fingers. Young Hunter understood. Crow would throw his snow snake first. Then it would be Young Hunter's turn. Young Hunter would have four tries to make his snake go half as far as Crow's. If Young Hunter did not succeed, Burden Carrier would lose his bear claw necklace.

Crow went first. He spoke to his snow snake and rubbed it with his palms to warm it. He took a stance with one foot raised high and then ran. When he reached the line he hurled the snake, doing a forward roll into the snow and coming back up on his feet. The snow snake buzzed down the trough of ice. It was like a hummingbird whirring through the air. It was a fine throw and watching the snow snake run lightened Young Hunter's heart. Some of the cares that had weighed on him seemed to lift like mist lifting from a field at dawn. Far down the trough, Walks Soft marked the spot where Crow's snow snake finally stopped.

Young Hunter walked to where he had seen Burden Carrier start his run each time. He had been watching closely as the game went on, imagining how it would feel to stand there, to run with the snow snake in his hand, to hurl it down the runway. He had noticed how each player held his snake near the tip, balancing it with a finger at the very end. He had seen how a good throw would send the snake quivering with life down the icy track, how a badly angled throw would flip it out or bury the nose of the snake in the wall of the track. Young Hunter held up the snow snake. Crow stepped forward and stopped him, sliding Young Hunter's hand a finger's width forward. Young Hunter nodded. The balance was better now. Crow held up his right hand, showing four fingers. Young Hunter nodded again. He had four tries.

On his first throw, he stumbled as he released the snow snake and it stuttered back and forth in the groove before stopping. Young Hunter knew he had not put all of his strength into it. It was not the same as casting a spear or using his atlatl. Still, the distance was not bad. His second throw was better. It went almost a third as far as Crow's throw!

Burden Carrier held up both of his fists and shook them. *"Henh! Henh!"* he shouted in approval. The crowd of young men answered him. *"Henh! Henh!"*

Young Hunter's third throw was even better. This time he felt the energy pass down his shoulder, through his arm, out of his fingers, and into the snake. He felt its life as he threw. It was longing to carry his spirit. The snow snake shot straight, tail quivering. Burden Carrier and the other young men shouted again. Crow's voice was the loudest of them all.

When Burden Carrier brought the snow snake back to Young Hunter for his final throw, Young Hunter walked off a few paces from the others. He sat down in the snow and held the smoothly formed stick to his cheek. "Long Brother," he whispered, "I know you want to help me. My friend has loaned you to me. Let us share our strength on this throw." He felt the snow snake throb against his cheek. It seemed to twist in his hands and it felt warmer. All of the supple strength of a young tree was within it. It wanted to run!

275

Young Hunter stood and went to the starting place. He held the snow snake lightly in his right hand, held his other hand out before him. He sent his eyes and his mind down the length of the ice groove, past the place where the marker indicated the length of Crow's throw. He breathed in and out slowly, feeling the pulse at the center of his being, feeling that pulse rise until it reached his hand which held the snow snake. Then he ran, but could not feel himself running. He threw, but could not feel his throw. It was as if the snow snake were pulling him and then, suddenly, he broke free of his own hand. He felt himself quivering with life, his own long limbless body whipping down the smooth surface, wind streaking about him as it streaks past the head of the diving hawk. He was all speed and long strength, swifter than breath, the sound of scraping ice a sweet, high sound, everything around him bright with sunlight.

Young Hunter opened his eyes. He was face down in the snow. He lifted himself up. It was strange to feel arms and legs again. He looked down the track. Far, far down in the distance, Walks Soft held up the snow snake. It was a spear cast beyond the throw Crow had made. Everyone was shouting. Young Hunter stood and was suddenly grabbed from behind by someone who lifted him as if to crack his ribs. It was Burden Carrier, shouting his praise. The other young men were pounding his back and shoulders.

"Brothers," Young Hunter said, trying both to catch his breath and shape his words in their speech at the same time, "I-run-gauntlet-already."

The crowd of young men began to laugh. Burden Carrier dropped him and leaned against Crow, as if his laughter were making him too weak to stand. Then the two of them went over to their wager. Crow picked up the bear claws and Burden Carrier picked up the strung stone. They brought them over to Young Hunter and hung both necklaces about his neck.

As they walked back up the hill toward the walled village, Burden Carrier tugged at Young Hunter's arm, let go, and then held his own arms out. Young Hunter understood. Burden Carrier wanted to try wrestling him one more time. The look on Burden Carrier's face was very serious. He was going to try even harder this time. His new brother deserved nothing less than his best effort, even if it meant breaking his new brother's ribs!

"Hunh!" Young Hunter said. "Let us wrestle." His heart was feeling light. It would be a good match.

The two of them walked to the place where the grass had been deep before the snow fell. They began to circle each other, arms held out. The other young men formed a circle around them. Young Hunter breathed in the cold dry air. He kept his eyes not on Burden Carrier's feet as his balance shifted from one to the other, or on the weaving motions of his hands, but on his eyes. His eyes would tell Young Hunter where the attack would focus. The sound of their breath and of their feet shuffling the snow was like the rhythm of a dance. Young Hunter felt that rhythm deep within himself. Deeper and deeper, like the sound of Bear Talker's drum. Deeper and deeper, and then he felt a part of himself begin to slip away. Part of him slipped and fell from his body. Before Burden Carrier could touch him, Young Hunter's knees folded. He fell on all fours, his face touching the snow. All of the sounds around him became very faraway as he fell into the mouth of a cave that opened beneath him.

Little Brother. The voice that was not a voice vibrated through him. It shook his body as the wind shakes a tree. And it was not a single voice that touched him. It came from all four directions. All around, heavy snow was falling, but did not touch him. Then he saw that it was not snow, but small stones. They grew larger and larger, but still they did not touch him. Four men were coming toward him. They came from each of the four directions. He saw all this without turning his head. He did not see it with his eyes.

Little Brother. The voices that were not voices shook him again. The storm had ceased. The four were close now. They carried Long Throwers in their left hands, small spears in their right hands. They wore caps like the cap worn by Even Tempered, each cap crested by two eagle feathers.

Older Brothers, Young Hunter said. He felt the words coming not from his lips, but from the center of his being, pulsing from him like the light from a fire at night. *I see you and I greet you. You are the* Bedagiak, *the Thunder Beings.*

This is true, Little Brother, the voices said. *You see us now as your new relatives see us.*

The voices were strong. Young Hunter understood why they shook him, for those voices were the deep spirit of the thunder. *Older Brothers,* Young Hunter said, *why have you called me?*

They are coming, the Thunder Beings said. *They are close to this village. You must walk out and meet them.* The Thunder Being who came from the north pointed with his Long Thrower to the pass in the hills above the village. Young Hunter looked. He remembered the cave, and high above it, he now saw a great stone that he had not noticed before. Its shape was almost like that of a huge man, and next to the stone was a dead tree, blackened from being struck by lightning. Young Hunter turned to look back at the Thunder Being. It nodded its head to him. *There is the place where you must wait.*

Young Hunter looked to the north, and suddenly, he was there in that place. It was the narrowest place between the hills. The cliffs rose to either side, and on the southern cliff, there was a deep cave. Seeing it again, he remembered the strange feeling that had come over him as he had passed through that place on the rocky trail. He had looked into that cave, seen how large it was. The roof was so high that a man with a spear in his hand could not touch it.

278

Here is where you must wait, the voice of the Thunder Beings said. *You will meet your enemy here. Here you will meet the one who does not know he is your friend. He will help you.*

I hear you, Older Brothers, Young Hunter said. The Thunder Being who came from the north placed a white stone point on the ground in front of Young Hunter. Young Hunter bent to pick it up, but it slipped through his fingers. He tried to hold it more firmly, but the stone point was gone. His hands held only melting snow. He tried to stand and he felt hands on his arms and a robe over his shoulders. He looked at the robe. It was the wolf skin robe that Burden Carrier had been wearing. He looked up. The Thunder Being from the north was gone and Burden Carrier squatted in front of him. There was concern in his eyes.

Young Hunter stood. "I am … " He struggled to remember the right words to say he was well in Burden Carrier's language. "I am … *ka-ien kwa-la-lee-tohn.*"

Burden Carrier stared at him and then began to laugh. The other young men around were laughing, too.

Young Hunter repeated the words he had spoken. Then he realized what he had done. He had remembered the words wrongly. Instead of saying he was well, he had said he was smoked meat!

279

CHAPTER THIRTY-FOUR
HELPERS

"*Ona-oh*," Reed said. "She is one of our helpers, the eldest of the Three Sisters."

Young Hunter listened. As she spoke, Reed ran her hands along the many food plants which hung braided together from the rafters of the lodge. She explained how the men did the work of clearing the new fields, girdling trees with their axes, and then setting fires to burn away the brush. Those fields would not be used until the second year, after the girdled trees had dried and could be burned away too. Then, with their hoes made of deer antlers, the women planters would come and make the hills for the seeds to be planted.

There was much that the People of the Long Lodges knew about plants. His own people knew about gathering medicine plants, knew to put the seeds back into the earth so that more would grow in the coming seasons. But the Only People did not know about this way of keeping the seeds over the winter, of readying the fields and growing so much food that they could feed a big village. Young Hunter understood now why there were so many of the Long Lodge People. He thought of the places along the river valleys and by the banks of lakes in the lands of the Only People—places where the Three Sisters, corn, squash, and bean, could be grown.

"This is the story," Reed said. Young Hunter leaned forward to listen. Children were gathered all around and a few others of Young Hunter's own age who wanted to listen to stories. The fire was burning in the lodge and it was dark outside. It was time for stories.

Reed spoke of how long ago a woman fell from the Sky Land, down toward the waters where there was no earth. She was given a place to stand when the animals and birds shaped earth and placed it on the Great Turtle's back.

Reed spoke slowly and moved her hands as she spoke. Even when the words were unfamiliar, Young Hunter understood.

"*Ho!*" Reed said.

"*Henh!*" everyone answered, showing they were awake and listening to the story. If no one answered, then the storyteller would know that it was time to end the storytelling for that night.

Among the chorus of voices that said, "*henh!,*" one voice spoke from close behind Young Hunter. That voice was very familiar. It was Redbird's voice. She had come into the Bear Clan lodge along with a number of children from the long lodge of the Deer Clan, her own clan. When Young Hunter heard her voice so close behind him, so close that he could almost feel the warmth of her breath on the back of his neck, it made him sit up straighter. His shoulders began to feel tight and he rolled them to loosen his muscles, turning his head slightly as he did so. He was also able to look for just a moment at Redbird as he did that. Her hair was nicely combed and her braids were wrapped in deerskin. He rolled his shoulders and turned his head again, and then very quickly turned back. Redbird had leaned even closer, edging two other young women aside. Her eyes were on him and not on the storyteller.

Young Hunter understood. Reed had explained to him how adoption worked among the Long Lodge People. He was now her son and had taken the place of her son of that age who had disappeared many seasons ago. That son had been a friend of Redbird's husband. Now Young Hunter had taken that son's place. And who would take the place of Redbird's husband? He had learned that here, as among the Only People, it was common for an older woman whose husband had died to marry a younger man. It must only be someone of another clan. Redbird was Deer Clan and Young Hunter had been adopted into the Clan of the Bear. Among these Long Lodge People, it was the women who decided who and when people would marry.

He had now heard all of Redbird's story, of her escape from the tall hard man who walked with the grey giants and who killed as they killed—like one without a human heart. Young Hunter wondered who that man might be, and wondered even more when Redbird described his language as being much like Young Hunter's. Some women would have been made crazy by what Redbird saw and experienced. But her strength was like that of a supple tree that bends in a strong wind and then stands tall once again. Her spirit would still sing, like the bird she was named for, even though her song might be—for a time—one of sorrow. He admired Redbird for her courage. Like most of the men of the Only People, Young Hunter found a woman who was strong and brave more attractive than other women. As a woman of the Only People should do after her family had been killed, Redbird was mourning her dead. Yet she was continuing to live, and thinking of what the next dawn would bring. When the Moons of Spring came, it would be time for her to choose a new husband. And she was making it clear to the other young women of the village who her choice would be.

This was all very difficult. Young Hunter tried to turn his thoughts in another direction. He thought of Willow Girl, then realized he should be keeping his mind on Reed's story. He thought of the message that had come to him that same day as he was about to wrestle with Burden Carrier. Then he thought of how brightly Redbird's face shone in the firelight.

He thought, very quickly, about his dogs. Had he remembered to put food out for them?

"*Ho,*" Reed said.

"*Henh!*" Young Hunter shouted, a bit too loudly. Someone giggled from very close behind him and her breath brushed the back of his neck. Young Hunter moved a little closer to the fire and sat up very straight indeed. He listened intently to Reed's voice.

"So it was," Reed said, "that the daughter of the Sky Woman died when her twins were born, and Flint forced himself out through his mother's side while Good Mind was born in the right way. Good Mind, whose thought was always good and caring, was the one who buried his mother in the earth. From her grave, these good things grew. The squash grew from her belly. The beans grew from her fingers. And from her breasts grew the oldest of the Three Sisters, *Ona-oh,* the corn, the food which is our life. So it is that the milk of the corn when we make our first harvest is as sweet as a mother's."

Reed finished her story. Before another began, Young Hunter stood and slipped out of the group of people. He walked over and sat on the bed that had been given to him as his place in the big lodge. It was his private place, and no one would disturb him there unless invited. It was that way among the Long Lodge People. Whenever people needed to have space for their own thoughts or to do some work which was best done alone, they could go to their own place. Young Hunter picked up the piece of deer antler he had been carving and the small blade made of shiny black stone given to him by Even Tempered.

He glanced back toward the circle of people around the fire. Someone else was telling a story. Redbird sat in the exact place where Young Hunter had been. The thought of her sitting where he had been, of the warmth of her body sharing the warmth of the floor where he had been sitting—that thought both disturbed and interested him.

Young Hunter turned his mind to other things. He thought of how *Ona-oh,* the corn, made it possible for so many people to live in one village. The ears of corn hanging overhead were so many they could not be counted. Burden Carrier had shown him how the seedstones of *Ona-oh* were stored under the earth in bark-lined granaries. Enough normally would be stored to feed a village for the whole round of seasons. If another village did not have enough, then they would share their seedstones with that village. Until recently, the Long Lodge villages had kept in close touch with each other. Now, though, the nearest villages had been deserted to come to the safety of the walled stockade here in the place among the hills. And though messengers had been sent to the farther villages, none of those messengers had ever returned. Only well-armed parties of warriors—like those led by Redbird's brother who had met her and Young Hunter—would go out from the stockaded town, and then only during the day.

Young Hunter put down the black knife and looked at the shape coming out of the antler as he carved. It was the shape he had seen in his dreams, the shape of a Thunder Being. He took the antler and the knife and placed them in the box under his bed. Leaving something out in plain sight meant that anyone was welcome to take it and use it, returning it afterward. It was like that too among the Only People. Sharing was important for people to live together in peace.

Young Hunter stood and began to walk back toward the fire. Someone reached out and took his arm from behind. It was Even Tempered, who motioned with his head toward the door of the lodge. Young Hunter followed him outside. The night was clear, the distant ones far overhead were bright. Their many campfires glittered to every side of the wide Sky Trail. Young Hunter found himself wondering if those who walked that trail to the last happy home looked down for one last time to see the small shapes of the lodges and the people they left behind. The air tasted sweet. Their feet made crunching sounds in the crisp snow that had fallen that evening. It was too cold now for more snow to fall.

Even Tempered led Young Hunter to the eastern gate through the stockade wall. The poles of the wall were all more than twice a man's height and the thickness of a man's upper leg. They were sunk deep into the earth and lashed together. At night, the door was placed in that opening, wedged in with other poles and lashed tight with basswood rope. The gate had not yet been shut. Though it was dark, it was not yet time for sleep. Before sleeping it was common for the people to go outside the wall to empty their bowels in the place downwind of the village.

Even Tempered went through the gate and Young Hunter followed. They walked to a place where the wall curved and the sentries inside could not see them. The old man squatted and touched the new snow with his fingertips, pointing out the footprints there. It was easy to see them in the moonlight.

"Wolves?" Even Tempered said. "Wolves come here?"

In the new snow, the evidence was clear. The old man lifted his sharp eyes to look at Young Hunter. Young Hunter sighed. The new snow held the paw marks of his dogs. He had forgotten to feed them. He felt them watching, even now, from the small trees on the other side of the field where dry stalks of the Oldest Sister rattled softly in the wind.

Even Tempered continued to look at Young Hunter. It seemed as if there were amusement in the old sagamon's face. *It is time,* Young Hunter thought. *These people have adopted me. I must trust them.* He lifted his head and whistled. Three dark shadows appeared at the far edge of the field and made their way quickly, following the darkest shadows, weaving their way across the field. They stopped a few paces away and then crawled on their bellies to Young Hunter, stopping at his feet. Young Hunter looked over at Even Tempered. The sagamon did not seem surprised. Instead, he nodded his head.

"Ah," Even Tempered said, "I am glad to meet your family." He held out his right hand and Pabetciman sniffed at it.

Once inside the lodge, Danowa lay with his head in Reed's lap as she rubbed his back with her right hand. Agwedjiman was on his back next to the fire where three of the small children were sprawled on top of him. The littlest of them, a girl of no more than three winters, was sitting on his stomach and bouncing up and down. The look on the dog's face was one of tolerant disgust. But Young Hunter knew how much his dog, how much all three of his dogs, enjoyed being back among human beings. Among the Only People, it was Agwedjiman who allowed the little children to ride on his back. Pabetciman sat, head erect, between Young Hunter and Even Tempered.

"The last of our dogs," Reed said, "was taken from us at the end of the last moon. Before our dogs began to disappear, each of our lodges had their own dogs. They belonged to our clans. They went with us into the fields and warned us of danger. They would drive even a bear away if it came too close. They would scout outside our villages each evening before coming in for the night, making sure all was safe for us. But then they began to disappear. Our scouts searched for our missing dogs. Only one of them was found by a party of our men. That dog was named Bear Tooth. He belonged to the Eel Clan. He was the leader of all the village dogs. He had managed to get back close to our village before he died of his wounds, many wounds all over his body. That was when we knew a terrible monster was killing our dogs. We tried to keep our dogs within the lodges, but they were too brave. They would not hide when they knew danger threatened their village, even those who were only a few seasons old. At last, something crept into our village and killed the few puppies that remained. It was then that we knew we must wait no longer to build the wall."

Even Tempered sighed. "It has been too long since I have seen a dog. It is very good to see these members of your family, Young Hunter."

Even Tempered placed his hand on Pabetciman's head and stroked it.

"Tomorrow I will introduce the dogs to the rest of my new family," Young Hunter said. "When I travel back to the village of my grandparents, I will see if some of our dogs are willing to have their children be adopted. Then I can come back and bring you new friends to join your clans. They may grow up to be as brave as those who gave their lives protecting your people."

"Your words are good," Even Tempered said. "But you must remember that you have been adopted. One who is adopted can never leave the lands of his new people. You will not return to the village of your former grandparents. You will spend the rest of your life here."

Weasel Tail looked down from One-Eye's shoulders at the few blackened sticks, all that was left of the village among the standing stones. Snow had covered the graves where Young Hunter and Redbird had buried those who had died a moon ago. The place was familiar to Weasel Tail. He remembered what had happened here and his hand went up to his missing eye.

One-Eye was walking in circles, as if looking for something, as if seeing something no one else could see. The Ancient Ones had almost completed the great circle they had been making. At its center was one remaining large village. It was now the Moon of Long Nights. Soon it would be time for Weasel Tail to help them again, to lead the warriors out of the village for an ambush. Already they had sent the Hunter ahead of them, to kill any scouts who might warn of their approach. When the Hunter came back, then they would send out Weasel Tail. He would have a single day in which to complete his mission. If he failed, they would release the Hunter upon his trail. One-Eye knew that his dog's fear would lead him back quickly.

This time, though, Weasel Tail thought, *this time it will be different.* The packet of medicine, his Little Helper, was hidden in his loincloth. This time he would not come back quickly. He would kill a rabbit, stuff it with his medicine, and hang it where the Hunter would find it when following his trail the next day. The Hunter would not be able to resist. It would tear apart and swallow the rabbit before continuing to catch bigger game.

Weasel Tail knew that his time was short. With only one eye, he was not as useful a dog as he had been before. After they wiped out the big village among the hills, their use for him would be done. They would kill him or give him to the Hunter. But Weasel Tail wished to live. If he could kill the Hunter, then he might be able to get away, to go far to the west where he could not be found, not be sensed by One-Eye's mind. But first he must kill the Hunter. He thought of its eyes watching him across the fire, like a bobcat looking at a field mouse, waiting for the moment to leap. *But this field mouse,* Weasel Tail thought, *this field mouse has a Little Helper.*

CHAPTER THIRTY-FIVE
HOLDS THE STONE

Young Hunter rose long before dawn. He had done little sleeping, and when he slept, his sleep was filled with voices. He heard the voices of many of the People of the Long Lodges, the voices of Redbird and Reed and Even Tempered. Once again Redbird walked beside him on the long trail, looked over her shoulder, and smiled that faint smile. Once again he felt the cut of the switches and the thud of the sticks against his back as he ran the gauntlet. Once again he wrestled with Burden Carrier, threw him, and heard his new brother's laughter. Once again he whipped the snow snake into the trench, and it sped as swiftly as a small spear from the Long Thrower, while the young men shouted their approval. Reed leaned over the fire and told the story of the twins and looked hard into his face when she spoke of the one with the good mind, looked toward the north when she spoke of the hard-hearted twin, Flint. Then the voices of the Long Lodge People blended into one voice, telling him again that he was now one of them, no longer a Dawn Land person, but one who belonged to the place between the hills.

He shifted in his restless sleep and his face turned toward the east. Other voices came to him, voices he had heard all of his life. He heard Willow Girl and Rabbit Stick and Sweetgrass Woman telling him that they were awaiting his return. Old

Muskrat stood in his dugout and held up the muskrat call for Young Hunter to see. Fire Keeper showed him the killing throw, a sad look in his eyes. Red Hawk and Blue Hawk called to him: *Brother-cousin, are you afraid to return and wrestle us again?* He turned again in his sleep and his ears filled with the drumming of the hooves of the bighead herd. Then he was deafened and paralyzed by the awful cry of the fire hunters as he smelled the smoke which reached for him like the long arms of a giant, trying to strangle him. His dogs whimpered as they pressed close to him and he grasped them in his arms. They were small puppies again and he pushed his back against the moist earth, pushed back, and then fell into the cave. He was still holding tight to his dogs and to the Long Thrower, but he was falling, falling, down to the very heart of Mother Earth. And as he fell into that darkness, last and strongest of all, he heard his own inner voice. That voice blended with the voices of Bear Talker and Medicine Plant and the voices of the *Bedagiak*, the Thunder Beings. And now all the voices said only one word as he fell, said it again and again. *Now. Now. Now. Now.*

As he slipped out of the village, wrapped in a deerskin blanket, he was sure that no one saw him go. He moved on his belly like a soft shadow, slid past the watchful eyes of the young men posted at the eastern entrance, the narrow gate. When he reached the bottom of the hill, he made tracks in the snow, a trail leading toward the south. Then he left the trail and turned north, wiping out his tracks behind him. By the time it was discovered that his first trail was a false one, he would be too far away for them to risk following him.

But Young Hunter's departure from the village had not gone unobserved. From her sleeping place, Reed had watched as Young Hunter slipped out of the Bear Clan lodge. As he turned toward the north, she was still sitting silently, looking toward the eastern door through which an adopted son had left her life. She had lived long with the story passed down to her from her father's father. She understood his dream. Although she made no sound which anyone could hear, she was singing, her song a prayer for his success against all those with hearts of flint.

By the time Young Hunter reached the hollow tree where the Long Thrower was hidden, the sun was reddening the edge of the eastern sky, even though the full moon still showed clearly on the horizon. It was the Moon of Long Nights, the shortest of all the days in the year. Young Hunter knew that he would not have long to ready himself. He slung back the deerskin blanket from one shoulder, bent the Long Thrower, and strung it. When he plucked the sinew string it sang a powerful note. It gave him heart.

The dogs ranged about him, circling, making sure the path was safe. No danger yet, but it was coming. He followed the trail to the narrow way between the cliffs. As he climbed, Danowa appeared on the trail before him. The dog looked at Young Hunter, a look which said the way was clear, then whined once and disappeared back into the snowy land.

Bear Talker looked into the fire. He reached out his callused palms and gathered a handful of glowing coals. He spread them on the earth in front of his lodge and looked at the shape they formed. He looked up and nodded at the people gathered there before him.

"I must go into my small lodge," Bear Talker said. "I must speak to the Below People. I must ask the ones who live under the earth to be ready to help."

Medicine Plant stood on top of the hill above her lonely lodge, her eyes turned toward the west. As she watched, a snow owl glided up from the trees below her. It flapped its wings and rose higher. It was white as a cloud come to life. The owl flew straight toward Medicine Plant, its eyes on hers. It landed on the ground at her feet, its wings spread, crouching on the snow. Its yellow eyes were like two moons. Medicine Plant motioned with her chin toward the west. The owl burst up from the snow and began to fly in the sunset direction, its wings strong and steady.

The trail grew very narrow and Young Hunter climbed from it to enter the big cave. He walked around inside it, touching the walls with his hands. He could feel the presence of the Thunder Beings. They had brought him here in his dream four nights ago. He placed the sticks he had carried with him on the floor of the cave to make a nest for the fire. He took out his fire-making kit. Soon smoke rose from his fire. He took some of the smoking herb from his pouch and placed it in the flames.

"Older Brothers," he said, "I have come to this place. I offer you this fire because I know fire makes you glad. The old story tells us that you gave fire by sending your spears down from the sky, sending fire down to burn in the heart of the cedar. I offer this fire and this smoke to thank you."

Young Hunter sat without speaking for a time. Then he placed more of the smoking herb into the flames. "Older Brothers," he said, "I want my people to live. I want my new relatives to live. They are real human beings too, even if they cannot speak real human speech. I want to help them. Their enemies are all around them. I am small and weak. I need your help. I need the help of our Creator. Older Brothers, I thank you. Owner Creator, I thank you. *Oleohneh.*"

Young Hunter paused and then, remembering the word for thanks which had been given to him by the People of the Long Lodges, he spoke again. "*Niaweh,*" he said. "*Niaweh.*"

When he came out of the cave, he looked up. That was where he had to go. The dogs looked at him as he approached the steep face of the cliff. He signaled them to conceal themselves, slung the Long Thrower over his back, and started to climb.

It was not an easy climb. His feet slipped often, but his grip was strong each time. He scraped his knees on the stones as he climbed, yet it seemed as if these stones were helping him, thrusting themselves out to steady him as he climbed. He remembered how certain stones would spark like lightning when struck together. These stones were friends of the Thunder Beings. His hand ached where his finger had been dislocated by the gauntlet club, but it was the smallest finger and he did not need it to use the Long Thrower. At last he pulled himself over the top and stood on the cliff high above the narrow way between the hills. The great stone stood on the edge, just as he had seen it in his dream. A single dead tree was close to it, one branch almost broken off. He pulled the branch free. It was strong and smooth, as big around as his calf, and as long as his own height. He wedged it under the boulder so that the leverage would be exactly right.

Something moved to his right. He turned and looked. A big white bird was coming toward him from high in the eastern sky. It came closer and closer on silent wings: a snow owl. As Young Hunter stood there, he could see that its eyes were focused upon him. Closer it came, and its eyes seemed as large as two moons. He felt as if he were in another place, on another hilltop. He was not afraid of that owl. He felt a surge of strength and he breathed deeply. Its wings almost touching his face, the silent bird passed him and swooped down over the edge of the cliff. It turned back again to the north and flew down into the forest of white birches. The birch trees bore the marks of the Thunder Beings on their trunks, those dark shapes on the white bark, like birds with outstretched wings. Because of those marks it was said that the lightning would never strike a birch tree and that places where the birches grew were places well liked by the Thunder Beings. *It is right,* Young Hunter thought, *that birch trees should grow in this place.* But as he lost the snow owl from his sight, he saw something else moving on the other side of the birch forest: a small figure was coming quickly

along the birch-lined trail which paralleled a rushing stream
that cut its way out of the rising northern hills. Now the
figure was coming to a little clearing.

Young Hunter shaded his eyes. It was far away, but he
could see as it crossed the clearing that the running shape
was a human being, a man. The man was running up the
trail, toward the still-distant gap in the hills. He was bent as he
ran, running as a hunted animal runs, as a rabbit runs from the
fox.

Young Hunter cast his eyes back behind the lone man,
trying to see what was following him. He breathed in and out
as he watched, waiting. In and out. In and out. Then he saw it
as it crossed that same clearing. It was not moving swiftly, but
steadily. It followed as a hunter follows an animal that will soon
run out of strength. Young Hunter recognized that night-
black shape which chased the fleeing man. He remembered its
eyes of flame staring at him as he pushed his boat out to safety
on the Waters Between the Mountains. He remembered the
awful scream of the Black Longtooth.

"Agwedjiman, Pabetciman, Danowa," Young Hunter called.
He unslung the Long Thrower from his shoulder and then swung
his hand in the signal he knew they would understand.

His breath tore at his throat and he gasped as he ran
across the clearing. The poison of the medicine plant had not
done its job. He had watched from his hiding place high in a
tree as the Hunter found the rabbit, tore at it, and then
swallowed. He had felt fierce joy in the center of his being as
the huge black animal choked and twisted with pain, clawing
at its gut before falling to the ground. But as he came close to
its still body, its eyes opened, and it saw him. Its eyes had been
blurred, but suddenly came into focus. Weasel Tail's knees
weakened. Then the Hunter began to rise. It retched and
vomited out what it had eaten. The poison that would have
killed three men had only weakened it.

Weasel Tail had scrambled back to the tree and climbed high. He would be safe there until One-Eye came and called the Hunter to heel. But the Hunter had not waited at the base of the tree. It began to climb. Weasel Tail went higher, but the Hunter did not stop. It followed him into the highest branches. Branches had broken beneath it, but it continued to come and the tree began to bend from its great weight. Weasel Tail leaped, grasping at the branches of other trees, twisting and falling. He landed in deep snow and scrambled to his feet. He began to run, hearing the *whumph!* of the Hunter landing in the snow behind him. He did not look back. He ran knowing that it followed. It would play with him, but it would not stop until it caught him.

As he ran, Weasel Tail kept a small hope. There was a cave in that narrow pass between the hills. He had scouted that pass and knew it well, for it was the way he meant to lead his masters along. The cave was large, but inside it there was a narrow passage, a place where a man could just barely squeeze through. It was too small for the Hunter to pass. Its head, with those long fangs, was twice the size of a bear's head, its shoulders twice the width of a man's. The Hunter was following, but perhaps the poison had weakened it. And even if it were strong, it would play with him, letting the fear fill his body before finally catching him. If he could just stay far enough ahead, he might be able to reach that place.

The trail was very steep now through the birch trees. Far below, a stream washed down over the rocks. He slipped, fell, rolled, and barely stopped himself before going over the edge into the stream below. He climbed to his feet, his eyes wild, as he searched for the trail. There, above him. But even as he crawled back up onto it, he saw the trail in front of him disappear. There was only blackness there, a spear's cast ahead of him. The Hunter had cut in front of him and it lay across the path.

It was not looking at him. Its only motion was its small tail, twitching from side to side. Then, slowly, it turned its head.

295

Weasel Tail felt its eyes upon him and he turned into ice. There was only one thing within its eyes. His death. It yawned, exposing its long fangs. Its mouth seemed wide enough to swallow the sky. He could smell its breath. It began to stand up, and as it did so, it coughed, retched, and then vomited. Its back arched as it vomited and then it struck with its front paws at a birch tree by the trail's edge. The tree was as thick as a man's waist, but the blows broke it like a small twig.

Weasel Tail took a step backward, whimpering as he did so. Shudders ran down the length of the black monster's body. The Hunter shook itself and then looked again at Weasel Tail. It took one slow step toward the pitiful man it was about to tear slowly into pieces. Then, behind the Hunter, Weasel Tail saw—he did not know what he saw. *Another animal?* It was creeping in close. Suddenly, the smaller animal leaped, bit at the Hunter's haunch and sprang back, twisting its body to avoid the sweep of the black monster's claws, which came as swiftly as the strike of a hawk. Another animal came running from behind Weasel Tail, past him on the trail. It tore at the Hunter's side. The black monster turned again to strike, but a third animal attacked from the other side.

Dogs, Weasel Tail thought. *They are dogs.*

They darted in and out in the narrow place on the trail among the birch trees. The Hunter struck at them and missed, struck and missed, as the dogs drew the creature away from the man.

Weasel Tail watched it all without understanding. It was as if he had left his body and was standing somewhere above it now. He could see the whole strange scene, the black creature, the three dogs, the skinny, filthy man with the terribly scarred face. The dogs moved as if they had a single mind, but the Hunter was quick and was beginning to see the pattern to their attacks. As one of the dogs drove in and another crept close from the back, the Hunter spun and struck at the dog that was creeping in. It hit the dog, which yelped and rolled over, the black monster following to leap upon it and drive in its great fangs. But another of the dogs leaped up onto the Hunter's back, where it fastened its teeth deeply in the loose skin and held on. The Hunter tried to strike at it and then rolled over onto the dog, its weight crushing the attacker, breaking the hold. The dog whimpered and crawled down the trail toward Weasel Tail.

Then, perhaps because he too had been a dog, Weasel Tail reached out a hand. It was the first time in more seasons than he could remember that he had made any gesture not born out of fear or hunger, lust or anger. He reached for the dog as one would reach for a wounded brother. He felt the warmth of its body and that warmth seemed to travel up his hand into his chest. Something inside him broke and a weight seemed to lift from his heart. A terrible cold began to leave the center of his being. There was a stone there by the side of the trail, a stone the size of an ax head. Weasel Tail bent down and picked up that stone. As he knelt to do so, the wounded dog at his feet licked his hand. He stroked its head and then stood between the dog and the black creature that faced them, crouching to leap, ignoring the last dog nipping at its haunches.

Weasel Tail looked into the Hunter's eyes. Again he saw his death there, but this time he was not afraid. He saw now that he had already been dead. There were things more to be feared than death. A mist cleared from in front of his remaining eye and he saw more than he had seen when he had had two eyes. He saw through the dark cloud that had hung over him since the death of his parents. He saw back to the time before that hard hand like stone had lifted him and One-Eye had scarred him across the chest and shoulder, marking and claiming him. He saw back before he had eaten the food of the Ancient Ones and accepted their darkness as his own. He saw that he was not theirs. He saw all this so clearly that laughter filled his throat. Everything around him was clear and new— the trail, the black animal, which no longer filled him with

297

fear, the snow owl that sat in the top of the tree above the black, crouched shape that would soon claim his life.

Weasel Tail stood straight. He held the stone in his hand, ready to strike one final blow before he died, ready to die defending this brave dog that had risked its life for his own worthless life. In a voice louder than he knew he owned, he shouted, "*Whaayeeh! Alnobah!* I am a human being!" He waited for the leap that would strike him down. But it did not come. Instead, the Hunter turned suddenly and bit at its left flank. Something had stuck there. The Hunter spun to face back the other way, and something came whirring down through the trees. Weasel Tail heard it before he saw it. Its flight was swifter than a hummingbird's. It dove straight for the side of the Hunter, its beak striking. It buried itself deep in the black animal's side, just behind its front leg.

The black monster leaped again and screamed. It rolled and clawed at the feathers of the small birds which had struck it, but it could not reach them. It rose up on its hind legs and another small bird darted in and struck its neck.

It was not a bird. Weasel Tail saw this now. A spear. A small spear, the size of the spears the Little People might throw. Were the Little Ones protecting him too? The Hunter fell back to all fours. It coughed and blood came from its mouth. Weasel Tail looked up the slope, in the direction from which the small spears had flown. The sun was coming from up there and it was bright. It outlined the shape of a broad-shouldered man holding something in his hands. A small spear flew again from whatever he held. It grazed the Hunter's throat. The black creature snarled, looked up the hill. It saw its enemy and howled. Its howl seemed to shake the earth. Then it leaped up the hill, three long strides in that direction. But as it leaped, another small spear struck home, struck at the base of its spine, and the beast's hind legs went limp. Clawing at the earth, it crawled up the slope, dragging itself, its eyes on the one it would kill, the pitiful human that was its food.

But Weasel Tail saw that the man stood without fear. He stood as if he were one of the Thunder Beings. The Hunter clawed up the slope and now it had almost reached that man. The man pushed out his left hand which held that long object, drew his right hand back. There was a small twanging sound and one final small spear drove through the air. It went into the black creature's throat and cut the cord of its breath.

CHAPTER THIRTY-SIX
THE NEW MAN

Young Hunter's heart was beating so fast that it seemed as if a bird were caught in his chest and beating its wings to escape. Each of his seven shots had struck the monster, but it had refused to die until the final one. It had fallen so close to him that he could reach it with a single stride. He knew that he had cut its breath. His last small spear had pierced its life. Yet he could not move. He felt as if he had turned into stone. His legs were so weak that he knew he would fall if he took a single step.

He stood there looking at it. Even fallen to the earth it was as tall as a man. It was as big as Fear Bear in the old stories. Its teeth were as long as the length of a man's hand. Its claws were four times as long as those of the long-tail and it was built something like that hunting cat. But he knew its prey was not the deer. This was one of those Ancient Ones that had escaped the eye of the Owner Creator and not been made smaller to protect the real human beings. This was one that hunted humans. It was something from the old stories.

Young Hunter's breath came more slowly now. He felt the strength returning to his limbs. He looked down beyond the huge shoulders of the dead monster, down the slope to the trail. There a gaunt, dirty man sat rocking back and forth, stroking the head of his wounded Danowa. Young Hunter began to make his way down the hill, to see if his friends were alive.

The sun still shone behind the broad-shouldered man as he came down the hill. Its light circled him as if he were a sky being. Weasel Tail watched as the man came closer, but he did not stop stroking the head of the dog that had saved his life. The broad-shouldered man stopped and looked down at him without speaking. It was as if the man were looking into Weasel Tail's soul. For a moment, as he started to stand, Weasel Tail felt afraid at what the man would see. Then he remembered. He remembered seeing the snow owl; he remembered the coldness leaving his chest as he had picked up and held the stone; he remembered the words he had shouted. Then a feeling different from fear or shame came over Weasel Tail. He straightened and stepped back. The broad-shouldered man knelt by the dog and gently began to examine its wounds.

I am a human being, Weasel Tail said to himself. *I am a human being.* He looked down at his right hand. It still held the lance-shaped stone which he had picked up to defend the dog. The stone felt warm in his hand. *This is my name,* he thought. *I am Weasel Tail no longer. That one has gone. I am Holds the Stone.*

The lone man who had been crouched over Danowa was the most pathetic human being Young Hunter had ever seen. He wore only a filthy loincloth of torn deerskin, bound around his waist by a belt of woven basswood black with filth. There were new scratches and old scars all over the man's arms and legs and chest. His hair was so matted and tangled that it looked more like snakes than human hair. The man was skinny, yet his thin muscles looked tight and strong. The man was tall and as he straightened his back, stepping back from the dog, he seemed to grow taller still. He was the tallest human being Young Hunter had ever seen. His face bore the worst signs of abuse the man had known. A great scar crossed the left side of his face and his left eye was covered with moss and caked mud. There was a strange smell to the man. Young Hunter

301

remembered that smell; he had smelled it the day when the fire had almost claimed him and his dogs as they hid behind the leaning stone. It was the smell of the fire hunters. Somehow this man must have escaped from them. Though his face was ruined, as the man straightened up a look of peace had come over that broken face. Danowa glanced up at the tall man with gratitude. Young Hunter knelt to examine his wounded brother.

The terrible animal's claws had raked Danowa's side, but they had not cut deeply. Its weight had rolled upon him, but the snow had cushioned that weight and the dog's ribs were sound. Young Hunter ran his hands along the dog's flanks and then felt each leg. Danowa whimpered softly, almost like a puppy, when he felt the right front leg. It was broken, but in a place where healing could come easily. Young Hunter put his face close to his dog's head and breathed softly in his ear. "You are brave, my brother. You will be well and strong." As Young Hunter stood and stepped back, the tall, ragged man knelt again by Danowa and put his hand on the dog's head.

Young Hunter searched his memory for words in the language of the People of the Long Lodges so that he could say something to the man. He spoke the words of greeting. Asked the man how he was. The man shook his head. He could not understand. *Stay*, Young Hunter signed to the man. *I go, return.* The man nodded.

He found Pabetciman a stone's throw down the hill from the trail, lying on his side against a birch tree. He was breathing, but his breath was shallow and quick. Young Hunter felt the dog's side. The ribs were badly broken. The blow of the black monster's paw had been a hard one.

Young Hunter put his hand in front of Pabetciman's muzzle. The dog licked his hand weakly. He did not whimper, even when Young Hunter ran his hand farther down his body where the hips were shattered. There was frothy blood in the dog's mouth. Breath blood. Young Hunter found it hard to see as his vision blurred with tears.

"My brave one," he said, "Pabesis. You are the bravest of all dogs, Brother." He stroked the dog's wide skull and Pabetciman's right eye looked up at him. The look went into Young Hunter's heart. It spoke to him. It said, *I know I have done well.* It was a look that was calm and deep and knowing.

"My brother," Young Hunter said. "We will hunt together again. When you reach the top of the trail into the Sky Land, you wait there. One dawn, your brothers and I will join you. We will hunt together across the sky."

Pabetciman sighed, the same sigh he had always given each night as the four of them huddled together along the trail. It was the same sigh he had made when very small and lying on his back against his mother's warm side. It was the sigh that accepts the arrival of the Sleep Maker.

Young Hunter continued to stroke the wide, silent head. His left hand was in front of the dog's mouth. No breath warmed his hand. He knelt there a long time. Was Danowa the only one of his three friends who had survived? Would he find Agwesis broken by the side of the trail? He did not have the strength to rise and search for him. It was as if part of his own heart had ceased to beat when Pabesis's last breath left him. Suddenly, a dog's muzzle shoved under his arm and he turned to see Agwedjiman. The dog stepped back and sat on its haunches, awaiting his command. There was blood in his mouth, but it was the blood of the terrible creature.

Agwedjiman looked at Young Hunter and then looked down at the body of his dead brother. He did not nuzzle him or sniff at him. It was as if he knew that the spirit was gone. The look in the dog's eye was sorrowful, but understanding, like the eye of an old sagamon.

Young Hunter did not ask the dog where he had been. He knew his friend well enough to understand. When the black creature had fallen at last, Agwedjiman had gone to scout the trail in each direction, to be sure no other enemy was close enough to strike them. The mind of the great dog was clear, that of a war leader. Young Hunter reached out both arms and embraced the dog. He held him close and Agwedjiman bowed his head to press it against Young Hunter's chest.

Together they walked back to the place where the tall, ragged man sat with Danowa. The man looked up as they came close. It was a strange look. It made Young Hunter think of the look on a small child's face after waking from a dream and seeing, not monsters pursuing him, but the face of his mother or father leaning over him. A thought came into Young Hunter's mind, and he spoke to the man in the language of the Only People.

"*Kuai, nidoba*," Young Hunter said. "Hello, friend."

The man looked up at him and opened his mouth. It was as if something were caught in his throat. He closed his mouth and opened it again and then, very slowly, as if his tongue were not used to human speech, he answered, "*Kuai, nidoba.*" Then the man looked down at the stone that he held in his right hand. He looked back up at Young Hunter. "I am a human being," he said, his speech halting. He held up the rock. "I am Holds the Stone."

"Holds the Stone," Young Hunter said, "are you hurt?"

"*Nda.* But my friend here ... hurt."

"His name is Danowa."

"Danowa's leg broken. And ... the other one? Three dogs came. Saved me from ... the Hunter." He motioned with his chin toward the huge black body that lay in the snow on the rocky slope above them.

"Pabetciman has given up his breath. He died as a warrior." Young Hunter stopped and took a deep breath. His throat hurt and he could not speak.

"I ... help you," Holds the Stone said. "I help you bury ... our brother."

Together they carried Danowa up the trail to the narrow pass and into the cave. Young Hunter brought more wood and made a second fire, a larger one this time. Danowa would need the warmth. Holds the Stone looked about the cave as he sat by the fire. He leaned very close to it, as if he could never get warm enough. It made Young Hunter think of another old story his grandmother had told him, the story of the man who was taken by the Forest Wanderers, the giants who ate human beings. That man had been like them until a hunter and his wife showed him kindness. Then he had them make a fire and used it to turn himself back into a human. He coughed up the lump of ice that was his heart, and as it thawed he became a real human being again.

Young Hunter looked closely at Holds the Stone. His voice had sounded familiar, a way of speaking much like that in the village of the Only People. Young Hunter stood. He walked over to the tall man and grasped him by the hand. "Come," he said, "come with me."

Holds the Stone rose. Though he was head and shoulders above Young Hunter in height, he was like a small child following his father. *And what am I about to do?* one part of Young Hunter said. He was two people again, one walking a spirit trail and the other following and watching. Somehow, though, to both parts of Young Hunter, what he was doing seemed right. For a moment his vision blurred and he was no longer two people but one, one person moving with certainty, drawing the tall, thin man behind him. He led Holds the Stone down the trail until they came to the stream. He led him down to a place where the current kept a swirling pool of water free of ice. Their feet broke the thin ice at the edge of the pool as they walked in. They stood together hip-deep in the cold water.

Young Hunter reached up and pulled down on Holds the Stone's shoulders. The big man bent his knees until he was in the water up to his neck. Young Hunter grasped him firmly and pushed his face beneath the swirling current, then lifted him, and much of the filth was washed away. Holds the Stone was relaxed and his weight seemed no more than that of a little child. Four times Young Hunter immersed him in the water and when he lifted him back to the surface for the fourth time, the last of the mud and moss had washed away from Holds the Stone's blind eye. It washed away from that eye and he could see. The eye was not gone. His vision was weak, but he saw light and color. What he saw was simple and beautiful. Holds the Stone knelt in the pool and Young Hunter began to draw his strong fingers through the tall man's tangled hair. Gradually he combed it free, combed out the tangles and the snakes. As this was done, Holds the Stone felt the last of his anger and confusion leave him. His thoughts were made straight again.

Young Hunter led Holds the Stone from the stream. When he reached the bank, the tall man fell to his knees and vomited. All that he held within his belly came out of him. All of the fear which had gripped his belly left him. He reached out for handfuls of clean snow and wiped his mouth and his face. Then he stood. His feet were no longer heavy on the earth. He walked to a place where the last light of the Day Traveler slipped between the hills. He faced that light and opened his arms to embrace it. In the trees around him the warmth of the evening light was still enough to melt the snow on the branches of the trees. All around him was the sound of dripping water and branches lifting as the weight of snow left them. He heard the songs of the small black-and-white birds as they fluttered nearby. He saw again how beautiful everything was around him. He turned to look at Young Hunter.

Young Hunter looked at him and knew him. He saw that this man was the one who once had been called Weasel Tail. But now he was a new man; he was Holds the Stone.

"Brother," Holds the Stone said, "I have a long story to tell."

CHAPTER THIRTY-SEVEN
DAWN

The light from the big fire reflected off the faces of the stones around it. It leaned back against the largest of the stones and closed its single eye. It breathed in and out slowly and then sent its spirit forth. It walked out in the same giant shape as its body, going past the other shapes which sat without moving around that big fire. The spirit shape moved quickly across the wide plain toward the hills. It moved with great steps which covered even greater distances than One-Eye's strides when the spirit shape was inside its body. As it traveled, it felt the pull from the northeast, from that place by the ocean where the Ancient Ones once had sat with their children and women by the deep-sounding sea. But its spirit did not turn that way. It would not travel ever again in that direction. There was only one way for it to travel now, travel as surely as the old mountains of ice had traveled, crushing all before them.

One-Eye's spirit body carried it quickly, rushing like the cold wind across the plain. Its spirit mind reached out, but could not find the Hunter, that black one which followed its mind's bidding. Ahead of the spirit body were the hills that circled the place where the small, weak ones were gathered. Toward this place it had sent his dog. Toward this place it had sent the Hunter to chase its dog back to him.

One-Eye's spirit body sensed something. There under the newly fallen snow. Something buried above the trail under branches and stones and snow. It tried to move closer, but something suddenly stood between it and that buried shape. It was a white-winged spirit shape. It spread its wings wide and blocked One-Eye's path. A storm wind blew from those wide wings and One-Eye's spirit body could come no closer. The spirit fingers tried to grasp it, to tear it, but it slipped away from it. Then another shape was there beside it. It rose to its hind legs in the snow. It was a bear, one of the Ancient Ones, and yet within its shape was the shape of a man. It too blocked the way and One-Eye's spirit body retreated.

One-Eye's spirit body sensed something else. The presence of a familiar shape, the small shape of that pathetic one that was its dog. It sensed it on the trail, returning as it had been told to do. Then the spirit shapes of the bear and the white owl rushed against One-Eye and it retreated. They pressed it and it pulled back through the forest, back across the plain, back into its own body leaning back against the cliff. It opened its eye. It had not found the black one, the Hunter, but its dog was returning to it. When it arrived, they would travel to the place in the hills. They would set the ambush and they would kill. They would kill and burn. They would continue to do so until they had wiped all of the small, weak ones from the face of the earth. And within their separate lodges far to the east, Medicine Plant and Bear Talker each lay back in exhaustion. Their battle to keep the Ancient One from seeing that which was hidden, that trap which had been set for the grey giants, had spent them and they knew it would be a moon or more before they regained the strength to do more than watch whatever battle would soon happen. And both of the deep seers prayed that they had helped Young Hunter enough.

It was almost dawn. From his vantage point on top of the cliffs he could see down into the valley to the west and back along the trail to the northeast. Snow was no longer falling. Everything was silent. Behind him, in the small wigwom that Holds the Stone and he had built, Danowa slept, his broken leg carefully bound and held in place with splints of ash. Agwedjiman sat by Young Hunter's side. Crystals of ice had formed about his mouth and his breath was a white cloud. Only his breath moved as he leaned against Young Hunter, lending him warmth as they sat there. The deerskin blanket draped over them was covered with the new snow and it seemed that they were part of the clifftop.

Three sunrises had passed since Young Hunter had left the Village Between the Hills. Three sunsets had passed since Pabetciman had died and been buried beside the trail to the northeast among the birch trees. Two sunrises ago, their plan had been made and Holds the Stone had started on the trail back to those who had been his masters.

"My mind," the tall man said, "is straight now. I never forget ... I am a human being."

Young Hunter had nodded, his right hand gripping that of Holds the Stone.

"I ... cover my eye with moss and mud. I will dirty my face and they will think I am ... still their dog. I will bring them back ... show them the cave to hide in. They will hide there. Though Ancient Ones, they are cowards. Afraid of the Day Traveler's light."

So Holds the Stone had spoken. And now it was the night when he had said that the Ancient Ones, the grey-skinned giants who wished to wipe out all the human beings, would come to the cave below this cliff. The eastern sky was beginning to redden and Young Hunter wondered if they would still come. He had felt the presence of Bear Talker and Medicine Plant two sunrises ago, felt it so strongly that he thought he would look up and see them standing next to him. The sense of their being with him had come soon after he had again felt that coldness at the base of his spine, the same chill he had felt three moons before, when he was starting out on his journey and had not yet reached the village of his brother-cousins. He had seen then, as now, that hostile eyes were watching him. But both the feeling of that enemy gaze and the reassurance of the presence of his teachers had vanished as quickly as the wind that swept over him, pushing the clouds toward the northeast.

Now, as he waited for the Ancient Ones to come, he wished that he felt less alone, that the two deep-seeing elders were indeed with him. He knew that what he had done, taking Holds the Stone to the water, had been the act of a deep-seeing person. And he accepted now that the second voice, which seemed to be with him all the time, was the voice that a deep-seeing person was said always to hear. But if he were a deep-seeing person, didn't that mean that he should be more certain of himself? Didn't that mean that he should be less fearful of what would happen? And the second voice spoke to him even as he was thinking, saying that being fearful was part of the burden of being human, that seeing what is coming does not always mean knowing what to do when it arrives. Young Hunter shook his head and laughed at himself. He had just remembered the words his grandfather, Rabbit Stick, had said to him more than once. *The only people who have a hard time with their lives are those who are still alive.*

Agwedjiman pricked forward his ears, sensing something that had not yet reached Young Hunter's ears. Young Hunter looked intently toward the northeast. Then he saw them on the trail, coming through the trees. They seemed large, even from this great distance. There was a long line of them and they carried clubs, striking idly at the trees as they walked, breaking branches from the living trees. The one in front seemed taller than the others, his head strangely shaped. Then Young Hunter saw that the one who led was carrying Holds the Stone on his shoulders.

Their strides were huge. Walking, they went almost as fast as a man could run. They looked to be more than twice the height of a man and their skins shone like flint in the thin light before dawn. Young Hunter gripped the Long Thrower more tightly. Perhaps his small spears would just break against that tough skin. Holds the Stone had told of seeing spears bounce off their bodies. But as he held the Long Thrower, it gave him courage. It was for this that he had been given the weapon. Already it had struck down one of the old ones which hunted humans. The line of giants came past the place where he and Holds the Stone had hidden the body of the Hunter. Since it was too large for them to move, they had mounded stones and branches and snow over it and then more new snow had fallen—a gift from the Owner Creator. It hid their tracks and the tracks of the dogs. It hid the graves of Pabetciman and the black monster.

The Day Traveler was just beginning to show himself in the east when the line of giants reached the cave in the narrow place between the cliffs. One-Eye reached up and pulled the little one from his shoulders, dropping him roughly on the ground. Holds the Stone rolled as he struck the ground. He was stiff from the long ride, bruised by the fall, but he rolled to his feet. He made motions with his hands. This was the cave where they would hide. He would go now to the village and stay hidden outside its walls. Here in the cave his masters could hide unseen by the Day Traveler. That night, when it was dark, he would lead the warriors of the village into ambush. Here, in the narrow pass, his masters could block their escape, kill all of the small ones.

Young Hunter watched from the clifftop as the Ancient Ones began to enter the cave below him. One by one, they went inside. Now all of them were within except for their one-eyed leader. His eye swept up the cliff face, toward Young Hunter. Young Hunter closed his eyes and held them closed. It seemed as if he could feel that piercing gaze upon him, feel a voice speaking inside his head, saying to him, *Show yourself. I know you are there.* His own inner voice helped him keep his mind silent, free of all thoughts. But he did not open his eyes until that feeling had passed. One-Eye was no longer to be seen. Young Hunter continued to sit without moving. They had agreed that he would wait until Holds the Stone was able to circle back up to the place where Young Hunter waited. Then it would be time to tip the great stone.

The sun was almost clear of the horizon. It was moving away from the days of less light. Already Young Hunter had felt the nights begin to shorten, the Day Traveler's face to shine down from the sky longer with each new dawn. Another time of snow and cold would pass and green would return again to the land, the birds would return from the southern lands, the sounds of new life would fill the air. All day Young Hunter watched and listened for any sign of Holds the Stone. At last when the sun was low again, Agwedjiman lifted his head slightly, sniffing the wind that was coming to them from the northeast. It was not the direction from which Holds the Stone had planned to come, for the cliff was steep and hard to climb there, but as Young Hunter lifted his head up to look down over the edge, he saw the tall man running. Something was wrong. Holds the Stone was still far below, scrambling as fast as he could up the narrow path that led up the face of the cliff. He had wiped the moss and mud from his eye and as his gaze caught Young Hunter's, he waved his hand and motioned to Young Hunter. *Look behind.*

Agwedjiman shook himself free of the snow-covered blanket with a growl and whirled. Young Hunter stood, turning as he did so. There, just coming up over the edge of the cliff to the southwest, was a sight which froze his blood. Its body beginning to block out the light of the setting sun as it climbed, One-Eye, the Forest Wanderer, the Stone Coat, the Cannibal Giant, the Ancient One, was there, only a spear cast away.

312

Young Hunter looked at the still face of the Ancient One. He felt something cold and thin pass from the giant's one great eye and into his own, touching his mind, as if long sharp fingers were piercing through the bones of his skull. He wanted to raise the Long Thrower, but his hands were frozen. Agwedjiman too seemed unable to move. He crouched with hackles raised, even his low warning growl frozen.

The Ancient One took a great step toward them. The sun was behind its back and it cast a long shadow over the clifftop. The shadow covered the man and the dog and spread past them, filling the whole of the valley beyond.

Young Hunter searched for his voice. "Older Brothers," he said, his voice small as a child's, "Thunder Beings. Have you forgotten me?" A sound rumbled out of the west. It rolled over the hills, crossing the sky above them. Thunder. Even though it was the Moon of Long Lights, the sound of thunder growled overhead. One-Eye stopped in its tracks. It looked toward the sky. As the giant looked up, Young Hunter felt his own arms and hands come back to life. He notched the small spear onto the sinew of the Long Thrower and raised it slightly, taking half a step backward. All the many days of practice steadied his hands as he saw the one place where an arrow might pierce home. One-Eye saw the motion and looked down. Its mind sought again to control this small one, but Young Hunter had already released the sinew. The small spear whipped through the air like a bolt of lightning. It struck deeply into the Ancient One's wide-staring eye.

One-Eye threw its hands up to its face and screamed, a scream that seemed to split the stones. It drove Young Hunter to his knees, his hands over his ears. The scream echoed over the hilltops, almost as loud as the thunder. In the cave below, the other Stone Coats heard the scream. They stirred and looked toward the mouth of the cave. But the light of the Day Traveler was not yet gone. They would not go out until it was dark. They would wait for One-Eye to call them.

313

As the scream died away, Young Hunter began to inch toward the great rock at the cliff's edge, where he had wedged the branch so that a push would send the big rock toppling down. It would cause an avalanche which would seal the cave mouth, trapping all of the cannibal giants. But as he moved, his feet made a small sound in the snow and One-Eye moved also, moved closer to Young Hunter and the great boulder.

Young Hunter stood still. One-Eye reached up and plucked the small spear from its eye. Slow blood throbbed down the giant's face. One-Eye hurled the small spear aside and cocked its head.

It is listening, Young Hunter thought. *Listening to hear me.*

Young Hunter signaled with one hand. Agwedjiman moved, his nails clacking on the bare stone. One-Eye turned its head toward the sound, cocked its head again, and then opened its mouth in what seemed to be a smile. Blood from its eye dripped across its thin lips and long sharp teeth. One-Eye turned its head away from the sounds of the dog and turned toward the direction where Young Hunter still stood.

Young Hunter understood. *It hears my thoughts.*

One-Eye took a step toward Young Hunter.

If you hear, Young Hunter thought, *know that you cannot catch me.* Young Hunter stepped to the right. The giant turned that way also. *Know that I have killed your black creature,* Young Hunter thought, and stepped again. He kept the boasting thoughts loud in his mind, while below those thoughts he tried to keep hidden his plan to signal Agwedjiman so that both of them would run at the monster at one time, confuse it, duck under its arms, and try to drive it off the edge of the cliff. *You cannot defeat me,* Young Hunter thought. *I have stolen your dog from you.* One-Eye opened its arms and crouched lower, as if waiting for them to attack.

Then a stone came sailing through the air and struck One-Eye in the face, struck it in the eye that had been pierced by the small spear. One-Eye screamed again, and turned in the direction from which the stone had come. Holds the Stone stood there at the cliff edge. He did not run away, but picked up another stone.

"One-Eye," Holds the Stone shouted, "I am a human being. I am not a dog."

Young Hunter darted forward quickly. There was space now to slip between One-Eye and the edge of the cliff. As he passed the giant, it swung a long arm. Young Hunter dodged low. A single sharp fingernail knifed across Young Hunter's back, cutting through the skin. Young Hunter stumbled but did not fall. Agwedjiman bit at One-Eye's ankles, but the giant paid no attention to the dog.

"One-Eye!" Holds the Stone shouted again. "A dog cannot throw a stone!" Another rock struck One-Eye on the side of its face.

Young Hunter dropped the Long Thrower and threw himself onto the wedged tree. The great boulder rocked, but did not go over. He pressed down again, rocking it, trying to reach that point where it would overbalance. Behind him he felt the presence of One-Eye growing closer. He knew that giant hands were reaching for him to cut his breath cord before the boulder rolled.

Now a shout came from behind him, the shout of a real human being. It was a strong sound, a sound filled with courage and with love for his people. It was the battle cry of a man who is ready to throw his life away to save others. It was the cry of one who knows his heart is not made of cold stone. Young Hunter turned to see the bloody-faced giant leaning closer to grasp him. He saw Holds the Stone running toward them. As he ran, Holds the Stone seemed to grow larger with each stride until he, himself, was a giant. He ran with the power of a Thunder Being. When he struck the back of the Ancient One's legs it was with such force that the giant fell. Young Hunter rolled to one side and the two—the Ancient One and

315

the human being—fell past him. Their weight thundered down on the lever and the great boulder tipped and fell. One-Eye fell with the boulder, and Holds the Stone, his arms still grasping the giant's legs, fell also. They disappeared over the edge of the cliff.

The ground rumbled beneath Young Hunter where he lay as the cliff began to give way beneath him. He felt himself about to fall when something pulled him from behind. Teeth grasping the strap of Young Hunter's shoulder pack, Agwedjiman braced his feet as he pulled. The sounds of thunder were all around them. The thunder rolled from the falling stones and echoed back from the sky above. The valleys and the forests and the plains filled with the sounds of thunder. The face of the cliff was falling and the earth shook as boulders filled the pass between the hills and the hills themselves shuddered. The one deep within the earth had wakened and shook the ground. The ancient Great Turtle who supports the earth with his back stretched his limbs. The solid ground beneath Young Hunter's feet was no more solid than the surface of a pond when the ice on it suddenly tilts and breaks. Above them, below them, around them, the thunder roared. And then stopped.

Young Hunter lay there, his arms wrapped about Agwedjiman's neck. He looked around. The hills had fallen lower and the cave was buried deep. The Ancient One was gone and Holds the Stone with him. The Long Thrower was gone also. He missed its feel in his hands. But Young Hunter's second voice spoke clearly to him. *It was meant to be this way.* He knew that he held the shape of the Long Thrower and its making in his mind, but he knew—as Bear Talker and Medicine Plant had known before him—that the time was not right to give it to the people. It was too great a weapon to be used by people whose minds might not be straight. He unslung the pack which held the small spears and dropped it down into a crevice between the fallen stones.

316

He looked back toward the west. The People of the Long Lodges in their hidden valley were well. He could not return to them, lest they try to persuade him to remain as one of them. He closed his eyes and saw them clearly. They were standing in front of their lodges, standing outside their walled village, looking toward the east where the hills had shaken and fallen. He saw the faces of his second mother, Reed, and of Even Tempered. *Good-bye, my elders,* he whispered. *I will not forget you. But I have a family of my own.* He saw the face of Redbird and it seemed as if she felt his gaze, for her eyes opened wider and she took a step in his direction. *You will marry again when spring comes, my sister,* he thought, *but it will not be me.* He saw the face of Burden Carrier and smiled. *You will have strong children and they will live long. Someday the children that Willow Girl and I will have may come to your lodges to wrestle your sons.*

Young Hunter opened his eyes and turned his face away from the sunset. A bird called from the birch trees to the east where the light of the Day Traveler would shine brightly. It was the call of a small black-and-white singer, one of the Owner Creator's messengers of life.

Bear Talker came from his lodge. He had seen much and he let the great bearskin slip from his shoulders. He was bone weary, but he would walk now to the lodge of Rabbit Stick and Sweetgrass Woman. He would tell them their grandson would return soon. Bear Talker nodded to himself. *Perhaps, too, I will take a longer walk. Go and see that woman, that Medicine Plant. It is time that we spoke.* He smiled. *Neither of us is getting younger.* As he stretched his arms, a snow owl flew up from the trees behind his small lodge and flapped on silent wings toward the village of the Salmon People. Bear Talker saw the owl and laughed. He looked toward the east and thought of how the Day Traveler would appear in the new morning that was about to come, radiant with life. Dawn. Dawn. Dawn. Dawn. The same dawn Young Hunter saw as he turned his eyes back toward his home.

317

13's

- plates on turtle back →
- # of moons
- 13 bands (